Contents

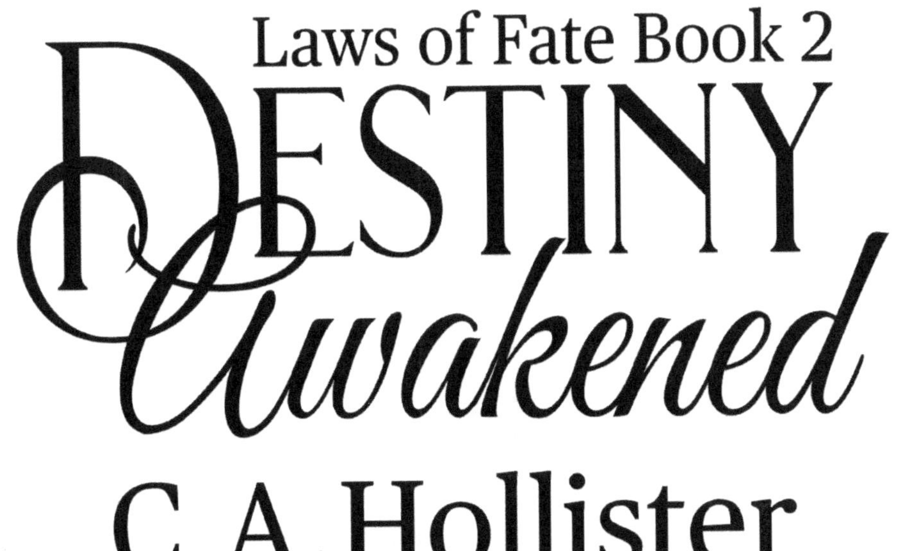

C.A. Hollister

Dedication

For a wonderful father and beloved Pop Pop. The world is a little less bright since you've been gone. You are dearly missed every day.

I WOULD LIKE TO thank my husband for encouraging me to finish the book. Your unwavering patience, understanding, and support throughout this entire journey is the only reason I had the courage and perseverance and get this far. Thank you, dear. I couldn't have done it without you.

Chapter 1

THE ANIMALS WERE UNUSUALLY vocal that morning. Their chatter filled the quiet, predawn air, not with their usual greetings, but with something else. Their voices chittered in her head like a hive of angry bees, vying for her attention all at once.

She shook off the incessant noise, determined not to get distracted from the path that lay ahead. This was the only time she had to herself, a time to let down her guard and not have to hide from the rest of the world. Out there, among the grass and trees, she could pretend the last five years hadn't happened.

Up ahead, the path forked in two and she veered off to the right, readying herself for the steady climb to her destination atop the overlook on the ridge above the lake. No matter how hard she tried to ignore the constant whispers of the forest animals, the way they skittered among the underbrush made their presence even more known, keeping pace with her long strides.

They insisted she stop and talk to them. They had something important to tell her, but Darya still ignored them. To the little animals, everything was important.

She settled her sights on the trail that lay ahead. Already, she was running behind schedule. Usually, by the time the sky showed its first signs of the coming dawn, she was at the halfway point of her run. That morning, however, she got a late start, thanks to another restless night. Her dreams were getting more and more bizarre, with faces of people she didn't know and places she'd never seen before.

And the dragon.

Always, there was the dragon soaring across a pastel-shaded sky. Its wintergreen scales reflected the lush landscape of the surrounding fields and forests. Sometimes, she stood at the peak of a cliff overlooking an unfamiliar view of a vast, open sea, beckoning it to her with outstretched arms. In that moment, right before they came together, she would wake.

Echoes of the dream stayed with her in the waking world, like the briny breeze of the ocean that would sway through her room even though her window remained closed. Sometimes, her clothes carried the lingering scent of a fire that lay abandoned on a deserted stretch of beach. The rolling surf colliding against rock played in her memory long after she'd awakened. When the images finally faded from reality, they left her with a profound sense of loneliness and loss for something she never had.

Even as a child, she had these strange visions come to her in her sleep. There was only one person she trusted in her commune to share her secrets with. Though he wasn't her real grandfather, he was the closest thing to a paternal figure she'd ever known. He listened to her fanciful tales with the fascination of someone enamored with her overactive imagination.

The other children often treated her like a freak because of her strange affinity with the animals and nature. Even some adults kept her at a distance, including her own mother. The man she called grandfather had tried to shield her from most of the taunting. She missed his infectious smile and easy laugh. She missed a lot of things from her old life.

The pang of sadness and regret brought her back to the present, and she spotted the trail up ahead. She gave the sky another swift glance. If she expected to make it to the summit before sunrise, she needed to pick up the pace.

Muted tones of orange and gold showed through the trees ahead, and she quickened her steps up the winding pathway, careful to keep her sights on the ground to avoid slipping on the spongy dirt and dead twigs that snapped underneath the weight of her feet. She stopped at the top of the hill and rested a hand on the smooth bark of a nearby maple tree, taking in the heavy, wet breath of the forest.

Along the horizon, the water mirrored the towering build-ings against the calm surface. The refracting sun's glare against the glass shot orange spears of light across the lake. Warm light splayed across her face when it bore itself from the Dallas city skyline.

Light filled all the hollow places inside her where remorse and sadness dwelled. She fought to hang on to those few precious moments of peace while taking in the glorious sight of dawn until volatile emotions threatened to shatter her serenity. She forced out one last, heavy breath, releasing all the unwelcome feelings with it.

Her gaze lingered on the brightening sky a moment longer. In the distance, she heard the screech of a bird shatter the peaceful morning. A streak of white darted out of the trees on the other side of the lake, melting into the backdrop of the sky as if it had disappeared altogether. She wasn't sure what was more disturbing? The fact that the falcon seemingly vanished, or the stark sense of foreboding its presence left behind.

Darya glanced above her, studying the branches overhead. Maybe she was standing too close to the bird's nest. Despite her connection with them, not all of nature's creatures appreciated a human disturbing their domain.

Shaking off the odd encounter, she started back the way she came.

More joggers had appeared on the trail since her arrival. She tried to make herself small, so she wouldn't be in anyone's way. She made it to the fork in the path when she realized that she couldn't hear the animals anymore. It wasn't unusual for them to quiet down when other people were traipsing among their home, but the sheer and utter silence was a little disturbing.

A flash of light to her left distracted her from her thoughts and she peered into the sky, expecting to see dark clouds that accompanied the lightning. Yet not a single blemish marred the pristine pastel beauty above. She didn't have time to ponder the strangeness of the light or what it could mean when someone yelled out to watch where she was going.

Darya mumbled a half apology and sped up, ready to be away from the park and the chatter of animals.

Boudica stepped through the portal, corn-silk-colored eyes scanning the surrounding clearing before landing on an oversized, brown-speckled hawk perched on a high branch across the field. He preened his soft feathers, unbothered by the woman who was glowering at him. If she'd brought a bow, he was sure she would have tried to shoot him out of the tree.

Frowning at the dry grass that crunched under her bare feet, she took a few steps forward, ignoring the family of rabbits that scattered in the wake of her intrusion. Her frustration manifested as a disgusted sneer. "Come here."

The bird lifted his head. A set of round, golden eyes regarded her with bored indifference. He let out a high-pitched screech and launched himself in her direction. When the hawk reached his target, a man now towered over her in its place.

"I told you to wait for me," she barked.

Tiernen frowned and raised a single umber-colored brow. "Here I stand."

She shoved a piece of paper at him. "This is the woman you seek. Kill her quickly," Boudica said. As if it were that simple.

He looked down at the woman's name and address. He did not know the unfortunate soul who garnered the wrath of such a vengeful god, but it was not his place to question his orders.

Before relinquishing the note, she added, "I went to a lot of trouble for this information, so don't screw it up."

His face relaxed into a toothy grin. "Is your back sore, harlot?"

She slapped him so hard and fast, the air crackled around them. Anyone that might have been watching would have missed her movements. "I will feast on that shriveled thing you call a heart if you ever speak to me like that again." The fire in her eyes blazed as hot as her temper.

Despite her inhuman strength, the sting of her palm did little to hurt Tiernen. He laughed and wrapped a hand around her throat. Rather than squeezing her fragile neck, he ran a thumb along the raised scar that marred her otherwise flawless flesh. It was the same sigil etched into the side of his head.

Tiernen leaned into her, ignoring the sweet scent of roses emanating from her very pores. "You forget we serve the same master. His will is ours." Then he snatched the photograph from her fist and shoved her away. "Run along, now. Fulfill whatever depraved needs Cernunnos demands of you."

She didn't get the chance to levy a response to his insult before he took off into the air, his feathered body soaring west toward a line of high-rise buildings. They pierced the sky like glass and metal mountains on the horizon, making him long for the white-capped peaks of a home he abandoned long ago.

He swept his sharp gaze along the bustling streets below, trying to pick out the best place to land and start his search. He wanted to finish the task as quickly as possible and get back to the peaceful, familiar trees of his prison.

When Darya walked through the front door of the cramped two-bedroom apartment, she expected her roommate to still be asleep. It was a feat to drag Annie out of bed in the mornings when Mark stayed the night.

The aroma of roasted coffee beans steeping in hot water was a pleasant distraction from her strange morning. "You're up early," Darya said, bypassing the open newspaper on the tiny, two-seater table separating the kitchen from the living room.

Annie pushed her hair up into a loose bun and grabbed a cup from the counter, eyeing the magic brew that spilled in a dark stream into the glass pot. Her tired eyes seemed to will the machine to work faster. "I have an exam in an hour and lab for the rest of the afternoon. Mark stayed over to help me study."

Darya didn't know if she would call the pounding of Annie's headboard against her wall last night 'studying', but she kept the observation to herself. Sometimes, Annie seemed more worried about being a policeman's wife than about her declining grades. Unless she started focusing on her studies rather than her love life, she'd flunk out of the nursing program.

Every time she felt the urge to voice her concerns, Darya would bite her tongue. It wasn't her place to dictate Annie's life choices. Especially since Darya could count on one finger how many serious relationships she'd had, and it ended in a flaming disaster of betrayal and heartache.

In her room, Darya picked out a pale blue sundress before heading to the bathroom for a shower. She took off her clothes and unbraided her hair while she waited for the water to heat.

She stood naked in front of the full-length mirror of the sliding glass door, following the same routine she did every morning after a run. Forcing her eyes downward, she studied the long, thin scar on her lower abdomen.

Over the years, it had faded to a near-translucent line against her alabaster skin. To Darya, the scar wasn't just a mark on her skin. It was a lasting testament to a twisted form of maternal hatred. One that had the power to wound deeply, both physically and emotionally. Each time she looked at it, she was reminded not only of her mother's capacity for cruelty but also of the difficult road she traveled to break free of an unwarranted guilt.

She met her own gaze, scrutinizing the tortured woman she kept locked away. She took some comfort in the fact that she didn't have to look into the eyes of her would-be killer every time she peered into a mirror. Her sapphire eyes, which held secrets and regrets of their own—and those of a man she'd never known—were like shuttered windows, blocking the rest of the world from her inner shame. Her hair, though, was the same deep shade of black as her mother's had been.

Tearing herself from the woman in the mirror, Darya stepped under the water, letting the heat melt away those terrible memories. The phantom pain of that night left her skin tender, so she avoided touching the scar while she washed off the morning run.

She rushed through the process of drying and dressing so she wouldn't be late for work. She'd gotten through the kitchen and had the door open, grabbing for her purse when she heard the chair scrape against the vinyl floor.

"Mark wanted me to ask if it was okay to bring a friend over for movie night," Annie said. "It's that cute paramedic, Ronny."

"I promised Janine I'd stay late. Help with a new shipment." Darya hoped her lie didn't sound as obvious as it sounded to her ears. "Some other time," she added, rushing through the door.

"You can't avoid dating forever," Annie called out.

In the elevator, Darya frowned at her reflection. The idea of a date didn't bother her. She didn't like Mark or his friends. He had antiquated ideas of how a relationship between a man and a woman should be. That was the reason Annie was being manipulated into dropping out of nursing school. It was nineteen eighty-two, for the goddess' sake. Women weren't relegated to simply keepers of the home. That was never their place to begin with, but the modern world had molded itself to a strange ideal of the family unit.

No matter how many years she spent away from her old home, she couldn't let go of her values. In her commune, the roles of men and women were chosen by their strengths and weaknesses. Some men were better protectors. Some women were better leaders. Sometimes the opposite was true.

The one constant in her community was the respect for each other's roles in their lives. A wife didn't submit to her husband because he demanded it. She gave herself as freely and completely as her man did to her. That was the devotion Darya longed for. It's what she thought she'd had for a while.

The elevator shuddered to a stop, and the tinny bell announced her arrival on the ground floor. Would it be so bad to spend the night in the company of another man? How long had it been since she'd gone on a proper date? Eight months? Nine? It was even longer since inviting anyone into her bed. After patching together her broken heart, she pretty much gave up on dating. Maybe it was time to break out of her comfort zone and have a little fun.

On a normal day, Darya's commute to the flower shop was a short one. That morning, however, the foot traffic on the sidewalks was unusually congested. It took a lot of effort to ignore the incessant engine noises, horns, shouting, and all the other obnoxious sights and sounds that came with living in the city. The chaos was so different from the small commune, and she longed for a simpler life.

She kept telling herself she would move to the suburbs, where at least she could get away from all that congestion. Unfortunately, her budget wouldn't allow for her to live anywhere else but the rent-controlled apartment she shared with Annie.

Darya turned the corner of the alley behind the flower shop and caught Janine struggling with an armload of paper bags. She fumbled with her keys while balancing the awkward load.

"Let me help with those." Darya grabbed a bag so the other woman could get the key in the lock. She followed

Janine inside and sat the bag down on a wooden bench just inside the door.

"Thanks. I had to pick up a few last-minute things for Chris." She went to the far wall and flipped two switches. The shop came alive with the soft glow of incandescent bulbs. "I love it when the kids tell me they have a project due the day before it needs to be turned in. Not to mention I still have to go to the dry cleaners after work, so Jerome has clean suits for his trip tomorrow." She blew a strand of hair out of her face. "I remember when I was a single woman your age. I miss those days."

Darya closed the door and motioned to the photo frame sitting by the register. Janine and her husband walked hand in hand with their two young boys at their sides. Behind them was a windswept ocean with frothy waves protruding from the surface. "Yeah, but look how beautiful your family is."

"They are precious, aren't they?" She stared at the picture for a few more seconds, then said, "I was going to surprise you this weekend when you came by, but you know me. I'm terrible at keeping secrets." She pulled an envelope from her purse. "Jerome and I wanted to do something special for you, for everything you've done to help with the store."

"You did me the favor, giving me this job."

"Are you kidding? I would have closed the shop a long time ago if not for you. Don't argue. Just accept it as the gesture of appreciation it is."

Darya opened the envelope and withdrew a plane ticket. Her mouth hung open as she tried to comprehend what she was seeing. Along with the plane ticket was a printed itinerary, and a pamphlet covered in picturesque scenes. "This is too much."

"You said you wanted to see the beaches of Broughied for yourself." Janine nodded at the photograph of her family. "Pictures can't do it justice."

Darya put everything back in the envelope and held it out. "I can't take this."

"Fine. I'll let you tell Jerome you're turning down his generous gift."

Darya feigned a grimace. "I'd rather not poke that bear."

Janine peeked at her watch. "Do you think you can handle the store today? If I leave now, I will have all my errands finished in time to get something taken out for dinner. I might even have time to grab the boys for T-Ball practice after school."

"Sure." It wasn't like she was in a hurry to go back home to an encore of the previous night.

After Janine was gone, Darya started placing the planters along the sidewalk in front of the store. The lilacs she chose were in full bloom, permeating the entire shop with their sweet scent. It transported her to the past, to the gardens she had cultivated with her own two hands. Living in such a confined space made it impossible to recreate those beautiful arrangements.

That was yet another reason she wanted to leave the city. She considered talking to Janine about renting one of her rooms but couldn't bring herself to put that kind of burden on her friend and their family.

She was on her second trip with more flowers when she spotted a couple pushing a stroller across the street. Her pleasant mood melted onto the pavement in a pool of bitter heartache and regret as she stared at the man she once shared her heart and bed with.

It had been over a year since she'd last seen Harvey. His hair was different. When they were dating, he'd kept it long enough to pull back in a ponytail. She noticed his hair was shorter now, giving the once light chestnut color a darker hue.

She recognized the woman at his side. Grace still had the blond bombshell waves that fell over her slender shoulders. Apparently, pregnancy hadn't affected her figure in the slightest.

They looked happy together, walking arm in arm, pushing their twins in the double stroller. The smiling mother bent forward, fussing over the child sitting in the front compartment. Darya couldn't help the fierce surge of animosity that made her want to march up to them and gouge those pretty brown eyes out of her pretty little head.

It took Darya a long time to come to terms with the truth of her feelings. She understood now that she never really loved Harvey. The resentment that festered inside her was more ardent.

Grace gave him what Darya could not. Children.

She could have forgiven him for the affair. Sure, her heart would still have been broken, but witnessing his excitement when he told her that Grace was pregnant with his baby was an unnecessary slap in the face.

Darya hurried inside before one of them caught her staring. She stood off to the side, away from the window, until the happy family was gone from view. The thought of having to interact with them made her clutch her stomach in a vain attempt to quell her rising panic. What if he came into the shop to buy a bouquet for his lovely wife?

She would sell him the damn flowers, that's what. It didn't matter that their relationship was a miserable failure. She had been blinded by a love she craved so badly that she ignored the warning signs of its impending doom. No matter how badly she wanted to share her heart and life with someone, she would never again let a relationship destroy her inner peace. No man would hold her heart without first proving his unconditional love and devotion.

Janine sat in her black S-10 pickup, watching Darya from across the street. It took all her willpower to hand over that ticket to Broughied, knowing what it meant for her. If she had waited until the weekend, she would have chickened out and done everything in her power to keep her friend from the destiny that lay before her. Of course, the others would never let that happen. Not after all the sacrifices they made to ensure Darya reached this moment.

The passenger door of the truck opened, and a woman wearing a charcoal leather jacket sat down in the seat beside her.

"Is it done?"

Janine's head snapped to the side. She hadn't expected to see Ronwen so soon. Much less have her pop into Janine's truck in the middle of the day in front of gods and mortals alike.

Janine curled her lips into a disgusted sneer. "Yes, it's done. I gave her the ticket. Everything is as it should be."

"Good. By next week, you will be relieved of your duties."

Janine tried to keep her expression from betraying the disappointment she felt. "Yeah."

"Why do you sound so sad about it? This is what we've been waiting for."

Turning back to her shop, Janine said, "We are sending her into this blind and unprepared."

"Once she's in Broughied, we will tell her the truth of who she is."

"She should have been preparing her whole life."

Ronwen sat forward, catching Janine's eye. "It would have left her even more vulnerable. Everything is happening the way it's meant to."

Janine refused to meet the other woman's cold gaze. "I hope you know what you're doing."

"We've kept her alive and unharmed so far."

A sharp laugh filled the small cab. "Unharmed? Is that why you sent her to me after she almost died?"

Ronwen waved a hand, dismissing the comment. "You really can't blame her mother for what happened. She was a victim in all of this, too."

Janine laughed again. "You all are so damn sure of this crusade of yours. Do you even care that there's a real person with real feelings you're manipulating for a ridiculous cause?"

The air in the cab dropped a couple of degrees. "Tell all those women brutalized and murdered for the sake of one god's broken heart how ridiculous our cause is. I will not let their deaths be in vain. When Darya learns of her true purpose, neither will she."

"It's too much to put on one person's shoulders."

"She won't be alone. She's never been alone."

Janine rested her head in her hand. There was nothing more she could do. Her role had run its course. It was time for Darya to face what was to come.

At the end of the day, Darya locked the front door and flipped the 'open' sign to 'closed'. Long fingerlike shadows curled around the streets, announcing the end of another day. She made sure everything was clean and tidy before she left through the back door, eyeing the flow of pedestrians that passed by. The early June air was still heavy with heat and humidity, making her shirt cling to her skin. The prospect of having to fall in with the dense crowd made her let out a disgusted sigh.

She turned the deadbolt and had barely gotten the key free from the lock when a couple of kids rushed past her, knocking them from her hand. The keys slid across the pavement, disappearing under a dumpster on the other side of the alleyway. She muttered a curse, then raised her voice. "Watch where you're going."

The taller of the boys looked over his shoulders. His mouth split into a mocking grin, flipped up a middle finger, and kept running after his friend.

She took three steps across the alley to the dumpster and bent down to retrieve the keys, keeping her eyes locked on the teens. A rush of something cool and sweet, like a summer wind, rolled through her body. The dumpster closest to the teen jerked away from the brick wall and slammed into his left hip. His friend skidded to a stop, catching the other boy before he fell.

Darya stared after them until they disappeared into the bustling crowd. A flutter of nausea rolled through her, making her aware of the mistake she'd just made. Giving the alley a quick once over to make sure no one else saw what happened, she snatched the keys from the ground and made a hasty retreat in the opposite direction of the street. She needed to do a better job of reigning in her temper.

Her apartment building came into view, and she hurried forward, ready to change out of her sticky clothes and relax with a good book. She stepped inside the lobby to be greeted by a familiar chuff and wag of an excited nub. All thoughts of the rude teenagers and rolling dumpsters left her mind. At the mailboxes, she held out her hand to the eager Rottweiler.

"Well, hello, handsome Dash," she said, scratching behind one dark ear. He looked up at her with an adoring gaze that stood out among the fawn fur that surrounded his eyes and muzzle.

His owner was a short, robust man with thinning salt and pepper hair and hazel eyes more brown than green. Hard lines punctuated the downturn of his mouth. To the random passerby, the perpetual frown he wore on his face was off-putting. But Darya saw through his grumpy exterior.

He was a good man who liked his privacy. Dash thought very highly of him as well.

Mr. Bilyk grunted, not taking his gaze from the paper in his hand. "You're making his head big." His thick Slavic accent was even more pronounced with the unlit cigar hanging from the side of his mouth. "He is a worthless pooch already."

She leaned forward. "Don't listen to him. You're the best boy."

Mail in hand, she pressed the call button, and after a few seconds, it announced its arrival with a tinny ding. They stepped into the waiting elevator, and she took up her place beside the Rottweiler, stroking his velvet fur. When the doors opened again, she parted ways with Mr. Bilyk and Dash.

She walked inside to Mark and Annie cuddling together on the couch, watching a movie. The smell of buttery popcorn filled the small space, making her stomach complain that she had missed dinner.

"Hey, Darya." Mark held up a hand to her, not taking his focus off the television.

"Hi, Mark. Annie, I'm putting your mail on the table." She strode to the fridge to grab water and some yogurt. On her way back, she asked, "What movie did you get?"

"Clash of the Titans," Annie said. "Do you want to join us?"

"It's not really my thing."

Mark laughed. "I would have figured you for a hardcore fantasy buff, considering how you grew up."

The comment froze Darya in place. She stared at the back of his head, chewing on a snide reply sitting on the tip of her tongue. Wanting to keep the peace, she said, "I've had a long day. I'm going to bed. Enjoy the movie."

She fought the urge to go back out there and confront Annie for revealing those things about her private life. Comments like the one Mark made were the reason she didn't tell people about her druid ancestry. The path she followed was none of their concern. Maybe it was her own fault for thinking she could trust her roommate.

Most people assumed her upbringing made her a crazy heathen pagan who dabbled in sorcery and witchcraft. It couldn't be farther from the truth. Darya's way of life celebrated the sanctity of nature and the gods and goddesses that protected them. It was ignorant to fear or belittle what they didn't understand.

She changed into a tank top and a pair of cotton shorts, readying herself for the nightly routine of misting the planters she had scattered around her room. Once her flowers shimmered with a fresh layer of water, she leaned against the windowsill, trying to get a glimpse of the stars through the light pollution of the city. It was times like this she wished she was back among the sacred lands of her tribe. She missed lying beneath the unencumbered skies, following the moon and stars through their journey across the cosmos.

She twirled the silver ring on the middle finger of her right hand. The delicate knot-work was comforting. It had been a gift from the same man who taught her many of the old ways and was one of the few belongings she took with her. No matter how many times the others made her feel like an outcast because of her ability to speak to the animals, he called her a diamond among glass. She pretended to be annoyed at those kinds of comments, yet she loved each and every show of affection he gave her.

The dingy orange glow of the street lamps made her face fall into a somber expression. She wondered if she could return to that old life and her people. Would they accept her into their fold after what happened? Would they blame her for what her mother did?

In the end, it didn't matter. She wouldn't have the courage to step through those gates again. There was no resurrecting the past from that kind of death.

She finished her yogurt and threw the empty container in the trash before sliding under the comforter. The warm breeze from the streets swept her into the escape of her dreams and those places her subconscious longed to get back to.

Chapter 2

TIERNEN KEPT TO HIMSELF on his way through the sleepy cityscape, sticking to the shadows of the high-rise buildings. He avoided the more populated areas, not because he didn't want to be seen. He didn't want to take the chance of encountering other people. Human touch made him uncomfortable. He still felt the lingering trace of the young woman who promised him a terrible demise. Every time he closed his eyes, her visage haunted the darkness there. How long did he have to wait for her prophecy to come to fruition? Whatever wrath waited for him in the next life couldn't be any worse than the miserable existence he had to endure in this one.

Night steadily retreated from the new day, urging him forward. He glanced at the paper in his hand. The sign on the corner matched Boudica's elegant script. He scanned the buildings across the street, and after making sure the way was clear, he strode through the crosswalk to the apartment building he was looking for. The thought of abandoning his mission and losing himself to the city's underbelly tempted him. Would that be where his terrible fate awaited?

Even now, he could feel Cernunnos lingering in the back of his mind, watching him. Tiernen feared little in this world, but he knew all too well the creative punishments in store for him if he disobeyed his god. There were worse things in life than death. Being cursed to an eternity as a slave to a sadistic deity was close to the top of the list.

He pulled on one of the glass doors of the apartment building, frowning when they didn't budge. He could have easily yanked them off their damn hinges, but he couldn't chance drawing that kind of attention to himself. At the end of the block, he turned into a shadowed alley. There, he found an open window on the second floor. After a quick glance over his shoulder, he shifted into a hawk and flew to the rail of an empty fire escape. From his perch, he heard robust, steady snores that assured his safe passage through the room.

The purple sky foretold of the coming dawn, and with time pushing at his heels, he hopped into the bedroom before taking on his human form again. The sleeping man didn't stir when Tiernen crept across the carpeted floor and into the narrow hall. He was a couple of feet away from the front door when a sound made him turn. There, on the couch next to the tiny kitchenette, sat a little girl that couldn't be any more than six or seven. She faced the bare window in the living room, but he must have made just enough noise to get her attention.

She turned. "Daddy?" Her eyes were open and searching, yet she did not see him.

Tiernen returned to the door.

"You're not my daddy." She pushed herself farther into the couch, wrapping her arms around herself. Her lips parted, and she drew in a breath. He was across the space between them in the span of a heartbeat, resting a hand over her mouth.

"I'm not here for you, little one." With his other hand, he smoothed down her pale hair. An act that surprised even him. "No harm will come to you or your father if you stay quiet."

When he moved away, her lips were white from the pressure she used to keep them locked together. "Good girl."

He left the apartment, knowing he should have made sure neither the child nor her father derailed his quest, but he didn't want their blood on his hands. Not when so much of it already stained his soul.

He passed by the elevators where a young couple waited with their infant, but he bypassed them in search of the stairs. A tinny bell rang out behind him, announcing the elevator's arrival.

"Oh, this one is going up," a woman said, holding the door for the young couple from inside the elevator.

Tiernen glanced back at the elevator, where a man was staring at his watch. "I don't mind making an extra stop," he said. "We have another hour to kill before Vincent's doctor's appointment, anyway."

"Here, let me help with that." The first woman said, picking up the edge of the stroller.

"Thanks, Darya," the mother said.

Tiernen's footsteps faltered upon hearing that name. He had to force himself to continue toward the red exit sign denoting the stairs. He paused just inside the door of the stairwell, contemplating his next move. Had his target been alone in the elevator, he might have gone after Darya right then, but the couple and their child added unnecessary complications. Surely, she was on her way to her apartment. If he was quick enough, he would be there waiting for her.

The elevator bounced to a stop on the third floor. Darya said her goodbyes to the Bakers before turning left toward her apartment. She passed by Mr. Bilyk's open door, where Dash waited for his owner to return from the trash chute.

"Good morning, Mr. Bilyk," she said to the space on the other side of his apartment and stepped in for a quick ear tussle with the excited Rottweiler.

"Good morning, Miss Pless." He stepped inside, past Dash.

She backed into the hall again, ready to head to her apartment, when Dash let out a growl from deep within his chest, followed by a strange warning.

Mr. Bilyk muttered a quick reprimand in his native tongue before switching to English. "Sorry, sorry. I don't know what has him so agitated."

But Dash wasn't looking at her. Wary eyes peered through her legs down the dimly lit hallway. Mr. Bilyk snapped his fingers before shutting the door on the agitated dog.

She glanced over her shoulder at the empty hall. Why would Dash try to warn her of a stranger in the building? The residents brought guests in all the time. Still, she wouldn't discount the hounds' warning altogether, so she hurried to her apartment, locking the deadbolts once she was inside. Annie was at the kitchen table reading the morning paper with a fresh cup of coffee in her free hand. She didn't have the same half-dead look from yesterday. Mark must not have stayed the night.

"Do you mind if I jump in the shower first?" Darya asked.

Without looking up, Annie waved her away. "Go ahead. I don't have class until noon."

After Darya finished in the bathroom, she walked through the kitchen, heading to her room to hang her towel to dry before putting in the laundry hamper. When she didn't see Annie at the table, Darya assumed she'd gone back to her room. She almost fell backward when her foot slipped in something warm and viscous. If not for the table, she would have fallen over backward onto the dead woman crumpled in a ball at the base of an overturned chair.

"Annie?" Her voice sounded detached, like it wasn't her own.

She felt a presence approach from behind and flung herself around in time for the knife to miss her chest, grazing her shoulder instead. The cry that left her mouth was more from surprise than pain.

Clutching her wounded arm, she scanned the room, desperately trying to find something; anything to use as a weapon. "We don't have any money," she sputtered.

If her words affected the man, he didn't show it. His smoky gaze regarded her in the same unfeeling stare the women in her commune wore when it came time to slaughter chickens for a meal. He made a move toward her again.

With the speed only blind panic allowed, she snatched the hideous green, orange, and white swan candy dish that sat on the table. It was heavy in her hand, and the weight helped her gather even more momentum when she swung it up and around at the man's face.

He saw the incoming blow, and his attempt to block the solid chunk of glass cushioned the force of it, striking his open palm and shoving his knuckles into the base of one eye. He grunted and shifted half a step to the side. That small opening gave her a chance to push past him and run out the door.

She didn't dare look back once she was across the threshold and into the hall. Footsteps thumped at her heels, pushing her faster toward the stairs. She was only a few feet from the top step when fingers tangled in her hair and yanked her backward onto the ground. Her mouth opened, ready to let out a scream, but the curved blade poised above her chest stole her voice.

A blur of black and brown shot over her, knocking the man off his haunches. She heard the sickly crunch of teeth on bone and an ear-piercing roar from somewhere behind her. She didn't realize she'd gotten to her hands and knees and started crawling for the stairs until she was hugging the banister, trying to work herself to her feet.

Behind her, the screaming stopped. She should have kept pulling herself down the stairs instead of turning around. The gruesome scene would be forever burned into her subconscious.

Dash loomed over Darya's would-be killer, his powerful teeth embedded into the man's neck so far; he'd ripped most of the flesh away from the muscle. Dead gray eyes stared at her. Or were they blue? In the dingy yellow light of the hall, she thought they shifted from one hue to the other. His body shook in violent spurts as Dash continued to shake him and squeeze his jaw even tighter on his throat.

She blinked and broke the trance, then continued her slow descent. The second she pushed through the door on the ground floor, there were two policemen rushing through the front lobby. She nearly barreled through two police officers rushing toward the stairs.

One of the uniformed men she recognized and fell into his arms. "Oh God, Darya, what happened?" Mark moved her hair from a tear-stained cheek, looking her over for injuries. When he found the cut on her arm, he called for his partner to get the paramedics. "Where's Annie? Is she okay?"

Darya opened her mouth, but nothing would come out. Her silence told Mark all he needed to know, and he ordered his partner to keep an eye on Darya, then disappeared up-stairs.

She tried to keep her focus on the paramedic that joined them. He spoke softly, reassuring her she was going to be okay. Her whole body shook in sporadic jolts from the shock of the attack. There were brief moments of lucid aware-ness where people were talking to her, asking questions she couldn't answer. At one point, she remembered watching her apartment building fading from view from the back of an ambulance window.

The sight of blood on her arm dragged her back to the day her mother tried to kill her. She had to relive those horrible memories from her past like a nightmarish movie she couldn't get away from. The last thing she recalled was the sting of a needle before the wonderful drugs enfolded her in the blessed darkness of sleep.

Janine's heart pounded as she sped through the city streets. Her fingers clutched the steering wheel, fighting to stay composed. When she received the emergency room call about Darya's near-death experience, Janine had left her groceries in her cart and took off for the hospital.

By the time all the pertinent paperwork was filled out, the detective that had been talking to Darya walked out of the small, curtained bay with a frustrated look on his face.

He handed Janine a business card. "When she comes to her senses, have her call me."

"I sure will." She put on her most endearing smile, and when he was gone, she gave the card a disinterested glance before throwing it in the trash bin beside the nurses' station.

Janine collected Darya's belongings; her relief tinged with worry. Darya's fugue state could be masking some deeper, undiagnosed trauma. Janine urged her into the passenger seat of the truck idling under the emergency room awning.

"Why do these things keep happening to me?" Darya's voice sounded distant and lifeless. "What did I do to deserve this?"

Janine's throat tightened, her lips trembling with the effort to hold back the truth of the situation. "You don't deserve any of it. Sometimes, life just sucks."

"I don't have anywhere else to go. All of my things are in the apartment."

"Of course you have a place to stay. You can use our spare bedroom for as long as you need." She rushed around the front of the truck and climbed behind the wheel. "Don't worry about the apartment. We will get everything as soon as we can."

Darya let her head fall back on the seat and closed her eyes, giving in to the medicine the nurse gave her before being discharged.

As Janine weaved through the labyrinth of streets, she agonized over past choices and looming decisions. Finally, she spotted her two-story Tudor home and whipped into the safety of the garage.

She leaned back in the driver's seat of the truck, watching Darya sleep. There was a small part of her that was relieved all of this was coming to an end. She wouldn't have to hide her pregnancy from Darya anymore for fear of feeling guilty about her joy. Maybe this time, she and Jerome would have their daughter.

Janine gently prodded Darya awake and guided her to the guest room, slipping off her shoes before tucking her into bed. She sat on top of the comforter until Darya was asleep again, knowing she could do nothing to lessen the horrors the poor girl was going through.

There was no question who sent that man after her. Janine smelled the stench of that whore god all over this mess. Now that he knew where she was, Darya couldn't stay in Dallas, yet she loathed the thought of giving her over to the others.

She told herself she had made a grave mistake befriending the girl. She was only supposed to look after Darya until it was time for the girl to fulfill her fucking destiny. A destiny she never asked for. But over the last few years, Janine had grown to care for Darya like a sister, and the boys loved her like an aunt.

Janine surveyed the living room, her gaze sweeping over a simple house that, over the last ten years, had become a home filled with love and laughter. It hadn't been her first choice, this life she had. She'd entered into an arranged marriage to a man she barely knew for the sake of their bloodline. Her dream had been a secluded home enveloped by forests and mountains. A sanctuary to raise their children, far from potential threats of the outside world.

But Jerome made it clear he had no plans of moving. Already a junior partner at a prestigious Dallas law firm, he insisted they stay in the city. He wasn't willing to sacrifice his career for a forced marriage. Yet, as the years passed, and she gave birth to their first son, they found a genuine affection for one another. Jerome promised that one day, when he was ready to retire, she would have her cabin in the mountains.

A weary sigh shattered the silence of the room, and she went to the kitchen. She was rummaging through the top shelf for a beer to give her a little liquid courage for the call she was about to make.

Amber bottle in hand, she grabbed the cordless phone when someone said, "How did they find her?"

Janine raised the beer, ready to lob at the woman sitting at the island bar.

"How the hell did you get in here?"

Ronwen sat forward. "You were supposed to make sure she stayed hidden."

"I did what I was told. For nearly five years now." Janine put the phone back in its cradle. "I don't know how he found her."

Ronwen crossed her arms and looked away. "He's getting desperate. I think he is using other means of tracking her down."

"What other means?"

"The bastard is moving into the modern age."

Janine joined Ronwen at the bar. "I thought your mother foresaw everything that was supposed to happen."

"That's not how it works."

Janine glanced over her shoulder to the room where Darya slept. "What do we do now?"

"Move up her flight. She will be safe in Broughied until the solstice."

"After what she just went through? I doubt I can convince her to go back to her apartment for her things, much less travel outside the country."

"Figure it out." Ronwen stood. "Until then, she does not leave your sight."

Janine rushed around the corner of the bar. "Are you sure you want to send her to them now? To him, now?"

Ronwen's mouth worked into a half frown. "They are aware of what's at stake. Unless they want to screw up her destiny, they will let her follow the path laid out for her."

Mark rested his head on the door of the coroner's office. He didn't know how long he'd been standing there, working up the nerve to go inside and face the reality of Annie's death. If he didn't do it now, he wouldn't get another chance to say his goodbyes before her family flew her back home to Minnesota.

Stepping over the threshold was like taking on the weight of the building above, and it threatened to crush him under its oppressive load.

The coroner was in his office, scribbling something on a notepad. He didn't see Mark at first. When he did, he removed his glasses and donned the sympathetic expression those in his profession perfected for mourners.

"I'm sorry, Mark," Dr. Stanley said. "I never thought I'd be seeing you on this side of the table."

Mark nodded, not trusting himself to speak.

The doctor took him to the far wall, pulled open a stainless-steel drawer, and stepped back. "Take all the time you need."

Again, all he could do was nod. When he was alone, he drew back the sheet to the top of Annie's collarbone. His gaze wandered to the slit going across her neck, piercing his heart with a fresh wave of sorrow that manifested in a choking sob. He reached for her hand, but the icy feel of her lifeless flesh was too real, forcing him to replace the sheet. After another long minute, he returned his lover to her temporary place of rest.

He stopped by the coroner's office on his way out. "Do you have any of her personal effects?"

"I haven't received the okay to release them yet."

"I thought the killer was dead. It's not like you need it for evidence."

The doctor was about to reply when his colleague stuck his head in the door. "Dr, Stanley, there's a lady out here demanding to speak to you."

"Tell her I'm with someone."

"She insists on speaking with you. I think it's important."

He sighed. "Will you excuse me for a moment?"

"Sure," Mark said. When he was alone, he studied the placards on the wall before settling on a stack of papers in front of him. A note in an evidence bag caught his attention because it had Darya's name on it.

He glanced around, making sure no one was watching, and snatched up the baggie. According to the scribbled note on the front of the plastic, it had been found at the crime scene next to Annie's body. He studied it more closely. Not only did it have Darya's full name, but her address as well.

This wasn't some random break-in. Darya was the target all along, and Annie was an innocent victim. Bag in hand, he rushed out of the office. Dr. Stanley was out in the hall, speaking with a tall redhead. She had a hand resting on one of his crossed arms.

"Were you going to tell me about this?" Mark asked, holding up the evidence bag to the man.

Dr. Stanley's stare was distant and glassy at first. His pupils slammed back into focus when he turned his attention to Mark's raised fist. "Where did you get that? Did you go through my desk? Do you know what kind of trouble you can get into? What kind of trouble I can get into?"

"That lunatic was after Darya, and Annie had been caught in the crossfire. Jesus, Daniel, this changes everything."

Dr. Stanley paused, lifting a hand to halt the conversation. He turned back to the mysterious woman. "I'm sorry, miss, but unless you are family, I can't release any details."

The woman's lips twitched, as if she were suppressing a mocking smile. Her honey-colored eyes met Mark's, and a chill ran through him. His mouth went dry, his knuckles whitening around the evidence bag. In that moment, he felt as if she were weighing him, measuring the depths of his grief and anger.

"That is a pity," she said, her voice dripping with disdain. "Good day to you, gentlemen."

As she exited, Mark felt a strange combination of relief and heightened alertness, as if a predator had just left the room. He looked at Dr. Stanley, who seemed equally unsettled, and realized that this woman was a piece of a puzzle he couldn't yet see but was determined to solve.

When they were alone, Mark continued, "Tell me everything you know about this case."

"There's nothing to tell. I'm sorry, Mark. Really, I am. Annie's killer is dead. Justice has been served. What more do you need to know?"

"How did he know Darya? What did he want with her?"

"Does it really matter? It won't bring Annie back."

"It matters to me. Will there be an investigation into this?"

"To what end?"

Mark threw the bag at Daniel's feet. "You people are useless."

"Go home. Get drunk. Grieve for your girlfriend."

He would go home. He would probably get drunk, but he wouldn't let this go. One way or another, he was going to find out what role Darya played in Annie's death. His wounded heart demanded justice.

Chapter 3

Darya watched the last of the eastern continent fade into the distance. When it disappeared from view, she settled into her seat for the eleven-hour flight overseas to the small seaside village of Broughied, grateful to have the two first-class seats to herself. She was still trying to figure out how Janine had convinced her to go after all that had happened with Mark at her apartment.

She'd witnessed a fraction of his temper before, but nothing like what he'd shown her that day. The stench of alcohol on his breath, coupled with his grief, turned him into a man she didn't recognize. She didn't know where his vitriol came from, but it scared her.

How could he blame her for Annie's death? No matter how many times she denied the knowledge of the man who attacked them, he refused to believe her. His sorrow and anger were all-consuming.

"You're the reason she's dead," he'd spat at her, each word accentuated with a jab of his finger. The accusation filled her thoughts, making her question just how innocent she really was in all of this.

Was Mark right? Had that crazy man been there for her all along? He claimed there was evidence but refused to show it to her.

She didn't know what she would have done if Janine hadn't been there to save her from Mark and his drunken madness. After the incident at her apartment, Darya knew she had to get away from Dallas for a while. She needed a break from the horrible nightmares that plagued her sleep and Annie's mangled memory that lingered in her waking thoughts.

Raindrops splattered across the window, shattering her thoughts. She peered at the bloated clouds in the distance, reminding herself she wasn't afraid of flying. The sudden shudder of the metal tube made her gut clench involuntarily despite the magnificent display of nature. Closing her eyes to the storm outside, she let the rumble of the engines lull her into a half-sleep until a bolt of lightning brought her back to full consciousness.

She scanned the darkness, captivated by the diffused celestial light show. There, an odd shape stood out to her in a thick clump of clouds. With every burst of wind that molded the cloud into a new form, it remained a constant shadow despite the ever-changing swirl of the storm. It was hard to make out the shape, given the sporadic glimpses when the lightning brought the sky to life, so she leaned forward, squinting at the dark figure. Her heart thundered in her chest when she realized it wasn't some random trick of the light and it was moving closer to the plane.

"Nervous flyer?"

Darya jerked her head around to the seat that had been empty at take-off. "No," she said to the stranger staring past her out the window. "Just watching the clouds."

"It's not that bad." His accent was exotic, like his Nordic features. His eyes were a striking shade of green, almost unnaturally so, and when she met his stare, she was struck with a peculiar sense of familiarity. "I've flown in worse."

She reached under her seat to grab a book from her carry-on bag, hoping it would convey the universal sign of wanting to be left alone.

But the old man didn't take the hint. "Are you traveling for business or pleasure?"

If she was more of a confrontational person, she might have asked him if that was his assigned seat, but she didn't want to make a scene in such a confined space with so many hours still until they landed. "Pleasure."

"Me too. Well, I guess you could say it's a little of both. I'm on my way to see my family. While I'm there, I have other business to take care of."

She nodded, keeping her sights on the pages in front of her. "Sounds nice."

"It wasn't your fault."

Her vision blurred before she turned her head to meet the stranger's illuminated gaze. "What did you say?"

"Her death. It wasn't your fault."

The book sank to her legs. "How do you know about that?"

"I regret we didn't save her, too."

She tried to break away from his stare. "Who are you?"

He made a move like he wanted to reach for her, but stopped himself. "You are going to be safe now. Your destiny waits for you across the sea." His eyes glowed a brighter shade of jade.

"I know you," she whispered.

"Safe travels, Darya."

She shook herself awake, knocking the book from her lap. The seat beside her was empty, and there was no sign of the man who'd been sitting there before. Had there been a man sitting there? She reached for the paperback, and by the time she sat back up, the image of the old man was all but gone from her waking mind. Setting the book on the empty seat, she turned her attention to the star-speckled sky outside the tiny window. At least the weather was clear. Maybe she could get a little rest on the long flight after all.

She leaned back and picked up the book again, trying to concentrate on the printed words. Her thoughts inevitably returned to Annie and Mark, and his accusations. Knowing that some random maniac had her information left her feeling vulnerable. The terrible truth of her situation hit her like a punch in the gut. As much as she hated leaving the shop and Janine and the boys, she would have to find a new place to start over, just like before.

Darya was unprepared for what awaited her when she exited from the plane at Heathrow. The bustling airport was a lot like Dallas since they both served international flights, but jet lag and the excitement of being in a new country had her discombobulated and made her nearly miss her connecting flight. According to the itinerary Janine gave her, someone was supposed to meet her at Sholford for the last half-hour drive to Broughied.

The little puddle jumper that carried her from the outskirts of London to the west coast of Wales wasn't nearly as comfortable as the one she'd taken across the ocean, but it got her there in one piece and only slightly shaken from the inside out.

After collecting her luggage, the glass of wine she had downed on the last flight had caught up to her, and she had to make a quick stop in the bathroom. When she made her way to the exit, she set her suitcases down, scanned the deserted area, and didn't see a driver waiting for her as Janine had planned.

A cold ball of dread started from in the pit of her stomach. What if no one was coming for her? Should she call the inn? What if the itinerary Janine gave her was wrong? The days could have gotten mixed up.

Someone tapped her on the shoulder. "Excuse me, miss?"

Darya whirled around, her face set in a wide-eyed expression of panic and uncertainty.

The man took a quick step back when he saw her reaction, but the easy smile on his face stayed in place. "Are you Darya Pless?"

She nodded.

"I'm Dino. I'm here to take you to Broughied."

The fear melted from her features, replaced by a grin of her own. "Oh, thank God. I thought I was on my own for a second there."

He moved to the side, eyeing the suitcase and overnight bag. "Is that everything?"

"Yep."

"Good." He snatched up her bags and said, "The car is just out front. Follow me." He led her to a late seventies model black Audi with tinted windows so dark.

She didn't know if they would have been legal in the states. Once Dino put away her luggage and she was settled in the back seat, he got behind the wheel and drove away.

"Are you hungry or thirsty? It's going to be a hike to Broughied. I don't want to be accused of starving our guests before you get checked into your room."

She shook her head. "I'm fine. Really."

Even though she couldn't see his smile, she knew it was there by the way his eyes crinkled with deep-set laugh lines when he looked at her in the rearview mirror. He sped onto the uneven road and bounced toward the coast, out of town. "How long was your flight?"

"A little over thirteen hours."

He let out a slow whistle. "I go stir crazy after a two-hour car ride."

A grin split her lips. "You must not travel much."

"I'm happy with what I have in Broughied. It's a peaceful life."

What she wouldn't give to have that again. To live a life unburdened by the constant fear and regret, and heartache that simmered just beneath the surface. Maybe if she had made different choices, ran away from home at the first hint of her mother's true feelings for her. Perhaps then, she could have changed the way things played out between them, and she wouldn't carry this mark of hate on her body.

"Miss Darya?"

Darya shook herself out of those dark thoughts. "I'm sorry, I must have spaced out."

"I asked how long you were staying in Broughied."

"A couple of weeks."

Again, Dino's eyes revealed his grin. "I can show you around some lesser-known points of interest. There's a beautiful island not far from shore called Didean. You have to see it at least once before you leave."

"I'd like that."

The car pulled up to a striking two-story building made primarily of slate and stone. Its placement atop a rolling hill imbued it with a sense of permanence, as if it had grown naturally from the Welsh landscape itself. Dark, weathered tiles covered the roof, which featured a dome of glass inlaid into intricate pewter filigree that caught and reflected the late afternoon sun. A scattering of dormer windows, framed by wooden tracery, punctuated the low-hanging tiles.

A tall sign at the outer edge of the cobblestone circle drive welcomed her to "The Dragon's Rest." Where Dino parked the car and opened her door. "You can head inside. I'll bring your luggage."

She ascended a set of cobblestone steps to reach a pair of massive double doors. Recently refinished, they emanated a rich, dark glow and filled the air with the comforting scent of linseed oil. Brass hinges captured the glow of the sinking sun, radiating brilliant shades of orange.

Something tugged at a memory from her past, and she paused, trying to remember where she'd seen a door like that before.

Inside the narrow entrance, filtered through the sheer curtains, casting a diffused glow on the stone floor. Her gaze wandered upward to the domed glass-paned ceiling that let in more of the overcast light from heavy clouds blotting out the sun.

Farther up the hall was a potted ivy, its vines twisting around themselves and hanging over the table it sat on. She fingered a leaf, pleased to see it doing so well despite the soil being so dry. She would have to come by sometime and sneak it a drink of water to help stave off any more potential death.

Photographs and painted portraits lined each wall in between the windows. She took a moment to look at each image. There was so much history in those frozen moments in time. One of the sepia pictures appeared to be an old nineteenth-century photograph. It was of two men standing on a beach in front of a calm sea. She struggled to make out a lot of detail in the poor-quality photo, but it was clear they were related. They shared the same square jaw and off-kilter smile.

A melodious voice drew her attention to the waist-high counter on the other end of the walkway, where a matronly woman stood with her back to Darya. Her body was tight, with her arms wrapped around herself. She stared at a small black and white television, so she didn't see the new guest approach the front desk.

Darya rested her hands on the smooth marble surface, admiring the way the sunlight reflected off silver flecks in the sporadic pattern. Before she could announce her presence, the old woman spoke.

"Go, go, go," she whispered, willing the men on the screen to do her bidding as they fought to control the soccer ball. Her head moved to the side, and she glimpsed Darya standing opposite her. She did a double take before slapping the power button. "Forgive me, love. I didn't see you there."

Darya gave the hostess a friendly smile. "I have a reservation. Darya Pless."

"Oh, yes. Everything is ready for you." She looked past her. "Dino, be a dear and take her things up to room four."

He nodded and headed up the stairs.

She readjusted her silver bun and motioned her for her to follow. "I hope Dino didn't talk your ear off on the drive out here. I think he misses adult conversation since it's only him and that boy of his. He needs to get out there and experience life. There's more to the world than this little village. But what do I know? I'm just some old woman that hasn't had her share of worldly living. Well, I know plenty. Take this place, for instance."

Darya kept a polite expression plastered on her face while being regaled with tales of the inn and how it had been owned by the same family for generations. In fact, the village of Broughied was one of the oldest settlements in the area.

When they stopped in front of room four, she ended the conversation with, "Anyway, my name is Mrs. Beal. If you need anything, give me a ring."

Dino stood to the side of her door, trying and failing to hide an amused grin. "She is a lovely woman, but she can be a bit long-winded."

"I think she's sweet."

He hesitated a moment longer before pushing off the wall. "I guess I should return to work. I'll see you around."

"That would be great." Darya fought to keep the pink out of her cheeks when she saw his own face redden.

She leaned against the door for a few seconds, taking in her accommodations. The room may have been small, but it was clean. Her feet whispered across the stiff cream-colored carpet on her way to the bathroom.

She was glad to see the clawfoot tub on the far wall. Its porcelain surface had a pearlescent shine to it, and the pewter fixtures gleamed in the soft glow of the lights. The thought of relaxing in a hot bath left her staring longingly across the room.

She backed out of the bathroom and bypassed the bed to a set of curtained double doors that promised a breathtaking view. She pulled them open to a narrow balcony big enough for a single chair and a tiny round table.

Judging from where the sun sat in the sky, this would be the perfect place to watch the sunrise. Salty air washed over her when she stepped onto the wood decking overlooking the ocean. Closing her eyes, she let the brine of the sea sink into her weary body.

She pushed off the rail and went to bed. The part of her that had been cooped up in a metal tube for thirteen hours begged for sleep, but she knew if she laid down now, she'd be up all night, so she gathered her purse and headed downstairs. A lazy walk was just what her stiff legs needed.

On her way outside, Mrs. Beal was kind enough to remind her that dinner was promptly at five and rattled off a medley of delicious-sounding food.

Darya eased toward the door. "That all sounds amazing." And slipped outside before the old woman could stall her any longer.

The village wasn't the sprawling metropolis she had grown used to over the last few years in Dallas. She wandered through the narrow streets, enjoying the lack of noise and traffic. Cobblestone sidewalks flanked the main road in and out of a picturesque town center. Despite modern amenities like power lines and electric streetlamps, most of the storefronts and houses had the feel of a long-ago time when life had been much simpler and more untamed. She was in awe of medieval architecture, imagining what the world must have been like back then.

She passed a window with elegant script painted on its imperfect surface, denoting it as a sweet shop. The smells coming from inside lured her through the front door. A bell announced her arrival, and the little boy sitting behind the counter glanced up from his comic book to assess her with the indifference of a distracted child before shoving his face back into the colorful pages.

She didn't see the man walking through the swinging door at the back of the shop until he said, "What can I help you with today?"

Darya stood up, shocked to see Dino standing there.

He leaned on the glass. "Isn't this a pleasant surprise?"

"When you said you had to get back to work, I thought—" She shook her head. "I don't know what I thought."

He grinned at her. "I wear many hats around here, but I own this candy shop." He motioned to the case. "Would you like to try something?"

"What pairs well with jet lag?"

His smile turned to laughter, and he pulled out a tray. "I think you will enjoy this one."

The second the rich chocolate touched her tongue, she closed her eyes and sighed. "Outstanding. Is that a hint of strawberry I'm tasting?"

"I told you everyone would like it." The little boy said.

Dino motioned to the boy beside him. "Darya, I'd like you to meet my son, Marcos. Say hello to our guest. She is staying at The Dragon's Rest for a couple of weeks."

"Nice to meet you, Miss Darya."

"It's nice to meet you too, Marcos."

She glanced at her watch. "I will come back for more of that chocolate. First, I want to get a little more exploring done before Mrs. Beal calls out the calvary on me. I can't be late for dinner."

"Yes," Dino agreed. "She is fastidious about her meal-times."

Darya followed the sidewalk past other shops that offered an array of services and goods.

She refused to let herself get distracted again, wanting to get a feel for the layout of the village before returning to her room. Tomorrow she could take her time exploring the beautiful landscape. She turned the corner into a narrow alley and was about to go back the way she came, but the field that lay beyond drew her forward.

She broke free of the alley and caught sight of a cluster of oaks and maples across a meadow of reedy grass. There was an inaudible thrum, resonating from beneath her feet, that spiraled up her spine, beating in time with her own heart. It drew her forward, one hesitant step at a time, inching her closer to the ever-shifting shadows beyond the branches.

A hand grabbed onto her arm, shaking her out of the daze. When she came back to herself, she was already halfway to the patch of trees.

"You shouldn't be out here," Marcos said, pulling her toward the street. "There are things that can hurt you."

She studied the tree line. Whatever had been there before was no longer calling to her. A wave of fatigue washed over her, and she forced her mouth into a smile that she hoped didn't look like a grimace. She blew a strand of hair from her face, wondering if this was what everyone experienced on such a long flight.

Turning to the boy, she said, "Thank you for saving me, young man." She gave his chin a light brush with her fingers.

With a newfound urgency, driven partly by her body's desire for rest and partly by the disquieting experience, Darya rushed back up the alley, taking the same familiar route back to the inn.

Having washed her hair before taking her flight, she wrapped her braid around itself in a bun and secured it with a hairband before settling into the scalding water. She lost herself in the sounds of the faucet dripping into the tub and soon forgot about the strange incident in the village. A couple of times, she had to jerk herself awake when her head started to sink onto her chest.

About the time her fingers began to wrinkle, and the water started to cool, she huffed out a disappointed sigh and pushed herself out of the tub.

With a towel tucked around her body, she reached for the porcelain knob on the bathroom door and was overwhelmed by a surge of panic. Annie's bloody visage filled her mind. Her sightless stare locked on Darya, blaming her for letting her die. After a few seconds of steady breathing, she finally made herself open the door.

The room beyond was just like she had left it. One suitcase lay on the end of the bed. The overnight bag sat on the chair by the closed balcony doors.

There was no dead woman there. No crazed maniac waiting to jump out and try to stab her. She was thousands of miles away from that horror. The comfort of the silver band she twisted against her finger helped to banish the rest of her fear.

She grabbed a bright yellow off-shoulder sundress and a pair of taupe sandals from the suitcase on the bed. She let down her hair and brushed it out of the braid with her finger before sweeping half of it back in a loose updo, letting the lower half fall down her shoulders.

After checking herself in the full-length mirror in the far corner, she headed downstairs, scared she would miss the deadline that Mrs. Beal set.

She wandered around until she found the dining room, where the cheerful hostess greeted her with a wide smile. "There you are. I was beginning to wonder if you had fallen asleep. I wouldn't blame you if you had after the day you had." She motioned behind her. "Have a seat wherever you like."

Darya's gaze wandered to the double doors leading to a set table on a balcony overlooking the ocean. "Am I allowed to sit out there?"

"Of course, deary."

Mrs. Beal brought her a glass of wine while she waited for her food. Darya lost herself in the waves crashing against rock and the echo of gulls calling to each other. Golden hues of twilight warmed her face, and the potent bite of the alcohol heated her blood. She was so enraptured by the scene before her she didn't notice the man approach until he rested a hand on the chair across from her.

"Pardon me, Ms. Pless?" The way he spoke her name was reminiscent of her childhood.

When she looked up, she expected to find a druid elder from her tribe standing over her. Instead, a man with emerald jewels for eyes smiled down at her. His gaze held the wisdom of someone whose age was beyond his appearance.

She matched his grin. "Yes."

"My name is Horsa. I am the proprietor of this establishment." The laugh lines that crinkled his face told of years of happy memories, yet there was a sadness he carried on his weathered face. A perfectly trimmed beard covered his lower cheeks and defined jaw and matched the burnished walnut hair that sat with a slight swoop in the front of his head. With the sweeping gray feathers that crested his temples, he looked like he could have stepped right off the cover of a magazine from the sixties. Even his dark suit had the dapper look of the era.

"I wanted to personally welcome you to my inn." He held out a hand to her.

She fought an embarrassed giggle when he brought the back of her hand to his lips for a chaste kiss. "Thank you," she said. "It's lovely."

His gaze lingered on the ring on her finger before turning his head to the horizon, watching the sun make its final descent into the sea. "I couldn't imagine living anywhere else."

She fidgeted with her hair, avoiding those all-too-familiar eyes. She was glad when her food arrived, so she had something else to focus on.

"I'll let you get back to your meal. It was nice to meet you, Miss Pless."

"I'm not that formal. Call me Darya."

"Enjoy your stay, Darya."

Despite the awkward encounter, she enjoyed the plate of grilled salmon, asparagus, and fingerling potatoes. Once she had her fill, she pushed her plate away and sat back in the chair, sipping at the last of her wine. Its rich, fruity flavors mingled with the memory of the food and left her full and content.

Two new shapes appeared on the beach. Dino and Marcos wandered along the water's edge. The boy bent down every so often to pick up a shell. The older of the pair glanced up at the hill to the inn, waving at her. She returned the gesture, fighting a silly grin.

Maybe it was the wine or the salty air stirring in the twilight, but seeing his masculine shape against the shimmering water stirred a heat inside her. It had been too long since she felt the touch of a man, and as she admired Dino's lean form, she wondered if there was a woman in his life.

Mrs. Beal suggested that Marcos' mother wasn't in the picture for whatever reason. It was possible Dino was dating someone, yet if he was, she doubted it was serious. Not when he so openly flirted with her.

She pushed away from the table and made her way down the sandy path to the beach.

"Miss Darya." Marcos ran up to her with an opalescent shell in his hand. "Look what I found."

"It's beautiful," she mused.

The little boy grinned at her and took off after more treasures.

Dino approached her. "I was going to say the same thing about you." Even in the low light, she noticed his tanned complexion redden. "That was so lame."

"It's not the worst line I've ever heard. Who doesn't like a compliment?"

"You are beautiful." He held her stare for a few heartbeats before clearing his throat. "Would you care to join us for a walk?"

"I'd like that."

He reached for her, but before he could take her arm, he spun to the side with a loud yelp and slapped a hand over his left arm.

"Daddy!" Marcos ran to his father's side.

Dino scanned the dark landscape before peeking under the hand. Rivulets of blood oozed through his fingers.

Darya grabbed his uninjured arm and dragged him to the inn. They made it to the dining room, and Mrs. Beal met them at the double doors. "What happened?" She sat Dino down at an empty table inside the door.

"I don't know," Dino said. "One minute Darya and I were talking. The next, I'm bleeding."

Mrs. Beal muttered something in a language Darya couldn't understand, but she recognized the inflection of someone cursing. "I swear these men get themselves into some of the worst pickles." The old woman practically pushed her to the staircase. "You go on to the bed, dear. I'll take care of him."

Before she could argue, Dino said, "It's fine. I'll see you in the morning."

"Okay. Goodnight, then." Darya donned a confused frown before disappearing upstairs.

HORSA COULDN'T SLEEP AFTER the incident on the beach. Dino had been a fool to be so cavalier, knowing what was at stake. He was there to ensure Darya's safety, not to try to date her. He's lucky the wound was as minor as it was, given his trespass.

Instead of brooding in his room over the ordeal, Horsa chose to ruminate on the patio overlooking the ever-rolling waves of the ocean, listening to the sounds of the endless song of the sea washing ashore. He usually enjoyed quiet times like these when he could be alone with his thoughts.

That morning, however, he couldn't find comfort in his solitude. He almost couldn't make himself approach the girl the previous night. Seeing her again nearly broke him, knowing what still lay in store for her.

"I hope you addressed that stupid stunt last night."

Horsa kept his sight on the faint telltale signs of dawn, catching a glimpse of Ronwen approaching the table. "I did."

She plopped down in the chair across from him. "And?"

"And what? Nothing came of it. Dino is fine. It was a simple scratch. A reminder of his place."

She poured herself a cup of the dark liquid from the decanter and took a sip, making a sour face. "What is this stuff?"

"An old family recipe."

"It tastes like dirt and feet."

"You have an unrefined palate," he scoffed.

Ignoring the teasing barb, she said, "We've come too far and sacrificed too much to let something like this derail everything."

He understood her frustration and reached for her hand. "Fate is fate. It will come to pass one way or another."

A hint of fear clouded her already dark eyes. "There is no set path to one's destiny. There are ways to cheat it. Cernunnos nearly found a way to cheat it when he sent Tiernen after her."

"Yet, she still made it to us."

They sat together in silence until the sun was well over the horizon. His attention drifted past Ronwen to the woman stepping outside. "Good morning, Darya." He stood and held out the empty chair next to him.

Darya hesitated before accepting the offer.

He motioned to the woman beside him. "This is a dear friend of mine, Ronwen."

Darya went to shake her hand, but Ronwen gave her a curt smile, ignoring the friendly gesture. "I wish I could stay and chat. Unfortunately, I have a full schedule. Horsa, I will be in touch regarding our meeting tomorrow."

When she was gone, Darya said, "She seems lovely."

He smiled. "She is once you get to know her. Are you hungry? Mrs. Beal makes the most exquisite black truffle omelets."

"Actually, I was hoping to find Dino. I wanted to check on his arm and ask if he was up for taking me sightseeing today."

"I believe he will be gone most of the day."

She frowned. "I guess that means I'm on my own."

"If you don't mind some old guy cramping your style, I can show you around. I've lived here far longer than Dino." He could see her ready to decline his offer, but her gaze wandered past him to the dining room. The smile on her face fell into a confused frown.

"Mark?" She got up from the table and rushed inside. "What are you doing here?"

The man she referred to as Mark jabbed a finger at her. "I told you I wouldn't let this go. If you had nothing to do with Annie's death, why did you run halfway across the world?"

She crossed her arms and leaned back from his imposing posture. "What are you talking about? I'm not running from anything. I just needed to get away for a while. How did you find me, anyway?"

"You weren't hard to track down," he said. "Not for me."

"What's going on here?" Horsa stepped up beside Darya.

Mark's heated gaze flicked from Horsa, then back to Darya. "This isn't any of your business, old man."

Her voice rose a few octaves. "Why are you doing this?"

"It's your fault she's dead," Mark growled.

Horsa held up a hand. "Sir, you need to leave."

Mark attempted to move around him, but the simmering fury he saw in Horsa's face made him take a step back.

"If you are not off my property in the next thirty seconds, it will give me great pleasure to assist you myself."

Mark backed away and pointed at Darya again. "I'm not done with you."

Horsa made a move to grab him, but Mark was already quickly walking toward the front entrance. Darya pushed past the older man and disappeared around the corner, ignoring his calls. Horsa shot a confused look at Mrs. Beal, who was carrying an armful of crisp white linens for the tables.

"What was that about?" she asked.

"I honestly don't know," he said. "This is all wrong." He walked to the front desk and rang up his room, hoping Ronwen had made it there already. Less than a minute later, Darya bound down the stairs with her luggage in her hands.

"Will you please have someone take me to the airport?" She was wiping at her eyes.

Mrs. Beal looked from Darya to Horsa, unsure of what she should do. "You're leaving?"

Darya set the suitcases down at the front desk. "I don't want to be here anymore. I need to go home."

"Please, take a moment to calm down," Horsa begged.

She glared at him. "Will one of you give me a ride to the airport, or do I have to walk?"

"We can't let you leave."

Everyone turned toward the entrance to find Ronwen blocking the front entrance.

Darya snatched up her bags. "Excuse me? You're not going to stop me from leaving."

"I didn't foresee that man coming here, or I wouldn't have let him get near you." She looked at Horsa. "I didn't know about him. What does that mean?"

Darya tried to push her way past the other woman, but Ronwen seized each side of her head, sending Darya to the ground, screaming in pain.

Horsa gathered the unconscious woman in his arms. "Was that necessary?"

"We couldn't let her leave."

He brushed the dark strands of hair away from her face. "The solstice isn't for another four days. We can't keep her knocked out for that long."

"We have to open the way now."

"You said it had to be the right time to keep everything in order."

"It'll still work," she bit at her lower lip. "I think."

"Are you sure? We still have so much to tell her."

"I'm not sure of anything at this point," she snapped. "If we don't do this now, we may not be able to save her from what's coming. She has the ring. It is the key to her identity."

Horsa's gaze fell on Darya. He had to believe her destiny would continue on the path she was meant to follow. Everything they planned for, everything they worked to make come to fruition, had to happen the way it was supposed to. It had to. "We need to tell—"

"No." Ronwen's tone left no room for argument. "Not until she's gone. It will only make things worse."

He let out a frustrated sigh. "I'll get the boat."

Mark slammed his foot into the side of the rental car, letting out a curse. He forgot about the pain in his leg when he spotted the size twelve dent he had left in the driver's door.

As he stared at the costly damage, he contemplated going back inside and confronting Darya again. She knew more about the man that killed Annie than she claimed. Why else would he have her name and address?

There was no way that old bastard would ever let him near her, not after what had just happened. Unless he wanted to get his ass put in the local jail, he needed to be smart about this. He couldn't take the chance of being seen, so he opted to come back later in the evening to catch her outside.

He took off down the narrow road leading back to the city. A shadow passed overhead, and he leaned forward, thinking he saw a giant bird flying into the row of fluffy white clouds. When he looked at the street again, he had to slam on the brakes to keep from hitting a woman standing at the next intersection. She went around to the passenger's door and slid into the seat next to him.

"What the fuck, lady?" He turned, and recognition silenced any further protests. She was the same redhead he'd seen talking to Dr. Stanley.

She nodded to the road ahead. "Just drive."

"I don't think so, you crazy—"

Her head swung around, and a set of golden jewels flared in the bright morning sun. She brushed her fingers across his cheek. "I said drive, love."

Mark reached for his door handle, but he no longer had control over his body. His hands moved of their own accord, taking hold of the steering wheel. Despite his desperate attempt to press the brakes, the dented Ford Cortina crept forward.

"Don't worry your handsome little face. You're going to like what we have in store for you." She relaxed into the seat.

Mark watched, helpless, while she flipped through the radio stations.

"Take a left up ahead." Her words jolted him back to the road ahead.

A sheen of sweat broke out on his forehead from the effort of trying to get control of his faculties. He couldn't even open his mouth to scream at her. He drove through the lush summer countryside while his captor rummaged through the car's compartments. When she reached for his pockets, his physical reaction was wholly opposite to fear and anger that coursed through him.

She moved away once she had the wallet in hand, eyeing the bulge in between his legs.

"Oh my. That little tart of yours must have been one satisfied lady."

The mention of Annie distracted him from the erection that was pinched at an odd angle in his jeans. He tried to pry his mouth open and ask her how she knew his dead girlfriend, but again, nothing came out of his damn lips. They were welded together by whatever witchcraft she used to subdue him.

"Mark Abernathy," she cooed. "I knew I chose the right man for this." Her fingers traced his polished badge. "With your background and training, you will be an adequate replacement."

She threw the wallet on the floorboard and glanced out the window. "We've arrived. Turn up here."

He turned onto a dirt road, sending the car bouncing along a winding drive through sloping hills until they reached a moss-encrusted wooden gate. The pale sun struggled to break through the canopy of intertwined branches.

He didn't have time to get to a complete stop before the gates swung inward. A group of men stood on either side of the entrance, bows slung across their backs and wicked-looking blades at their waists.

"Pull over here." The woman got out, ordering Mark to follow.

"Where's Tiernen?" someone asked.

"Dead." She led Mark through the camp past a stone hearth with a fire pit where men and women convened. No one looked particularly hostile, yet they didn't look happy either. Everyone shared the same resigned expression about them. Even the children lacked that spark of life that was prominent in the faces of most youth.

An old woman who had spent too many years out in the sun came into view. She carried a covered basket in one hand and a clay pitcher in the other. Something about how she held her mouth sparked recognition in him, but his captor took hold of his arm before he could dig for anything more.

"This way."

They approached a set of bone markers stacked on top of one another. The yellowed skull that crowned the pile was definitely human, leading him to assume the others were as well.

"This is going to be unpleasant." The woman warned. "You'll probably be nauseas, but it will pass quickly."

The surrounding air warbled and pressed down on his skin, sending a warm sensation throughout his body. The breakfast he'd eaten that morning rose with such force he was on his hands and knees before he comprehended what was happening.

Her lips peeled back in a disgusted sneer. "That killed any thoughts of the yummy things I wanted to do to you."

To his surprise, he had control of himself again. "I wouldn't fuck you with my worst enemy's dick."

She snatched a handful of hair, yanking him to his feet. Her breath warmed his neck, and his body's reaction was instantaneous and all-consuming. The hard-on he had experienced before was nothing compared to the engorged erection threatening to explode from his jeans. It throbbed with each quickening beat of his heart. She pressed into him, and he let out an involuntary shuddering moan that ended in an unexpected orgasm.

"I will have you when I want, how I want, and for as long as I want." To prove her point, she ran a hand down to the moist front of his jeans. Already, he was painfully hard again.

"Boudica."

She glanced to the side, keeping her body tight to Mark.

"He is not here to be used for a plaything."

"He insulted me."

"You place too much value between your legs. Not everyone cares to taste the sweetness of your fruit."

Her features morphed into a seething glare. The man behind her stood in a relaxed manner, uncaring of the ire he invoked. The mask that covered his face stopped short of a mocking smile. Eyes the color of summer storm clouds looked past her to the man who was trying to cover the shame that soiled Mark's jeans.

Boudica worked her peach lips into a thin line before backing up a couple of steps. Mark slumped forward once he was no longer under the spell of her salacious touch.

"Leave us," the masked man ordered with a wave of his hand.

After a brief hesitation and one last glance at Mark, she sauntered into the forest. He kept his gaze glued to the ground, so all he saw was a pair of leather boots appear in his vision at the newcomers' approach.

"Careful," the other man said, his tone holding a hint of amusement. "She will eat your mortal soul if you give in to her."

Mark lifted his head, assessing his captor. He wore tanned animal skin pants that were held together at the waist with a triple-braided leather cord, much like the other men in this hippie commune. His linen shirt clung to his upper torso, revealing black tattoos that snaked up his arms in the shape of peculiar symbols. What he found particularly disturbing was the deer skull he wore over his face and the set of wide, thick antlers that sprouted from his head like some beastly crown.

"Who the fuck are you, people? What are you? Why did you bring me here?" Mark tried to give his voice authority, but the humiliation that bitch forced on him drained his strength.

The other man motioned over Mark's shoulder to where a woman lay naked on a stone slab. Her matted blond hair lay flat around her shoulders, caked with blood from the neck wound that killed her. Her once sun-kissed complexion was now pale and lifeless.

All the fear, humiliation, and anger that had heated his blood drained from him, leaving only longing and regret. "Annie," Mark whispered. He trudged to the stone, fearing that she was an illusion. When he touched her bare arm, he recoiled from the shock of her frigid flesh. "This is about Darya, isn't it?"

"She is the reason your Annie is dead. Her existence is a blight on this world."

Tears clouded Mark's vision, and his chest squeezed against his lungs, making it hard for him to breathe. "Why am I here?"

"I wish you to finish what the other could not. Kill Darya Pless. If you do this for me, I will give your woman back to you."

Hearing that impossible promise made his heart beat a little faster, but the cop inside him refused to believe in such a ridiculous fantasy. "How?"

The horned beast stepped up to Annie and laid a calloused hand on the arm Mark couldn't stand to touch.

Her pallid flesh brightened to the golden hue it had been in life, and her eyes fluttered open before landing on Mark. Lips flushed with fresh blood parted into a smile when her vision came into focus.

He bent forward, pressing his mouth to hers. The warmth of her kiss soon turned to ice. When he pulled away, she was again the lifeless shell he visited in the morgue. "No. Bring her back."

"I will. If you do what I ask."

He tore his gaze from his lover. "You're asking me to kill another human being in cold blood."

"She is an abomination." The creature cocked his head. "Do you wish to have your Annie back?"

"Yes."

"It is a fair trade."

It was a fair trade. What did he owe Darya? Annie didn't have to know the bargain he made in exchange for her life.

The man beside him let out an exaggerated sigh. "I can find another for this task. Return to your life, broken and alone."

Mark closed his eyes, silencing the voice inside his head, pleading with him to leave this place and let Annie rest in eternal peace. "I'll do it."

The monster's lips curled upward in a carnivorous smile. "Come. Allow me to bestow my blessing on you."

The monster took Mark by the side of the neck. A pain like nothing he'd ever felt before raced through every nerve under his skin. He thought he was screaming but couldn't be sure with all the burning agony boiling inside his veins. He heard bones snapping against each other, filling his lungs with the fire of his torture.

After the agony faded, and there was no more feeling left in his body, Mark blinked open his eyes. He looked down at the horned man from one of the nearby trees. His head darted around, taking in the crisp, clear images of the surrounding area. From across the field, he spotted a tiny mouse scurrying along a patch of dead leaves. He struggled to resist the urge to swoop down and snatch the delicious morsel in his quivering claws.

"It will take time to get control of your powers," the horned man said. "Boudica can help you." He lifted his face to the sky, his gaze wandering to the horizon. "They think to hide the seedling from me. When I find her again, you will fulfill your end of the bargain."

Mark was left alone to contemplate the speckled wings where human arms used to be. His sharpened gaze went to the rock where Annie no longer lay. Soon, he would get the chance to put right the terrible wrong that Darya caused and bring back the woman he loved.

The slow and steady roll of the ship rocking through the rough waves pulled Darya out of unconsciousness. Each gust of wind that swept past her face carried strands of hair that had come loose from her braid and tickled her nose and cheeks, further drawing her back to wakefulness.

Her head bobbed in time with the sway of her body. She stared at her hands resting in her lap, and there was a moment of panic when she tried to raise them and knock away the annoying hair, only to find herself unable to move them off her legs. After a few attempts, she managed to tuck the stray strands behind her ears.

Horsa and Ronwen stood at the helm, their backs to her. She couldn't understand the hushed whispers that came from their direction, nor did she care what they had to say. Her only concern was getting off the boat to dry land so she could call the police and report these lunatics.

"I'll open the portal when we are closer to the island," she heard Ronwen say.

Horsa turned, sensing Darya's gaze. "I know what you're thinking," he said in a calm, placating voice. "We're not going to hurt you."

"She's about to do something stupid." Ronwen kept her hands on the overside helm, her sights fixed on the waters ahead.

Horsa gave Ronwen a warning shake of his head before refocusing on Darya. "Please, let me explain why we brought you out here."

Darya jumped to her feet and took off for the cabin. Horsa was faster than she expected and cut her off before she made it to the top step.

"I told you," Ronwen muttered.

"Let go of me, crazy old man." Darya's voice shook with equal parts anger and fear.

Something big and heavy slammed against the sailboat, sending a spray of salt water over the bow. The taste of the sea was strong in her mouth, and the sudden impact of the waves spewed in her face took her breath away.

Horsa pulled Darya from the slick deck. "We need to open it now."

Darya wriggled in his arms, desperate to get free of his grasp. The call of the whale below gave her hope of escape.

"Not until we are closer," Ronwen insisted.

The boat rocked from another heavy blow.

"Or not." She started speaking in a language Darya recognized but hadn't heard since leaving her commune.

"Why are you doing this to me? What do you want?" Darya pleaded.

He hugged her tight to him. "I promise you are going to be alright. We only wish to protect you."

She stopped struggling long enough for him to relax his grip. When he did, she shoved an elbow into his ribs, but she lost her footing when the sailboat jerked again. Horsa latched onto her waist, knocking her farther off balance.

"Hurry," he called over his shoulder.

"Bring her here. I can't hold it for long."

Darya stared in disbelief at the shimmering swirl that split the air before her. The ever-changing spectrum of opalescent colors pulsed in oblong streaks like an open mouth waiting to swallow her whole. She struggled against the man at her back. "Please don't do this."

Too much in shock to resist, Darya was helpless to fight when she was raised toward the glowing rift in reality. She'd never felt such horrible pain like the liquid lava that filled every cell of her being. The lights of the portal flickered around her, racing faster and faster until the sensation of falling came to an abrupt stop.

Then there was nothing.

Chapter 5

DARYA CHOKED ON THE gritty saltwater rushing into her mouth. The assault on her senses forced her eyes open to the searing, angry glare of the sun. She let out a whimper and slammed them back shut from the sting of the blinding light. Her arms wobbled, and she struggled to keep her face out of the strong, unrelenting waves that tried to yank her into the sea.

Grit crunched in between her teeth, and no matter how much she spat, she couldn't get it out of her mouth. The sea's continuous, greedy pull ignited a primal fear of being sucked back underwater. She used what little strength she had left to dig her fingers into the soggy sand and dragged herself out of reach of the water.

Blind, weary, and free of the waves, she fell to her side. Time passed, counted only by the steady whispering of the ocean's advance and retreat. It was a long time before she could open her eyes without setting fire to her corneas. Her clothes were dry to the touch, but still held a hint of dampness. She barely had the strength to push herself to a sitting position, moving her head in a slow half-circle and studying the desolate surroundings.

Her vision was still bleary, making it impossible to discern anything more than general shapes in the distance. There was a bend in the beach that disappeared beyond the view of a sloping cliff. The clacking of rock on rock drew her attention to a narrow trail hidden among the patchy weeds on the far side of the cliffs.

A little girl peered around a small boulder. Wild brunette hair framed a curious face. The sight of another person made Darya scramble to her feet. The girl's inquisitive expression morphed into fear, and she retreated behind the rock.

"Hey." The vibration of her voice made Darya's throat burn. "Little girl. Wait." She started loping after the child on unsteady legs across the uneven terrain.

The chase wasn't a long one, but it felt like an eternity with the way her legs burned from the steep incline. She followed the trail up and around a steep hill to a grassy meadow that overlooked a shallow valley surrounding a village where a few dozen houses lay in neat rows. At the crest of the ridge, she saw the girl speaking to a couple of men.

Darya's vision had cleared enough for her to see they carried weapons at their sides. When they spotted her, the taller one yelled something she couldn't make out and started in her direction.

Panic propelled her toward the sanctuary of trees across the valley. The rolling terrain of rock gave way to the wonderful relief of soft grass, allowing her to ignore the pain that still blistered the soles of her bare feet.

Despite her terror, she spotted a thicket of underbrush and ducked inside. Adrenaline drove her forward, gnarled branches clawing at her clothes and face. She had to throw up her hands to stave off their sharp edges.

A few seconds later, the sound of men's voices and heavy footsteps cut through the pounding of her own heartbeat in her ears. One of her pursuers called to his companions. When she looked behind her, the sight of more men chasing after pushed her to run faster, even more desperate to get away. The swell of relief from the distance she put between her and the other men was short-lived, though.

Too late, she glimpsed the edge of a ravine. Before she could reverse her momentum enough to turn from her current course, she slipped on a moss-covered rock, sending her rolling and bouncing down the steep embankment. She clawed at the earth to slow the dangerous descent, but there was no stopping the cluster of rocks that came up to meet her at the bottom of the gully.

A deafening crack of bone on stone echoed inside her head, sending white-hot pain radiating out from the point of impact. Agony surged through her, so intense it stole her voice. Paralyzed from the shock of the fall and the subsequent abrupt landing, she lay on her stomach with her mouth hanging open in a silent scream, choking on her own gasps.

A pair of dark boots came into view, slow to approach her. She managed to get her arms in front of her in a feeble attempt to pull herself away, only to be scooped up in a pair of sweat-drenched arms. Already, darkness was encroaching on the outer periphery of her vision. She had no choice but to relax into the man's arms and the coming black wall of nothingness.

Consciousness rolled in and out of Darya's vision like some nightmare of flashing images and faces until everything slowed into a single point of awareness. She lay nestled into a soft bed, running her hands over the silky furs that covered her lower body. This time, she was careful to ease her eyes open, remembering the painful sting of the sun on the beach. The warm orange glow of late afternoon light eased her the rest of the way out of sleep.

The arched window next to the bed let in a tangy breeze from the surf crashing against a rock. Her gaze roamed over the pockmarked stone until a twinge in her neck reminded her of the fall she'd taken. A shaking hand reached up to her scalp. She traced a tender split in her hair, making her suck in a breath from the pain. She was relieved when she didn't pull back bloody fingers.

She focused on a set of glass-paned doors that led to a stone balcony. There was another closed door across the room from the bed. Cast iron hinges embedded the weathered wood of the door in the stone frame. She lost any higher brain function and flung the blanket to the side, thinking it was a way out.

Her stomach advised against making any more sudden movements when she sat up too fast. She obeyed the warning by swinging one leg at a time onto the floor. The cool rock was soothing on her sore feet.

She made a detour on her way through the sparse space, peeking around the open doors overlooking the rolling hills below. Wispy white clouds dotted the sky, and another warm gust of wind brought with it the tart taste of burning wood and other potent spices. From where she stood, anything beyond the terrace was impossible to see. She didn't dare risk being caught out in the open, so she backed inside again and continued her trek across the room.

Leaning against the door, she listened for any sounds of movement. The heavy handle made a loud clacking noise when she lifted it. She held her breath until she was sure it was quiet outside the door.

At one end of the hall was a narrow window. Opposite was a set of stairs and a possible means of escape. Her bare feet made soft slapping sounds against the stone as she made her way to the top of the landing that rounded out of view below.

She eased forward onto her toes but couldn't see anything beyond more than the half-dozen steps. After a few harrowing heartbeats of hesitation, she eased down, one stair at a time. She made it to the bottom of the stairs and rushed around the corner, bumping into a young woman carrying a tray of food and drink.

Darya grabbed the tray to keep it from spilling onto the floor, then put a finger to her lips. The girl nodded, but it was too late. Another woman was already rushing toward them.

Unsure of where to go, Darya took off for a large swath of light, hoping it was her way to freedom. Had it not been for the two armed men blocking her path, she might have made it outside.

The taller of the men drew his sword, making her shuffle back a few steps to keep from skewering herself on its vicious tip. She followed the distinct Damascus patterned blade past the hilt and up the arm to the owner of the weapon.

A scowl was half-hidden beneath a straw-colored beard sculpted around a face that looked to be chiseled from the very stone of the surrounding walls, hard and imperfect. A pair of furrowed brows shaded malachite eyes that promised to bring forth their wrath if she so much as took in a heavy breath.

"Where might you be off to, girl?" His rich, basso voice didn't hold the mirth of the crooked smile that could have been a scowl, given the rest of his demeanor.

Darya's gaze darted from the sword to the promise of freedom beyond the open door.

His smirk fell. "Go on, try to run again," he said.

She fought to keep her breathing shallow, so the vicious tip of the blade didn't dig into her chest.

The woman who started the chase came into view and put a hand on the hilt of the sword, pushing it away from Darya. "Is that necessary?"

He frowned at Darya and asked, "Was it necessary for her to run?"

She held out a hand to Darya. "I will not harm you." Eyeing the man beside her, she added, "None of us will."

Darya glanced from her hand to the woman at her side, noting her eyes were a lighter shade of the same as the man who tried to run her through, though her hair was darker, and her smile was much more sincere.

Darya clasped her hands to her chest when the other woman reached for her.

"Come," she said. "I only wish to talk."

With no other choice, Darya relented and followed her to a small room with two chairs facing a rumbling fire. The warmth of the hearth was comforting, making it easier for her to relax in the high-back chair, despite its stiffness.

In between the chairs was a set of wooden cups and a carafe sitting atop a round table. Thin wisps of heat rose from the dark liquid. The pleasant woman poured the tepid drink into a glass and motioned for Darya to have a seat. "This will make you feel better."

She sipped at the stout tea in quiet meditation while the other woman watched on.

"Do you think you are ready to talk to us now?"

The soothing voice broke through Darya's thoughts. She looked away from the flames and nodded.

"Good. Let's start with our names. I am Gita. This is my brother, Edwind, of the house, Wodehal." She motioned behind Darya.

She looked over her shoulder. The angry man stood to one side of the door, eyeing her with the same scowl.

"What is your name?" Gita asked.

She took another sip before saying, "Darya."

"How did you end up on our island?"

She opened her mouth to tell her, but when she went to pull at the memories, there was nothing to recall. A blank wall stared back at her.

"Where do you come from?"

Again, Darya peered into the nothingness of memories that weren't there. The cold crept back into her bones. Aside from her name, she couldn't remember anything from her past. Not where she came from or how she got there. Not a single detail about herself. "I—I don't know." Fearful tears blurred her vision.

"No, child. Don't cry. The little girl who found you said you washed up on shore. Do you recall the ship that carried you?"

There was a flash of water and a boat. She had a sense of danger, but nothing tangible. "No."

Gita took Darya's hand, fingering the ring there. "This is unique. Do you recognize it?"

She cocked her head to the side. "I'm sorry. I don't recall." She set the cup aside and rested her face in her hands, trying to remember something of her past other than a name.

"I'm sure it will come back to you in time. Until we can find your people and get you home, we will care for you."

Gita's motherly demeanor put her at ease, unlike her brother.

"What island is this?" Darya asked.

"Didean."

The words slithered inside her mind, nudging the part of her brain that housed her past.

"Is the name familiar to you?"

"I don't know. I mean, no, I don't think so." She went to stand, but Edwind was at her back before she could get free of the chair.

Gita shot him a warning glare. "I imagine you are hungry," she said to Darya. "Would you care for something to eat?"

"I'd like to lie down if that's alright?"

"Very well. Though you are a guest in our home, you are still a stranger among us. For your protection and our peace of mind, I must insist you have an escort if you expect to roam the grounds."

She couldn't imagine she'd be doing a lot of exploring. All she wanted to do was take some time to process everything that had happened to her.

Gita nodded to someone out of view. "This is Wynfrid. She will see you to your room."

The young woman Darya collided with on the stairs waited in the doorway. Her tawny hair was pulled back in a tight braid and hung over one shoulder. Vibrant blue eyes drew the afternoon light into their depths, making them practically glow in the dim corridor.

Darya followed her out into the hall. When they were away from the others, Wynfrid whispered, "You are safe among these walls."

Safe was not the word she would use to describe her current situation, but she had no reason to think she was in immediate danger if that man, Edwind, kept his blade put away.

"She is lying," Edwind insisted. "She remembers her name, but nothing of her past?"

Gita ran a finger along the rim of the cup, staring out of the window. "Did you notice the knot-work of that ring?"

Her question threw him off his train of thought. "Her ring? I didn't pay any attention to it. Why?"

"I'm sure I've seen it before," she said, lifting her gaze. "She is being truthful."

"How can you be so sure?"

Gita nodded to the mug Darya had been drinking from. "You may not walk the same path as our ancestors, but I do.

The herbs I put in her tea would make it nearly impossible for her to lie."

"Even if I trusted in the potency of those herbs, she could still be untruthful under its influence."

"That poor girl has no memory of who she is or how she came to be on this island. I am trying to appease your untrusting nature. I insisted she have an escort by her side at all times, but she will be allowed to roam freely among the common areas."

He opened his mouth to argue until a single raise of Gita's sharp eyebrows quieted any further protest. "Fine," he grumbled.

"Naven is a suitable companion. See that he is put at her door."

He followed his sister outside. In the courtyard she joined Saebbi near the gardens. He watched them disappear down the path to the beach, past the southern cliffs where the girl washed ashore. He was tempted to join them. Maybe he could find some clues that could tell them more about this mysterious woman and how she ended up on his shores.

He studied the open balcony doors of Darya's room. Everything about her was unlike anything he'd ever experienced in his travels. She spoke in a dialect he'd never heard. Even her scent was reminiscent of the strange and exotic.

Gita thinks she is some poor helpless creature, but he knew there was something dangerous about her. He wasn't about to let an unknown threat loose around the people he was sworn to protect. Despite what his sister demanded, he would not give that woman an opportunity to be free of her room.

"I left food by your bed." Wynfrid pointed to the same tray Darya almost knocked out of her hand. "I imagine you must be famished after being spat out by the sea."

Darya attempted a smile to hide the unease she felt at the thought of putting something on her sensitive stomach. The gash on her head still had her guts clenching. "Thank you."

Wynfrid led her to the balcony. She pointed through the gates of the wall to the village. "I stay there among the houses, but I come here every day to care for this place as my mother did before me and her mother did before her."

Darya's gaze swept over a man disappearing past the outer wall. She recognized the hilt of the sword at his side. "Are Gita and Edwind royalty?"

"Never call them that to their face," Wynfrid whispered. "They hold a strong seat of power here, but only because of who their mother was."

Darya watched the girl's expression fall into a sullen sadness that told of loss and grief.

Studying Darya for a moment longer, she said, "We follow a different path than those druids on the mainland." She nodded to the small houses in the distance. "Gita and Edwind's grandmother was a priestess among her people. On one of her pilgrimages, Niamh met a young man who fell instantly in love. He was so devoted to her that gave up his claim to his throne and traveled across the sea to live among her people."

Wynfrid motioned around the room. "In return for his devotion, Niamh agreed to raise their daughter among these walls as the druid princess she was."

Wynfrid returned to the valley below. "That's the story my grandmother tells me, anyway. Love can bring forth the most unlikely of compromises." She met Darya's stare. "I tell you this because I see the old ways in you. You may not know where you come from or how you came to be here, but I sense the hands of the gods in this. I think you were meant to find us."

Darya stared after Wynfrid when she left, wondering if there was more meaning to her words. She stepped onto the balcony, resting her hands on the waist-high railing of the balcony. Bright colors caught her attention, and she looked over the beautiful array of flowers that flanked a narrow walkway circling the courtyard.

At first sight, the flowers were a beautiful spectacle, but the longer she stared at them, the more she noticed wilted petals and drooping stems. She wasn't sure how far into the season it was, but they shouldn't be so sickly.

Their scent carried on a soft breeze, and it triggered a hint of a memory that slipped out of her grasp as quickly as it manifested. She fought to bring the images to the forefront of her mind. The harder she snatched at them, the more they dissipated.

Frustrated, she folded her arms together and stared at the garden. Movement in the sky took her attention to a bright streak racing through the air toward a parapet attached to the stone wall surrounding the keep.

A white falcon landed on an outlying stone. There was a thin line of brown that ringed a set of pale moon-shaped orbs and accented its otherwise crisp pale feathers. She was drawn to the beauty of those eyes and was acutely aware of being pulled across the expanse of the courtyard.

The bird's shrill cry echoed inside her head, and she jerked free of the hypnotic trance. It flapped its wings a few times before taking flight and fading into the fluffy clouds that rolled past the tall tower at the far side of the outer wall.

She pushed off the rail, wanting to get away from the odd feeling still skulking inside her head. It was bad enough that she lost her memory. She didn't need to lose her mind, too.

She wandered around the room, stopping in the corner near the arched wooden door. There was a table with a basin of water on one end and a clean cloth folded in a neat square beside it. Behind the clay bowl was a cloudy, rectangular mirror that reflected a stranger's face.

She fingered the dark locks hanging loose over her shoulders. Unfamiliar cobalt eyes looked to her for answers she could not give. How could she know her own name but not recognize the person staring back at her?

"Who are you?" she asked the stranger there.

Laughter echoed through the window, distracting her from the image in the mirror. She eased to the sill, peeking out over a long stretch of beach. She recognized Gita's tall frame, strolling at a casual pace along the shore. The man at her side was the same one she encountered with Edwind when she tried to escape earlier, though his complexion was much darker and contrasted with rust-colored hair that swayed in the breeze.

Gita leaned into him, listening. Her head fell back, and she laughed again. He turned his face to whisper in her ear and saw Darya standing in the window. His smile was genuine, like Gita's. He gave her a quick wave of his hand. Gita followed his gaze and did the same.

Darya moved out of view of the opening, embarrassed at having been caught spying on such an intimate moment. After a couple of long breaths, she eased forward. They were walking away toward the ocean once again.

Turning back to the room, she suddenly felt the walls pressing in on her. The need to isolate herself from the potential dangers on the other side of the door was out-weighed by an even greater desire to get away from the drab gray stone that surrounded her. Gita had insisted Darya have an escort with her if she wished to explore, so when she opened the door and found no one waiting for her, she wondered if she was supposed to ask for an escort. Perhaps, Wynfrid would agree to go with her.

Ignoring the fear of the unknown, Darya headed for the stairs.

Sunset settled over the quiet meadow, dispelling the late summer afternoon. Murky water rippled around Cernunnos' chest, synchronized with the sweeping movements of his arms over the pond's surface.

Dark thoughts churned inside his head, thoughts of his past and the family he once had. Even after countless years of this pitiful existence, he clung to the memory of his Etain's beautiful visage. Her eyes had been the color of the clearest blue sky. He ached to taste her soft lips and run his fingers through the silken hair that carried in it all the colors of the changing leaves before the first snowfall; how he missed the melody of her voice when she called his name.

Cernunnos shut his eyes against the painful memories, but they still came. He was taken back to the day his mate had been so brutally murdered by those disgusting hunters. Cernunnos watched Etaine move through the trees, her belly big and round with their child. She often took the form of a graceful deer and grazed among the herds that passed through their home.

Her terrified wails shattered the very air around them when the arrow pierced her breast. With all the power he wielded, he was helpless to save her or their seedling. He begged his uncle to return them from the dead, but Arawn had refused.

Grief soon gave way to an uncontrollable anger, burning through him until there was nothing left but an all-consuming fury directed at the men who dared trespass in his domain. He hunted down those men that took his mate from him. They were a small clan of pitiful humans. He'd torn through their midst, demanding the souls of their women and children for the lives they plundered.

An elder of the tribe begged him for mercy, offering his own life in their stead. But a single life would not sate the need for vengeance. They had to suffer for their transgression, and suffer they would, along with their descendants. He cursed them to an eternity of servitude to his will and desires. Every generation, he would come to them and choose a bride. When he'd had his fill of them, he would offer their lives as a sacrifice to Etain.

And so that is how it has been, for longer than he cared to remember. After a few hundred eons, he understood that the curse he laid upon that tribe became his own prison of retribution and revenge he couldn't escape.

Then the Weaver dared to lay her own prophetic blight on him, foretelling of his death by the hands of his own seed. He'd laughed at her words. No child would come from the dead he left in his wake. Yet here he was, fighting Fate for his very life because somehow one of his brides survived to spit out his offspring.

Cernunnos felt the subtle shift in the air behind him. He turned, frowning at the two figures shadowed against the horizon. Boudica stood next to a robed man. An unnatural shadow fell across the cowl that was pulled over his head, hiding his face in the darkness.

"I brought the summoner you asked for," she spoke the words as if she had eaten a piece of rotten fruit.

Cernunnos strode out of the water, unbothered, when the newcomer turned his hidden face from his naked form. The ancient god kept his gaze set on the last of the sun's golden light on the western horizon as he fastened his pants and slung his shirt over his torso. Turning, he pierced her with a sneer, annoyed at being disturbed.

She visibly struggled to look him in the eyes, finally breaking their hold and turning her gaze to the ground. "The summoner says he can do what you ask."

"The magic will be trickier without a talisman." said a deep, melodious voice from within the black pitch of the hood. "Your blood should be strong enough to bind you to her."

"And what of the price?" Though he didn't see the smile that spread across those hidden lips, Cernunnos had to make an effort not to shudder at the sickly wave of power that permeated the air between them.

"Your spawn is destined to bring forth tragedies for us both. Her death will be sufficient."

Cernunnos cocked his head to one side, his eyes narrowing to tiny slits. "Her reach is that great?"

"You do not know the dangerous force you've unleashed upon this world. She cannot be allowed to live."

The summoner's words heightened the need to find Darya and kill her. Cernunnos' mouth twisted into a feral smile. "Then let us begin the ritual."

Chapter 6

Darya stood at the end of the foreboding hall, considering her options. She'd gotten so wrapped up in exploring that she lost herself in the labyrinth of passageways and dark halls. She was about to retrace her steps when she caught sight of an open doorway spilling sunlight into the hallway.

Though her instincts were telling her to turn back the way she came, her legs carried her forward. She peeked inside, making sure the room beyond was empty before pushing the heavy door all the way open. It was definitely a woman's bedchamber. The once bright and cheerful decorations were dulled by years of neglect dust and neglect.

On the far wall sat a double bed with sheer linens hanging across a delicate canopy frame. Gracefully carved filigree had been etched into the four posts by the hands of a master woodworker. The swooping lines and flowing curls whispered to that place in her mind where her lost memories remained locked away.

A brisk breeze swept through the room, pulling her focus to the open window where there sat a small square table flanked by two low-back chairs positioned across from each other, one of which was turned at a slight angle as if waiting for its occupant to return.

She crept closer to the board to get a better look at the figures methodically placed on each dark and light square. Every piece was carved from a pale timber. Age marred the brittle surface with tiny fissures, but she could still see the sloppy knife marks that told of someone who wasn't very confident with their blade.

Opposite the table was a stone fireplace that made up most of the wall separating this room from the one beyond an arched doorway in the far-right corner. Judging from the layers of dust, the cold, lifeless hearth hadn't been used in some time. Dried husks of what had once been roses sat in a clay vase atop the mantle.

At the end of the bed, she spotted a wood trunk that was as wide as the bed and half as tall. Milky, translucent stones gathered what little light came through the window, giving them a luminescent appearance.

She forgot about the rest of the room and strode to the chest. Dropping to her knees, she carefully traced the gems with her fingertips. There were symbols etched deep into the aged iron that held it together. The flowing designs were almost readable, but their meaning kept falling away as quickly as the rest of her memories.

No matter what the sigils said, they wouldn't stop her from operating the latch. She tried to flip the hook to the side, but it didn't budge. Her brows furrowed, and she pulled harder until it gave way with the sound of iron scraping on iron.

The surrounding air grew colder, sending a brisk breeze over her skin. The soft hairs of her arms stood on end with an ethereal energy that emanated from the smooth wood she was touching.

After a few heartbeats of hesitation, she lifted the lid. She had it halfway open when it occurred to her how incredibly inappropriate she was being. Here she was, a guest in this house, and she was rifling through their private things like they were her own.

Someone grabbed her by the shoulders, snatching her up with so much force they hoisted her into the air before bouncing her back onto the ground.

She stood nearly nose to nose with a face twisted in anger. "What are you doing in here?" Edwind's eyes appeared to glow in the filtered light coming through the curtained window. "You were told not to leave your room."

Darya didn't have time to find her voice before being dragged out into the hallway. Her gaze dropped to the hand that gripped her arm too tight. The pain from his fingers digging into her muscles brought her back to her senses. "Let go," she demanded, surprised at the authority in her voice. "You're hurting me."

He looked down and relaxed his grip, but didn't release her. "How dare you mock our hospitality? I will not be made a fool and treated with such disrespect."

Taking advantage of the loosened hand, she jerked herself free. His words stung her pride. No matter how true they were, she refused to give him the satisfaction of her guilt. "No one said I couldn't leave my room. I was told I needed an escort, which I was trying to find."

He snatched her arm again. "Is that so? It didn't look that way just now."

He quickened his pace, and she had to practically run to keep from being dragged along behind him. After shoving her into a small room, he moved himself into the doorway, blocking her escape. "You will wait here until I decide what to do with you."

She took a step toward him, and he leaned into her advance. "Or I can lock you up as a prisoner in a much less accommodating place."

Clamping her lips together, she chewed back the string of protests waiting to be unleashed. His pompous smile sent an irrational sense of indignant rage through her. When she heard the bolt engage, she pounded on the unwavering wood. "You're an arrogant ass!"

Frustrated, she stomped to the lone window and calculated her chances of getting through the courtyard to the outer wall unnoticed.

Edwind's looming shape exited the front entrance and headed for the gate. He turned his head and spotted her watching him and called to someone out of view. When a new man stepped up beside him, Edwind pointed to her. Any hope of a grand escape vanished.

And what if she had gotten away from the castle? Where would she go? She was on an island in the middle of the ocean. There was no telling how far the mainland lay from those shores. Even if by some miracle she made it across the sea, who would she turn to?

With no other choice, she threw herself into a chair, staring daggers at the door and wallowing in the stupidity of her actions. Her gaze wandered to a shelf inlaid into the stone behind her, with tomes of all sizes filling each tier. She strode to a random row of books and pulled a leather-bound tome from the middle. Ever so gently, she pried it open to the first page, only to be disappointed by the same undecipherable words that were carved into the chest.

Instead of reading, she studied the pictures that were sketched on the outer edges of the soft vellum. Their drawings depicted strange flora she wasn't familiar with. Other sketches showed exotic animals that were just as foreign to her. She put the book away, choosing another random text.

This volume was dedicated to a single creature. Each winged beast had the same distinct hatching. The detail was exquisite. Though they all shared the same shape, they had their own unique features. One of the drawings stood out to her more than the others. She reached out to run a finger over the sketch. Behind her, the lock on the door disengaged.

She slammed the book closed, then shoved it back in place before rushing to the chair in time to meet the trio coming into the room. Gita was the first to enter, followed by the man she'd been walking with on the beach. Darya mused how fitting it was for Edwind to be bringing up the rear, being the ass he was.

"Edwind told me what happened." Gita's tone was hard but not hostile.

"I bet he did," Darya said before she could stop herself. She drew in a deep breath, letting it out just as heavily. "I needed to get out of that room."

"I thought I made it clear you were to have an escort at your side if you wished to explore the grounds," Gita said.

"I was searching for Wynfrid when—."

Edwind snorted.

Darya skewered him with a look before returning to Gita. "I was searching for Wynfrid, but I got lost."

The priestess frowned. "Was there not a man at your door?"

Darya shook her head.

Gita stared at her brother in a way that stopped him from smiling. "We will be but a moment." She dragged Edwind from the room.

Darya and the other man shared awkward glances, pretending not to hear the angry, hissing whispers coming from outside the open door.

When Gita returned, she wore a forced smile, making her lips thin and tight. "I'm sorry for the misunderstanding, Darya. Edwind was supposed to have someone assigned to be your escort. I suppose he forgot to do as I asked."

The implication of Edwind's actions sent a range of emotions through Darya. When she cut her eyes at him, he shied away from her outrage.

"I'll make sure it doesn't happen again," Gita assured her. She motioned to the man beside her. "If he agrees, I would like Saebbi to look after you."

Saebbi nodded. "Of course."

Gita gave a curt nod. To Darya, she said, "We are eating soon. Would you join us?"

Darya felt herself shutting down both emotionally and physically. She didn't have the constitution to deal with these people anymore. "I'd rather be alone in my room." She held onto the anger that chewed at her guts, refusing to give them her tears.

Once out of sight, she clamped a hand over her mouth to hold back the tears that threatened to burst out of her. In her room, she sat on the edge of the bed and gave in to the fear and sadness, letting all her frustration out in silent sobs.

"I cannot believe your audacity," Gita said. "As priestess of Didean, my word is the law. I don't care if you are of my blood. I will not have you disregard my authority."

Edwind poured himself a drink, bracing for his sister's verbal lashings. Cup in hand, he wandered to the window and let Gita continue her tirade.

"I entertained your ridiculous notions and put a guard on her, but even that wasn't good enough. I swear I don't know what to do with you anymore."

He took a long pull of the ale, letting her rant. It was better to let her vent; then come back with logic.

"Don't play this game with me," she said. "I won't let this go because—"

"She unlocked the chest," he said, feeling the weight of Gita and Saebbi's eyes.

"She did what?" Gita's anger vanished, replaced with disbelief.

Edwind turned a self-satisfied smile on her. "How is it we haven't been able to find a key or magic of any kind to unlock that damnable box in the years since our mother's death? And now, this stranger who claims to have no memory can achieve this miraculous feat?"

"Is it still unlocked?" Gita asked, ignoring Edwind's questions.

"I didn't go back after confronting the girl."

"Bring it here," she ordered.

Edwind and Saebbi returned after a few minutes with the unlocked chest. Gita rested her hand on the latch before pushing it open.

Saebbi whispered a quiet curse.

"Do you think she is so innocent now?" Edwind asked.

Gita pushed aside the dress that sat on top. "I doubt our mother would have made a ward easily dismantled by someone who means harm."

He frowned, not wanting to contemplate the possibility. "If she meant it to be opened at all," he muttered.

She pulled out an oval box Edwind recognized. It was the one he had carved for his mother when he was a young boy. His mood shifted from irritation to nostalgia. "I thought she got rid of this stuff."

Gita handed him the box. "Mother kept the things most precious to her."

He ran a thumb over the crude knife marks on the outside. His skill had grown significantly since he made it for her. A smile pulled at the edge of his mouth at the thought of their mother treasuring his clumsy keepsakes.

Saebbi cleared his throat. "I don't mean to disturb your memories, but what if Darya doesn't know the power she possesses?"

The siblings stared at him.

"Perhaps she, too, is a priestess. Gita, you recognized that ring of hers. Did Diana have one?"

"It doesn't belong to any druid I know of, but I am sure I saw something similar when I was visiting our father years ago." Her eyes slid out of focus. "She could have been on a pilgrimage to another island. What if her ship encountered a storm?"

Edwind shook his head. "You didn't find any markings when you mended her wounds."

"That means nothing." Gita countered.

"Why can't you, for once, accept that I may be right?" Edwind's frustration came through in his words.

"When you stop assuming the worst in people, I'll believe in your instincts again."

"She needs to be returned home. I'm sure she has family worried about her."

Gita shrugged. "When she regains her memory, we will take her there."

Edwind looked to his friend for help, but Saebbi held out his hands and shrugged his shoulders. "I cannot abide treating Darya like a prisoner."

Edwind slammed down the cup of ale and stormed out of the room. Outside, he glanced from the gardens to the cliffs before deciding to follow the outer wall to a set of stairs leading to a walkway around the inner courtyard. At the top, he stared out over the village of the people who entrusted their lives to his family for protection.

Gita could be so naïve at times. Even if Darya was telling the truth about her memory loss, it didn't make her any less dangerous to them. How could his sister not understand this?

Muffled sobs carried on the wind, snapping his head around. Darya stood on her balcony, gripping the banister so tight her knuckles were stark white against the gray stone. Her body shook with the effort of trying to hold back her pain. Even in the dim light of dusk, he could see her tears falling on clenched hands.

Watching her in that state made him wish he'd chosen a different place to brood. He felt sorry for the woman, sure. However, he still believed she wasn't the innocent victim she claimed to be.

Darya drew herself up, wiping at her face. Her tear-glazed stare swept over the horizon before landing on him. Sadness hardened into ice. She backed into her room and shut the doors, holding him with a stony glare until she was out of view.

Edwind rubbed a hand over the back of his neck, a heat running up his spine. He told himself it was because she caught him spying on her, and not the way her shimmering eyes bore into him, as if trying to peer into his mind and pluck out his most private thoughts.

He climbed the stairs to the tower that overlooked the island to distance himself from her presence. On a clear day, he could glimpse the blurry shapes of the closest shore. He wondered if that was where the woman came from.

Casting a final glance at the closed doors of Darya's balcony, he moved to the opposite side of the tower so he wouldn't be tempted to seek out her shadow.

Darya leaned against the wall beside the balcony. Indignant anger bubbled under the surface of her emotions at the thought of Edwind seeing her tears. She didn't want him to know how scared she really was. And she was so very scared.

The black wall of nothing still held her memories hostage, with no sign she would ever get them back. What if her past never returned? Would she be stuck on the island indefinitely? There had to be someone looking for her.

She worked the silver ring around her finger. Though she didn't know the significance of the knot-work, she had a sense of it being a precious memento for her.

Peeking around the corner, she watched Edwind disappeared into the door of the tower that loomed over the castle. She waited a few more seconds to make sure he didn't return before going to bed. Exhausted, she slumped forward, her body surrendering to fatigue. Almost as soon as she lay down and closed her eyes, a light breeze brushed tendrils of hair over her nose and cheeks, tickling her back to consciousness.

She blinked and squinted against the sun shining through the swaying branches and leaves of trees overhead. She raised a hand to her face, blocking the harsh glare. At first, she thought she had sleepwalked her way outside, but the peculiar landscape didn't belong to the island.

A smooth, gray path sliced through the surrounding swath of trees. Beyond some of the taller pines lay tall structures that reflected shards of the midday light. Though unfamiliar, this strange place wasn't completely foreign to her.

"There you are." A man's voice startled her upright. She couldn't make out his features until he was close enough for her to touch him. He was wearing a red and gold plaid button-up shirt tucked into a pair of light blue pants. His clothes looked nothing like what Saebbi and Edwind wore. Dried mud encrusted the bottoms of his dark boots. There was a friendly smile on his face that didn't quite reach his chestnut eyes.

"Do I know you?" she asked.

The man sat down next to her, handing her a small, lidded cup. "I should think so. We've been friends for years. You, Annie, and I."

Annie.

That name sent a chill down her spine.

"It's me, Mark. Mark Abernathy?"

She stared at him, waiting to remember who he was.

"What did they do to you?"

Her eyes narrowed on him. "Who?"

"It doesn't matter. Look, I need to know where you are. I think you're in danger."

She dropped her gaze to the cup. The writing swam in warbled patterns, much like the words of the tome she studied earlier. "I'm on an island."

"I know. What year?"

"The year?"

"What is the year, Darya?"

Her gaze wandered past him to a set of deer antlers floating in the distance. She glimpsed a yellowed bone mask half-hidden behind some trees. The masked man held on to a low-lying branch, watching her.

Mark snatched her by the wrist when she tried to stand. "Tell me where you are."

She pried at his fingers, but his grip was like a vise. "Let go of me."

His friendly demeanor was gone, replaced by something wild and dangerous. "Tell me, seedling."

Darya was no longer sitting in front of the man who called himself Mark. The masked creature from the trees had materialized in his place. His eyes lay hidden in the black shadows of the mask, but she felt them boring into her, demanding the answers she couldn't give him.

She yanked her arms down and out of his grasp. "Get away from me!"

Her body spasmed, and she sucked in a terrified breath, scooting herself to the wall at the head of the bed, trying to free herself from the monster that was no longer there. Though the room was dark, the sky outside cast enough light to show she was alone. She tried to remember what had scared her so badly, but the dream slipped through her conscious mind like fine sand through open fingers.

After unfolding herself, she moved to the balcony. The air was heavy with morning dew, and there was a faint hint of dawn filling the eastern sky. Deep in her soul, she yearned to be outside so she could greet the waking sun. She glanced at the bedroom door, telling herself she wouldn't break Gita's trust again.

At the bowl of water, she undressed and cleaned herself. Her fingers skimmed a raised scar on her belly, and she was overcome with a horrible sense of rage and disgust. She snatched her hand away and finished dressing so she didn't have to see it anymore.

At the bedroom door, she paused, wondering if someone was waiting for her on the other side.

If Edwind had his way, she would stay a prisoner in the room. She stuck her head in the hall. There was a chair stationed to the right of her door with a man leaning back, slicing a fist-sized purple fruit.

Saebbi lifted his gaze from his work. His expression softened, and he said, "You're up early."

"I wanted to watch the sunrise."

His lips split into a wide grin. "Follow me."

Edwind woke to his back pressed against the tower's cold, unyielding stone. The stars gave way to the first hint of dawn. He winced and clamped his mouth shut on a pained moan when he sat forward. He hadn't meant to fall asleep up there, but like so many nights before, he'd lost himself in an endless dance of thoughts about the past and how simple life had been when he was still a young boy, unaware of the dangers beyond the island.

Sometimes, he wished he could speak to his mother one last time. He missed her words of comfort and wisdom. Gita strove to be the kind and wise priestess that Diana had been, yet Edwind was resentful of her title, giving her undue strife with his stubborn ways. Where his sister led with a soft hand, he sought to take on his problems with logical brute force. There was no place for emotions or frivolous feelings in his world.

Which made his current situation that much more frustrating. Last night, no matter how far away his mind wandered, it had always brought him back to the stranger who had washed up on his shores. He didn't care for the sensations she invoked every time she snared him with her gaze. Staring into her eyes was like peering into the deepest depths of the very sea that surrounded the island. He imagined when she smiled, the fire he saw within that fierce stare of hers would be tenfold.

He ran his hands over his face, trying to banish those ridiculous notions from his mind, and pushed to his feet. The sight of Saebbi climbing the slope halted his approach to the stairs. It wasn't Gita walking with him that time. Darya followed in his wake that morning. She kept her sights locked on the infinite colors of the sun, trying to break free of the horizon.

When they reached the peak of the cliff, Saebbi motioned for her to join him. She crept close enough to the edge that a strong wind could have carried her away, yet she stood there, unafraid.

Edwind moved closer to the half wall surrounding the top of the tower. Below, daybreak overtook the night in a brilliant orange and pink light. The moment dawn touched her body, all the sadness and tension leaked from her tight features. He hadn't realized he was grinning until his cheeks tingled from the effort of holding it in place. Smiling wasn't something he did often anymore, and he was out of practice.

He pushed off the wall and followed the stone steps down the spiraling stairs to the gardens. His sister watched Saebbi from the archway as Edwind looked past her to where his friend was making his way down the hillside, with Darya in tow. Gita glanced over her shoulder. Over the years, Edwind learned to read her thoughts in the subtle ways she moved her mouth or arched her brows. He didn't like the unspoken accusation he saw in her gaze.

Ignoring her unspoken words, he disappeared inside before being confronted by the woman chipping away at his resolve.

Sunrise stayed with Darya until she reached the gardens, where Gita waited for them. The smile on her face reflected the deep love she held for Saebbi, who greeted her with a kiss on the cheek.

Gita returned the kiss, then slipped her hand into his. "Why are you two out so early?"

"Darya wanted to greet the dawn."

Gita looked over Saebbi's shoulder to Darya. "How did you sleep?"

Darya shrugged. "I dreamed, but I can't remember what it was about."

"Perhaps it's your mind trying to tell you of your past."

"I wish I could recall what they were. Maybe I'd be able to piece something useful together."

"Would you like to join us for our morning meal?" Gita asked.

Darya considered declining the offer. She dreaded the thought of another encounter with Edwind and his temper, but her stomach let out an angry protest at being ignored for so long. "I guess I'm a little hungry."

She followed Gita to the dining hall, relieved to find the table already set and food waiting for them. She was especially glad it was only the three of them. They ate in silence while Darya stared out of a window, studying the mountain in the distance. Sounds of life drifted through the open windows, drawing her out of her seat.

In the valley below, people went about their lives. They weren't the ones stranded with no memory of their past.

Watching them made her long to be anywhere but stuck wandering aimlessly with no purpose.

She didn't know what Gita expected of her, being a guest in her home. The thought of sitting around being waited on was uncomfortable. She couldn't imagine being accustomed to that kind of treatment where she came from. Her gaze wandered to the gardens near the outer wall.

"Who takes care of the flowers?" The question was out of her mouth before she knew she was going to ask it.

Gita's lips turned up into a pleased smile. "That was our mother's sanctuary. Since she's been gone, Edwind and I try to keep it up, but we don't have the touch she did."

Knowing how precious it was to her hosts, Darya rethought her idea of mucking around their delicate blossoms and possibly doing more damage.

Her silence prompted Gita to say, "You are welcome to work in the gardens if you wish." Before Darya could say no, she added, "You cannot do any more harm than we have. I would be ever so grateful for whatever help you can give."

For the first time since her abrupt arrival, a spark of purpose ignited inside Darya. After finishing her meal, she excused herself so she could go outside and assess the flowers.

The blooms drooped like sad teardrops on their dreary stems. She ran a finger over the dulled thorns. "You poor things," she whispered. Despite the sad state they were in, the air was thick with their sweet scent.

She looked to where Saebbi was pretending not to be her warden. "They need better soil. How often are they watered?"

He glanced at the cloudless sky. "It's the dry season, so I'd say they only get a drink every few weeks when it rains."

"Can you live with that little water?"

Laughter accompanied his grin. "No, I cannot."

She took another moment to study the flowers before moving to the far side of the courtyard, where a path led outside the walls to the forest. "Am I allowed out there?"

His reply was to motion for her to follow him toward the trees.

She rushed down the slope to catch up to his long strides. She didn't know what kind of soil she was looking for, but for the moment, she enjoyed the quiet serenity the surrounding landscape provided. All around them, she watched small creatures go about their day, jumping from branch to branch and skittering along dried grass and leaves.

At a nearby stream, she swept her fingers through the earth. "This is perfect, but how will we get it to the garden?"

"Leave that to me," he said.

By the time the sun dipped beneath the horizon, Saebbi had set the last bucket of dirt at Darya's feet. Her whole body ached, but the pain and filth were all worth it when she looked at what she'd accomplished already. After only a few hours of taking the nutrient-rich earth, the blooms were looking much healthier.

He wiped at his neck and face with a stained piece of cloth. "We've had a long day. Wynfrid will take you to get cleaned up."

The muscles in Darya's back screamed as she stretched her arms up and over her head. "Thank you for helping me."

"I'm glad to see the garden is getting the attention it needs."

Darya didn't know what to expect when she was told she'd have a place to clean up. She stood at the rim of the tub, inlaid into the stone floor of a small windowless room, staring into the milky opaque water. Faint tendrils of steam drifted off the surface, and her body begged to be enveloped in its warmth.

Taking in the sweet floral fragrance, she said, "It smells wonderful."

Wynfrid set a clean dress on the lip of the rock and covered it with soft white linen.

"Get out of those dirty clothes."

Keeping her back to the door, Darya undressed and stepped into the water.

Grabbing the dirt-encrusted dress, Wynfrid said, "Enjoy your bath. You deserve it after what you've been through."

When she was alone, Darya settled against the outer edge of the stone tub and laid her head back, relaxing in the heat of the water. Her mind drifted into a place of half-sleep before she shook herself awake. The last thing she needed to do was fall asleep and drown.

She took her time running the warm water over her arms and neck before rinsing her face and sinking under the surface to wash out her hair. The weight of the water pushing at her body made her relax even further, and she sank to the bottom, enjoying the feel of weightlessness for as long as her breath would let her stay under.

The unexpected brush of a leg against her side shattered her tranquility. She flung herself upright, wrapping an arm over her chest, and used her other hand to push the hair out of her face. A naked Edwind sat across from her. His expression was that of slack-jawed bewilderment.

They stared at each other for what seemed like an eternity. In that forever moment, she had time to study the hard, lean lines marred by numerous scars of untold battles. She didn't expect to see a man who carried himself like a spoiled heir to a throne to have such a dangerous past carved into his flesh.

Edwind's eyes wandered from her chest into the milky water.

Darya found her voice. "What are you doing here?"

Her question yanked his gaze back to hers. "I saw the tub was recently filled, and I thought—" His mouth opened and closed like a fish struggling to breathe. "I didn't see anyone in it." He looked away. "Can you please do a better job of covering yourself, woman?"

She peered down at her exposed breast but wasn't as embarrassed as she was infuriated by the man staring at her. Working her arm over herself, she dipped lower into the water. Her own gaze drifted to the hidden depths and felt her cheeks flush.

She averted her eyes before he caught her wandering stare.

They sat in uncomfortable silence, refusing to look at each other. She kept expecting him to get out of the tub and let her finish cleaning herself, but he didn't move. "Why aren't you leaving the bath?"

"Me?" He almost sounded insulted by her question. "This is my home. My water. My fire that heats it."

"It was made for me."

He glared at her, unmoving.

The nerve of that man to bully his way into her private space was too much. Anger muddied her mind, and she dropped her arms so she could pull herself out of the water. "Fine. Keep your precious bath."

She felt a petty sense of satisfaction when she saw his eyes go so wide, she wondered if they were going to pop out of his pig head. It took her only a few seconds to snatch the dress from under the linen towel and throw it over her body. On her way out the door, she grumbled over her shoulder. "Insufferable, arrogant ass."

Edwind stared after Darya, fingers clutching at the sides of the tub to keep from chasing after her. What had he been thinking, assuming the bath wasn't already spoken for? He should have fled the second he saw her pop up out of the water, but his brain didn't quite send the right message to the rest of his body. Nor did he want her to know how the mere sight of her affected him.

The memory of the sunrise reflecting off her beguiling features turned rational thought into incomprehensible passion and need. When he glimpsed her exposed breast, it was all he could do not beg her to let him worship at the beauty of her sacred temple. Then she had to show him her whole glorious, naked body. He'd never experienced such an intense desire for another woman. It left him feeling vulnerable and unsure of himself.

He found the will to resist her only because of the vicious scar that marred her stomach. He recognized the intent behind such a scar. It was meant to be a death blow. Was that the danger she was running from when she appeared on the island?

His hands started cramping, so he released his hold on the stone and flexed his fingers. Part of him wanted to run upstairs and ask her about the wound, but the image of her curves and those breasts he longed to touch kept him in place. If he went to her now, he wouldn't be able to stop himself from confessing the fire she set ablaze inside him.

Perhaps Gita would be the better one to speak to her. Tomorrow, after he and Saebbi finished their hunt, he would talk to his sister about his theory. If Darya was fleeing from an enemy, he didn't want them to find her on his island, putting his people at risk.

Despite the oils used in the bath, Darya's earthy scent still permeated his senses. With a resigned sigh, he surrendered himself to the warmth of the water, hoping the milky depths could cleanse his thoughts of her.

Chapter 7

Mark teetered on the precipice of madness. He tried to hold on to his belief in the solid foundation of the sane and rational world that didn't have seductress witches and mask-wearing gods with the power to transform mortal men into shape-shifting beings. Yet here he was, perched on an outlying branch of a thick maple tree, watching another day give way to twilight. His acute vision picked up the subtle shift in the ever-darkening sky. Even the calls of the night creatures resonated in an ancient place inside his new body.

"Are you ready for your training, helot?" The sound of Boudica's voice slithered through his mind like the muck that bubbled out of a putrid bog. It made him ill and aroused at the same time.

He was disgusted with himself for being so helpless to her touch. She'd already taken him into her body, and though he tried to make himself loathe the feel of her, she let him do things Annie would have never allowed. The beast he found within was not Cernunnos' making. He'd been fighting against that thing his entire life.

With the succubus, he didn't have to hide his true nature, and it was glorious to set the monster free. He delighted in the pain he inflicted on her when he indulged in his darker fantasies, and she encouraged him to go even further each time.

She wasn't alone that evening. The man that stood by her side was one he recognized from the hippie commune he'd been avoiding for days. Those unfortunate souls were captive to the demon god, like he and Boudica were. He witnessed the harsh reality of their people when, after the birth of a new child, Cernunnos came to the infant boy and laid his sigil upon him. Now he was cursed with the same fate his ancestors suffered.

She pushed the other man forward to meet Mark when his feet touched the ground. "Tiernen was a warrior whose feats echoed through the ages. There will never be another to match his skill on the battlefield, but we must train you to hold your own so you don't die the first time Cernunnos sends you out into the world." She nodded to the man beside her. "Josef trained with him. He will help you stay alive."

Mark kept his face neutral, but her words sparked irritation. "I'm a cop. I know how to handle myself."

Without warning, Josef was behind Mark, driving a fist into one of his kidneys, dropping him onto the ground in a heap of guttural heaving from the force of the punch and the shock of the attack. He glared at the asshole, now standing stone-faced, watching over him. "What the fuck, man?"

Boudica's mouth turned down into a disgusted sneer. "When you're finished, come to me. I'll bandage your cuts and help take the sting from your damaged pride."

Josef helped Mark to his feet. When the succubus was gone, he said, "She will grow bored with you soon enough."

"Good to know." Rubbing at his aching back, he added, "Hey, what's the deal with Tiernen? If Cernunnos can bring Annie back from the dead, why doesn't he do that with him?"

Josef's gaze stopped short of Mark's eyes. "I know nothing of the way of the gods. Now stop talking before we both get in trouble."

By the time Josef finished their training, Mark could barely walk, yet the thought of going to Boudica excited him. He had a lot of pent-up frustration and could think of no better person to take it out on.

Darya was pulled from sleep on the cusp of an orgasm. She could still feel Edwind's calloused hands roaming her body while he moved inside her. The heat from his breath lingered on her neck, and her chest heaved as she lay there, covered in a sheen of sweat. Her head fell to one side, and she let out a frustrated groan at the empty space beside her.

For a long time after coming back from the bath, she watched the door. A part of her wanted him to chase after. She liked to think she would have had the willpower to resist him and spurn his advances so she could see the disappointment roll across his face, but if he had shown up at her room, there was no doubt in her mind she would have given in to whatever he asked. She craved the feel of running her hands along his sinewy frame, tracing the raised scars that told the story of a savage past.

She was even more disappointed that the sky was already turning a pale purple. It was too late to make it to the cliffs for the sunrise. After dressing, she paused at the door for a few seconds before pulling it open. She expected to find Saebbi on the other side, but the hall was empty. She wondered if this was yet another attempt to keep her confined to her room.

A wave of embarrassment snaked up her neck. After the stunt she pulled in the tub, she deserved it. Edwind probably thought she did it to seduce him. The truth was, she'd been so flustered by his presence she couldn't think straight.

"Darya." Gita was walking up the hall. "I was hoping you would be awake. Saebbi said you get up before dawn."

"Is there a problem?" She didn't mean to sound so defensive. "I'm sorry. That was rude."

"I take no offense. I came by to let you know you will no longer be required to have an escort when you leave your room. It is a waste of everyone's time to have you followed when you are no more dangerous than anyone else on this island."

"What about—I can't imagine everyone is happy about this decision?"

"As priestess, it is my choice to make." She turned to walk away and paused. "Edwind's distrust of strangers is a trait he inherited from the men in our family. His mistrust of you comes from something else entirely."

A hint of heat worked into Darya's face at the implication of her words carried. Pushing those thoughts out of her mind, she skipped down the stairs to the courtyard to check on the flowers. They looked even more lively than they had when she left them last night.

Before long, the blooms would fill the garden with their vibrant array of colors and sweet smells. She grabbed the bucket Saebbi used to gather soil, starting down the same path from yesterday.

She breathed in the cool air under a canopy of tight-knit limbs where the sun didn't fully reach the ground. The earthy smell of dirt and leaves was invigorating. All around her, the animals of the forest skittered about their homes, unbothered by her presence. She watched a pair of rabbits running across the shadowed earth.

At the stream, she got to her knees and began scooping up damp soil into the bucket. Movement from the far side of the water drew her attention to a fallen tree, where a set of dark eyes watched her work.

The fox craned his neck to get a better look at the human in his domain. His fur resembled that of a summer sunset, with hints of maple in his undercoat. His gaze was full of curiosity and mischief. He made his way to the opposite bank, matching her movements, inching closer to the water's edge.

They sat staring at one another. She tilted her head, astonished when the fox imitated her movements. When she changed positions, it did the same. They played that game for a while until she heard someone bark out a loud laugh from somewhere in the distance.

She turned back to her new furry friend, and he was sitting atop a bolder half-hidden in a steep embankment across the stream. He leaped from the rock onto the ground, glancing over his shoulder.

"Do you want me to follow?"

He twirled in a circle and bound up the hill, stopping occasionally to see if she was still behind him. She used the trees for leverage, pulling herself up the incline. She slipped a few times on the thin layer of leaves blanketing the slope.

By the time she reached the summit, the fox had disappeared. Instead of heading back down, she stepped out onto a rocky embankment, giving her a perfect perch to observe the valley below. She walked to the edge and grabbed hold of the tall oak that weaved its way up and around the protruding stone.

The morning wind rolled through the hills, pushing plump clouds across the sky, sending sporadic rays of light over the cluster of houses. She grasped onto a low-hanging branch with one hand and held out the other arm over the rock.

Her mouth turned up in a mystified smile when she saw the breeze sweeping over her open palm in a faint, ethereal glow. She followed the trail to where a familiar white bird flew into view from around the mountain in the west. The falcon swooped down and circled back to Darya. It came to rest on a limb above her. Silver disks studied her, giving the same strange feeling they had the first time they met.

Voices carried up the side of the hill from somewhere below, breaking the bird's hold. A group of men ambled out of the trees. Between the six of them, there was a small bounty of kills, which consisted of two deer and a handful of smaller rodents. She couldn't quite understand what they were saying, but their laughter echoed back and forth between them.

She recognized Saebbi's lean build. The sun brought out rich auburn and orange highlights in his bronze hair. He carried a string of what looked like rabbits in one hand and his bow in the other. Edwind's basso voice rumbled through the air before he came into view with a buck slung around his neck and over his shoulders. The sight of his burly frame stirred a reminiscent spark of her dream, but she quickly shook herself out of those forbidden thoughts.

Edwind motioned to the men, and the group burst out in another raucous round of laughter. She had a hard time believing that man even had a sense of humor. He turned to say something to Saebbi and caught sight of Darya watching them. Even from that distance, she saw Edwind's mood shift from jovial to somber.

Saebbi followed his friend's stare. When he saw her, he lifted his hand in a cordial wave.

She returned the gesture.

One of the younger men spoke, and Edwind shot him a look that stopped him from smiling, but he quickly recovered and grinned at Darya once more before heading toward the village.

The white bird chittered beside her. She threw it a curious glance, and when she looked back at the group of hunters, they were already disappearing into another clump of trees. Edwind was the last to walk into the shadows. His stare sent her moving a few steps away from the edge of the overhang.

Once she was down the hill, she forgot about the bucket and the flowers and followed the sounds of the men. She thought she heard someone call her name, but when she turned around, there was only the fox watching her with its curious gaze. "Was that you?"

It didn't answer.

Shaking her head, she started walking again. She really was losing her mind if she heard the animals talk to her.

Boisterous crooning echoed through the forest. Most of their bluster was tales of hunting exploits the men had achieved. She laughed aloud to herself at a rather raunchy comparison of the aim of their bows and escapades in the bedroom.

She eased through the trees to the back side of the houses, watching Edwind hang the buck on a tall scaffold. Saebbi handed the smaller rodents to a couple of young women.

"Are you going to stand there and watch us do all the work, or are you going to help?"

Darya whirled around, looking down at an older woman with a pair of stout arms crossed over an ample chest. "I don't know what I can do."

She motioned a weathered hand at Darya's head. "You're not feebleminded, are you?"

"No."

"Good. I have just the job for you. I hope a little blood and innards don't hurt your feminine constitution."

"Minerva," Edwind was passing by, carrying a curved blade in one hand. He spoke with an agitated undertone. "What are you doing?"

"I'm taking advantage of an extra pair of hands." She pulled Darya over to where the squirrels and rabbits had been laid out, ready to clean.

Darya hesitated before accepting the knife. If she'd ever handled such a thing, she couldn't remember and was worried about ruining their food. "Are you sure there isn't something else I can help with?"

Minerva rested her palm on the back of Darya's fingers. "These are the hands of a woman who's worked the land. You may not have your memory, but your body knows what to do."

After being shown how to make the first few cuts, Darya was still reluctant to accept the blade. Her initial strokes were cautious and sloppy, but after finishing with her first hare, she was much more confident.

"Not bad," Minerva mused and handed her a stack of pelts. "Take these to Naven." She pointed to a young man sitting by the fence with a pile of furs next to him. It was the same man who'd garnered Edwind's irritation earlier.

"Minerva wanted me to give these to you."

Without looking up from his work, he pointed with the knife in his hand. "Set them there." When he lifted his face, his scowl melted into a dimpled grin.

"What are you doing with them?" she asked.

His mouth widened into a full smile. "Sit down. I will show you."

Edwind's concentration kept faltering, sending his blade to the side, nearly ruining the precious cut of meat. He let out a soft curse before stabbing the knife into the scaffolding so he could shove his hands in the bucket of water, searching for the stone inside.

Saebbi stood back, wiping blood on the cloth at his waist. "I haven't seen you this careless since that night your father brought in his special brew from the mainland."

"My blade is dull." He snatched the knife from the wood and started running it across a small stone.

Laughter broke through the sounds of others in the vil-lage, bringing Edwind's head around. Darya and Naven were sitting together, their heads bent close. He pointed to something on one of the brown scraps in his lap before taking her hand and moving it over the soft fur. Her lips split into a pleased grin, and she handed him another pelt.

"I thought Darya was helping Minerva," Edwind said, forgetting the task of cleaning the deer. "Shouldn't she be with the other women?"

Saebbi walked into his friend's line of sight. "Shouldn't you be concentrating on your kill?"

Edwind threw the stone back into the bucket and turned his back on his friend. "It was a mistake to let her roam so freely among our people. She shouldn't have the same privileges as the women of our tribe, especially when we know so little about her. What if this is not the path she follows?"

Tracking Edwind's stare, Saebbi said, "You speak as if she intends to take Naven to her bed."

"That will never happen." Edwind snapped. A simmering heat worked up his neck, and he wasn't sure if it came from anger or embarrassment.

Saebbi seemed unaffected by the outburst. "If she wants to bed the boy, it is her decision to make and his honor to accept or not. If you want it to be you in her bed, may I suggest you stop treating her like your enemy?"

"I want nothing of the sort," Edwind said a little too quickly. Too late, the image of her naked form invaded his thoughts, making his body react on its own accord.

"I have known you long enough to recognize the desire you harbor. Darya is a beautiful woman. Any man would be lucky to earn her favor."

Edwind pushed past his friend. "No one will be earning anything from her."

Darya stood up from the stack of furs, and Edwind locked onto her when she walked by.

Her beguiling eyes snared him in their oceanic depths. The world slowed around them. In the hidden periphery of his vision, images danced just out of focus. Some he recognized, and others were strange and enigmatic, like the woman before him. He wanted to turn his head and catch a clear view of the phantoms, but didn't dare relinquish the hold she had on him.

She blinked, releasing him from their grasp, and he forced his gaze to the ground before grabbing the deer carcass and started slicing the buck again. His skin crawled with the force of the other man's stare.

"What?" he asked, keeping his focus on the dead animal.

Saebbi breathed out a long sigh. "You're a stubborn damn fool."

Darya stood at the table with the other women, listening to them talk about an upcoming solstice celebration. Most of the meat they were preparing was going to be made into a feast for the fire. They kept talking about the dance, which she came to understand was the most anticipated part of the night. Minerva gave a few disapproving sounds when they got too distracted from their duties, though from time to time, the old woman would throw in a tale or two of when she was younger.

"Are you going to join us for the solstice?" One of the women asked Daray.

"Becca, keep your focus on your work." Minerva shook her bloodied knife at the girls, but when she looked at Darya, there was a twinkle of curiosity in her gaze.

Darya glanced around at the other questioning stares. "I don't think I'd be welcome. I'm a stranger here."

Minerva grunted something unintelligible, then said, "Our ceremonies are open to anyone who wishes to celebrate with us."

Becca raised an eyebrow. "But will she choose someone to dance with?"

Another girl motioned to where the men worked. "She would be a fool not to make the obvious choice."

Darya glanced at the man still cleaning the furs. "Naven?"

The two girls shared a look. One of them said, "No." And pointed to Edwind's back. "Him."

Minerva cleared her throat. "That's enough of this talk. You have work to do before the fires are lit."

Becca shrugged. "Even if she wanted to choose him, Edwind hasn't joined our celebrations since before we—"

"Becca, you and Layla gather some water to clean up this mess." The frown on Minerva's face left no room for argument.

Darya lowered her gaze and continued carving the squirrel. If she decided to join them, she certainly wasn't interested in doing anything with Edwind, but the part of her that longed to finish what her dream had started called her out on the lie.

Movement at her feet made her jump back. The orange fox from the river squatted on all fours, black eyes beckoning her to drop a few morsels. She glanced up, making sure no one was looking, and snuck a couple of meaty bits into her furry friend's mouth. The fox nabbed its prize before loping for the safety of the trees.

When she stood again, Minerva was watching the fox disappear into the forest. She pushed a dish at. "Gather what meat Saebbi and Edwind have ready."

Darya set the bowl on the table next to Saebbi. He said, "I'll take care of this. You should wash up."

Nodding, she wiped the knife on her apron. The glint of steel caught the sunlight, and when it sparked in her eyes, she was no longer standing outside. She was in a room she didn't recognize. Her vision was locked on the massive blade being thrust at her gut from an unseen foe.

Helpless to stop the incoming blow, she jerked forward when the blade disappeared into her flesh. Though the pain wasn't real, she still felt the cold steel yanked from her stomach. She doubled over, heaving out a voiceless cry. A spray of blood flecked across the yellow floor. Phantom agony burned her from the inside out.

A pair of hands dragged her out of the vision and into the present. Tears rolled down her cheeks, and her mouth hung open in a silent scream burning the back of her throat. Her eyes darted around the surprised faces staring at her.

"Darya, are you alright?" Saebbi's voice broke through the shock, and she threw the knife on the ground before backing out of his grasp and running for the trees.

At the stream, she dropped to her knees and dunked her hands below the surface to scrub the gore from her skin, trying to erase the horror from her mind. Her scar ached and burned under the pressure of her dress. Muffled whimpers struggled against her closed mouth.

Saebbi knelt beside her, helping her clean the crimson viscera embedded in the sides of her nails. "What did you see?"

"I saw—" She took in a long slow breath. "I was stabbed. Someone tried to kill me."

"Do you know who did it?"

She shook her head.

"You don't have to hide the truth from us." Edwind watched her with a thoughtful frown, pulling at his mouth.

She looked from Edwind to Saebbi before pushing to her feet.

Saebbi tried to reach for her. "Where are you going?"

"I don't know how else to prove I'm not lying. Send me away. I don't care anymore."

The waves rushing to shore sang of their journey across the sea, while Darya kept a steady pace along the soft, white sand that threatened to swallow her feet if she stopped walking. She wasn't paying attention to where she was going or how long she'd been traveling the same stretch of beach.

After cleaning off as much blood from her body and clothes as possible, she couldn't bear the thought of being cooped up in that room, alone and trapped in her own thoughts. She needed to distract herself from those horrible images that swirled inside her mind. She wished she had never learned how she got the damn scar. Even worse, she still didn't know anything substantial about her past or who might have wanted to kill her.

Tomorrow, she would speak to Gita about traveling to the mainland. There, she would have a better chance of finding her people. At this point, being thrust into an even scarier unknown was better than facing more of Edwind's mistrust.

Turning to the ocean, she waded into the surf up to her waist, letting the waves rock her in a steady push and pull of their dance. She rested her hands atop the choppy surface, letting the warmth remove some of the chill from her blood. Having the force of the water pressing around her lower body was strangely comforting, as if being held by an old friend who only wanted to give comfort in this time of upheaval.

Her gaze wandered to where the moon reflected off the choppy surface, musing how the light appeared to pulse in time with her heartbeat. What seemed to be indiscriminate patterns of luminescent moonlight moved with purpose and glided along the tops of frothy waves, culminating in pale circles around her body.

She blinked a few times and rocked herself out of the trance of rolling lights, backing out of the water to the beach. Behind her, the moon's reflection had returned to how it had been before she trekked into the ocean. Whatever solace she'd felt before was replaced with unease.

At the outer gate, she saw movement from the path leading from the village. Edwind's gaze was stuck on the ground, so he didn't see her at first. Part of her was curious to know why he was out so late among those dark houses. Did he often spend his free time there? Was there a woman he went to each night? Some secret tryst, perhaps?

Why did it bother her so much to even consider the answers to those questions?

As if feeling the weight of her stare, Edwind lifted his head. Their eyes locked on one another, and even in the dim light of the moon that hadn't yet reached its zenith, she could make out the hardened lines of a man who was lost in his own thoughts.

She rushed inside in case he wanted to accuse her of something else she had no control over. It was obvious no matter what she said, he would always see her as a threat.

She continued to the balcony in her room. There, she balanced herself on the wide rail, bracing her back against the pitted, gray stone. The moon was pulling itself over one of the shorter mountains, giving it a look of a winking eye. She followed its slow ascent, wishing she could join in on the celestial journey among the stars, even if it was only for a night.

A knock on her door jolted her out of her ruminations. She wasn't up to talking to anyone and contemplated ignoring the intrusion. Pushing out a heavy breath, she went to the door. The hall beyond was dark and empty. She looked down to find a single linen towel with a vial of milky liquid nestled on top. Stepping over the strange gift, she rushed to the stairs, but there was no sign of light or the sound of footsteps retreating down the stone.

Back in her room, she bent down to pick up the towel and vial. She knew what the offerings were meant to represent, but the thought of risking another awkward encounter in the bath sent her pulse racing.

Who would have left something like that at her door, and why? It couldn't have been Wynfrid. She had left for her own bed a long time ago. Did Gita watch Darya come back inside, and this was some kind of peace offering to soothe a scared woman's fractured life?

If it was meant to be a simple act of kindness, how rude would it be for Darya to let it go to waste?

Clutching the towel to her chest, she squeezed her hand around the small vial and made her way downstairs. There was a newly filled tub of steaming water waiting for her. She opened the bottle and brought it to her nose. The scent reminded her of the flowers she cared for, along with the dirt in which they lived. After adding the fragrant liquid, she eased into the milky water, letting out a closed-mouth moan as the heat threatened to scorch her skin.

She dunked herself under the surface for only a few seconds, and when she popped up, she stayed submerged up to her neck until she was sure no one else decided to join her. Laying her head back, she gave into the hypnotic beating of her heart and let it lull her into a meditative state. Finally, the horrible visions of an incomplete past drifted away on the rising heat of the water.

Chapter 8

A COOL, SALTY BREEZE drifted through the open windows, sweeping over Darya, where she sat in a chair, watching the stars gradually disappear. She'd been tossing and turning for half the night, despite the soothing bath, so she moved to the window for respite.

In the valley below, soft rumblings told of people going about their morning chores. She studied the horizon until the first hint of daybreak appeared in the east. After slipping into the still-clean dress from the night before, she headed downstairs, hoping she wouldn't run into Edwind on her way to the cliffs.

Instead of waiting on the peak for the sun to make its appearance, she followed the bluffs overlooking the sea, breathing in the briny breath of the ocean. The smell was intoxicating. She wandered to the end of the cliffs, letting her gaze drift along the brightening horizon.

Despite the beauty before her, the horrid images from the day before kept creeping into the forefront of her mind, but, like the other lost memories, she could only recall cloudy details and strange visions that left her even more confused.

Knowing now how she'd gotten the scar on her belly, she wondered how she could've possibly stayed in a place that offered her such violence. Was that why she was on that ship?

Despite the warm glow of the sunrise, it didn't lighten her mood. She had too many unanswered questions plaguing her; Questions that would only be answered when or if her memory returned.

By the time she wandered back to the village, the narrow dirt paths were alive with men, women, and children going about their daily tasks. She decided the night before that she wouldn't let one man drive her away from these kind people.

Yesterday, Minerva gave her a purpose that was more than merely busy work. Darya would accept her role in their lives if they were willing to welcome her into their homes so graciously.

The smell of freshly baked bread floated to where she came down the hill. Minerva was directing two younger kids toward the fields, and Darya skipped down the steep incline in her direction. The first sounds of fighting were so faint she thought she had imagined the noise.

Her gaze strayed from Minerva to a group of young men clustered at the base of a grassy divot in the valley. She veered off the trail to the houses and sought the source of the distinct clang of metal on metal. No one else seemed to pay much attention to the raucous.

She approached from the northern side of the incline to get a better look without getting too close.

"Your stance is sloppy."

Darya's pulse quickened at the sound of Edwind's irritated voice breaking through the gathered crowd.

"If we are ever attacked, you will be the first to die," he said.

Naven and Edwind stood a few feet apart, both holding swords in opposite hands. The battered metal glinted in the mid-morning sun, showing off dangerous, sharp edges.

The young man rolled his sword and moved in a slow circle around Edwind. His expression was no longer lighthearted and mischievous. The man she saw glaring at his opponent was full of hostility and anger.

Edwind kept his weapon lowered at his side, unbothered by the other man. He held still, following Naven with a calculating gaze. Edwind knew what was coming.

The younger man made one more complete circuit before rushing forward with such speed she didn't think Edwind could move out of the way of the coming blow. He kept his body tight and stayed calm, easily sidestepping the young man's attack. He used the hilt of his sword to strike Naven in the small of his back, sending him staggering over his own feet.

Naven forced out a heavy breath, and the rage that permeated his features foretold of the reckless attack he was about to unleash.

The two men came together in a clash of metal so loud, Darya flinched with each impact.

Each man fought for control, testing each other's weaknesses, searching for an opening to strike. The beating of her heart kept time with the cacophony of the rhythmic clanging of their weapons.

Darya was so entranced with the swordplay she didn't realize she was sidling around the crowd to get a better view of the vicious dance of body and blade. Naven feigned left but, at the last second, pivoted in the other direction and brought his sword up across Edwind's back, slicing him from shoulder-blade to hip.

Edwind glanced over his shoulder. His expression wasn't that of pain. A calm fell over him, darkening his features. Naven held up his weapon, moving a couple of steps away from the infuriated man.

Without warning, Edwind rushed into Naven with a flurry of quick movements, landing each nonlethal blow, opening small, precise wounds along the front of him. Naven stumbled and tripped over his feet, holding up the sword to shield his face.

Darya's heart hammered against her chest in fear of Naven's life. Why didn't someone stop this madness before one of them got seriously hurt? Edwind stood over the cowering man on the ground, heaving with anger. He turned from Naven to search the sea of faces until his gaze landed on Darya. The anger there melted into confusion, but was soon replaced with a blanket of indifference.

"Enough," he said, and shot an irritated glance at Naven, who was still on his back. "I have made my point."

Darya backed away when Edwind started in her direction. His stare bore into her back, and it took every ounce of willpower not to look over her shoulder. She sensed his presence brush past her like he had his own gravitational pull. With her head down, she rushed to where Minerva stood, eyeing them.

"What was that about?" Darya asked.

The old woman's eyes flicked from Edwind to Naven, then back to Darya. "Pride."

She raised a dark brow. "Why do I get the feeling it wasn't Naven's pride that started the fight?"

Minerva huffed out a laugh and motioned for her to grab a basket at her feet. "Take that and help Becca gather some herbs. I'm going to need them for those two stubborn men."

Darya stood outside the door to the room, where Gita and Edwind argued. She thought about going back to helping Becca gather herbs, but Gita took her in and gave her shelter. What kind of guest would she be if she ignored her host's request?

"I can tend to my own wounds," Edwind grumbled.

"If you could reach them, I'd let you." Gita's tone held little comfort for her brother's plight. "I should leave you to suffer after what you did to that poor boy."

"He is a cocky young buck who needs to learn his place."

Gita moved into view of the hall. "There you are." She motioned with a hand. "Can you finish with this stubborn man while I prepare more herbs? Between Edwind and Naven, Minerva's supply will be depleted."

Inching her way into the room, Darya said, "I can go back to the village and help her," She hoped to be given a reason to retreat to a safer distance from Edwind's annoyed demeanor.

Gita pushed a pile of rags into her hands. "I don't understand why men need to beat on one another so fiercely."

"You will understand when we are able to protect you from an attack on our land," Edwind called after her.

With a roll of her eyes, Gita continued to walk away, leaving Darya staring at the bloodied mess of Edwind's back. She set the rags on the table where a bowl of clean water waited.

After wetting the first rag, she stepped around him. The gash where Naven's blade had split the skin at the side of his neck was minor, having barely bled. His left eye was showing the first signs of bruising from a blow that the younger man was lucky enough to land.

"I'll try to be gentle," she said, blotting away traces of the fight from his back.

"They are but scratches. This was friendly sparring."

She had a small sense of satisfaction when his body tensed, and he fought to hold in a pained grunt when she cleaned away a pool of dried blood. "If this is what you consider a friendly sparring, I'd hate to see what you do to each other when you're angry."

"Our enemies won't show us mercy. We must be prepared to face any foe."

She nudged his head further to the side to make it easier to clean the gash on his neck. "Your enemies? Do you have a lot of those here on the island?"

He eyed her from his periphery. "You could be one."

Her eyes strayed from his neck to his face. He pretended to ignore her glare, but she saw the way he kept following her movements.

She let her hand slip and roll into the open wound, and he jerked away, trying to stand. She grabbed onto his arms to hold him in place. "I thought it didn't hurt," she muttered.

His eyes narrowed on her, but he stayed silent.

She moved to his back and the more serious wounds. "Do you treat all strangers this way?"

He turned his torso so he could look at her. "As a matter of fact, I do."

"That's a ridiculous way to live."

"It has kept us safe thus far."

Pushing him around, she grabbed a fresh rag. His tight muscles rolled under the pressure of her fingers as she worked them down his back, cleaning away dirt, sweat, and blood. He let out an involuntary noise that was a mixture of pain and pleasure.

"Do you need a break?" she asked.

"Gods no," he sighed.

She hesitated before continuing. This was supposed to be an unpleasant experience for him, but his reaction to her touch surprised her. She kept applying the same heavy pressure along his spine, moving outward.

Her fingers rolled over his tight muscles, and she had to remind herself repeatedly how terrible a task this was. Yet with each passing of her hands, his body relaxed even more. Knowing it was her touch that broke through his sour demeanor sent a warmth through her that was unwelcome, but not entirely unpleasant.

When she got to his uninjured shoulder, he reached over and put a hand on hers. "I don't recall having a wound there."

Her face bloomed with the heat of her embarrassment, and she withdrew her hand from his. "That friendly sparring did more damage than you realize."

"Like I said, our enemies won't spare us, so we need to learn to fight through the pain."

She cleaned around the split in his skin, thankful it was shallow. There were a few minor scrapes and cuts on his side that needed a quick cleaning, but every time she tried to apply any kind of pressure, he jerked away.

She had to put a hand on his arm to steady him. "Come on, you big tough man. Don't tell me it hurts that bad."

"No," he said through clenched teeth. "It tickles."

She barked out a sharp laugh. "Are you serious?"

He sat forward, grabbed his shirt, and slung it over his head. Without another word, he walked out of the room.

She stared after him, taken aback by his abrupt departure. "Thanks for cleaning my wounds," she said in a mocking tone.

"You're welcome," she replied in her own voice. "I'm sorry for laughing. I didn't realize a grown man your size could be so ticklish." She threw the dirty rags in the crimson water and grumbled, "What an insufferable man-child."

"Thank you," Edwind was leaning against the stone frame of the door, staring at her with an amused expression on his face. "For cleaning my wounds."

She stared at him, unsure if she should be angry or embarrassed.

"This is where you say, 'you're welcome,'" he said.

Instead of answering, she snatched up the rags and water and met him at the door. "May I get by?"

He studied her for a few more seconds. "Did you enjoy your bath last night?"

She opened her mouth, then closed it again. Setting her face in a frown, she said, "You did that for me?"

He gave her a crooked half-smile that sent a flutter through her stomach and disappeared around the corner, leaving her staring at the space he no longer occupied.

On her way back from rinsing out the bowl and rags, she saw Wynfrid and Naven under a shaded patch behind a group of houses. He had his face turned away to make it easier for her to get to the smaller scrapes on his neck.

Darya watched him reach around his side and put a hand on the one Wynfrid steadied herself against him with.

"I suppose you won't die," she said, spreading a green paste on one of the longer cuts. "You're lucky Edwind didn't run you through."

"He shouldn't have left himself vulnerable." His gaze wandered to the path leading to the castle. "It seems poor Darya got stuck caring for him."

Wynfrid shrugged. "She's not covered in blood, so he must not have pushed her to the point of murder."

Darya approached the couple. "Almost."

Wynfrid returned to wiping at Naven's neck. "I'm surprised he let you even get near him with those rags. Usually, he's content to wallow in his own pain or swim out into the sea and let the waves clean him up."

Naven dropped his hand to the ground, turning his vigil across the valley while Wynfrid gathered the rags and poultice. "There's still much to prepare for tonight. Darya, would you make sure this stubborn man here doesn't let his tongue get him into any more trouble?" Her hand lingered on his shoulder. "At least wait for the pyre to be lit."

After Wynfrid walked away, Darya asked, "She's the one you fancy?" He'd mentioned a woman he cared for but never spoke her name.

He avoided her gaze.

"Have you told her how you feel?"

"I feel a lot of things about a lot of people." His mouth turned up into a playful grin. "Even for you."

"What you think you feel for me and what lies in your heart for Wynfrid are not the same."

His eyes slid back to the place where Wynfrid walked up the hill to the castle. "She chooses to keep herself unattached to any man. She thinks she will leave here one day and never return."

"And what if she does? What's stopping you from going with her?"

"I have my family to care for. My mother and sisters. I won't ask her to give up her happiness for me."

"I may not remember a lot about old life, but I know a woman's heart. Love isn't only about the sacrifices we make for one another. It's surrender. It's trust. It's giving over that part of ourselves we are afraid to relinquish the most." Darya took his hand. "What if she is waiting to be given a reason to stay?"

He gave her hand a squeeze. "You sound like Gita. Maybe you are a priestess of your own tribe."

"What are you two younglings doing out here?" Minerva watched them from the edge of a cluster of houses.

"Nothing like that, old woman," Naven said.

Darya let her arm fall to her side. "I'm trying to convince this big dumb man to tell Wynfrid he loves her."

"She already knows. She wants to hear it from his mouth. Big dumb man, indeed."

Naven backed away from the two women with his hands up in a placating manner. "I will tell her the truth of my feelings in my own way and in my own time."

Darya raised an eyebrow but kept silent. When they were alone, she turned to Minerva. "Is there anything I can do to help prepare for tonight?"

"Of course. Since you can't remember where you come from, we will treat this as your first solstice celebration."

They made their way through the row of houses to the village center, where Edwind was splitting a pile of wood for the fire that night. Without missing a swing, he said, "I hope Darya doesn't think she is taking part in tonight's solstice fire."

Confused by his comment, Darya stopped walking. "Why wouldn't I?"

"You know nothing of our customs. You don't know what tonight's celebration means for our people."

Minerva stepped in. "Boy, you need to remember the path you walk."

"I walk my own path," he snapped. "I won't allow her to join them. Not when she may not share in our ways."

Darya opened her mouth to argue, but he was right. She didn't belong there, nor was it her place to intrude on their sacred rituals.

Yet the thought of having him dictate her movements made her want to fight him for the sake of her pride. Instead of arguing, though, she looked at the old woman and said, "I can still help with the preparations."

Minerva motioned toward a group of young people. "Becca will tell you what to do."

Darya had resigned herself to spending the evening alone, watching the fire from on top of the wall of the gardens, so it surprised her when Wynfrid came to her room at dusk.

"I was told I couldn't join the solstice fire," Darya began.

Wynfrid held up a gown with bright hues of reds and blues and greens that swirled in sporadic patterns. "I am only doing what Gita bade of me. Now put this on."

The dress fit her tall frame as if someone had tailored it, especially for her. It hung from her shoulders with thin straps, gathering at her waist and spread in loose pleats around her knees. She looked in the mirror, comparing herself to the other woman whose gown shared the same hues.

"You are not the outcast you think you are," Wynfrid said. "I consider you a sister, even if you don't walk the same path we do."

Darya followed Wynfrid down the path around the village to where the others were already celebrating. Heavy drumming shook the ground, resonating up her feet into her legs. The vibrations dispersed throughout her body in waves of chaotic beats that spoke to a place hidden behind that wall that locked her memories away.

Naven met them with two cups of pungent liquid. "I was beginning to think you weren't going to join me." He moved in to brush his lips against Wynfrid's mouth. She lingered on his kiss before taking the drink and gulping down half the contents. He grabbed her by the hand, leading her toward the raging pyre, leaving Darya to stare awkwardly at the revelry.

Wynfrid glanced over her shoulder. "Are you coming?"

Anxiety and nerves had Darya second-guessing her decision to join them. She shouldn't be here, imposing herself on these people. Wynfrid called to her again. Dousing the last of her reservations, Darya followed her friends through the crowd of people, sipping conservatively at her drink.

The spice that permeated the ale warmed her blood and lessened the unease of being a stranger in their midst.

By the time she finished her first drink, the warm spice flowing through her had her swaying in time to the music. She wondered if this was the same celebration her own people partook in. There was a faint sense of familiarity to the music. Maybe she wasn't as much an outcast as she thought.

Naven's sudden appearance from the crowd was so fast, she didn't have time to fight him when he took hold of her free hand and pulled her into the wild group of dancers.

Soon, Darya found herself swept up in the frenzy of bodies and movement. She forgot about the fear of being an out-sider with no memories of her past and gave herself to the rhythm that spoke to the deepest parts of her being.

When her cup was empty, another appeared in her hand. She was swept up in the dance, being drawn from one body to another. The world spun in and out of focus, faces rolling from one to the next until she found herself in the arms of a man she recognized but couldn't recall his name.

The trepidation that seized her muscles wasn't because of the hands that ran down to her hips. She enjoyed the way he pressed himself against her. What gave her pause was the nagging voice inside her head that kept telling her he wasn't the person she wanted to be dancing with.

She stifled the hesitancy and leaned into him, ready to meet his kiss with the same fervor of the drums thundering through her blood. He lifted his eyes to somewhere behind her, and she felt his body stiffen. She squeezed his arms, trying to keep him with her, but when he looked at her again, it was with regret. He let her go and backed into the crowd, never looking back.

Her skin heated with embarrassment, wondering if she had made a mistake coming to the solstice fire after all. What if her presence wasn't as accepted as Wynfrid and Naven claimed?

She made a wobbly half-turn, ready to forgo the rest of the dance and go back to her room. A familiar figure stepped into view from around the raging pyre. She couldn't be sure if it was the heat of the flames that set her blood ablaze, or the man peering at her through the flickering light.

Edwind's presence split the other dancers like a ship through the ocean waves. Her relaxed mood vanished, replaced with the fear of his anger that she disregarded his demands for her to stay away. But there was no outrage in his features. Lust and desire burned in that malachite stare.

She stiffened, and her breath caught in her throat when he reached out, putting a hand at the small of her back, pulling her into him. She expected him to drag her up the hill and lock her inside her room. Part of her wanted him to do just that. He could keep her imprisoned in her bed the entire night.

Eyes that were once the color of the hills of his home reflected the fire in such a way it cast them in an amber glow. She lost herself to their blaze, giving into his embrace. Their bodies swayed to the beat of the drums. Every movement drew them closer together until his heart was pounding against her, in time with her ragged pulse.

He spun her around, pressing her back into his chest. An arm snaked down one of her thighs, and with his other hand, he slid her hair away from her neck. Tendrils of lightning raced through her veins when his lips rested against her skin. Each time his mouth broke from her flesh, she made a small sound of protest. The palm at her thigh roamed up her stomach to her breasts, testing their firmness while curious lips continued their sensual exploration across her shoulders and neck.

The weight of his hands and body left her so quickly she stumbled backward, nearly falling to the ground.

She whirled around, fearing she'd hallucinated the whole thing, but Edwind was still there, standing a few feet away. Uncertainty and disbelief now marring his shadowed face.

"Why did you stop?" she asked, reaching for him.

He took another quick step back, shaking his head, unable to give her an answer. He backed into the sea of people, disappearing in their midst.

The alcohol sitting heavy in her stomach stymied her gait as she stumbled through the crowd, trying to catch up to him. When she had broken free of the other dancers, he was gone. She turned in a slow circle, but there was no hint of where he might have disappeared.

Despite the desire that still burned inside her like an out-of-control wildfire, she knew she'd nearly made a horrible mistake. She couldn't let herself give in to her desires. Not for that man.

Shame and confusion kept her from rejoining the others again. She trudged up the trail to the castle, shoving the disappointment and humiliation down into the pit of her stomach, only to have it all come up again when she fell to her knees and lost the battle against all the alcohol she consumed.

She vaguely recalled hands grabbing her shoulders. Wynfrid's voice sounded hazy to her drunken senses. Her body was urged upward, and the world wobbled before the ground was swept out from under her. Her vision swayed as her head fell back against the arm that carried her away from the sounds of the drums.

The feel of the heavy blanket on her body was a welcomed sensation, and she dove into the peaceful embrace of unconsciousness that enveloped her.

"Are you sure it was our tribal marking?" Gita asked. She sat in front of the cold hearth of her room, staring at the bleak stone. Saebbi stood in the open doorway of the balcony, watching over the celebration in the valley below.

Edwind crossed his arms. "I know what I saw. How is this possible?"

"Our ancestors migrated from the mainland a couple of generations before we were born. There could be another tribe with a marking similar to ours."

"It isn't similar to ours." He motioned to Gita's shoulder, where she had the same symbol etched into her skin. "It *is* ours. There's more to this woman than she's telling us."

"Because she doesn't remember."

His lips pursed together in thought. After a few seconds, he said, "I think we need to get word to our father. If anyone can find the truth about her, he can."

The look she gave him betrayed her shock. "You really want him involved?"

"I do."

"Very well. I will go to him myself."

"Why you?"

She leaned forward to the fireplace, blowing gently on the dried logs, sending smoke and flames across the back of the stone. An orange glow lit up her face. "I know where he spends his time. He will come more easily at my request."

Saebbi joined Gita at the newly awakened fire. "Why were you at the bonfire tonight? It's been years since you last took part in our celebrations."

Edwind turned away, heading for the door.

"How was it you found that marking on the back of her neck?" asked Gita.

Refusing to look at them, Edwind said, "Why do you ask questions you know the answer to?"

"Because I want to hear you say the words."

He paused at the threshold. "When you return with Father, he can take Darya to the mainland to search for her people."

Gita stood. "You cannot make that decision for her."

"She doesn't belong here. She's dangerous." He turned to the hall.

"She's dangerous to you, don't you mean?"

Edwind met her stare. "She will be leaving with Father."

Chapter 9

SUNLIGHT PIERCED THE VEIL of Darya's eyelids, and the unrelenting glare of the mid-morning light made her remember what a hangover was. Her head threatened to crack wide open, spilling forth its scrambled contents on the soft pillow on which she lay.

The knock on the door hammered at her skull.

"Go away," she croaked before burying herself in the blankets. "Let me die in peace."

A gentle hand pulled back the covers. Wynfrid had a cup in her hands and a sympathetic smile. "I thought you might be in this state, so I brought you something to help with your suffering."

Darya closed her eyes against the harsh glare of the sunlight, trying not to gag when she caught a whiff of the potent liquid. "What is it?"

"Just drink."

She held her breath, gulping down the pungent tea. When the cup was empty, she was glad it stayed put in her belly. To her relief, the pounding in her skull dulled to an annoying ache.

She could even open her eyes without invisible fingers trying to gouge them from their sockets.

"What is that stuff?"

"A special blend Minerva concocted."

Images of last night broke through the drunken fog shrouding her mind. The only things she could pull from her foggy memory were flashes of dancers and the feel of drums awakening her blood.

Wynfrid took the mug. "You'll want to put something on your stomach."

"That's asking a lot right now."

"When you finish eating, gather your belongings."

"Why?"

"You are going to stay in the village with me while Gita is gone."

"Gone? Where did she go?"

Wynfrid shrugged. "She didn't say. I am simply doing as I am told."

"By whom?"

"Edwind."

More of the celebration swam to the surface. The memory of his hands and lips roving across her skin made her flush even without the alcohol running through her blood. Then came the sting of his rejection.

And the anger. "I don't think that will be necessary. I'm not going anywhere."

Wynfrid gave her a pleased grin. "I knew you wouldn't be happy with the arrangement."

Soon after dressing, her belly was making small protests for food, so she headed downstairs where Wynfrid told her there would be food waiting in the dining hall. Upon entering the room, she stopped short of the table. Edwind shifted in his seat, turning from the window. His expression morphed from calm contemplation to irritation.

"I thought Wynfrid was supposed to take you to the village for a few days."

"I will not be put out when I have a perfectly good bed right here."

He sat forward. "It's best if you stay in the village until Gita returns."

"I have to be banished from these walls because you can't decide how you feel about me?"

He turned back to the window.

"You accuse me of being your enemy, but last night, your lips said something else."

"They lied."

"Which time?"

He ignored the question.

"I may not have my memory, but I know I'm not one to be told what to do by any man. You hold no say over where I lay my head. That is in Gita's power as the priestess of this island. Until she returns, I will stay here and sleep in the bed I've made my own since arriving."

He stood, and despite being only an inch taller, his presence towered over her. "While my sister is away, my word is law."

She crossed her arms and leaned into him. "If you want me gone, you'll have to remove me by force."

He raised his hands to do just that, then thought better of it and shoved them back down at his side. "Fine. Stay. I will leave."

She grabbed for his hand, but he snatched it out of her grasp. "Don't touch me."

The bite of his words was enough to snap her out of whatever fantasy she had about his feelings for her. Her face fell into a neutral shroud of indifference to hide the pain he elicited.

Not trusting what would come out of her mouth, she lowered her arm and headed for the stairs.

"Darya," He followed her into the hall. "I didn't mean to speak so cruelly."

His presence pushed her legs faster through the halls. She needed to get away from him, away from that place.

"I won't make you leave." He followed her up the stairs. "I'm sorry."

She spun around. "No, Edwind, I'm sorry. I'm sorry I got stuck on this damn island. I'm sorry I can't remember who I am. I'm sorry for whatever I did last night to make you push me away."

He opened his mouth, but she put a finger in his face. "I don't care about what else you have to say. You're a heartless man, Edwind Wodehal." Unable to hold back the tears, she ran for her room.

Edwind stood at his bedroom window watching Wynfrid lead Darya to the village, glad to be rid of her finally.

That's what he kept telling himself, anyway. Her words stung that place inside his chest that he fought so hard to keep cold and unfeeling. He spent so many years trying to make himself into the cruel man she saw him to be, but to have her bestow that title on him hurt worse than the blows he'd gotten from Naven.

This was for the best. She didn't know the truth about them. If she did, she wouldn't be so eager to explore those silly feelings of hers. Instead, she'd be begging to be sent away.

Her presence was already dangerously close to slipping past the last of his defenses. If he saw her beautiful smile or heard that musical laughter one more time, the walls around his heart would come crumbling down. He'd be standing in the ruins of the promise to never leave himself vulnerable to the inevitable pain that kind of love brought with it.

The sound of footsteps approaching his door made him turn from the window. Saebbi stood in the hall, staring at his friend with a disappointed expression on his face.

"What do you want?" Edwind asked.

"I was going to take the ship out for a couple of days. It's perfect weather for fishing. Perhaps if I'd come to you sooner, Darya wouldn't have been forced to leave."

"I told her she didn't have to go."

"I heard what you said to her."

Edwind sighed, turning back to the village. "Gita and I are not meant for people like her."

"Like me, you mean?" Saebbi asked. "Yet here I stand by your side. And Gita's. Your sister and I have accepted the path that is laid before us. Instead of fearing the uncertainty of that future, we are taking advantage of the life we have with each other."

"Gita is stronger than I."

"Not stronger. She is unafraid to let herself care for another. Heartache is not something reserved for you and your father. It lives in us all." He backed into the hall. "Meet me at the docks when you are ready to leave."

Edwind didn't want to go fishing. He wanted to find Darya and finish what they had started last night. The memory of her body against his and the way she fit into his arms was almost too much to resist, even now. He balled his hands into fists and closed his eyes against his fragmented resolve. A few days away from the island would help clear his mind. Once his father arrived, he would send her to the mainland and rid himself of her siren's call once and for all.

Darya watched the ship disappear over the horizon, carrying Edwind and Saebbi away from the eastern shore. Instead of easing the ache in her chest, his absence left her more hollow inside. She tried to stay bitter toward him for what he said, but self-loathing and sadness took the place of her anger. How foolish of her to believe a man like Edwind could think her worthy of his heart, this half-woman she was.

She wanted to run to the sea and swim far away from this place and these people and never look back. She wanted to go home, wherever that was. Why couldn't she fill those dark chasms where her memories should be? If only she could remember something, anything, about her past, maybe she would find her way back to where she belonged.

There was some comfort to be had while he was gone. She was free to come and go from the castle and the gardens. She worked too hard to bring those blooms back from the brink of rot to let her hard work go to waste.

When she wasn't in the gardens, she was in the village, helping Minerva and the other women in their daily tasks. No one spoke of the way she'd shown up so suddenly in their midst and accepted her in their lives. They treated her like any other person in their clan.

The little girl who found her on the beach that first day followed her around, even up to the castle where Darya showed Shannin how to care for the flowers.

At dusk on the second day, Shannin had eagerly and dutifully weeded what few sprouts were peeking through the soil, so Darya sent her home for the evening while she went inside to grab the comb she'd left behind. The truth was, she just wanted an excuse to be in that familiar place. She craved the comfort of the stone walls she'd called home since waking on the island.

She bound down the steps to follow the little girl back to the village when she spotted a faint glow from a room she'd never noticed before. As far as she knew, Gita was still gone, and the men hadn't returned from their fishing expedition. By this time of day, Wynfrid was back in the village.

She approached the open doorway and peeked inside. A fascinating collection of exotic totems and sculptures decorated the walls. She crossed the threshold to examine the smaller items arranged on plain wooden shelves around the room. On her way across the stone floor, she noticed a table much like the one in Diana's bedroom. Instead of wood, the figures on the board looked hand carved from smooth, glass-like stone. The white pieces had a milky hue to them, and the black ones had the shiny sheen of onyx.

Something about the layout of the carved stones stirred a memory in her. She picked up a statuette and ran a finger over the glossy surface. A fleeting glimpse of an old man's face smiled at her, but it was gone before she took hold of any significant details. She replaced the figure and lowered herself to inspect the table more closely, hoping to reclaim the memory, but nothing else came to her.

Noise from outside the window above made her raise back up. From where she stood, she watched children flocking to their homes. Having spent the last few days in the village, she had grown to care for these people like they were family. Maybe when she got her memory back, she would stop standing out like this broken, stitched-together shell. When her past returned, then Edwind might accept her into his life.

She pushed out a silent laugh at the fanciful notion. There was no place in his life for her.

The siblings stood apart in a way Darya didn't understand. Though Gita and Edwind spent much of their time in the village, sharing in the responsibilities, they kept themselves separate from the others. She tried to ask Wynfrid about the unusual arrangement, but the woman would change the subject.

It was obvious Edwind held himself to a higher standard than some fractured woman with no memory of her past. Why else would he fight the fire that burned between them? Every time their eyes met, she saw brief glimpses of what it would be like to share a life with him.

She pushed out another heavy breath before turning to leave. Her legs froze mid-step, and her heart fluttered at the sight of Edwind's silhouetted form against the glow of firelight from the hall behind him. How long had he been standing there watching her?

"I didn't realize this was your room." She started for the hall. "I didn't mean to trespass."

He moved toward the table. "Have you ever played?"

She shot a glance in his direction. "If I have, I can't remember."

"I can teach you if you wish." He picked up the pieces and started arranging them around the board. "Sit."

She didn't move at first. "I don't want to bother you."

He kept working at the game. "It's no bother."

His ambivalence was unnerving. She turned all the way around so she could better scrutinize his intention. "Aren't you angry that I'm in your room?"

"Do I seem upset?"

"No, but I expect you to be, given how we left things between us."

He looked up, snaring her with that dangerous stare of his. "I'm not upset. Now, would you please have a seat so I can go over the rules of the game?"

Still not trusting his calm demeanor, she walked across the room and sat down. "The last time we spoke, you made your feelings clear." She didn't bother pretending his words hadn't cut her. "Why are you so eager to be around me now?"

"What I said to you—" He paused a moment. "Gita is the only woman who's ever spoken to me like you did. I was frustrated."

She leaned back in the chair, staring at him.

He lifted his gaze and let out a sigh before pushing back from the table. "This was a stupid idea."

Her hand shot out before she thought better of it and took hold of his wrist. "It looks like a fun game."

He didn't pull away, instead moved his chair back in place. With a heavy reluctance, she let him go.

Edwind set up the board and went over the basic rules, moving each piece to demonstrate. "Do I need to go over it again?" he asked, resetting the figures.

"I don't think so."

"You may have the first move."

Her defeat came quick, but she accepted the loss and was eager to start another game. He went over the rules again, but she stopped him. "I get how to play. It's not that complicated."

"Very well."

The second game lasted a few more moves than the last, and he kept eyeing her after every turn. When she lost again, there was visible irritation in her frown while she stared at the board.

"You are playing too recklessly with your knight," he offered.

Something in the way he spoke sparked another flash of the old man, and she giggled to herself.

"Did I say something amusing?"

"No. Maybe. I don't know. The way you said that almost made me remember something." She waved a hand. "Let's play again."

They started the next game, and she took the time to study his moves, anticipating what he might do to counter her own. While he looked over the board, her gaze wandered up his arm to a jagged scar that disappeared under the sleeve of his shirt. She noticed it when she cleaned his wounds and made up her own scenarios.

As if reading her mind, he said, "I got that when I was a foolish young boy."

"It must have been a horrible accident to leave a scar like that."

"It nearly severed my arm." He spoke as if it was an everyday occurrence. "Your move."

"What happened?"

"A nasty fall."

She stared at him, expecting a more detailed explanation. When he didn't give her one, she turned her attention back to the game. "I suppose you got all of your scars when you were a foolish young boy."

His laughter was soft and breathy. "No. I got a lot of them as a reckless young man."

She feigned shock. "You, reckless?"

He shrugged, looking over the board. "I haven't always been the mature, level-headed person you see before you." His gaze lifted to find her gaping at him. "What? I am very sensible."

"Among other things," she muttered, making her move. The smirk on his face told her she hadn't offended him too badly.

They played another few rounds in silence, and he said, "I shouldn't have come to you at the bonfire."

She kept her eyes on the board. "Why did you?"

He tapped a finger on the table. "Your move."

She contemplated pushing him for an answer, but he'd left himself open to attack. She pounced on his folly, belting out a laugh. "There's a nasty blow for you."

Edwind sat up in the chair, his own expression turning somber.

"Don't act so shocked. It's not like I beat you."

He cut his eyes at her, and her smile faltered. "I won? Wait, did you let me win?"

"Of course not. No one learns that way."

She grinned again.

"You must have played before." He kept looking over the board.

"Maybe I have." She stood up and started dancing around in a circle.

Her movements distracted him from the game. "What are you doing, woman?"

"A celebratory dance," she said.

He was on his feet, grabbing for her wrists. "No one likes someone who flaunts their win."

"I still beat you." She accentuated each syllable with the swing of her hips.

His kiss came so quick, she didn't have time to register his coarse beard scraping at her chin before the lingering taste of ale bombarded her senses. His tongue demanded entry between her lips to parlay with her own eager mouth. She flung her arms around his neck, pushing her fingers into his hair. He backed her into the wall, rocking into her.

With every touch, each kiss, she burned ever hotter until she thought her blood would burst into flames. He broke from her lips, tracing his mouth across her jawline to her neck while at the same time working a hand into her bodice, freeing one of her breasts. The feel of his coarse palm against her sensitive flesh made her shudder.

"Take me to your bed," she demanded. "Now."

His breath was hot against her skin. "Yes. Now." He drew her away from the wall and backed toward the door. And just like the night of the solstice, he was gone from her. He squeezed his eyes shut. "We can't do this. I can't—"

She took a few seconds to catch her breath. "I don't understand."

"I don't dare take you like this."

She tried to make him lift his gaze, but he refused to look at her. "You coward. You're too afraid of your own fucking feelings to take what you want. What I'm trying to give you."

"How can you want to be with me when you don't even know who you are? What if there is a husband waiting for you?"

"I think I'd remember a husband."

"You can't even remember who tried to kill you. There's so much you don't know about your life." He looked up. "There's so much you don't know about me. I can't take advantage of you like this."

"How very noble of you."

He hung his head, shaking it back and forth. "I don't mean to hurt you, Darya."

She took a step toward him, offering her hand. "I am giving myself freely to you, and I'm prepared to face the consequences of my choices. I want to be with you."

He looked from her face to her hand but made no move to take it.

Curling her fingers into a fist, she drew her arm into her body and wrapped it around her stomach in a vain attempt to hold back the pain inside her. She ran from the room, trying to stifle the cries he wrought from her yet again. She almost slammed into Saebbi on her way outside. He tried to stop her, but she ducked out of his grasp.

The night air hit her face, and tears came rolling down her cheeks. A cacophony of emotion churned inside her, and all she could think to do was flee to the one place she knew she could be alone. When she got to the top of the tower, her whole body trembled as she tried to keep the tears at bay.

She stared into the darkness of the sea, wishing she was out there in the middle of those rolling waves. She could sneak aboard the ship and take it to the mainland. It didn't matter that she didn't know where she came from. She didn't belong there.

But he'd been right to stop what was sure to be a horrible mistake. What if she did indeed have a husband? And children? Until she got her memory back, she would be a fool to give herself to anyone.

The door to the tower opened. Saebbi stepped out on the walkway and leaned on the rail, breathing in the crisp air. "It is magnificent up here."

She returned to her vigil over the island. "I'm not here for the view."

"You need to understand that there are things about Gita and Edwind that could alter how you perceive them."

She turned on him. "What could possibly change how I feel about them?"

"It's not my place to share that burden."

She turned to face him. "Why are you people so secretive?"

Before he could give an answer, her gaze floated over his shoulder to the sound of heavy wings beating in the air and the red dragon soaring right for them.

Chapter 10

Darya backpedaled, refusing to believe what she was seeing. Her feet tangled together, and the momentum sent her over the ledge. Saebbi made it to her just in time to latch onto her hand, only to have her slip out of his fingers from the momentum of her fall. Fear locked the scream in her throat, and all she could do was squeeze her eyes shut against the impending doom.

Instead of death, a rush of air enveloped her, and her head whipped back, her body clenched inside a vice-like a cage of something cold and hard. When she pried open her eyes again, she was staring into the belly of the same crimson dragon she'd seen flying toward the island. One of its dark claws cradled her in its grasp. It turned its sunburst yellow orbs toward her before swinging around to land.

The dragon dropped Darya onto her back a few feet from the earth, knocking the wind out of her. The taste of blood bloomed in her mouth from where she'd bitten her tongue on impact. Despite the pain, she rolled onto her hands and knees, ready to sprint away from the vicious beast.

Gita and Edwind sprinted to where she struggled to get her footing. Saebbi burst through the door of the tower, joining his friends. Darya watched the dragon shrink into the form of a man. His familiar features jarred her mangled mind, flooding her with memories like a fast-moving slide show.

"You!" Darya screamed. Whatever residual fear thrummed through her blood paled to the anger and frustration that had been building since waking on the island.

She launched herself at Horsa, hoping to knock him off balance with the weight of her body, but he was a solid man and easily held his ground. "What did you do to me?"

His wide-eyed expression was quickly replaced with something darker. He reached out, took her by the throat, and squeezed, cutting off Darya's ability to take in air.

Darya fought against him, clawing and slapping at his arms. Her voice was strangled against his grip.

The dragon turned man looked at Gita and Edwind. "Who is this crazy woman?"

Darya's struggle grew more labored, her breath more ragged.

"You're killing her," Gita pleaded. "Father, please. Let her go."

Horsa's eyes didn't leave Darya. "She attacked me first," he rationalized, yet he released his grip as Gita asked.

Darya swayed, but kept her footing as she gasped for air. Her eyes darted from Gita to Edwind, then back to Horsa again. A horrible realization constricted her chest even tighter, making her skin prickle with a cold sensation.

Gita saw the panicked expression on her face and said, "There is no need to fear us. We are the same people who took you in and cared for you."

Darya flinched away when Gita reached for her.

"How do you know our father?" Edwind asked.

Darya jabbed a finger at Horsa. "He and that crazy woman of his are the ones who kidnapped me, drugged me, and left me out in the middle of the ocean. Oh, and he's not a man. He's a dragon. You're all fucking dragons." Still unsteady from shock and lack of air, she wobbled to her feet. "What am I saying? I've gone insane. Dragons aren't real. None of this is real." She ran a hand down her face. "Get it together, Darya. It's nineteen eighty-two, for the goddess' sake. Stuff like this doesn't exist. There's got to be a logical explanation. There's—"

"What year did you say?" Horsa asked.

She blinked at him, confused by his question.

He took a step toward her, seemingly unfazed by the fighting stance she took.

"Don't you dare come near me." She'd taken a few self-defense classes with Annie, but she knew her basic skills wouldn't help her against a dragon. Still, she wasn't about to let him touch her again without a fight.

Horsa held up his hands. "What year do you come from?"

Something about his question made a chill snake down her spine. She glanced at the castle before looking over the valley at the village. Understanding swept over her like a frigid winter wind. She turned a fearful gaze to the village past the walls.

When she came back around, she whispered, "Nineteen eighty-two."

Horsa and his children shared a look of shock and uncertainty. It made her stomach roll with the same force her that her chest constricted against her lungs.

"I think we need to go inside so we may speak about this calmly," Gita said.

Darya shook her head. "No. What I need is to get back to the mainland, find a phone, and call the cops on your crazy dad." She refused to entertain the idea of being thrust back in time. "I need to get—I have to go home. You seem like a nice person—dragon—whatever you are. Please, let me go home."

Edwind's shoulders fell with the exhalation of a long sigh. "If what you say is true, there is no home for you to return to. The year is nine eighty-two, not nineteen eighty-two."

"No." She fought back frightened tears. "No, this can't be real. I'm in a coma or dead."

"Edwind speaks the truth," Gita said.

"No!" Darya said even louder, pulling herself upright. "First, you expect me to believe dragons are real. Now you're telling me one of those dragons sent me a thousand years into the past?"

Her fear fed the anger that bubbled under the surface. She turned that frustration on Horsa. "You did this to me, and you are going to stand there and tell me you don't know who I am?"

"I have never seen you before this night."

The hold she had on her temper snapped, and she rushed the elder dragon again. Edwind intercepted her, wrapping her up in his arms and simultaneously spinning her away from him.

"Let me go," she snarled.

He hesitated before releasing her. She whirled around so she could keep them in her sights and stumbled backward toward the slope that led to the beach.

Gita stepped forward. "Come inside. We can talk about this over a cup of tea."

"I'm not stepping foot back in that place." She backed away, ready to run.

"Where will you go?" Edwind's voice broke through her panic.

Her pride still blistered from his rejection. "Why the hell do you care?"

His expression hardened into something that tried to hide the sting of her words.

"Please, Darya. We only want to help you," Gita said.

"Help me?" She glared at Horsa. "He sure as hell wasn't helping me when he threw me into this godforsaken primitive land."

She turned in a half-circle, looking for a place to run. No matter how far or fast she ran, there was no escape. Even if she made it to the mainland, there was nothing for her there.

Everything—her home, her friends, her life—was gone. All of it was a thousand years away.

Darya summoned the resilience that had carried her through unimaginable tragedies; tragedies no person should have to go through in their lifetime. If Horsa sent her here, he could send her back to nineteen eighty-two.

Ignoring Gita's outstretched hand, Darya strode past her and the men, prepared to face whatever waited for her inside.

The cool breath of the evening breeze swept over Darya, easing her anxiety and made it more bearable to tell the others the story of how she ended up thrown ten centuries into the past. Their faces fell into the same expression of shock and disbelief that overwhelmed her when she found out what year she woke up.

Trying to explain modern things like cars, airplanes, and electricity were some of the more challenging hurdles, but she pushed through until she got to the part where she washed up on their shores. It was a relief to learn that Horsa and his children were the only dragons on the island.

"I can't believe such things exist in the future," Horsa said after finishing his ale in one long swallow.

"Well, you get to experience it firsthand." Darya looked away from the star-filled sky. "How is it you live in this time and a thousand years into the future unless you figured out how to time travel?"

He and Gita shared a look. "There is no time travel involved for me. Because of what I am, I will live an infinite number of years."

When Darya glanced at Gita, she said, "Edwind and I won't live near as long. Since our mother was human, the mortal blood that runs through our veins will shorten our lives significantly compared to our father."

"Your mother was human?"

Gita nodded.

"I'm going to gloss over how that is even remotely possible because I'm having enough trouble believing how any of this is possible." But was it so hard to accept, given what she was? What could she do?

"Did I—" Horsa frowned, releasing a tired breath. "Did my future self tell you why I—he sent you here? To this time?"

Darya turned back to the open door. "No. When Mark showed up, you and Ronwen refused to let me leave. That's when she knocked me out. I woke up in the sailboat. Now, here I am." She leaned forward, as if to take a step toward him, then thought better of it. "Are you sure you don't know her?"

He shook his head.

"You said you were trying to protect me."

"From what?"

"I don't know. Mark, maybe? But he's harmless. He was grieving for his girlfriend and wasn't in his right mind."

They sat in silence until Gita leaned forward and asked, "Could he have been protecting you from another like the man who tried to kill you?"

Darya wondered about that. The maniac that broke into her apartment had her name and address, according to Mark, but who would want her dead? Is that why Janine pushed for her to get out of the country? Was she somehow involved with Horsa and Ronwen?

"Darya," Gita said.

"It's possible, I guess."

"Can you describe the portal?" Horsa asked.

She threw a harsh glare over her shoulder. "Not really. I was too busy fighting for my life," she snapped.

His expression darkened. "Watch your tone."

"Or what? You'll throw me into another time portal? Make sure this one sends me back home."

"I can do worse," he grumbled.

She rolled her eyes. "Oh, please. If you were going to kill me, you would have done it already."

"If not for my daughter, you would be dead now."

Gita stood between them. "Calm yourselves."

Darya pinched the bridge of her nose. "What does it matter what the portal looked like?"

Horsa shrugged. "I'm trying to understand the magic that brought you here."

"I don't care how I got here. I just want to get back home." She started for the gardens.

"Where are you going?" he asked.

"I need to be alone."

Edwind stood. "I don't think it's a good idea for you to be by yourself."

"Where am I going to go?" she asked, throwing his words back at him. "I'm stranded a thousand years from everything and everyone I've ever known. It's not like I can fly away."

He lowered his head. "I didn't mean it like that."

"I need to sort all of this out." Her voice sounded tired to her own ears.

Horsa sat forward. "I have more questions."

"I really don't give a damn about your questions right now." Darya stormed outside the door, unsure of which direction to go. She didn't lie when she said she had nowhere to run to.

Behind her, she heard Horsa say, "The gall of that girl."

"Have you no heart?" Gita's voice was laced with vitriol. "With everything she's been through because of you, I'd say she is being very accommodating in answering what she did. If I so much as hear a whisper of a crossword toward her, I swear I will skin the both of you alive and feast on your carcasses."

Saebbi's calm stoicism came through in his words. "Tread lightly for now."

"I should tread lightly?" Horsa scoffed. "That girl is lucky I didn't snap her neck."

Darya frowned at the unveiled threat and started for the path to the small beach beneath the cliffs. She stared into the vast ocean of stars, thinking only hours before, she wished so much to have her memories. Now that she was whole again, she wished she could go back to living in blissful ignorance.

Looking over the silent village, it amazed her how the islander's lives intertwined with her own. Their ceremonies. Their gods. Their rituals.

None of that mattered, though. She couldn't go back to the life she'd built there, nor would she expect these people to accept her, knowing where she came from; when she came from. She was being forced to leave the people she cared for due to circumstances that were out of her control.

She wandered to the tiny beach beyond the cliffs to watch the tide roll into shore. A scattered array of stars blanketed the night, falling into the horizon. When she was younger, she spent many nights among the tall pines of her home, watching the celestial heavens and all their infinite glory. Were these the same interstellar diamonds she studied when she was a child? Was there a twinkle or two missing?

She was now a lost vessel in the sea of time, with no means of finding her way back to where she belonged. Maybe if she knew why they brought her here, she wouldn't be so helpless. If only she understood why Horsa and Ronwen chose her.

All her questions would remain unanswered until she returned to her own time.

If she ever found her way back.

The prospect of being stuck in nine eighty-two for the rest of her natural life made a cold, heavy weight drop to the pit of her stomach. The ball of dread swelled inside her, and she covered her face to stifle the wail that clawed free of her open mouth. Her knees gave out, and she fell to the soft sand.

When the first cry faded, she sucked in a desperate breath, only to have another sob burst out of her again. She screamed until her throat ached. Her cries turn into muffled sobs that were lost to the roar of the surf crashing against the cliffs.

A pair of arms wrapped around her, pulling her up from the sand. She tried to break free of Edwind's grasp, but she didn't have the strength to fight him. He settled her in his lap, rocking back and forth. "I'm so sorry for all of this," he whispered.

His sympathy raked over raw wounds, forcing more tears to blanket her cheeks. God, how she wanted to stay enveloped in his arms for the rest of her life.

He sat there, taking her pain and fear and sorrow. When she was empty, she pushed out of his arms. He clutched at her hands, but she had to break free of him before she lacked the willpower to leave.

When her memory returned, so did the promise she made to herself. She wouldn't leave herself that vulnerable to another person again. Especially not to a man who so forcefully drove her out of his heart.

"I hate you all for doing this to me." The taste of those words on her tongue was disgusting, but she was already grieving for the life that would never be hers. "Especially you."

She shoved away what remained of her anguish and left Edwind alone on the beach.

Chapter 11

DARYA WOKE TO THE smell of freshly brewed coffee. The fragrance made her homesick. She wanted so badly to imbibe in a piping hot cup of that dark drink again. When she opened her eyes, she shot upright, taking in the strange surroundings. She expected to see the same drab gray stone she'd woken up to over the last couple of weeks. But there was no stone, no glassless windows, no furs covering the sleigh bed on which she now lay.

The walls caught the early morning sun, giving the yellow paint a muted glow and making the flowered border paper stand out even more. She looked down at herself. Instead of the off-white gown she'd been wearing when she fell asleep, she had on a light pink spaghetti-strapped cotton shirt and matching shorts.

Her feet landed on a plush eggshell carpet when she jumped out of bed. Though she didn't recognize the room, she knew it was the modern world and not nine eighty-two. Somehow, she was back in her own time, but this wasn't her apartment.

She made her way out of the bedroom and down the hall, following the enticing aroma of coffee and cooking food. The decorations had the same simple color scheme, with a sprinkle of bold hues on the furniture and portraits on the walls.

She turned the corner, bypassing the living room for a set of glass doors that led into a small dining room. Beyond the round pine table was the source of the wonderful smells.

A man stood with his back to her. He was intent on the bacon that sizzled in the pan, but when she got within arm's length of the counter, he turned around, greeting her with a big smile. "Good morning, lover."

She put up her hands, pushing away from him. "What's going on? Mark, where's Annie?"

His expression fell into one of confusion. "Are you feeling okay?"

"What is this?"

"You must have had too many drinks last night." He went back to the stove. "I made a fresh pot of coffee. The paper is on the bar."

"Where's Annie?" she repeated.

His body shook with silent laughter. "I swear I'm never letting you mix liquor and wine on the same night. How should I know where she is? She moved away years ago. It's not like I kept in touch after we broke it off." He shot her a quick wink. "You're not still jealous of her, are you?"

"I—" She put a hand to her head. Everything was so foggy.

He took the pan off the burner and pulled her into a close embrace, and kissed her cheek. "Are you alright?"

She forced a smile. "Yeah. I guess I drank too much, like you said." It was all she could do not to shudder at the feel of his lips against her cheek.

"Have a seat. I'll bring your plate when the biscuits are done."

Instead of going to the bar, she walked to the counter and poured herself some coffee. Bringing it to her nose, she inhaled the magical fragrance. "This smells so good. I feel like I haven't had coffee in forever."

She set down the cup and hopped onto a barstool. Her thoughts swam in and out of focus, and she looked over the kitchen, trying to find something familiar, but everything seemed off.

He placed a generous helping of bacon, eggs, and grits in front of her. "Eat up, darling. You need it after last night. I think you were more excited about my promotion than I was." He stepped to the stove and made his own plate of food. "You gave me my own private celebration when we got home."

Darya shut her eyes against disturbing visions of Annie's dead body on the floor of their old apartment. "Man, I had some strange dreams."

"Strange how?" he asked, sitting next to her.

"We—Annie and I were still in the city. Someone broke in and attacked us. Poor Annie was killed. After that, I flew to Europe, to this little village by the sea. You were so upset about her death you followed me all the way to Broughied." She brought the mug to her lips, taking a sip. Despite the powerful odor that emanated from the cup, it was like drinking hot, stale water. "Oh, god, what is this?"

"It's a new brand I'm trying," he said dismissively, then sat forward. "What happened when you got to the village?"

"It's gross. Don't buy it again." She set the cup beside the plate of food. "Anyway, there was this man and his lady friend. They kidnapped me and sent me through some time portal into the past. I wound up on an island called Didean."

"What year did they send you to?"

She shrugged. "I can't really remember. I think it was some time in the tenth century."

He grabbed her arms and turned her to face him. "What year? Specifically."

She stared at the fingers gripping her arm. "Why does that matter? What's wrong with you?"

His mouth softened, and he let go of her. "I'm just curious about your dream."

She rubbed her wrists and scooted away. "I didn't find out I was even in the past until I fell out of a tower and get this, a dragon saved me. His children had been taking care of me. One of them told me what year it was." She closed her eyes. "Nine eighty-two, I think. Yeah, it was exactly a thousand years in the past."

Mark leaned back from her. The grin on his face melted into a malicious sneer. His eyes shifted from brown to the shade of the deepest part of the sea; dark and cold.

He reached for her arms again, thick fingers digging into her flesh. "Thank you, seedling."

No matter how hard she yanked against his grip, she couldn't get loose. "Mark, you're scaring me."

His visage shifted, and he wasn't the man she'd known in her old life, but the monster that had haunted her dreams since being stranded on Didean. The fog shielding her mind disappeared, and she came to the horrible realization that what she thought was a dream was, in fact, real.

Gita. Edwind. Saebbi. They were all real.

The horned man laughed. "I am coming for you, girl. I won't let you steal what is mine."

"No!" she screamed and threw herself backward out of the chair.

Morning dragged Darya out of the nightmare and into the safety of the waking world. She pushed herself up to the wall, still trying to get out of the beast's phantom grasp. Her gaze darted around the empty room. Only after her heart slowed did she relax. The cool, rough surface of the stone reminded her she was in the real world and not the horrible nightmare.

Outside, the sky foretold of the coming dawn. Dread of the unknown world that waited beyond her door kept her in bed a few minutes longer. What was going to happen to her now? Where could she possibly fit in?

When she finally broke free of her anxiety, she slid out of bed and went to the balcony. The valley below was the same one she'd spent the last couple of weeks immersing herself in. Yet, in this new light of her reawakened memories, nothing would be the same again.

After dressing, she hesitated at her door. It wasn't feasible for her to stay in her room indefinitely. Nor did she want to remain in the quiet space where the nightmare still lingered, unnatural almost. Like the tasteless coffee she'd sipped in the dream. Besides, Horsa might have more questions for her—perhaps even some answers.

Downstairs, she was almost to the entryway when she noticed Gita step outside the dining hall. Darya wondered how the woman was aware of her presence, but the instincts of dragons were beyond her understanding.

Gita motioned her forward. "Would you care to join us?"

It would only put off the inevitable if she refused, so she nodded and followed her inside. Edwind and Horsa sat on the opposite end of the table. Edwind avoided looking at her, which she was thankful for. It meant he wouldn't see the longing in her gaze at the memory of his arms around her.

She sat in the empty chair next to Gita and across from Saebbi, who offered her a reassuring smile.

They ate in awkward silence for a few minutes until Gita asked, "How did you sleep?"

Darya kept her eyes locked on the tea in her hands. "I had strange dreams, but I guess that's normal, given the circumstances." She glanced at Gita. "I'm sorry for how I left last night. I was a little freaked out and angry. You've been nothing but kind to me."

"I understand your fear. We all do." Her gaze wandered to the other men in the room. "Don't we?"

There was a mumbling of agreement.

Horsa cleared his throat.

Darya looked up from her drink. "I hope you aren't expecting an apology from me."

"I saved your life."

"You're the reason I'm here."

"My future self is the reason you're here."

"Same difference."

They stared at each other for a few seconds.

"Ungrateful child," he muttered.

"Grumpy old man," she shot back. "Even if it was the future you that sent me here, I liked him better. He was a lot less bitter and angry."

Horsa tried to hide a smile behind his cup. Clearing his throat again, he said, "I have more questions."

Gita gave him a warning glare.

"If she wishes to answer," he clarified.

"I'll answer what I can," Darya agreed.

He glanced at Edwind. "He saw your tribal marking."

She ran a hand over the back of her neck before she could stop herself. She hadn't thought about that tattoo in so long that she almost forgot it was there.

"It belongs to our clan," Edwind told her. "When I saw it at the bonfire, I wasn't sure what to make of it."

Horsa nodded. "And you unlocked Diana's chest. I still don't understand why she would put a ward on it in the first place. There were a lot of things I didn't understand—"

Darya stopped listening. What he didn't know, what none of them knew, was why the elders made her hide it. That couldn't be the reason she was here, could it? Only a handful of people understood what she was. She left that world behind a long time ago.

Why now? Why wait nearly five years to come after her? She thought back to Mark and wondered if he might have had something to do with any of this.

No. His grief was genuine. He'd been an innocent victim in this, just as Annie had been.

"Darya." Gita sat forward, patting her arm. "Are you having a vision?"

She pushed back from the table and strode to the closest window. "I think I know why I was targeted, but I can't explain the reasoning behind it." She eyed Horsa. "Nor what part you and Ronwen played in it."

All four of them shared a look, and Horsa said, "Well?"

She studied the rolling hills and, after a few heartbeats, went on. "I always assumed I had to hide my mark because of what I am and what I can do." Her lips split into a bitter smile. "My mother liked to call me her little abomination."

"That's horrible for a mother to tell her child," Gita said.

"It wasn't the worst thing she did to me." Shaking her head, Darya continued. "After I came of age and received the mark of my ancestors, I didn't have the freedoms that the others had. They could come and go whenever they wanted, but I had to have an escort if I left the safety of our land." A sad smile pulled at her mouth. "No matter how sneaky I thought I was, there was one elder who always seemed to know where I was at all times."

She made herself meet Edwind's gaze. "He's the one who taught me to play that game. In my time, we call it chess." With a reminiscent smile, she said, "You play a lot like him." She turned back to the fields outside the window.

"What does this have to do with why you are here?" Horsa asked.

A light gray squirrel peeked its head inside and sniffed the air before leaping to the ground and bounding across the stone floor to Darya's empty chair. Another smaller squirrel with more red than brown in its fur soon followed. The orange fox from the river was the last to come into the room. It hesitated on the windowsill before racing to the table. She held up a hand to stop them.

"Don't be rude." She grabbed a piece of bread off her plate and doled it piece by piece to the little forest creatures. "This is my food. You cannot have theirs."

The fox yipped at her.

"I don't care if they feasted on the flesh of your brethren. That is the way of things."

Stunned faces stared back at her from the table.

"Druidae," Horsa whispered.

Darya rolled her eyes. "That's a pretentious-sounding name the elders called me. I never liked it."

"It is what you are."

"What is a druidae?" Saebbi asked.

Gita took his hand. "They are rare beings blessed by the goddess of the forest to speak to her creatures. I've heard stories of them. Never have I met one." She swung her gaze on Darya again. "Was this why you and your friend were attacked?"

"Maybe. Only a handful of people knew what I could do. To most of them, I was just a weird kid who pretended to talk to animals. I can't imagine anyone sending a hired assassin after me."

"What about the person who gave you that scar?" Edwind asked.

She frowned, letting a chipmunk hop into her open hand. "She would have to do so from the pits of the underworld, and I doubt my mother has that kind of pull with the gods."

"You poor child." Gita's face reflected the sadness she felt. "Did she have the gift?"

"As far as I know, she was a normal mortal woman. I didn't realize just how much she hated me until she got so drunk one night. She worked up the courage to shove that knife in my gut."

"How did she die?" Horsa asked.

"I was told she killed herself with the same knife she used on me. I guess she couldn't live with what she did. After I healed from the injury, I never went back. I couldn't. So, I moved away and have been trying to make a new life for myself." She glanced at Horsa. "Apparently, you and your people have been biding your time until you were ready to send me here."

Horsa tapped a finger on the table, deep in thought. "I may know of someone who can give us the answers we need. Gita, I want you to travel with me to the mainland. We should return before nightfall."

"We will do whatever we can to get you home," Gita promised.

Darya forced a grim smile. "I don't even know where that is anymore."

Darya stood on her balcony, watching the two dragons disappear into the western sky, thinking how surreal it was to be a witness to these mythical beasts of legends. Now that she knew what they were, she should have been able to quell the feelings she had for Edwind.

How could an outcast like her ever expect to be a worthy lover to such a beautiful creature? Even if he thought he wanted to be with her, eventually, he would find out how broken she truly was, and like Harvey, he would push her aside for someone else.

Back in her room, she sat down in the chair in front of the fireplace. She thought about going downstairs to find comfort in the gardens or help Minerva with her herbs. Yet knowing how far out of place she really was, she thought it best to be alone.

So, for the remainder of the day, she stayed busy with her own thoughts. She kept going over Annie's murder and the subsequent chain of events that brought her to this moment, but no matter how many times she picked apart her memories, she couldn't come up with a solution to get her back home.

By the time the sun was sliding into the ocean that evening, she had to get out of those walls, so she snuck downstairs. The halls were dark and silent, with no trace of Edwind or Saebbi. Wynfrid would have gone home a while ago. She kept her footsteps slow and silent on her way through the study that led outside, where the flowers waited.

She ambled at a leisurely, unbothered pace, taking in the peaceful twilight that muted the colorful buds that surrounded her. Every time she let her thoughts drift, they conjured a face that sent her pulse racing.

In a vain attempt to banish Edwind's presence from her mind and the memory of his touch, she got to her knees and picked at what little weeds were sprouting from the ground around the bushes. The tedious work was a convenient distraction from her ever-circling thoughts.

Faint whispers called to her from outside the garden walls. They warned of an interloper watching her. A ghost of a smile swept across her lips when she heard footsteps approach.

"Do you mind if I join you?" Edwind asked.

She fought the urge to lift her gaze from the ground. "It's your home. You can do whatever you want."

After a few seconds, he knelt beside her and plucked at the weeds from a nearby rosebush. He kept glancing to the side, his mouth parted, ready to say something, but couldn't quite get the words to come out.

After a minute of silent weeding, he finally said, "I was right. The moment you washed onto these shores, I sensed you were special."

She didn't try to hide the snarky grin that landed on her face. "Special? Not dangerous?"

His smile matched hers, making her pulse race. "You are very much both."

They returned to pretending to care for the foliage. It was her turn to struggle to speak. After a few failed attempts, she said, "Why didn't you tell me about the sigil on my neck that night at the bonfire?"

"I was too much in shock at first. After speaking with Gita, I wanted to bring Father here, hoping he could tell us what it meant."

"Is that why you tried to send me to the village?"

"That was part of it." He almost looked her in the eyes, but his gaze stopped short of her nose.

She stood to go back inside. "It worked out for the best. For both of us."

He was on his feet and blocked her path before she took another step. His hands encased hers, making her heart pound in her chest, threatening to break free of its mortal cage.

"Look at me, Darya." His voice was quiet, but it demanded to be obeyed.

When she lifted her face, her whole body stiffened at the sight before her. His once mesmerizing jade eyes were now glowing jewels of amber, swirling like molten pools of infinite desire. "Is there a husband or betrothed who waits for you?"

She shook her head, whispering, "No one."

He captured the sides of her face before laying claim to her lips, gingerly testing the softness of her mouth until their need for more pushed them together, fighting to consume each other. They broke apart, panting and breathless.

"I will not turn you away again if you choose to come to my bed." He caressed her tingling mouth one last time. "But I understand if you can't accept my offer."

She let him walk off, frozen with indecision. Of course, she wanted to be with him. Every feminine fiber in her body screamed at her to follow.

Yet that part of her that had suffered such horrible heartache kept her feet planted firmly to the ground like the flowers that surrounded her. She reminded herself of the promise she made to the broken woman left in the wake of the last man who shattered her world.

While she argued with herself, her legs broke free of their paralysis, carrying her forward toward the open doors where Edwind disappeared.

Her heart knew the right choice.

From the corner of her eye, she saw a brown streak shooting through the air. The second the hawk made contact, she was on the ground, being crushed by the weight of a man's body. Mark pinned her wrists above her head with one hand and used the other to cover her mouth.

"You thought you got away from me," he hissed through clenched teeth.

She stared at his crazed features in disbelief. The shock left her unable to move when he let go of her arms and wrapped his meaty hands around her exposed throat.

"You don't know what I've gone through to find you; what I've given up. It will all be worth it when I have Annie back." His expression kept morphing from glee, to sadness, to fear and anguish.

There was a moment of clarity in his crazed gaze, and his grip on her loosened. "I'm sorry, Darya. I really am, but I miss her so much. This is the only way I can have her back. He demands your life for hers." He tightened his grasp again, and fireworks exploded throughout her vision. "There isn't any other way." His voice took on a hoarse purr.

Somewhere above her, there came a fierce shriek, bringing Mark's focus from Darya to the sky. A pair of pale claws dove for him, followed by the sound of his shrill screams and the feel of something warm, wet, and viscous spraying over her face and torso. He let go of her neck, allowing her to suck in a desperate breath. She rolled onto her stomach, frantic to get away while Mark continued to scream in agony at her back.

Edwind paced at the end of his bed in anticipation of Darya's arrival. He wasn't used to being this nervous about bedding a woman.

He chuckled to himself. Darya wasn't just any woman. He couldn't pinpoint what it was about her that drove him to the point of madness with need when she was near him, but he knew her body alone wouldn't sate his desire. He wanted to find a place in her heart as well.

He searched his room for the best place to wait for her arrival. Should he be on the bed? Sitting at the table near the window? He certainly shouldn't be pacing back and forth like some nervous youngling waiting for his first lover. Finally, he decided to stand near the door, ready to take her in his arms and ravage her body the moment she stepped inside.

He expected her to be right behind him. What if she changed her mind? Surely not. He felt the way her pulse raced when they kissed.

She would come.

The shriek of a man broke through the silent calm of his room, making him snap to attention. He was in the hall and yelling for Saebbi on his way outside. When he reached the gardens, he saw a woman's arm on the ground, covered in blood. Darya was clawing at the dirt, trying to drag herself away from the stranger that was being attacked by a white falcon.

Edwind ran to her side, relieved to see she was alive.

The bloodied man knocked the bird away and turned his ruined face back to the woman on the ground. He jumped on her legs and reached for her hair.

Edwind rushed forward, kicking him off her, and latched onto his bloodied shirt. It was then Edwind saw how bad his injuries were. Crimson viscera covered one side of his face from the eye that hung by a single, meaty string. The blood-soaked man arched away from Edwind before trans-forming into a hawk and shooting into the sky.

Edwind looked from Darya to the bird of prey, torn between going after it and getting her to safety. The white falcon decided for him when it took off after the hawk.

He drew the sobbing woman into his arms, holding her close to his chest. "I've got you," he said, trying to ease her uncontrollable shivering. "You're safe."

She clung to him, still trembling.

Saebbi came running up behind them. "What's going on? I heard screaming." He saw the woman in his friend's arms and a hand went to his sword. "Who attacked her? Where are they?"

"Gather the men," Edwind ordered without looking away from the woman in his arms.

Inside, he carried Darya to his room, laying her on his bed so he could check her over for injuries. Other than the redness that would soon turn to bruises on her neck, he couldn't see any other wounds.

"How did he find me?" she asked through shaky whimpers. "It was a dream. Just a stupid dream."

He brushed blood-matted hair from her face. "You're not making any sense. What are you talking about? Do you know that man?"

"Mark," she sobbed. "It was Mark."

"But you told us he was mortal. I watched him transform into a hawk."

"I don't know. I don't understand any of it." She closed her eyes. "He said he was here to kill me. Someone made a deal with him. My life for Annie's. Who could do that? Is it even possible?"

"Only the gods have that kind of power." He backed away from the bed. "I will send Wynfrid to look after you."

She reached for his hand, but he was already walking out of the room.

"Edwind."

He closed his eyes to the desperation in her voice. His focus now needed to be on making sure the island and his people were safe.

A voice in the back of his head pleaded with him to go back, but he refused to yield to his heart and kept walking.

Chapter 12

DARYA STORMED PAST WYNFRID on her way to her room. Her chest ached at the memory of the expression on Edwind's face before walking away. Each step fomented more anger, overtaking the despair in her heart. By the time she was back inside her sanctuary, a seething rage made her skin flush.

In her room, she stripped out of her clothes and scrubbed Mark's blood from her body before donning a clean dress. Already the bruises around her neck were darkening against her pale skin. She stared into her reflection. Bitterness was fueled by how helpless she was to her circumstances.

Somehow, Mark traversed time to find her. Not only that, but he also had the power to transform into a hawk. The worst revelation of all was his willingness to kill her, hoping to resurrect Annie from the dead.

Only the gods have that power. Edwind's words echoed inside her head, compounding the helplessness she already struggled with.

Gods. Dragons. Time travel. It was all too much. What did any of this have to do with her?

In a fit of bitter rage, she pulled the wash basin off the table, watching it shatter at her feet. Pieces of pottery float-ed across the floor, and she stared at the ruins of the bowl until some of the anger subsided. The emptiness that swallowed the rest of her emotions was a welcomed reprieve from reality. She sat down in a chair beside the balcony doors, losing all sense of time when she became absorbed in a vicious cycle of spiraling thoughts.

She must have fallen asleep because when she lifted her head, she was leaning over one side of the chair. Her body ached from being twisted at such an odd angle. The sky held a dusky rose hue announcing a new day. Her gaze swept over the dry stone, then snapped up to the door at the sound of someone knocking.

Wynfrid stepped inside, eyeing the mess on the floor.

"I'm going to clean it up," Darya said.

"Gita wishes to speak to you. I'll take care of this."

Darya didn't argue. What was the point? Nothing was in her control anymore.

Everyone waited for her in the great hall. Gita and Horsa's eyes landed on the bruises around her neck. Saebbi stood off to one side of the doorway. Edwind was facing the window across the room.

There was a newcomer standing beside Horsa, watching her every move with eyes the same shade as the rest of the Wodehal clan, but much paler and more iridescent. His silver hair was gathered at the back of his head, leaving the sides of his head shaved, and the markings that decorated the exposed scalp tickled a hidden part of Darya's mind she still couldn't quite reach.

Gita took a step forward, but Darya held up a hand against the intrusion into her personal space. "I'm fine."

"How did that man get here?" Gita asked, backing away again.

"How should I know?" Darya snapped. "I don't even know how I got here. Ask your fucking father."

Edwind turned from the window. "Be mindful of how you speak to my family."

The older man took a step toward Edwind. "You should follow your own advice. Has she not been through enough because of you all?"

Edwind went back to staring out of the window, avoiding Darya's anger.

Horsa stepped forward. "Can we please not fight amongst ourselves? Not when we have a true enemy at our gates. Darya, this is my father, Hengist."

Hengist took her hand in his. The feel of his rough, calloused palms reinforced the nagging memory fighting to come to light. "My son says you've traveled a long way to be with us."

Her eyes were fixated on the fingers that covered hers. "You could say that."

"And he was the one who sent you here?"

"He and another woman."

"Is she a dragon too?"

Darya withdrew her hand from his grasp, offering a weak shrug. "I have no idea."

Hengist nodded. "You speak to animals? Which ones? Birds? Foxes? The bigger beasts?"

Darya cocked her head to the side, confused by his question. "All of them."

He turned to Horsa. "You didn't tell me she spoke to them all."

"You didn't ask."

Darya looked at the two elder dragons. "What's the big deal? So, what if I can talk to all of them?"

Hengist smiled. "It means you are the first of your kind in a very long time to hear the call of every animal."

Her gaze fell to her feet.

"What do you know of your parents?"

She crossed her arms. "Not much. My mother was a self-ish, cruel woman who hated me. I know even less about my father since I've never met him."

"No one ever mentioned his name?"

She frowned. "Every time I asked about him, the elders made it clear that he was never to be spoken of." A trickle of familiarity wriggled into her mind. She took hold of Hengist's right arm, turning it over and pushing up his shirt sleeve, revealing a scar on one of his biceps.

"What is it?" he asked.

"I get the feeling we've met before."

"Did you meet me in this future of yours?"

"Not in Broughied." She made a slow circle around him, reaching out with a finger every so often and touching him at specific parts of his upper torso.

"What are you doing?" Horsa asked.

"Each one of those places is a scar."

"How do you know of them?" Hengist's mouth dropped open. "Were we lovers?"

There was a collective gasp behind her, and she took on a look of disgusted shock. "Gross. No."

"How else would you have known of them? And it isn't so outrageous to think I could be a worthy lover."

Ignoring his bruised ego, she said, "You were an elder in my tribe." Realization bloomed across her face. "That explains so much. That's how you found me so easily, you sneaky old man."

"He's the one who taught you to play," Edwind said.

Without looking away from Hengist, she nodded. "You always said I was a better student than your grandson."

Edwind cleared his throat. "That still doesn't tell us why she is here or what we are going to do with her?"

"We are going to continue to protect her," Gita said. "As we have been doing."

Hengist looked to Darya. "Did Mark say anything else? Did he mention the name of this entity he works for?"

She searched her memory of the attack. Everything had happened so fast. All she could focus on at the time was the manic expression on his face. She recalled him having dark eyes before, but they kept shifting from a dark blue back to brown. There was a scar on the side of his neck that hadn't been there before.

She smudged her fingers in the soot from the cold fireplace. "He had a symbol burned into his flesh. It was the same one the other man had. The one who attacked Annie and I." She got most of it drawn out when the elder dragon snatched up her hand and wiped it away.

"You're sure that was the same marking?" Hengist asked.

"Yes."

"That sigil is a conscript of the gods."

"Which one?" Gita asked.

"I can't say for sure," Hengist said.

Darya pulled her hand free of his grasp. "This is ridiculous. First of all, the gods have better things to do than recruit people to do their bidding. Second, why would one of them want me dead? I'm not a threat to them."

"Given the circumstances," Edwind said, "I think it would be best if Grandfather took her to the mainland. Both for her safety and ours. There's no telling when Mark will return."

"If he returns at all," Horsa said. "He knows we will be waiting."

Edwind's words sliced through her. "He's right. I can't stay. Mark won't give up so easily. I—" She swallowed, pushing down her sadness. Edwind wouldn't get any more of her tears. "Out there, I will have a better chance of finding my way home." She kept her eyes locked on the ground and rushed out the door, pausing on the other side of the hall to swallow back tears.

"You may as well throw her into the sea," she heard Hengist say. "She is safe here. More so than out there."

After a few silent breaths, Hengist grunted and said, "Bah, you stubborn boy. Gita, do you have a room for your grandfather? I will need a place to stay until I can secure passage for us to the mainland."

"Of course."

Darya rushed around the corner so Gita wouldn't catch her listening to their conversation. She took off past the gardens to the fields on the other side of the valley. The animals were the only ones who could give her comfort now.

When Horsa and Edwind were alone, the older dragon said, "Are you really going to send her away to fend for herself?"

"She won't be alone. She will have Grandfather. He is the one who watches over her in the future. He can do so now."

"Your mother would have done all she could to keep her protected right here on the island. Gods be damned."

Edwind turned on his father. "Well, she isn't here, is she?"

"For once, I'm glad she isn't."

Edwind frowned and headed for the open doorway, stomping his way up the stairs of the tower. At the top, he rested his hands on the stone wall, looking over the beauty of his home. He saw so many of his mother's people born, grow up, start families of their own, and give in to the ravages of time. He and his sister were the protectors of this place. They were the ones who would endure when all others eventually left, either through travel or death. He would do everything in his power to protect them. Even send away the woman he'd grown to care so deeply for.

There was a storm coming in from the north, bringing with it bloated, purple clouds rolling toward the island. Hopefully, it wouldn't delay her departure. He contemplated trying to convince her to let his grandfather carry her across the ocean. His resolve to be rid of her was growing weaker with each passing moment.

No matter how much he tried to assure himself she would be better off on the mainland, he wasn't naïve enough to think she would be safer out there than if she stayed. His grandfather may be one of the most feared dragons in all of creation, but no one would protect her as fiercely as Edwind could. He was lying to himself when he insisted he was only looking out for her well-being. In truth, he was trying to protect his own heart.

Across the valley, in a meadow past the village, he saw a lone woman wander into view. She approached a group of grazing deer. He stared in awe when none of them flinched at her presence.

The largest buck of the herd lifted his head when she stopped a few feet from where he drank from the stream. She spoke, but Edwind couldn't make out what she said. One of the buck's ears twitched. It glanced at the other deer, then turned its dark eyes toward the water. She held out her hand, letting it nuzzle her palm.

Lifting her dress so she didn't get it wet, she crossed to the other side. There, she climbed to the top of a jagged cliff overlooking the ocean. Her dark hair whipped around her face and neck, carrying her scent over the valley to where he stood.

Edwind wondered if it was the druidae in her that spoke to him. Was it that part of her that connected to the dragon in him?

No. It was more than the power she carried inside her. He watched the moon reflect off her hair and wanted so much to run his hands through its silken strands. Every time she held him in her gaze with those beautiful cobalt gems, he wanted to stay locked in their grasp.

And her smile. How easy it would be to lose himself in that smile for the rest of eternity.

Before he could stop himself, Edwind was in the air, flying toward the woman he was trying to let go. The second his feet touched the ground, he regretted making the leap. What was he going to say? What could he possibly tell her that would ease the pain he caused?

Her head moved to the side, but she wouldn't look at him. "Did you need something?"

"We both know this is for the best." He closed his eyes and let his head drop when he heard the words spoken out loud.

"Do we?"

"Yes." Though he is voice was subdued, inside, he was screaming at himself to say no. To tell her he didn't want her to go, but his mouth was welded shut by his own selfish fear.

She turned. "Then why does it hurt so much to say good-bye?"

When he didn't respond, she started back the way she came, letting her fingers brush against his. Every time she touched him, it was like feeling the sunrise on his skin.

If he had been a stronger man, he might have stopped her and shown her how much she meant to him. He should have grabbed her hand, pulled her into his arms, and refused to let her go.

But he wasn't a stronger man. Instead, he let her walk away.

The promise of rain drifted through the window of the room Darya had been locked inside that first day. She smiled at the memory. It seemed like so long ago when, in reality, it had only been but a handful of weeks. She was going to miss this place and these people when she was gone.

Mostly, she was going to miss Edwind. His crooked smile. The way he thought, she didn't notice him watching her. His laugh. His kiss. His touch.

She wanted so much for him to tell her she didn't have to go. Yet if she stayed, everyone she cared for would be in danger. Mark would come for her again. The only option she had was to lure him away from the island.

At the bookshelf, she took down the same tome she'd been unable to decipher. The writing was no longer a jumbled mass of unfamiliar strokes. She was careful to turn each page with great care. Halfway through the text, she realized the book documented the Wodehal family lineage. She found Edwind's passage. The monochrome depiction of his dragon was so detailed that she could almost envision it circling the island in a graceful dance of wings and tail. Something about the drawing worked inside her subconscious, like she'd seen this very illustration in her dreams.

"Would you like to play one last game before you go?" Edwind's voice drew her gaze from the book to the doorway, where he held one of the opaque chess pieces in one hand.

At that moment, she could think of no other place she wanted to spend the rest of her time there. "I would love to."

He clasped her hand, but instead of leading her to where the chessboard waited, he walked her to his room. The door had barely latched closed when they came together with the force and intensity of waves crashing against the cliffs of the island.

Clumsy fingers worked at the strings of her dress, and she pulled his shirt loose from his pants, slipping it over his head. She got lost in his kiss while her hands explored his bare back, tracing over the imperfections of his scars.

He worked her dress off her shoulders, and she drew away from him, her lips swollen and flushed from the force of his kiss. Amber fire flared in his gaze.

She shimmied free of the dress, letting the fabric pool around her feet.

"You are the most exquisite woman in all of time," he whispered.

He carried her to the bed, laying her on the soft furs that intoxicated her with his scent. His mouth and fingers traversed her body like that of a voyager, driven to explore and conquer her delicate curves.

He took his time caressing the smoothness of her breasts and silken rosebud nipples, gently nipping them with his teeth to bring them to stiff peaks. "You don't know how badly I've wanted to touch you like this."

The heat of his breath sent waves of goosebumps across her skin. She shuddered and cried out when he used his fingers to part the flames of her desire, plunging them inside her, and used a thumb to sweep over the crux of her most sacred femininity. She arched into him, ready to meet the coming orgasm. Torrents of lightning and thunder rumbled through her body in the wake of his touch.

Trembling arms clung to his neck, afraid of being swept away by the relentless way he kept flicking and rolling and pushing inside her again and again until, at last, he brought her back down from that place of bliss.

He moved off the bed long enough to remove the rest of his clothes. She needed his body against hers. Skin to skin. Heat to heat.

His chest vibrated with a soft growl when she wrapped her legs around his waist, welcoming him inside her. They both shuddered at their joining. He arched forward, giving all of himself to her.

When she cried out, he pulled back. "Am I hurting you?"

She folded her legs around him again and worked her arms under his so she could grab onto his shoulders. "Did I tell you to stop?"

Grinning, he rocked into her, matching the urgent pace she used to meet his thrusts. The coming quake of another climax threatened to break her in two, but this time, she rode the waves of euphoria, writhing against him for every last ounce of pleasure.

When she was still again, he pulled her on top of him, so they were facing each other, smoothing back her hair. "Careful, druidae. I don't want to be done with you yet."

She rocked against him, nibbling at his lower lip. "Don't worry, dragon. We have all night."

He took hold of her hair and pulled back her head so he could rake his teeth across the soft flesh of her neck, making her thrusts grow greedier and more needful. She pushed him onto the bed so she could take him deeper inside her.

His hands were at her hips, grinding her into him for his own gratification until he could no longer stop the pleasure his body demanded. He jerked forward with the force of his orgasm, and she screamed his name when he dragged her over that cliff with him.

She fell on top of his chest, letting the rapid rise and fall calm her own thundering heartbeat. She lay there, enjoying the feel of his heartbeat against her. After a few minutes, he rolled her onto the bed and encased her in his arms, nestling his face into her neck.

They listened to the ocean whisper to them from the shores below until Darya thought he had fallen asleep. He moved a hand from where it rested on one of her breasts and ran a finger along the scar on her lower abdomen.

She wouldn't let another man touch her like that, but with Edwind, there was a trust she had never experienced with anyone else. "I made peace with what she did a long time ago. What I can never forgive her for is killing my children."

He shifted beside her so he could look at her eyes.

She took in a long breath. "Because of where she stabbed me and the damage it caused, I'll never be able to have kids of my own. At least I won't have to pass this curse onto someone else."

Edwind cupped her chin and pulled her face to his. "What you are is not a curse."

They got lost in their kiss, and their bodies soon demanded more than the simple touch of hands and lips. When they came together again, their lovemaking was more tempered. He moved inside her like a tender lover, yearning to reach the part of her she kept locked away.

And reach it, he did. She gave herself over to him. Her body, her heart, her love. All of it.

She sat up, admiring the way he glowed in the muted starlight. His jade stare reflected the stars, and she glimpsed the universe inside his eyes. "Will you go with me when I leave?"

"This is my home. These people are mine to look after and protect. Stay with me, so I can protect you, too."

"You were right when you said it's too dangerous for me to be here, but I don't want to do this alone."

"You won't be alone. Grandfather will be with you."

"I won't have you."

He let his head fall toward the window, as if unable to face the choice he was making.

She got out of bed and dressed. Her chest felt like it was being crushed under the weight of the surrounding stones. At the door, she said, "I will always love you. Even if I find my way back to where I started."

Sunrise didn't bring Darya the peace she hoped it would. She stood on the cliffs watching the rough waters of the ocean push the remnants of the storm back to sea. Soft whispers of light edged closer to the horizon, a bitter reminder of the journey that was to take her away from Didean and the man she loved. She wondered if she could ever watch another dawn, knowing this was the one that stole her heart.

Behind her, the village was coming to life. That meant the ship would soon be ready for the two-day trek across the sea.

There was no need for her to step foot back inside those stone walls again. She said her goodbyes to Gita and Saebbi already. Horsa would see them off at the docks. She wasn't naïve enough to think Edwind was going to reconsider and come with her.

So, from the cliffs, Darya made her way to where the small ocean vessel waited in the water. It floated in the calm waves, demanding she leave behind all she held dear for some unknown adventure she didn't ask for, nor wanted. She hated that ship, hated Horsa for abandoning her in the past, and she hated Edwind for making her love him. But mostly, she hated herself for being too weak to demand to take what her heart desired.

"We aren't leaving right away." Hengist stepped up beside her. "You still have time to say your goodbyes."

She kept her focus on the water, knowing who Hengist was talking about. "We've said all we needed to say."

"You both can't be stubborn about this."

She swung her frustration at the old dragon. Fresh tears made her eyes sparkle in the predawn light. "I did everything but get on my knees and beg him to come with me. I gave him my heart, but he chose to hang on to his."

Her heartache reflected on his face. "He watched his father struggle with losing his mother. He is scared to leave himself vulnerable to that anguish."

The way no one spoke of how Diana died led Darya to assume she met a horrible demise.

"How does he know he's going to lose me the same way?"

"Did he not tell you—" a sharp yell cut his sentence off from across the valley. Hengist's attention turned to the horizon.

She followed his gaze to the four massive ships cutting through the waves toward the island. They flew yellow flags with a red sigil emblazoned on the front. At the speed they cut through the water, they'd reach shore within the hour.

"Come, child." Hengist grabbed at her arm.

She glanced back at the horizon, a heavy stone of dread landing in her gut. She knew if those ships reached land, they were all doomed. Dragons or not, there was only so much they could do against a fleet like that. By the time she got to the top of the hill, there were men running from the village to meet up with Saebbi and Edwind. Gita was giving orders to Wynfrid and some of the other women to get the smaller children to safety.

"Go with Gita," Hengist said. "You will be safe in the caves."

She ran for where the dragoness directed the others, but movement in the sky caught her attention. A one-eyed hawk swooped down, heading straight for her. Edwind was running from the castle and took to the air after it. The smaller bird was quick, easily slipping through the dragon's grasp.

She watched Edwind in wonder. He was the dragon from her dreams, and he was every bit the magnificent creature she'd imagined him to be.

Having that knowledge crushed her heart even more. They were both meant for this moment, yet they would never be together again.

More screams brought her out of those miserable thoughts. Darya stared at where Gita was urging the other women and children to follow and knew she couldn't take the chance of luring Mark or the others to them, so she took off in the opposite direction, toward the cliffs. Horsa called out to her, but she ignored him.

Anger, frustration, and heartache welled inside her like a volcano filling with molten lava, ready to let loose its reign of fiery destruction. She could see the occupants of the ships now. There were way too many for the men of the island to defeat on their own.

This was all her fault. Her presence led them here, and these innocent people were going to suffer because of it.

Damn, Mark, for getting mixed up in this. Damn, Horsa, for sending her here. Damn her mother for not killing her when she had the chance.

Damn them all.

Unable to hold in the fury that consumed her, she blew out a wild bellow across the water.

Something inside her gave way, and the world shifted around her. No longer did she see the bright colors and vivid imagery of the landscape. In its place were golden, ethereal lines that snaked along the ground and in the rocks and trees and blades of grass and the sand down below into the sea.

The veins of light thrummed at different speeds toward her. They moved up her legs and into her body, filling her with a sensation she remembered from her life in the future, but it had never been so intense.

The magic flowing through her was like taking in a cool drink of water on a hot day, and she wanted more—needed more of it inside her. She dropped her hands to her side, pulling at the power that heeded her call. Flocks of birds took to the sky of one hive mind. They came to where Darya stood at the edge of the bluff, encircling her, waiting for her command.

"Don't let them reach land," she demanded.

Farther out into the ocean, a pod of whales surfaced, spraying spouts of water high into the air to announce their arrival. The melody of their battle cries was deafening. They dipped under the waves, swimming toward the ships that moved ever closer to the island.

The heartbeat of the earth raced inside her, a raging, unstoppable river, and she focused her sights on the closest ship. She held out her arms, pushing power into the already choppy waves. A smile curled the edge of her lips when the frothy ocean obeyed the movements of her hands, rolling and splashing up the sides of the ships.

She pushed and pulled their current against the wooden vessel until giant swells slammed the ship so hard it broke

apart. The men on board screamed in fear until they disappeared into the unforgiving sea.

The flock of birds swooped down on the second ship while
the whales pounded on its hull. She turned the momentum
of the first set of waves to the next boat in line, rolling the
ship back and forth against the raging waves.

Despite the current of the earth racing throughout her
body, her legs trembled from the weight of holding that
much power inside. She swayed to the side and had to lock
her knees in place to keep from falling over. But she refused
to relinquish her hold on the magic inside her.

With the third vessel destroyed, only one ship had survived
unscathed. The crew were desperately trying to turn around
and head back out to sea.

"That's enough!" someone shouted from behind her.

She glanced over her shoulder. Hengist was running down
the slope toward her, genuine fear etched in his weathered
features.

"It's too much," he said. "You're killing yourself."

Though his words should have scared her, she was prepared to make that sacrifice. Her life was a worthy price to
pay to keep the island and its people safe.

The smile she gave him was one of determination and
regret. "Thank you for protecting me."

He rushed forward, but she flung the power into the
ground and twisted his body in hundreds of thin vines. He
bucked at his restraints, letting his dragon free so he could
get loose of them. She sent more of the earth at him, snag-
ging his wings and holding him down.

Something thick and wet trickled down from her nose,
over her top lip and into her mouth, but not even the taste

of her own blood would distract her from what needed to be done.

"Darya!" Edwind's voice fought to be heard over the chaos.

She ignored him and turned her focus on the last ship that sped over turbulent waves. Her whole body ached, and she was having a hard time keeping upright. She knew once she released her hold on the earth, the tenuous tether to life would go with it.

A jade dragon dragged her attention from the water, its dark talons outstretched, ready to pluck her from the ground. Seconds before the beast made contact, Edwind was there, taking her in his arms. He leaned over her, his face betraying the fear that shook him.

She wanted to scream at him for stopping her from sinking the last ship, but she didn't have the strength. She tried to take in a breath, only to find the simple act of opening her mouth was beyond her depleted body. Darkness crowded in on her, narrowing her vision until the only thing she could see was Edwind's beautiful face.

"No," he cried. "Don't go, Darya. I never wanted you to go. I love you. Please stay with me."

I love you... Those words were forever trapped on her lifeless lips when death came to claim his prize.

Chapter 13

"You do not belong here."

Darya rested against the weeping willow, watching the pale hues of the dawn. The sound of the man's voice drew her gaze from the beauty before her to the person who had the audacity to interrupt her mediation. "What are you doing here? This is my private sanctuary."

"This is my realm," said the keeper of souls. "Nothing is beyond my reach."

She looked away from his mesmerizing pale prisms of blue and went back to the endless sunrise. "I'm where I need to be."

He took her hand. "This place is not meant for you yet. Nor is it meant for you alone."

Through his touch, she could feel the faint beating of her heart in the body she left behind. "I don't want to go back."

"If you stay, you will miss the life you are destined for."

"I'll miss what? Loneliness? Misery? Heartache? I don't want it."

Arawn pointed to the sunrise. "Look, druidae."

She followed his other hand to where images appeared over the water and began dancing across the waves like they would in a stop-motion movie. Her body moved of its own accord, getting to her feet and walking toward the tide. "That's what waits for me?"

"It is your destiny."

"Even after everything that's happened?"

He nodded.

"Will I remember it if I go back?"

Arawn laughed. "This is but a dream, girl. It will be gone from your mind as soon as you wake. I cannot promise you will not face heartache and pain. However, it is your path to follow. Do you wish to fight for it?"

She watched the images of her future fade into the waves of the ocean. "Yes. I want it more than anything. I want—"

Darya's eyes flew open at the same time she sucked in a heaving breath, choking on the air she was fighting to take in. She sat up, batting at the heavy blanket covering her, and threw herself to the side, almost falling off the bed that wasn't hers.

The scent that filled her lungs made her chest pull tight around her heart. She cradled her pounding head in her hands, trying to drag the memories out of the darkness of her fragile mind. Blurry images swam in and out of focus until a single man came into view.

Mark.

That bastard returned and brought an army with him.

The memory of the harrowing events floated to the forefront of her consciousness, drawing her gaze to the window. Remnants of the power of the earth still lay inside her blood, waiting to be reawakened.

But she died, didn't she?

She remembered Edwind holding her while she fought to breathe. Then there was darkness.

Darya stared at her hands. She didn't feel dead. Her skin was flush with the flowing blood in her veins. Her heart thrummed inside her chest at a strong pace. She took in a few breaths, filling her fully functional lungs.

From outside the open door, she heard a man shouting. The familiar baritone voice dragged her over the side of the bed, where she pushed up on unsteady legs. A soft orange glow came from the archway that led to the great hall, where the shouting grew louder.

"I don't care how big his army is." Edwind's words dripped with a barely concealed rage. "He dared send his ships to attack my land. My people. Her."

"You are one man," Horsa said, his wizened temperament trying to talk reason into his son.

"I am the grandson of a death dragon." Edwind's emotions made his voice tremble. "I'll burn his entire kingdom to ash. If you won't help me, then stay out of my way."

"Edwind, you must listen to reason." Gita's tone was low and soothing.

"She's dead because of him." His anger gave way to heartache, cutting off his words.

Darya inched inside the open doors, peering past the threshold. Gita and Horsa stood in front of a dying fire. Edwind stared into the glowing coals, resting his forehead on the arm laying across the mantle.

Darya stepped into the room, her movement drawing Gita's attention to where she stood. The dark circles lining her tired eyes exacerbated a weary sadness that pulled at her face. The sight of the dead woman made Gita sway to the side. Horsa followed her gaze. His mouth fell open, and his shoulders slumped in disbelief.

"I swear he'll pay for what he's done." Edwind's words, though just above a whisper, carried the heavy weight of his rage.

"Edwind," Horsa said.

"You won't change my mind."

"Dear boy."

"I will not be deterred."

Horsa grabbed his son and spun him around.

His red-rimmed eyes stood out against headed cheeks that were still wet from the tears he'd shed. His expression twisted into uncertainty when he saw the woman standing in the doorway. "Darya?"

Hengist stepped away from a window, his face twisting into a curious smile.

Darya looked at the old man. "I think I almost died."

"You were very much dead, girl," he said.

"How am I alive now?"

He shook his head. "I—I don't know."

She folded her arms around herself, suddenly chilled at the idea of coming back from the underworld. Edwind rushed to her side, helping her to the fire. He knelt in front of her, unable to break his gaze from hers. She wanted to stop him when she saw he meant to kiss her, but her heart craved his touch.

"I thought I lost you," he said.

She grabbed his wrists and pushed his hands down, and turned her attention to Hengist.

"What I did to those ships—No druidae has that kind of power."

"You are so much more than druidae. I believe I know why no one speaks of your father." He paused, glancing around the room before turning back to her. "I think he is one of the gods your people worship."

"That's impossible," she whispered.

"Like dragons and time travel are impossible?" Horsa said.

"Is that something they do? Mate with mortals, and pop out demigod children?"

"You wouldn't be the first," Hengist said.

Her gaze slid down to her hands. The weight of his words anchored her memories to the present. "She knew. My mother knew what I was."

Saebbi had taken his place at Gita's side. "Why would such a being want to kill Darya?"

"Who knows?" said Hengist. "Jealousy? Revenge?" He motioned to one of the windows. "There's a druid camp on the mainland. The priestess of that tribe can help unlock the secrets of Darya's bloodline."

Darya couldn't bring herself to meet Edwind's gaze, remembering what he said to her on the cliffs before she died. They were the words she wanted to hear, but if his love meant she had to stay on the island, she wouldn't agree to his terms. Nor could she deny herself the chance to learn the truth of who she was. "Of course, I'll go. I have to know who I am. What I am."

Edwind stood but kept a hand on her shoulder. "We should leave immediately. Only one ship escaped. They will return with reinforcements, but it will take time." He turned to his father. "Do you still hold favor with the Duke of Broughied?"

Horsa nodded.

"Can you convince him to send his men to our shores?"

"He will give me whatever I ask."

"Good. Grandfather and I will take Darya to the druid camp. Go to the Duke and secure protection for the island. Meet us when you can. Gita, if the ship returns before help arrives, take our people to the caves. They should be safe there until the duke's men reach our shores."

Everyone stared at each other until Edwind waved his hands. "I've given my orders. Go."

When they were alone, Darya kept her gaze on the fire. "You don't have to come with me. Gita and the others need you here."

He pulled her out of the chair and lifted her face. There was a hardness in his gaze, but it wasn't meanness or cruelty. What stared back at her was remorse. "When I watched the life drain from your eyes and held your lifeless body in my arms, my heart died with you. There is no force on this earth or beyond that can keep me from you again. If I must travel a thousand years into the future to stay by your side, that is what I will do."

"Even knowing who I am? What I can't give you?"

"Who you are is the woman that welcomed me into her heart and made me realize I am worthy of her love." He pressed his lips to her forehead and said, "I am not so vain that I will put my need for an heir above my devotion to you." His kiss was gentle, but it soon deepened, making her pulse race and her skin flush.

She wanted to give in to him, but she was terrified of being wounded again. When they stepped away from their embrace, she searched his face for the truth of his words. "I need to know that if I give you my heart again, you won't turn me away."

He drew her hand to his chest. "Do you feel that? Every beat is for you, my love. For as long as I draw breath in my body." He pulled her into him and swept her into his arms. "Let me prove how much I love you."

Cernunnos knelt at the shore of the murky water, steeping in anger and fear. Only a few hours ago, he celebrated his victory when Darya's thread crumbled into dust. At last, he no longer had to worry about Fate's cruel plans for him. His seedling was dead.

But she didn't stay dead. He knew the second her heart started beating again. The summoner's binding was strong indeed.

One of his ilk must have dragged her from the under-world. Not many beings would be so foolish to steal from Arawn unscathed. Cernunnos certainly wasn't bold enough to take from him. That little trick he pulled with Mark's woman was a simple sleight of hand. The grieving mortal had been too eager to win back his lover that he would believe anything the old god told him.

He could feel Darya's heartbeat through the veil of time mocking him. He bellowed at the helot that had failed him. Mark's fear of losing his chance to be with his woman made it easy to manipulate him.

Track her down, Cernunnos raged at him through time. Do not let her find her way back. Losing your Annie will be the least of your punishment if you fail me again.

Fury and fear filled the mortal man's heart, and he knew Mark would do what he commanded.

Footsteps crunched through the dried leaves behind him. "Is it done?"

He turned his head far enough to stop Boudica's approach. "She was dead, but those damn dragons found a way to wretch her from the underworld."

"Are you sure it was the dragons?"

The question made him turn all the way around.

She fought to keep her stare steady. "I saw the Weaver with them in the hamlet by the sea. She could have bargained for her life."

A wave of rage rolled through Cernunnos, threatening to incinerate him to his very core. How many centuries had he begged his uncle to give him back his family that had been so mercilessly stolen from him, only to be ignored?

But this abomination who sprang, unbidden, from his loins, was allowed to live? "I will feast on her pain as I did her mother's."

Edwind rested against the protruding rocks of the tiny beach, holding Darya against his chest. She clung to the arm that lay across her and ran delicate fingers along his skin, waiting for the sun to break through the sea. She'd urged him awake that morning, asking if he wanted to watch the sunrise with her. Of course he did. He wished to share so much with her.

The horizon foretold the coming dawn with its soft pastel hues of orange, pink, and purple. He worked his fingers into hers and pondered what it meant to have the blood of a god inside her. She escaped the hands of death himself. Surely it meant she wouldn't be doomed to a mortal's lifespan.

In the end, it didn't matter. Whether she lived fifty years or five hundred, he would love her every second of every day they were together.

Brilliant orange light reflected off the choppy waves of the sea, giving birth to a new morning. He didn't have to see Darya's face to catch the silhouette of the smile that bloomed across her lips. Her heart sang of the wonders that came to life before them, and he shifted so he could draw her closer.

"Is this why the sunrise speaks to me?" Darya wondered aloud. "Because of what I am?"

He brought her hand to his mouth, savoring the warmth of her palm. "When you find out who your father is, maybe we can understand why you have such a strong connection with it."

She wriggled out of his arms and settled into his lap, facing him. "I wish we could stay here in this moment." She looked over her shoulder. "Wouldn't it be the perfect place to spend the rest of our eternity?"

"When our eternity comes, perhaps it will be ours to enjoy."

She leaned into him, melting into the delicate dance of lips and tongue.

From the path leading to the keep, Hengist called to them. "We must prepare to leave."

Edwind broke from their embrace with a disappointed sigh. "Are you sure you don't want to travel by ship?"

"It'll take too long."

He helped her off the soft sand and led her toward the cliffs where Hengist waited. Gita and Saebbi made their way up the path.

Gita threw her arms around her brother, holding tight and refusing to let go.

"We will only be gone a short time," he promised.

She was reluctant to step away and pushed at the wetness that gathered at the corners of her eyes. "I know. Can I not be concerned about my brother and his beloved?"

Edwind turned his attention to Saebbi. "You will see to the safety of our people?"

"I've taken care of you this long, haven't I?" Saebbi took the big man in an embrace that was just as fierce, albeit much shorter than the one Gita had given.

Darya lingered around Gita's neck. "I'll make sure he comes back."

"Both of you," Gita corrected.

"Are you two ready for this journey?" Hengist asked, taking his place between Edwind and Darya.

Edwind looked to Darya, who nodded. "As we will ever be," he said.

"When you reach land, Darya will need to eat and rest. So will you, boy. I doubt you have flown such a long way at one time."

"I will be fine."

The old dragon smirked and shook his head. "The druid camp lies near the shore where you will land. Be mindful of eyes on the ground." Hengist took to the air; his silver scales shimmered in the orange glow of morning.

Edwind smoothed down Darya's wind-blown hair. "Are you ready?"

Her answer was to kiss him one last time before taking a couple of steps back. The transformation from man to dragon took but a few seconds. When his leathery membranous wings settled to his side, she approached him with outstretched arms. Tentative fingers traced over the bumps and crevices of his face. He let out a contented rumble from deep within his throat when she rested her forehead on his.

I love the way you feel against me.

She beamed at his unspoken words. "I didn't know if I would be able to hear you."

She took her time following the contours of his neck. The light reflected off him like countless diamonds mirroring the flames of a hundred suns. "This is how I saw you in my dreams."

Edwind lowered his body so she could climb on his back. Once she was in place at the base of his neck, she wrapped her arms and legs around him. His wings shivered, preparing for their launch, and her body went rigid. She tried to stop herself from shaking, but the fear and excitement of what was to come made it impossible for her to still her quivering muscles.

His head swung to the side, his bright yellow reptilian eyes regarding her with deep concern. I can carry you.

"No." She held tight to him. "I want to be up here with you. Just don't drop me, alright?"

Never, my love.

There was no preflight testing of his wings that time. He launched them into the air in a powerful leap. Her stomach stayed on the ground while the rest of her flew away. The thrill of being airborne dragged a cry from her that could have been mistaken for one he'd gotten the night before when reaffirming his love.

She loosened her grip on his thick neck when he lifted his head to provide a break against the onslaught of the constant, shrill wind. Though she still trembled against him, the longer she was up there, not falling to her death, the more she relaxed into him.

We should make landfall by the next dawn.

She ran her hand down the side of his neck, knowing her words would be lost in the wind.

"I saw her fall," the captain of the surviving ship insisted. "She must have been gravely injured for the dragons not to follow us."

"Or dead," another crewman said.

Mark stood on the bow of the battered vessel, staring at the rolling waves of the open sea. The salty wind whipped his unkempt hair. His knuckles were white at how tightly he was gripping the bow, and his head rang with the fury of Cernunnos' terrible words that promised him more misery than his mortal mind could comprehend.

"She's not dead." He spoke so quietly that he didn't think the others could even hear him. On top of the pulsing agony of the damn god's thundering voice, his face throbbed from where that white bird plucked out his eyeball. Whatever godly magic Cernunnos used to let him transform into a hawk also gave him the ability to heal at an astonishing rate, but it didn't give him back the lost eye.

Turning from the water, he said, "I won't have a surprise on my side if we attack again."

He wasn't sure if King Wilden would lend him more men for another attempt after losing all those lives. "Damn those dragons." He exhaled an exasperated snort. "Fucking dragons."

Had Cernunnos told him about them, he would have been more prepared. If he could believe in succubus shrews and psychotic gods, why not dragons as well?

And what of the powers Darya possessed? She glowed like a piece of steel in a forge when she sent the ships under the waves. He wondered if she could always do those things.

There'd been no hint of such power in the months of knowing her. What if she had a god of her own who imbued her with the same gifts Cernunnos gave Mark?

All he wanted was to hold Annie again. Instead, he found himself in a world of gods, magic, and mythical beasts of legend.

"Sir?" the captain said.

Mark shook himself out of his maddening thoughts, glowering at the other man.

"One of my men got word from our scouting vessel. They saw a couple of those winged beasts leave the island. They carried a woman."

Darya, he thought. This perked up Mark's mood. "Which direction?"

"North."

"That's where we will go."

The captain had a hard time meeting Mark's mono gaze. "You can travel there much faster than our ship." He handed him a polished silver disk, along with another satchel full of smaller coins. "Take this token. Go to one of the port cities and ask for a man named Eron Tyr. If anyone can find her, it is he."

Mark reached for the coin, but before he could, the captain added, "Be warned. Once you make a contract with him, you've made a deal with the devil himself."

He snatched the silver medallion and the coins from the captain's hand. "I've already sold my soul to one demon. He can't have what I no longer own."

Chapter 14

Daylight broke over the horizon, burning Darya's tired gaze. Edwind dipped down to the rocky shores and the blessed relief of solid earth. Her wobbly legs made her stumble over the unsteady ground. If not for the man at her side, she wouldn't have made it up the beach to the cluster of rocks that promised shelter.

"This looks like a safe place to rest," Edwind said, kicking away debris. He surveyed the landscape, then nodded to a cluster of trees in the distance. "I'll gather timber to start a fire."

Darya heard the concerned rumblings of a pack of wolves in the direction where he disappeared over a grassy hill. She craned her head, looking for any sign of Edwind; not so much worried about a potential threat, but she had another favor to ask the pack.

When Edwind returned with his bounty of firewood and kindling, he set everything up in a neat pile. She watched him with curious fascination. With no obvious means of spark, she was about to ask how he was going to light it on fire when he leaned in close to the tinder, and without looking away from her, he blew into the stack of wood.

A plume of pale tendrils rose between the empty spaces, followed by flames chasing the smoke through the logs.

"That is the most incredible thing I've ever seen." Her voice was full of wonder.

He chuckled. "Is this coming from a woman who commanded the power of the sea and destroyed three ships?"

"Two," she corrected. "The whales sank the third."

He wrapped her in a tender embrace, brushing his lips against hers. "Still, you protected my home and my people. For that, I am eternally grateful." He searched her face and kissed her again.

Returning to the fire, he said, "I would love to lose myself inside you, but I need to find us something to eat."

The sound of soft footsteps approached from the grassy hill behind them. A brown and silver wolf trotted up to the fringes of the firelight, out of Edwind's reach. It carried in its mouth a plump hare. Darya gave it a nod, and the wolf dropped the kill on the ground before looping back to his family over the ridge.

Edwind retrieved the rabbit and set it on the ground between them. "Did you ask it to bring us food?"

"You've done so much already."

"Now, that is amazing," he said, reaching for her. "Maybe I'll ravage you after all, sweet druidae."

She pushed him aside so she could start preparing their meal. "First, we eat. Then, we can discuss dessert. Hand me your knife."

When they had their fill of food, she settled against him. Despite the prospect of each other's bodies, they were far too tired and soon fell into a heavy sleep. The next time she woke, the sun was no longer visible in the sky. Everything appeared muted and overcast. The fire was still burning hot with the same neatly stacked logs, indicating she hadn't been asleep that long.

"Edwind?" Her voice sounded dull in the eerie atmosphere. Much like how the landscape looked.

"Your dragon is not here, druidae."

Darya was on her feet, spinning in a full circle. "Who's there?"

"Do you not know whose land you walk on?" The disembodied voice sounded closer.

Movement from inside the tree line farther inland caught her attention. A streak of brown hair passed behind one of the thick maples.

"I'm new to this place." Darya took a tentative step forward. "Whose sacred land is this?"

"All land is sacred to me." The answer seemed to echo all around her.

Darya moved even closer to the trees. "I didn't mean to offend you."

The woman's laughter was anything but merry. "Your blood reeks of your mortality, yet you carry his power within your frail flesh."

A quivering excitement made her body. "Are you talking about my father? Do you know who he is?"

A hand reached around a tall oak. Its pale skin was covered in a textured, mossy film. "Tread carefully this path you've chosen, seedling. Not all roads will lead you to the destiny you seek."

The use of that name sent a trickle of icy dread down Darya's spine. She expected the beast from her dreams to spring out of the trees and come after her, but a waif like, petite creature peeked out from behind the tree.

Only half of her face was visible, revealing a single yellow cat's eye that watched Darya from beneath a mass of wild matted hair caked in mud and littered with sticks and leaves.

"What are you?" Darya asked.

The forest spirit vanished behind the tree.

Darya poised herself to rush after the creature, but before she could move more than one step, she was back at the fire, staring at the dying embers.

"Did you have a bad dream?" Edwind's fingers were light as he ran them through her hair.

She kept her head resting on his chest but watched the forest for any sign of the strange being. "There are ancient things in these trees. I think one of them is trying to tell me something."

The weight of his lips pressing against the top of her head helped banish some of her unease. "What did it say?"

"Nothing useful."

He was gentle when he lifted her off him. "I've been awake for a while and didn't see anything moving in the forest except for the animals that belong there."

"Maybe it was just a dream." She mused aloud.

Stomping out the remaining glowing remnants of the fire, he said, "If you're rested, we should go to the druid camp. I do not wish to keep Grandfather waiting."

Hengist met Edwind and Darya at a set of ten-foot-high wooden gates that looked almost identical to the ones belonging to the commune Darya grew up in. The tribesman had carved the gates with tools that were much less sophisticated than those in the modern world. Even so, the craftsmanship was impressive.

"I was glad to hear you made it safely to shore," Hengist said, grabbing his grandson in a rough embrace.

Edwind eyed the surrounding forest. "How did you know we arrived?"

"Our eyes are everywhere in these trees." The woman who spoke came around Hengist, and Darya knew instantly that she was a priestess. She held the same authority about her that Gita did, but this woman wore hers like a cloak of armor to protect herself.

"Druidae." She greeted Darya with a friendly nod, taking her hands in a warm gesture. Dusky heather eyes took in every detail of the newcomers. "It's been a long time since our people have felt a presence as strong as yours. I am Mavae, priestess of this tribe."

Darya let her face fall into a neutral expression. From experiences, she knew that navigating a woman of Mavae's stature was tricky. Despite her youthful appearance, the priestess was wise and dangerous. "Thank you for accepting us into your home."

Mavae looked from Darya to Edwind, her demeanor growing more stern. "I have known Hengist for many years. I trust one of his bloodlines will show us the same reverence, even if you have abandoned your mother's path."

Edwind's gaze shifted to his grandfather, who took Mavae's hand. "Of course he will."

Without looking away from Edwind, she said, "Let the boy say it."

Edwind's mouth twitched, but he kept his expression neutral. "I will show you the respect you are owed." He leaned in closer to the petite woman. "And never speak of my mother again. You know nothing about my life or the path I walk."

For the first time since their arrival, the priestess showed genuine affection. "You have your grandfather's fire."

Hengist cleared his throat. "You two look like you could use some food."

"I'd rather have a place to clean off the last twenty-four hours." Darya picked at her crumpled dress.

"That can be arranged." Mavae motioned for them to follow.

She led them to the heart of the camp, where a stone hearth encircled the communal fire. She instructed someone to gather fresh clothes for the newcomers.

"Follow Cecile. She will take you to a place where you can bathe." To Darya, she said, "Tonight, I would like for us to visit the well. There, I will help you on your quest to find the answers you seek."

"Tonight?"

"Do you not wish to know who it is you come from?"

"Of course, but I didn't think it would be so soon."

Edwind squeezed her hand. "I'll be there with you."

Mavae's smile faded. "I'm sorry, young dragon. You are not permitted on this journey. It is one she must take alone."

Darya smiled at him. "It's why I'm here."

A young woman joined them at the fire with a handful of clothes. "Come with me."

In the spring, when they were alone and undressed, Edwind helped Darya into the water and sat her in his lap. She relaxed into his chest, and they spent a long time losing themselves to the feel of each other. It was hypnotic, the way her body rose and fell with each breath he took.

He pushed his fingers across her shoulders in heavy strides. The moan that escaped her parted lips turned into something more sensual when his palms started to warm her skin. "How are you doing that?"

His chest vibrated with a throaty purr. "I have many wonderful things to show you." He swept away the hair from her shoulder, followed by a light brushing of his mouth. The warmth of his fingers paled to the blaze ignited by his kiss. Everywhere his lips landed, a trail of goosebumps puckered in their wake.

"Even if your fingers didn't warm to the touch." His breath was hot on the nape of her neck. "They still sent a fire through my blood that day you tended to my wounds."

She turned her head. "Is that why you were in such a hurry to get away from me?"

"Yes." He moved his hands down the front of her, pausing at her breasts. His teeth gingerly bit at her shoulder, and he flicked the taut buds that bloomed beneath his masterful touch.

She nestled into his chest, moving against the hardness pressing into her.

He ran one hand down between her legs. The warmth of his fingers sent a torrent of wildfire up her body. She sucked in a sharp breath and latched onto his arm.

He drew her to the cusp of orgasm before pulling away. "Not yet. I want to be inside you."

She wriggled around, settling onto him, and his hand was between her legs again. He called back the heady storm, making her take hold of his neck to steady herself against the thunder that rumbled through her. She felt herself falling into the depths of his gaze, and the world around them faded away.

When she gave into the euphoria he demanded, they were no longer two separate beings. For eternity and a single moment, they were one. The air they breathed, their memories, their joy, their pain. Everything they had ever been or would ever be was encompassed in that one drop of time.

She knew what it was to fly among the clouds with the air flowing over her dragon body.

The will of the earth and the magnificent power it promised mingled with Edwind's blood, intertwining them even more. They floated in that endless river of time, basking in their love until it was time to return to themselves. When at last the world came rolling back into existence, they heaved against one another, two separate entities once again.

Darya rested her head on his shoulder. "Where did we just go?"

"I do not know, but I will travel to that place with you again and again." He nibbled at her neck. "I love you so very much."

"I'll never tire of hearing those words." She wrapped her arms around him. "Tell them to me for the rest of our lives."

"I love you," he whispered in her ear. "I will love you beyond the reach of time itself."

The two lovers came back from the spring in their clean clothes and wrapped in one another's arms. Edwind was disappointed to find Mavae sitting next to his grandfather at the communal fire. They leaned into each other, Hengist whispering something into her ear. She tried to keep her face neutral, but the color that rose in her cheeks told of the words he spoke.

Edwind wasn't fast enough to turn away before her gaze trapped him.

"Come here," Mavea said. "Both of you."

Edwind hesitated before letting her go, but she hung onto his hand when she walked forward.

"Sit." Mavae motioned beside her.

"Hengist says you are not only a rare druidae, but you come from a thousand years in the future." She looked at Edwind. "And you think to take her for your lover? Do you expect her to stay here with you?"

"Mavae." Hengist's tone was a warning one.

It was Darya who answered. "I don't see how that's any of your business."

The comment did not phase the priestess. "Have you children thought about your actions?"

"We aren't children."

"You're acting like it, letting lust make these important decisions for you."

Darya shot to her feet, so she loomed over the woman. "And what if I choose to stay? What do I really have to go back to? I have no family waiting for me." She glanced at Edwind. In all the times they spent alone, that was one subject neither dared broach. But after what they shared in the spring, it forever intertwined their lives together no matter when or where in time they stayed.

"I was afraid to ask," he said. "You don't know who your father is?"

"That doesn't matter." She turned back to Mavae. "Edwind and I share a bond beyond the mortal world. I will never leave him, and I would never ask him to abandon his family."

Mavae's smile never faltered. "Did he tell you why he fought against your union so hard?"

Edwind stood. "Hold your tongue, priestess."

"You cannot expect to keep such truths from the woman you claim to love so dearly."

Darya took Edwind's hand. "What is she talking about?"

He glared at Mavae, who met his gaze with the serenity of someone who knew the battle was won. He turned to his grandfather for help, but the old dragon nodded to Darya. "She deserves the truth, boy."

His anger leaked out of him in a defeated sigh. "Walk with me."

They made their way to the lake, where Edwind pulled her around in front of him. "Do you remember when Gita said our mother was human?"

"Yes."

He stared out over the water for a few seconds before going on. "It's one thing for a child to lose his mother, but I had to watch my father lose his heart. He loved her more than the sun loves the dawn."

Darya studied his tormented features. "He knew she would only be in his life a short time, yet he still stayed with her."

"There was no choice for him. He said she claimed his heart with a single smile. Much like you did with me."

Her brows creased in thought. "You and Gita won't live as long as your father, but you will outlive mortal humans."

He nodded without meeting her stare.

"By how long?"

"Others of our kind have been known to live for hundreds of years."

"Hundreds?" She blinked in surprise. "That explains so much. That's why you keep yourself so isolated and why you pushed me away."

"After watching my father go through the pain he did, I promised myself I'd never allow that kind of heartache to take me over. Then you came into my life and destroyed every damn defense I put up."

She stepped out of his arms.

He wasn't fast enough to hold on to her. "What are you doing?"

"How selfish of me."

"Don't say that."

She turned back toward the communal fire. He tried to reach for her again, but she pulled her hands into herself.

"Darya. There's more you should know."

Meeting his distraught gaze, she said, "That's what Hengist was trying to tell me. Edwind, I'm so sorry."

"Would you please listen to me?"

Unable to look him in the face, she said, "I need to—I have to prepare for tonight."

Mark pushed his way through the busy streets of the dirty city, keeping his head down to avoid the angry looks of its miserable inhabitants. He'd been traveling from one shit-hole village to the next, trying to find the right tavern where this Eron Tyr was supposed to be meeting him.

The last place he visited cost a man his life when some prick thought Mark was an easy pocket to steal from. There was still a hint of guilt nagging at him for having to kill the boy, but it was a case of self-defense.

He stepped inside the tavern and nearly doubled over at the mix of rancid smells of body odor, stale booze, rotten vegetables, and powerful spices. His one good eye clouded over with tears from the pungent aromas and smoke, and he had to use his filthy shirt to wipe away the moisture so he could see where he was going. At the bar, he asked about the man he was looking for.

The bartender pointed to a shadowed corner of the smoky room where a man sat alone at a table with a pint of ale and a single mug in front of him. He was far from the monster Mark pictured in his head. The well-dressed man before him looked like a soldier awaiting orders.

His clothes were spotless, with not a single belt or button out of place. He had what Mark would imagine was this era's regulation-style haircut for someone unlucky enough to be drafted into their military. Even in the foggy smoke of the bar, he could make out a scar running along the left side of the man's temple. It was an odd thing to see him watching the stage with such a relaxed demeanor.

Mark turned his attention to the petite woman who re-galed the room with a musical voice that matched the di-vine instrument in her hands. She plucked its strings with nimble fingers and sang a sad song in a language he didn't recognize.

He approached the table, ignoring the dangerous glares he got from eager gazes, calculating if he would make an easy target to glean a little extra coin. No sooner had he reached his destination, the man took a sip and, without looking away from the stage, said, "If you dare disturb this lovely bard's song, I will drive a dagger through that one remaining eye of yours."

His tone was lighthearted and jovial despite the overt threat.

Frozen with a hand on the only other empty chair at the table, Mark stood without moving, barely taking in a breath. When the song finished, the man with a dark stare raised a hand to the barmaid. "Give her whatever she wishes." He nodded to the chair. "Now you may sit."

He did as he was told, keeping the table between them. "Are you Eron Tyr?"

"Aye." He looked him up and down from head to toe, pausing at the burn on his neck. "Are you going to tell me what I can do for you, or will you continue to sit there and admire my handsome physique?"

Mark felt his face grow warm. It wasn't Eron's looks he was admiring. There was something about the man that put him on edge and not just the ease with which he threatened to blind him. He pulled out a pouch of gold coins marked with the king's sigil sewn into the cloth. "I am in search of a woman?"

Eron's laughter came quick and loud, drawing unwanted attention from those around them. "I'm afraid you've come to the wrong man for that. I am no matchmaker of the heart."

"That's not what I mean. This is no ordinary woman I am after. She is being protected by—" He moved in closer. "Dragons." He expected Eron to laugh again, but instead, his light mood dimmed into something darker, more feral.

Eron snatched the bag, dragging it across the table, and asked, "Do you know the names of these dragons?"

"No. They were keeping her on an island. It's called Didean, I think."

Eron's fingers unfurled from around the pouch. The way the light from the fire danced in the abyss of his stare made Mark inch back even further in his chair.

"You're one of them," Mark said.

"Why come to me for a simple woman? Did she spurn your advances? Are you a scorned lover?"

"That's none of your business. Can you find them or not?"

He ran a finger along the soft leather of the pouch. "The," he paused, "dragons you wish me to track are formidable. I will not accept a job unless I know what it is I am after."

Glancing around the murky room, Mark let out a weary sigh. He could have taken the coins and tried to find another mercenary to track down Darya, but he didn't know who else to turn to. "She has a price on her head. I'm not sure if I have to be the one to kill her. I think dead is dead to the one I serve. If she gives you too much trouble, take her out. Burn her body."

Eron shook his head. "No, no, helot. My talent is sub-terfuge. If you want this woman dead, her blood will be on your hands."

Mark bristled at his use of that word. He especially didn't like that Eron even knew he was bound to another like he was. "Fine. Whatever. Find her, and I'll take care of the rest."

Eron plucked the satchel of coins off the table. "Tell me more about this woman. What is her name?"

"Darya." Mark gave the man a rudimentary description of her, highlighting those features that would most likely stand out among other women he'd observed in this time.

Eron stood, readying to leave, and Mark asked, "When can I expect results?"

"I'll send word when I have her."

Mark stared after the man until he disappeared outside, leaving him alone in the tavern in a sea of unfriendly faces. He could hear Cernunnos inside his head. Always whispering. Always pushing him to hurry.

Kill Darya. Do it quickly. Make sure she cannot be resurrected again. There cannot be a body left for Arawn to bring life back to.

When he found Darya again, he would make sure she was indeed gone forever. Then he would, at last, have his god's favor.

The disturbing thought shook him to his core. It wasn't the favor of Cernunnos that Mark sought in exchange for killing Darya. He was trading his humanity for something greater, his love for Annie.

He closed his eye, conjuring the face of the woman he yearned to touch again. It swam to the surface of his mind in a dull vision against the constant hissing of the damnable being inside his brain. After a few minutes, he drew her visage from his memory and sat there for a long time, clinging to the fantasy of having her in his arms again.

DARYA SAT ON A pockmarked rock, lost in the flickering flames of the newly awakened fire. Somewhere in the deep recesses of her mind, there had been a nagging voice trying to get her to see the truth of things. When Gita told her about Diana, Darya assumed the siblings would live a somewhat normal life. As normal as a half-human, half-dragon could. How stupid she'd been to ignore the reality of their nature. Now she had forced Edwind to open himself to a pain he feared most.

And what of her own ancestry? What did it mean for her to be the daughter of a deity? Would she, too, live beyond that of a mortal? She came back from the dead, after all.

"It's time, druidae." Mavae stood at the threshold of where twilight met the firelight.

Darya looked from the fire to where Edwind sat with his grandfather at the lake. He glanced to the side, feeling her gaze on him. She had to believe that fate didn't bring them together, only to rip them apart in such a tragic manner.

Mavae took her hand, pulling her to her feet. "Come."

She followed the priestess away from the heart of the camp to a circle of stones with a staircase inlaid in the surrounding rock. The steps curved down and around an open cavern where a shallow body of water waited deep below the surface. The chamber at the foot of the stairs opened to a labyrinth of tunnels leading to hidden chambers beyond. Mavae turned her toward the shimmering pool that reflected the last of the day's light.

"If we had time, I would wait for the moon to be whole again. Its power would make the journey easier." Mavae tugged at the shoulders of Darya's dress.

"What are you doing?" Darya asked, pushing the woman's hands away.

"Would you rather fight your garments or focus your mind on what you need to find?"

Darya relented, letting the dress fall to the ground.

Mavae backed away. "When your ethereal spirit leaves the well, you must remain secured to your body. Do not lose sight of your tether."

Darya stepped into the cool water, letting it envelop her up to her waist. Mavae nodded to the other women in the room. They approached with bowls that overflowed with thick clouds of smoke, and let them float across the glassy surface. Darya laid back, giving herself to the weightlessness of the pool, letting the pungent herbs envelop her.

"The spirits of your ancestors will guide you to the place you need to be." Mavae's voice was muted.

Darya did as she was told, relaxing her body and breathing in the smoke. She wondered what to expect out of this quest. Would it be like watching a movie on the back of her eyelids, or was it going to be something more surreal?

Before she could contemplate her questions much further, her consciousness flew away.

She flailed at the darkness, desperate to find anything to hang onto. A pale white light split the sea of sparkling light, and she looked down to see it attached to her chest. It pulsed in time with her heart, and she followed the rhythmic light down a path of stars with no end.

Her flight slowed until she landed on solid ground, surrounded by tall oaks, maples, and ash trees. Nonexistent feet carried her forward into the vision. Even though it was dark, she could see everything in vivid detail. Ahead, there were torches lighting the way to a clearing where a blazing fire raged into the sky.

She followed the thrumming beat echoing in the frigid night. Half a dozen white-clad girls danced around a flickering bonfire. Darya stilled her ethereal body, peering out from behind a gnarled ash tree. The seductive movements of the maidens were something she'd seen before, but not quite like this. This dance wasn't a celebration. What these girls were doing was an invocation.

From somewhere in the shadows of the trees, a resounding horn bellowed forth. A swift gust of wind swept over the fire, whipping it outside of the bounds of the stones that held the logs in place.

A set of stag horns emerged from the woods and moved around the now calm pyre. The same set of horns from Darya's nightmares. Despite not being in her corporal body, his presence made her shudder. The man stepped around the fire, flames arching toward his powerful frame on his way by.

In the quivering glow of the orange light, she glimpsed a pair of familiar blue eyes behind his mask. A hungry gaze swept over each girl, dropping them one by one to their knees. He held out a hand, letting thick fingers trace the contours of their chilled cheeks. He wore a starving smile, as if trying to decide which delectable morsel he was going to choose to partake in.

On his first pass, he couldn't decide and strode past them a second time. When he came to the last girl in line, he wrapped his hand around the back of her neck and pulled her up to stand before him. He turned her around, and Darya came face to face with a ghost from her past.

Her mother stood silhouetted in the firelight. The horned monster put a hand behind Polly's neck and drew her in for a kiss that lacked any tenderness or passion. It was meant to humiliate, cause pain, and make her bleed.

"You will be my bride." His voice oozed from in between his lips like molasses. The sound of it made Darya's ethereal being tremble.

The other girls ran from the clearing, leaving the lone maiden shivering on a winter night.

Darya tried to turn her nonexistent head away from the horrid scene before her. She shouldn't have to witness this beast savagely rape her virgin body. Yet, no matter how hard she pushed against the unseen force keeping her there, she was stuck in that spot, forced to endure this torment alongside her mother.

When she thought the disgusting ordeal was over, she watched in horror when he wrapped one of his massive hands around Polly's frail neck. The broken girl didn't even try to fight him. Her death was a welcomed relief after the humiliating torture she endured.

Afterward, the beast disappeared into the forest the way he came, never to look back at the destruction he left in his wake.

Darya wanted to run to her mother, but she was cemented to that spot.

Her heart broke for the woman who she had spent much of her life hating. What she didn't understand was how Polly survived?

Movement from the trees drew her gaze from the dead woman and the fire. She recognized Ronwen when the light from the pyre lit up her features. She went to Polly's side, a disgusted expression etched on her face. Another man stepped up beside her. His eyes glowed with a power Darya was sure she'd felt before.

"You will do this for us?" Ronwen asked.

He nodded. "Your mother deemed it so." He touched Polly on the chest, and she heaved back to life.

Ronwen was on the ground at her side. "Easy, girl. No longer do you need to fear Cernunnos. The child that now grows inside you will bring forth the fate he so desperately fights to escape." She lifted Polly's head, looking at the place where Darya's spiritual body stood. "Go to the Temple of Gaia. There, your true destiny awaits."

The hold on Darya vanished. She clung to the glowing tether, following it through the trees. She hadn't gone far when a face appeared out of the darkness, halting her departure.

Sapphire eyes—her eyes—blazed with a dangerous rage. "Where are you hiding, seedling?" He squeezed her spiritual body, making her cry out in pain. He held not only her ethereal being but her physical body in the well.

"Show me where you are," he demanded.

Darya embraced the fury that rose inside her and fought against the monster's touch, but he was so much stronger. Her lungs burned, and she fought to get back to her physical body, only to come to the sickening realization that she was being sucked under the water by an unseen force.

"Get her dragon. Quickly," she heard someone yell.

What seemed like hours passed as her lungs demanded air. Then she felt a pair of arms yank her free of Cernunnos. Edwind's face came into focus, and she latched onto his neck, scared he was a mirage.

"I'm here, my love," he said, cradling her to his chest. "I've got you."

Edwind sat with Darya tucked into one of his arms. Despite the warmth of his body and the fur that surrounded them, she still shivered from the horrible visions that wouldn't stop replaying in her mind's eye. She leaned into him, gripping his hands, fearing she might fly away at any moment. He kissed her forehead, trying to ease her fear.

Hengist and Mavae sat near them, watching Darya with the same concern Edwind had etched on his face while she told them about her vision. She skipped the more gruesome details of her mother's rape and murder. That shame was something she couldn't share. Not yet.

"You say he wore the mask of a deer?" Hengist asked.

She nodded.

The smile Hengist gave her was more of a sneer laced with pitiful sadness. "You are indeed the child of a god. A powerful one."

Mavae said, "So, his end has finally caught up to him."

Darya met her stare. "What do you mean, his end?"

"Whose end?" Edwind asked. "Who is this god that is trying to kill Darya?"

"Cernunnos." Darya's voice was soft and small.

"That is one name for him," Mavae said. "Others call him The Stag. The Horned One. The God of the Hunt. He was many things to many people." She gathered a handful of timber to feed the fire.

"He is a vile monster," Darya hissed. She turned her face into Edwind's chest.

Mavae nodded her agreement. "Whatever he used to be, now he is but a vain, despicable being of lust and sex, demanding the purity and lives of his brides." She chucked a couple of pieces of wood on the dying flames, sending sparks and embers billowing into the air. "It makes me ill to think he is still torturing those pitiful people so far into the future."

Hengist took her hand, urging her to sit beside him.

"How long has he been doing this?" Edwind asked.

"Too long," Hengist said. "Cernunnos was once a benevolent and peaceful god, but a group of hunters murdered his mate. His grief and rage were all-consuming. He cursed the tribe and their descendants for some depraved need for vengeance."

Mavae chuffed out a sound that was a mixture of contempt and laughter. "Fate did not look kindly on the heinous crimes he committed against them, so it was prophesied that he would die at the hands of his own offspring."

"But he slays those women. His brides," Edwind said. "If he killed Darya's mother, how is she alive now?"

Darya left the comfort and safety of Edwind's arms. "Ronwen was there with another man. He brought my mother back to life with a touch." Her body shook with fresh tears. "Now I understand why she hated me so much. I was a constant reminder of that night."

Edwind pulled her into him again. "You are not to blame for what happened to her."

Hengist stared into the flames. "For Ronwen to hold the favor of Arawn...." His voice trailed off, losing itself to his thoughts.

"Why was my mother spared?" Darya asked. "Why were we allowed to live when so many other women died?"

"I cannot answer that question," Mavae told her. "Perhaps if you meet Ronwen again, you can ask her."

Darya looked at Edwind. "Ronwen knew I was there or that I would be there. I don't know. This is all so confusing. She told me to go to the Temple of Gaia. That's where my true destiny lay."

Mavae stood again, tossing the last of the limbs into the flames. "That is quite the voyage from here."

"It will take us a month or more by foot," Hengist said.

"Couldn't we fly?" Darya asked.

Edwind and Hengist shared an uncomfortable glance. "What?"

"Do dragons fly openly in your time?" Hengist countered.

She frowned. "I can't say I've ever seen one, but we flew over the ocean."

"We know of safe places to fly over the sea," Hengist said. "It's too dangerous to do so openly on land. There are too many perils for our kind. People who will go to great lengths to kill us simply because of what we are. When Horsa arrives, we will plan our route." Hengist took Mavae by the hand. To Edwind, he said, "Let the girl get some rest tonight, yes?"

Edwind enveloped her in his arms again. "Yes, Grandfather."

When they were alone, he watched Darya in the soft glow of the firelight. The popping and hissing of the burning wood filled the silence between them. She couldn't bring herself to meet his gaze and kept working her fingers in and out of each other to keep herself occupied.

"What are you thinking about?" he asked, wrapping his hands around hers.

She took a few seconds to compose her question. "Were you really willing to put your heart through the same misery your father went through? For me?"

He tensed around her. "I will walk through the deepest pit of the underworld to spend just one more moment by your side."

"Don't be so melodramatic." She nudged him with her shoulder. "I'm being serious."

"So am I. If you would have let me finish speaking earlier, I would have told you that the god-blood inside you means you could have the same extended life my dragon blood gives me."

Her face lifted from her feet to the hands that held hers. "I know."

He swept her chin up so their eyes met. "If you know this, why were you so upset?"

"You were willing to hold on to that enormous burden and carry all that pain alone. If we are meant to share our lives together, we must trust each other with everything we are. The good and the bad."

Edwind stood, taking her with him. "I've always been by myself. Sure, I had Gita, and later there was Saebbi, but I've never loved another like I do you." His face held a hopeful longing, and it took her breath away. "After what we shared in the spring, there is no doubt in my mind that our lives are bound together for as long as we both live in this world and into the next." He kissed the backs of her fingers. "So, while we exist in this one, I wish us to be united in the most sacred way I know. Will you marry me, my love?"

Her mouth fell open, but no words came out.

His hopeful expression twisted into uncertainty. "Do you not wish to marry me?"

"Yes," she blurted out. "Yes, you big dumb dragon. Of course, I'll marry you."

His smile returned, and her heart fluttered against him. "I will speak with Mavae. When Father arrives, she can join us together." His kiss was reserved and gentle.

She cupped his face in her hands. "Take me up to the mountain so we can be alone."

"You need rest, my love."

"I know what I need." She brought him close, consuming the last of his will.

He scooped her up in his arms and spent the night giving her whatever her heart and her body desired.

Darya stood at the head of the path leading to the altar, where Edwind waited for her to join him.

Horsa had arrived at camp earlier that morning, and when Edwind told him of his proposal, Horsa was overjoyed at his son's news.

Darya had been worried there would be tension between them, given the circumstances of her appearance in their lives and the uncertainty of her situation, but there was no changing her mind about where she wanted to be. She didn't want to go back to her old life. This is where she belonged.

Horsa leaned into her. "I want you to have this." He placed a leather cord around her neck, and she fingered the opalescent stone hanging from it. "I gave it to Diana when we were married."

She took the pendant in her hand, running a finger over the exquisite jewel. "I can't take it."

"No, sweet child. She would have given it to you herself if she were here." He cupped her face in his hands. "I am so happy to be gaining another daughter."

There was no fighting back the joyful tears that gathered in the corners of her eyes. "I wish I could have met her."

Horsa's eyes glistened when he spoke. "Her fierce spirit and selfless heart lives on in Gita and Edwind."

At that moment, she couldn't find the words to describe how much happiness her new family had brought her. She wrapped her arms around his shoulders. "Thank you for sending me here."

After a long minute, he cleared his throat. "Come, now. Edwind is waiting for you."

When she let go of him, she wiped at her salty cheeks. She took his hand and started her walk down the path to where her future awaited.

Edwind's lips split into that boyish half-smile, and it was like watching the sunrise reflect in his luminous gaze, filling her with a love she never thought she'd share with another person. When they stepped inside the stone circle, Horsa let go of her hand so Edwind could take it. His gaze went to the pendant at her neck, and his smile was whole again.

Mavae took her place under the dolmen. With a length of straw cord in hand, she began the rites by wrapping it around the couple's clasped hands. "I call on our ancestors who have walked this sacred land before us to bless this union between Edwind and Darya. As this cord binds your hands, so shall it bind your souls in this life and into the next."

Edwind ran a thumb along Darya's cheek. When he began his profession of love in the old tongue of the druids, she stole a glance at Hengist. He'd spent most of her childhood teaching her that very language, knowing one day her destiny would lead her to this moment.

She saw the surprise on Edwind's face when she responded in kind. The last of her vows barely left mouth when he took possession of her lips, not as her lover but as her husband.

"Easy, boy," Hengist muttered under his breath. "There will be plenty of time to consummate your union after the feast."

Ignoring the old dragon, Edwind continued the sweet exploration of his wife's lips. He and Darya were vaguely aware of the others when they broke apart and wandered away.

His smile filled her heart with unrivaled bliss. "I feel like I've waited a lifetime for this moment," he whispered.

"I'm sorry it took me so long to get here."

Running a hungry gaze along her body, he said, "Do we have to go to the feast?"

"You still owe me a dance."

"I will give you anything you wish, my love." Then his lips were against hers again.

Eron followed the narrow beach along the southern shore of the desolate territory. If his new employer was right, and the dragons fled north from Didean, this stretch of coast would be the most likely place they would come to shore. It was the shortest distance from the island and would give the least chance of leaving themselves vulnerable to any unwanted attention in the sky.

Had he not held the same fear of being seen, Eron would have simply flown the length of the coast until he found evidence of where the others landed. Edwind wasn't adept at hiding his tracks. It was but one of a dozen qualities that irritated Eron throughout their tentative friendship.

Questions kept circling in his mind. One of the most important of which was what kind of woman would earn the ire of an entity as powerful as the one that enslaved that Mark fellow. How had Edwind, of all people, gotten mixed up in that kind of danger? He wasn't known for his sense of adventure. In fact, Eron was surprised the man dared leave the comfort of his home.

Eron reached a part of the beach that was cut in two by a jagged rocky formation, so he trudged up the steep incline to keep from having to backtrack all the way around. He could have flown over the top, but there was too much of a risk of being seen, even in this remote area.

At the peak of the embankment, he took a few minutes to study the shore below. It looked the same as the other half-dozen beaches he'd searched. Maybe he had been wrong about the route his old friend took. The scout on the little worm's boat could have been mistaken.

He let out a long breath, ready to make the trek back down the hill, when his keen eyes spotted something peculiar under a rocky overhang. By the time he was close enough to examine the remnants of the fire, the sun was nearly gone, and the warm light cast long shadows across the landscape.

There was a whisper of leaves from inside the shadows of the woods, making him swipe a hand across the back of his neck at the sense of eyes on him. He studied the trees, but all he saw were small woodland rodents rushing about in their insignificant little lives.

Turning back to the fire pit, he studied the two sets of footprints leading away from shore to a cluster of trees to the west. One of those prints most definitely belonged to a woman. He followed alongside the trail until he reached the tree line. He didn't get the chance to follow their path when a burst of wind bore down on him from the south, washing a sea of dead debris and leaves through the trees. When the gust died down, he took a hesitant step back.

The footprints were gone.

"What have you gotten yourself into, old friend?" he muttered under his breath. Eron studied the surrounding landscape, but he no longer felt the heavy weight of those unseen eyes.

Despite the otherworldly wind wiping away Edwind's prints, he knew which direction they were headed. That was all he needed for now.

Chapter 16

"WE SHOULD AVOID ATLENY," Edwind said, shoving supplies into the satchel his grandfather handed him earlier. After the perfect night he spent with his new wife, he hadn't expected to be arguing with his father this early in the morning.

Edwind lifted his gaze to the lake, where Darya and his grandfather were saying their goodbyes to Mavae, glad to have this chance to speak to his father alone.

"That is the most direct route through the mountains. We will lose a week or more if we go around," Horsa said.

"I don't like the idea of taking Darya through such a populated area. What if Mark has people looking for us?"

"How can he possibly know where we are?"

Edwind's face puckered into a tight scowl. If anyone could understand his reason for not wanting to travel through that city, his father would. Before he could tell him, Darya and Hengist returned from the lake.

"Have you decided which way we are going?" She brushed her lips against Edwind's cheek.

Keeping his hands busy with gathering the last of their belonging, he said, "I think we should bypass any big cities. King Wilden's reach is a long one."

"Bah." Hengist waved a hand. "That's too much of a delay. We will go through Atleny."

"I told him as much," Horsa said, shrugging.

Edwind finished tying the twine around the woolen satchel and dropped it on the ground. "We need to keep ourselves hidden."

Darya put an arm in his. "I have three of the fiercest protectors at my side. I've never felt so safe."

He stared into her trusting gaze, and a heavy stone of dread settled into the pit of his stomach. "And I have never felt so insignificant." He moved his arm out of her grasp so he could finish gathering their belongings. "I tell you these things to protect you, and I'm treated as though I speak nonsense."

He pretended not to notice the way her hands balled into fists when they dropped to her side, or how he heard her heart speed up inside her chest.

She bent down to pick up the bundle of clothes, and he dropped down beside her. "Can't you see I only want to protect you?"

She ignored him and glanced at Hengist. "I'm going to ask Mavae if she will give me some of that tea you like."

"Darya." Edwind reached for her, but again, moved out of his grasp.

"I'm not a delicate flower who needs your protection all the time, Edwind Wodehal."

He worked his mouth open and closed, staring at the back of her head as she stormed off.

Horsa kept his laughter quiet. "Did you think it was always going to be easy, this love between you two?"

"Why does she have to be so stubborn?"

Hengist pretended to study the nonexistent clouds in the sky. "Why can't you tell her the real reason you want to avoid Atleny?"

Edwind shook his head. "There are people I'd rather not see inside those walls."

The elder dragons shared a look.

"It's a big city," Horsa said. "What are the chances of running into anyone you know?"

"It's not a chance I wish to take."

"And I do not wish to drag out this journey any longer than we must. We will travel through Atleny. That is the end of it."

Edwind threw up his hands, cursing in the old tongue, and snatched up the rest of their belongings. He kept his gaze averted from his new bride, who stared daggers at him. It didn't matter how angry she was. He would do everything in his power to protect Darya from what waited for them in that city.

They started their journey in brooding silence. Hengist was the only one who seemed unfazed by the awkwardness between the group. He kept the conversation going by regaling them with tales of the old world and how much it all had changed since the time when he was a young dragon. Darya asked him repeatedly how long ago that had been, but he breezed past the answer with more fanciful stories from his youth.

She eyed the sun inching its way across the sky. Her stomach grumbled and complained, but her irritation with Edwind kept her verbal protests trapped in silence.

Apparently, Hengist's stomach was making the same objections for food because he wandered off the trail and announced this was a suitable spot to stop for a quick meal. He unfurled the bounty Mavae had prepared for them before they left, motioning for them to join him.

Edwind stood back from the group, watching the valley behind them. He hadn't said more than a few words the entire morning. His frown made it clear he was still unhappy with their current route.

"Are you hungry?" Hengist asked, drawing Darya out of her thoughts.

"Starving." She sat beside him. "Do you think I can try to touch the power again? Like I did that day on the cliffs?"

"You mean when you died?" Edwind's tone was harsh, but he quickly forced the scowl off his face.

She tilted her head at him. "If I have it in me to do these things, I need to learn to control it."

"She's right," Hengist said. "I suppose we could try after our meal."

Edwind made a frustrated sound and went to a shaded spot on the ground.

When they finished eating, Hengist led her away from the others so she wouldn't potentially hurt them. His lack of trust didn't fill her with confidence, but she understood his concern.

"Do you remember what it was like to hold power inside you?"

She nodded. She could feel it still, sitting dormant in her blood, waiting to be awakened by her call.

"I want you to do the same thing now, but carefully. Let it in slowly. Don't try to use it."

She closed her eyes and blew out a slow breath. Starting with her toes, she relaxed her body, letting the warm summer breeze sweep across her face, tickling her nose, lips, and cheeks. She waited for the same sweet fullness of the power that filled her before. At the first trickle that pulsed through her veins, she opened her eyes to witness the same radiant light that snaked throughout the world just as it had on the cliffs.

Now that there wasn't a fleet of armed men racing to kill them, she took her time to study the ethereal link between her and the powerful configurations at her fingertips. Taking hold of the power, she ever so carefully tugged at the line and ran through the stone where Hengist sat. He jumped and leaped from the bolder when it rocked back.

She let out an excited yip and put a hand over her mouth. "I think I understand it now," she said. "It's connected. All of it."

He frowned at the rock he'd been ejected from. "What's connected?"

"What I can do. The power I wield. It's tethered to everything. The earth. The plants. The water. The wind. It's all within my grasp."

"There is a reason that kind of magic is reserved for the gods. The mortal blood you carry would explain why it overwhelmed you. Be careful if you ever try to call on it again."

Edwind leaned against a bowed maple, his face shaded beneath its full limbs. He watched her with an adoring fascination. Whatever frustration she'd felt for him faded into the background of the tenderness with which he kindled inside her.

She strode to where he rested under the tree, pretending to look over the leaves within her grasp. He pretended not to watch her pick at the limbs, his mouth opening and closing with unspoken words.

Pushing aside her pride, Darya dropped her arms and looked him in the eyes. "I'm sorry."

His brows furrowed in genuine confusion. "For what?"

"For the way I spoke to you earlier. I guess I'm not used to someone being so protective of me."

He pulled her into his lap. "I want nothing more than to see you safe, but sometimes this big dumb dragon needs to be reminded of what a powerful goddess he married."

She leaned in and kissed the tip of his nose. "And don't you ever forget it." Holding his stare, she added, "I want you by my side not only as my lover but as my husband and, yes, on rare occasions, as my protector."

His laughter came easily, and he moved a strand of hair from her face. "Every time you touch the power inside you, your eyes shine with the light of the very sun itself. You are an amazing woman, my love. I will always be with you, no matter where we end up."

When they started back on their journey, Edwind's mood was much more upbeat, and he even joined his grandfather in the stories of their past. Darya was excited to learn more about the man she married.

"Do you remember when I brought you to train with Parr?" Hengist asked Edwind. "You fought me the whole way. I've never known a boy so afraid of adventure."

Edwind frowned. "I wasn't afraid. I didn't want to leave Mother and Gita without protection." He glanced behind him. "Father wasn't exactly around a lot in those days."

Horsa frowned. "Someone had to secure trade routes, bring back livestock and seed."

"But you benefited from that experience, yes?" Hengist slapped Edwind on the back. "It gave you a little taste of the world outside that damn island."

"It also led me down a reckless path." He winked at Darya. "That's where I got several of those scars you were curious about."

Hengist made a disgusted sound. "That's because you fell in with the wrong group of boys. Especially that Eron Tyr."

At the mention of Eron's name, Edwind's face burned red, and she couldn't tell if it was anger or embarrassment. "We won't go into that," he insisted.

"Who's Eron Tyr?" Darya asked.

Before Edwind could answer, Horsa said, "I wonder if he's gotten himself killed yet? A man that built the reputation he did can't be long for this world."

Hengist shook his head. "You have little room to speak, my boy. I remember a certain dragon—"

"That's enough, old man. I may have had my share of mishaps, but I've never lowered myself to the deeds Eron has done."

Darya grabbed Edwind's hand. "And this was a man you used to hang out with?"

"We were friends at one time. Until I grew some sense and chose a better path for myself."

"How long ago was this? How old are you, exactly?"

"Old enough," Edwind said simply.

She wanted to push him for an answer, but let it go for the moment. "Does this Eron Tyr have mortal blood in him like you?"

"Yes. His mother is a true-born dragon. His father was human and a general in one of the most feared armies in the territory. When I met Eron, he'd already made a name for himself among Parr's men and took me under his wing."

Darya belted out a laugh.

The three men eyed her.

She stared back at them. "Don't you get it? Wings? Dragons?"

Edwind raised an eyebrow at her. "I don't see how that is funny."

"Fine. I still think it's an amusing pun." She waved a hand. "Go on. What kind of trouble did you and Eron get into?"

"The usual things young men do. Drinking. Gambling. Fighting."

"And women," Hengist added.

The red hue returned to Edwind's face. "Yes. That too."

"I bet you were quite charming with the ladies." She jabbed a finger into his side.

He snatched her hand and pulled her into him. "It wasn't like that." He laid a gentle kiss on her mouth. "Women were more Eron's game. My troubles came from drinking and gambling."

Darya wrapped an arm around Edwind's waist and took up a lazy pace beside him, content to spend the afternoon listening to her new family talking about the past and their plans for the future.

The moment Darya lifted her head off the table, she knew she was dreaming. She recognized the tiny apartment she used to share with Annie. When she looked down, she was wearing a pair of red and black flannel pants and a pale yellow spaghetti-strapped camisole. The sky outside the row of windows across from the kitchen table cast a warm, cozy glow on the small space.

"How can you stand to live in such a confined place?" The forest creature sat in a chair across the table from her, holding a newspaper in her hand, just like Annie used to do. She even wore Annie's fuzzy pink robe. The thing's dirt-encrusted hair and cat eyes were comically out of place among such modern amenities.

"You get used to it." Darya fidgeted with the empty cup in front of her, unable to meet the creature's shrewd gaze.

"I could never grow accustomed to such things," she scoffed and set down the paper and ran her slender fingers over the pink fuzz. "I do like the feel of this garment, though. What is it called?"

"A robe. What are you doing in my dreams again? Who are you?"

"I come with a warning, druidae. You are not too far gone on this path you follow. You can still turn away. Take your dragon and go back to his island among the waters of Llyr."

Darya sat forward, resting her arms on the table. "Are you one of Cernunnos' minions?"

The creature stopped petting the robe and turned an irritated gaze on her. "I am beholden to no one. As you should not be."

"Who do you think I'm beholden to?"

"Fate seeks to use you as her pawn. You walk this path to your destiny, yet your destiny has many roads for which you may travel."

Letting out a disgusted sigh, she sat back in her chair. "What is it with you people and your nonsensical riddles? Why can't you tell me anything in plain words? My destiny is to kill Cernunnos. How many roads can I possibly have to follow to get to that one?"

The creature's smile was too wide, making her look even more menacing. "Is that what fate's puppet told you? It was the cruel hand of the Weaver that cursed Cernunnos to this death you seek to give him, yet you do not ask why."

"I've heard the stories, and I've also seen what he's done to all those women, what he did to my mother. He deserves to die for that alone."

The forest creature stood and slammed her hands on the table, cracking it down the middle. "What of the pain and suffering he endured?" She flung the two halves aside and grabbed Darya by her shirt. "Turn away from this foolish quest of yours and live out your life with your dragon as it was meant to be."

In the distance, a horn blasted so loudly it vibrated the windows. The creature's expression went from anger to fear. "Please, druidae. Be happy with the life you have been given."

Darya's eyes flew open, and she was no longer inside her apartment in Dallas. She stared into a cloudless night sky with thousands of stars winking back at her.

"Bad dream?"

She looked across the glowing embers of what remained of their cook fire where Hengist sat drinking from a mug. "Yes."

"Do you wish to talk about it?"

"Not really."

He nodded, taking another sip. "Sometimes dreams are just dreams. Sometimes they carry a different meaning. These lands are filled with many ancient things that prey on those who slumber. Be careful what you choose to believe."

She turned over and moved into Edwind's arms. In a half-sleep, he kissed her forehead and murmured his love for her. There was no going back to sleep, so she spent the next few restless hours mulling over what she had been told. Until that moment, she hadn't doubted her duty to kill Cernunnos. She tried to banish the words of the forest creature, but what if she was right? What if, by continuing on this path, she was putting Edwind and the others in danger?

She tugged her husband's arms tight around herself in a futile attempt for reassurance. In the end, she didn't have a choice. If she didn't kill Cernunnos, he would continue to search for her. Even if they killed Mark, he would send more of his followers after her. No matter what decision she made, lives were going to be at risk. Killing the ancient god was the only one that guaranteed a semblance of hope for a normal life.

The next morning Darya didn't mention her dream to the others, and Hengist didn't push her to share it. There was nothing Edwind could do for her. In fact, he may even try to convince her to take the creature's advice and go back to Didean. That was something she wouldn't do.

She considered what Hengist had told her. What if she was being lied to? Something didn't sit right about how enraged the forest creature became when Darya spoke of killing Cernunnos. That alone told her she was on the right path.

It was well into the late afternoon when they approached the towering city walls of Atleny. The closer they got to the bustling ancient metropolis, the more Edwind rushed them forward. He practically pulled Darya through the gates, past vendors, and down narrow side streets, like he knew the direction he needed to go to avoid any heavy foot traffic.

"Have you been here before?" Darya asked.

"Yes," he said, not offering to elaborate. "If we hurry, we can make it to the base of the mountains before sunset."

"We need to find someplace to sleep in the city," Horsa said. "Your wife is exhausted. We all are."

He paused in an alley to look Darya over. She forced a smile, hoping to hide just how drained she really was, but he frowned at her attempt to hide her tiredness. "There's a tavern near here. We will get a room there for the night."

"I can make it out of the city if that's what you want to do," she insisted.

"Father is right. We are all tired and need a good night's rest in a proper bed."

"Edwind?" A man's voice cut through the background noise around them.

Edwind put an arm around Darya and urged her forward.

"Edwind Wodehal, is that you?"

"Do you know him?" Darya motioned to the man chasing them.

A set of heavy boots padded closer. "It is you."

Edwind let out a defeated sigh, his body visibly stiffening when the other man grabbed him in a rough embrace.

"It's been too long."

"It's good to see you again, Varic." Edwind returned the gesture.

Varic let him go, and his gaze fell on the others. "Who do you travel with?"

"This is my father, Horsa. My grandfather, Hengist." He took Darya's hand. "And my wife, Darya."

"Wife?" Varic's face matched the astonishment in his voice. He scratched at the red scruff along his jawline while a pair of faded denim eyes looked her over. "Congratulations on your beautiful bride."

"Thank you. Please excuse us. We are on our way to Gail's."

"I won't hear of it. You will not subject your family to that swill. Come to my estate. I have plenty of room."

Edwind gave him a hard look. "I won't put you out like that."

Varic laid a hand on his shoulder. "Don't worry. All will be well there. I have the whole place to myself for the next few days."

Something in his words made Edwind relax. "If you're sure it won't be an inconvenience."

"Nonsense. You're practically family." He put an arm around Edwind's shoulder and dragged him onward, beckoning for the others to follow. "A wife? Really? I guess it can happen to the best of us."

Varic hadn't stopped talking since they started their trek from the lower city. Edwind kept looking back at Darya, his expression twisted into an uncomfortable apologetic smile. Seeing how much he was enjoying the banter they shared warmed her heart. She stayed at Horsa's side, content to watch her husband in this new light.

When they arrived at Varic's estate, he waved over a young woman rushing through the halls. "Make ready Edwind's room and two more for his family."

The woman nodded before disappearing upstairs.

"You still hold a room for me?"

"This house will always be open to you, old friend. While your accommodations are being prepared, let's enjoy a drink and a hot meal." He held his arm out for them to go into the dining hall.

"Did I hear the name of the great Edwind Wodehal?"

The color drained from Edwind's face, along with his emotion. Darya followed his gaze up the rounded staircase. At the top of the landing, a woman rushed into view. Her soft features and supple curves filled the lavender gown in all the right places. A pair of porcelain breasts struggled to be tamed inside the plunging neckline.

She practically skipped down the steps straight for them, and her fiery locks bouncing over her shoulders. "You don't know how long I've wanted to feel your arms around me again."

Edwind turned his body away from her, throwing himself behind Darya.

Varic stepped in front of them, cutting the woman off. "Lerin, I thought you were on your way to Baron Rouet's estate."

She waved him off, trying to get past him. "I forgot something in my room. Now I'm glad I did. I'd much rather stay here now."

He looked over his shoulder, mouthing the words I'm sorry to Edwind. To Lerin, he said, "Don't be rude to our guests, dear sister. This is Horsa and Hengist. Edwind's father and grandfather."

Lerin gave them a slight bow.

"And his wife, Darya."

Her smile faltered before falling off her beautiful face altogether. "His wife? Isn't this a surprise?"

Darya side-eyed Edwind. A lot of his behavior made sense now. She stepped forward, taking Lerin's hand in both of hers. "It's so nice to meet you, Lady Lerin. You have a lovely home."

Lerin sneered at her hand as if it was on fire. "Yes." She snatched it away. "So nice."

Varic cleared his throat. "I could use a drink."

Edwind put an arm around Darya's waist to lead her into the dining hall, but held her back while the others made their way into the other room. "I'm sorry. I was under the impression she wouldn't be here."

Darya placed a hand on his chest to stop him from speaking. "There are a lot of things we don't know about each other. All I ask is you be honest with me. Even if you think I'll be upset. If you had told me this is the reason you didn't want to come this way, I wouldn't have fought you so hard." She planted a quick kiss on his lips. "In fact, I would have dragged us around the damn city myself."

"You give me yet another reason to love you, woman." He matched her kiss with one that lingered a little longer before they joined the others.

Varic sat at the head of the table, with Lerin lowering herself into the chair to his left.

Darya went to take the seat opposite her, but the other woman held up a dainty hand. "No, dear. That is Edwind's seat."

Darya smiled at her and sat down, anyway.

Lerin looked to her brother, who pretended to be enjoying his drink too much to be interested in anything else. When he put the cup down, he said, "Tell me, Edwind, how did you meet your lovely wife?"

Edwind rested his hand on Darya's. "She came into my life as if sent by the gods themselves."

Darya laughed. "It's not quite so dramatic. The ship I was traveling on ran into some bad weather, and I fell overboard and washed up on his shores with no memory. While I healed from my injuries, we fell deeply in love."

Lerin grabbed a piece of fruit. "The last time Edwind and I were together," she let the grape roll over her tongue, "he told me he would never give his heart to another. He said love was a fool's game."

Darya was aware of the trap Lerin was trying to lay, and Darya tried to keep her demeanor calm. "Maybe he hadn't found the woman he was ready to trust with his heart."

Lerin narrowed her eyes at Darya, looking her up and down. "What house are you from?"

Varic put down his drink and turned a sharp glare on his sister. "These are my guests. You will treat them as such."

Lerin ignored him. "I simply want to know more about our dear Edwind's new wife. We haven't seen him in nearly two years, and he shows up unannounced with a woman we were told nothing about."

Edwind sat forward. "My life is none of your concern."

Lerin kept pushing. "Do you know what he is?"

"Yes," Edwind snapped. "She knows everything about me and my family, as I know everything about her. Now heed your brother's warning."

Still, Lerin wasn't deterred. She took a sip of her wine, pretending to be indifferent to the threats. "Do you even hold a title? You have the look of a simple farm girl, raised among the filth and muck of animals."

Edwind sat forward, ready to push himself to his feet, but Darya was done with her games. She put a hand on Edwind's arm and let a smile curl the edges of her mouth. "What an astute observation for a woman with so little self-awareness. I did, in fact, grow up tending the land and caring for the animals."

Lerin sat back, satisfied to shame her rival.

"But do not think for one minute I am any less deserving of this man's heart because I walked a path that honors the very breath of life that gives you the food that sits before you and fills your ungrateful belly."

She stood, towering over Lerin. "I know the type of woman you are. You live in this lavish home with men lined up waiting to lie in your bed. You use them to fill this sad, empty life of yours. Now, you think you can take back the man who no longer wants you by insulting the woman he loves. His wife?"

Lerin shot to her feet. "How dare you say such things to me?"

"Do I lie?"

"You are a vile woman."

"This vile woman will be sleeping with her dragon tonight, won't she?"

Lerin turned to Varic. "Are you going to let her speak to me that way?"

"And have her cut me with that tongue of hers?" He hid his grin behind his drink. "You earned your humiliation."

Lerin narrowed her gaze on Darya, but instead of continuing their game of insults, spun on her heels and rushed up the stairs.

Darya stared after her. The feel of Edwind's hand brought her out of her anger and back to him. She looked around the table before returning to her husband. His expression was hard to gauge.

To Varic, she said, "Is our room ready?"

He motioned to someone she couldn't see. "Henriette will take you upstairs."

When Edwind didn't let her go, she forced a smile. "Stay and visit with your friend. You two have a lot to catch up on. I'm suddenly very tired."

Chapter 17

ALONE IN THEIR ROOM, Darya leaned against the heavy door, the pitted surface rough against her forehead. She inhaled what she hoped would be a soothing breath, but when she blew it out, she was still shaking with residual anger and disbelief. The woman she invoked downstairs was someone she hadn't seen in a long time.

It was rare for her to give in to her temper. When she was younger and would let her emotions take her over, strange, sometimes dangerous things manifested because of it. She knew now that the power inside her had been at her fingertips far longer than she realized.

Pushing off the door, she bypassed the bed for the balcony that overlooked the city. The audacity of that woman to lay claim to her husband. Her dragon. Lerin was lucky Darya hadn't brought out her newly awakened goddess to do more than cut her with words.

She lost herself in the rumble of people walking the streets of Atleny in the torchlight. The foot traffic had eased since their arrival, but it was still quite busy for being so late. In nineteen eighty-two, she could run down to the corner store and grab a pint of ice cream to drown her feelings in. She would just about maim someone for a spoonful of rocky road right now.

Edwind thrust open the door, letting it swing close behind him. His expression was as unreadable as the drab gray stone that surrounded them. She expected him to be furious with her after how she embarrassed him in front of his friend. And she was ready to meet his anger with her own rage for bringing her to his ex-lover's home without warning her beforehand.

"That tongue of yours." His tone betrayed little more than his face.

She turned her back on him. "If you've come here to tell me how angry you are, you can leave. I don't feel bad for saying what I did. She deserved—"

There was no sound of footsteps at his approach, so when he had her in his grasp and pushed her onto the bed, excitement tempered the surprise he elicited from her.

"There is no anger heating my blood." He climbed on top of her, nuzzling his face into her neck. His whiskers scraped over her skin, sending chills down her body. One of his hands fought to get between her legs.

She grabbed him, halting his hunt for her desire. "Is she the reason you're so turned on right now?"

For the first time since entering their room, anger tinged his features. He easily overpowered her and pulled her arms over her head. He bent close to her ears, whispering to her in the old tongue, repeating the vows he'd spoken when he pledged himself to be her husband.

Wriggling loose from his grasp, she took hold of the sides of his face, losing herself in the desperation of their embrace. They collided against one another again and again, pulling away for the briefest reprieve to take a breath before crushing each other once more.

She yanked at his shirt until she worked it over his head, flinging it across the room.

Every time he kissed her, she lost more of herself to him. His fingers fumbled with the strings of her dress. She was about to help him get the damn thing untied, but he grabbed hold of the thin fabric, ripping it apart, freeing her breast from their confines.

He took their delicate softness in his mouth, savoring them on his tongue. He used his teeth to tease her nipples to stiff peaks and ran his other hand between her legs, demanding she give herself to him.

She squirmed underneath him, trying to undo his belt. She didn't want to relinquish her pleasure until she had him inside her. "Take them off," she said between kisses.

He left the bed and yanked off the rest of his clothes. "You are the only woman my body craves," he rumbled.

Remnants of the dress were draped over the most sensual parts of her, and she ran her hands up her legs, moving the fabric aside so he could enjoy the sight of the goddess he gave his heart to. He returned to the soft curves of his wife, taking over her mouth and the exciting cry she made for him when he slid inside her.

Using one hand to steady himself and the other to play with her breasts, Edwind drove into her with slow, powerful thrusts as if he was starving for the feel of her around him. The pulsing sympathy of her orgasm gripped him and made him push harder until her cries and her body slowed.

He got to his knees, careful not to leave the heat of her and, using a thumb, he worked her swollen bud under the dark patch of curls while keeping his strokes steady. Already, she shuddered in anticipation of another wave of ecstasy.

She arched into him, twisting her fingers into the blankets. He rocked into her again and again until he propelled her into the ether of the universe. There were no rational thoughts or words, only the delicious rapture that filled every crevice of her being.

By the time he had taken what pleasure he could from his wife and allowed himself his own, they both lay across the end of the bed. Darya was on her stomach, and Edwind was half on the blankets and half on her back, where he fell on top of her.

She brushed his sweat-drenched hair from his face. "You are a beast."

"You knew what I was when you married me." He pulled a hand to his lips. "I'm sorry I brought you here."

"I'm sorry I made a fool of myself."

"You did no such thing." He pressed his mouth to her cheek and gathered her into his arms at the head of the bed. "Let us rest, my love. Tomorrow we will be gone from this place."

Silence greeted Darya when she woke. Moonlight bathed the room in a faint ethereal blue glow, with no hint of dawn in the air, so she must not have been asleep that long. In her half-awake state, she noticed that Edwind's usual rumbling snores weren't there. She rolled over, expecting to turn into him, but she fell into a cold, empty space.

She threw on a dress and went to the balcony to find it desolate as well. She tugged the heavy door open, glancing up and down the darkened hallway. When she stepped out of the room, the sounds of unintelligible whispers floated from somewhere around the corner.

Each room she passed in the seemingly endless hall was closed, except for one. Her bare feet were silent on the cold stone floors, careful not to trip in the dim light.

A faint glow spilled from the open doorway, and she eased around the threshold to peek inside. Judging from the soft hues and delicate décor, it was definitely a woman's bedchamber. There was a massive bed with ornately carved designs along the four posts that flanked each corner. Sheer curtains obscured the woman sitting upright on her knees. Her hips moved back and forth, and she had her arms outstretched, anchoring herself to something in front of her.

A hoarse moan drifted from the other side of the room, followed by, "I've missed the way you feel inside me."

Darya recognized Lerin's flowery voice and the flaming hair that bounced out of control down her bare back. When Lerin's head fell to the side, Edwind's face appeared over her shoulder. His mouth and tongue traced the length of Lerin's slender neck. He opened his eyes, revealing the burning embers of desire he once harbored for his wife.

Darya sucked in a breath, sending her backward into the door and pushing it all the way open.

Lerin's head snapped to the side. Her lips twisted into a satisfied grin, and she grabbed the back of Edwind's neck. "I have your dragon now."

Darya opened her mouth, meaning to scream. What came out was a hoarse sob, and she flung herself into a sitting position. The image of their room edged out the horrid dream. She gripped the reality of the furs that covered her lower body, yet no matter how hard she tried, she couldn't banish those terrible visions of her husband and that woman out of her mind.

She fell back, hoping to find comfort in his embrace, but she was confronted by the same empty bed from the nightmare.

A weak whimper escaped her parted lips. She closed her eyes, willing this to be a dream, just like before, but she knew it was real life. Edwind was gone from their room in the middle of the night with that woman still among those walls.

As she did in her dream, Darya dressed and checked the balcony before rushing into the hall. She stood outside Horsa and Hengist's room with her hand poised to knock. What if Edwind needed a drink or to relieve himself? It was a stupid dream. He would never betray her.

Not like Harvey.

The sound of raised voices brought her out of her thoughts, and a tight ball of nerves twisted her guts. She had to make her legs carry her to where the sounds grew louder. Nothing looked the same as it did in her dream, loosening the tight hold on her lungs.

When she reached the end of the hall, she spotted an open door to the left. More angry words drifted to where she stood, listening.

"I have nothing else to say to you." Edwind's tone was one she recognized when he was dangerously close to losing his temper.

"You don't mean that." The sound of Lerin's melodious voice made her stop walking. "After everything we've shared?"

"You are making a fool of yourself," Varic said.

"Shut your mouth," Lerin hissed. "You promised me to him. What did she offer you? Land? Money? I can give you that and more."

Darya tiptoed forward until she was at the edge of the threshold. The room in which her husband stood was much like the one on the island where she and Edwind played chess.

Varic was next to a board identical to Edwind's, except these pieces were silver instead of stone.

Lerin had her back to the door, standing uncomfortably close to Edwind.

"That was drunk talk between friends," Varic scoffed. "It meant nothing, and you know it."

"It meant something to me." Lerin sounded like she was on the verge of tears.

Edwind leaned away from her. "I've given my heart to Darya. I love her. Only her."

"How can you love that awful woman?"

Anger flared in Edwind's eyes. "Do not speak so cruelly about my wife."

Lerin took a step back, but she recovered by putting a hand on his arm. "Oh, Edwind. You know I'd give you whatever you want."

He jerked out of her reach. "Never lay your hands on me."

Fury drove any semblance of reasonable thought out of Darya's mind. She pushed her way into the room. On instinct alone, she held out a hand to the fire, pulling it to her. The flames snaked from the hearth along the floor and up into her open palm. All the rage, sorrow and disgust poured into that orange ball of hate. The intense heat threatened to burn her, but the will of her anger kept it from scorching her flesh.

She glanced at the flames in her hand, and when she lifted her gaze to Lerin, someone grabbed her wrist. She tore her eyes away from the woman who tried to seduce the man she loved into betraying his vows and his heart.

Hengist stared at her with a look of sympathetic under-standing. "There is no coming back if you lose control."

Her face twisted into a sneer, and her cheeks burned from the tears that streamed down her face. She turned her at-tention to the room again, wrenching her wrist free. Edwind moved in front of Lerin to shield her from any would-be attack.

A fresh wave of anger and betrayal made the fireball flare, and she choked out a sob through clenched teeth. She didn't know how she found the will to keep from lobbing that flam-ing ball of rage into the room. Instead of letting go of the flames, she closed her fingers around the fire, smothering it with the fury that burned hotter than the blaze in her palm. She opened her hand again to reveal only reddened skin.

She glanced at Hengist, unable to even look at Edwind. "I'm leaving. Right now," her voice was quiet. "Stay if you want, but I can't be here anymore."

She ran from the room. All she wanted to do was gather her things and leave that house and the heartache writhing inside her. She didn't care if she had to sleep on the streets of Atleny. If Lerin's offer of money and land or whatever else she promised was enough to tempt Edwind to break his vows, he didn't love her as much as he claimed.

"Darya." Edwind rushed to catch up with her.

His presence pushed her even faster until she was in their room. She tried to slam the door, but he was right behind her, catching it in his hands. "Would you talk to me?"

She couldn't answer him. Her throat was locked shut by all the emotions warring for control.

"I don't know what you think you heard, but I can assure you I only went to speak with Varic. I didn't know Lerin would be there." He crossed his arms. "How could you have reacted so recklessly? You could have hurt someone."

She whirled on him. "I could have hurt her, you mean. God forbid I hurt your precious, delicate Lady Lerin."

He threw up his hands. "How can you be so jealous? Have I not proven how much I love you?"

She clamped her mouth shut and turned away from him. The pain of the dream still dug at her heart, and she was incapable of rational thought at this point.

Only a few hours ago, she berated Edwind about being honest with her, and here she was, holding on to a part of her own past that almost caused her to lose control of herself and hurt another person. Even if that person was a horrible woman who tried to steal her husband.

She slumped to the bed, letting go of her anger. "I had a horrible dream."

"A dream?" His own anger faltered.

"About you and Lerin. Together."

"Is that why you acted so irrationally just now?"

Her head shot to the side, and she took on a defensive tone. "I wasn't acting irrationally."

"You nearly set us on fire."

Shaking her head, she went on. "It wasn't just the dream. When I heard her offer you the things I couldn't, it made me go a little crazy."

She refused to meet his stare when he dropped to his knees in front of her and took her face in his hands. "What could I possibly want from Lerin when I have this goddess before me?"

She stood and stepped around him onto the balcony. "A child."

"I told you how I feel about that."

"You're not the first man to tell me those things."

Edwind rested his hands on her arms.

She stared at his fingers, unable to look him in the eye. "I was almost married once before. He told me it didn't matter that I couldn't give him a child of his own. There were other ways to have a family. I guess he changed his mind." She shut her eyes against the coming tears. "A few weeks before our wedding, he admitted to having an affair, and the other woman was pregnant."

He spun her around. "Oh, my love. No one will ever come between us like that."

"What if you change your mind? What if you decide one day you want a real family of your own?"

"You are my family. You are the only family I will ever need. Please believe me when I tell you this." His kiss eased the ache in her chest.

She rested her forehead against his, but her muscles went rigid when someone knocked on their door. "I can't face anyone right now."

Edwind gave her another quick kiss. "I'll send them away." At the door, he let out a sigh. "We will leave as soon as we gather our things."

"You will do no such thing." Varic's voice carried a hint of irritation. "This is my house, and you are my guests. Lerin has overstepped her place one too many times. I suppose it's my fault. I've spoiled her too much." There was a pause. "Lady Darya, please accept my apologies for her behavior. I sent her away for the night. She won't bother either of you again."

Darya kept her gaze locked on the streets below.

"The choice is yours, my love," Edwind said.

She didn't know if she could stand to be in that house any longer, even if Lerin was gone, but it was selfish of her to expect the others to be miserable because of her stupid insecurities. "We are leaving in the morning, anyway. What's a few more hours?"

Edwind crossed the room and bent close to her ear. "Would you like to know the reason I went to find Varic so late?"

She met his gaze, her silence prompting him to go on.

The playful smile that split his mouth had her even more curious. "Perhaps you would be the better person to make this wager."

Turning all the way around, she asked, "What kind of wager?"

Lerin sat atop the gray and white dapple mare, seething from the tongue-lashing she received from her brother. He had some nerve in speaking to her like she was still a child.

Yet here she was, made to leave her home in the middle of the night to travel to the Baron's estate. It should be that horrid bitch Darya walking these desolate streets.

And what was that witchery she possessed? Was that the same magic that enchanted Edwind into her bed and her heart? Did he even really love her?

Love.

His kind did not love. Not when they were doomed to outlive everyone they will ever know. They are creatures of lust and sex. That's what Lerin found irresistible about him. Edwind's stamina was outmatched by no other man she'd ever been with. His body was meant to be hers until she grew tired of him. How dare he claim to love another woman?

In a fit of renewed spite, she spurred the horse forward toward the open gates, barely missing a man walking up the street.

His reaction was swift. He had the reins of the mare in one hand and a dagger poised at her belly with the other. Behind the man, three guards were at his back with their own swords, ready to skewer him at her command.

He held out his hands to show he was no longer a threat, despite still holding the vicious onyx blade. "Forgive me, my lady. My clumsy feet carried me directly in your path."

Lerin nodded to the men who returned to their posts at the gates. The firelight of the torches did little to refine his features, but the way it reflected off his dark eyes stirred something inside her. "Do you always go on the offensive when you are in the wrong?"

"Had you been anyone but the beauty I see before me, I may have followed through with my threat for such temerity." He held her gaze with those shimmering black eyes.

Breaking their hold was more difficult than she liked. "I should consider myself lucky, then."

"I hope you are taking an escort when you leave the city. It's late for a lovely woman to be out by herself."

"I've traveled this path many times. It is a short and safe journey."

"Given how the guards respond to your orders, I bet nothing happens in the city without your knowledge." His eyes lingered on her chest, and an eager smile bloomed across his lips.

There was an allure surrounding him that made her reconsider getting to know more about his mysterious man, but Darya's words still stung where they skewered her pride. "My brother and I are the keepers of its walls."

His smile turned predatory. "How fortuitous that you nearly ran me over."

A flaming eyebrow arched upward.

"I am in search of someone. A woman. Her cousin has been trying to find her for many weeks. He's spent a small fortune hiring men all over the land to seek her out."

"Oh? Has she been abducted?"

"No. Nothing so sinister. It seems she's run away from her betrothed. She doesn't want to marry into his family or some such nonsense. I am but a hired hand, so I am not paid to care about the inner workings of their family."

"I'm sorry," Lerin paused. "I don't believe you gave me your name."

"Eron Tyr." He gave a slight bow.

"I'm sorry, Eron Tyr. Atleny is a big city. Many young women pass through its walls every day. Perhaps you will have better luck in the morning asking around the markets."

"I will do that." He reached for her, brushing his lips against the back of her hand. "May I know the name of the woman that nearly ran me over, at least?"

"Lerin, of the house, Eweln."

"Ah, Lady Lerin. That is a beautiful name befitting a ravenous woman." He took a step back to let her by. "Travel safe."

She hesitated, not ready to leave his presence. "What does this girl look like? I can have a few of our soldiers scout the area and ask about her."

"I was given a rather vague description myself. Dark hair, blue eyes, probably about your age. She is closer to my height than yours."

Lerin slid off the horse, sidling up to the stranger. "And her name?"

"Darya. I'm afraid that's all the information I have."

Her face lit up with an excited smile. "You say she is promised to another?"

"Yes. Is this someone you know?"

Lerin clapped her hands together, unable to hide the giddy excitement in her voice. "Eron Tyr, it is indeed fortuitous that we met this night."

Darya kept her eyes locked on Varick. He studied the chessboard, his wildfire brows stitched together in irritated concentration. Each player was positioned to take the game at any moment, but Darya knew she was going to be the ultimate victor. She had a feeling Varic knew it too, from the way he drummed his fingers on the edge of the table and his gaze skipped from square to square. His other hand worked at the braided leather chord around his neck that held a thick silver ring with the letter 'W' etched into it.

Edwind wandered the room, sipping at the pungent ale he carried with him. At the fireplace, he picked up a wood sculpture. "I can't believe your grandfather kept this."

Varic barely looked up from the game. "Didn't you carve that out of the tree that once stood on this very spot?"

A reminiscent smile passed over Edwind's lips. "Josephine was furious with him for destroying such a magnificent thing. You're lucky to be alive. I'm surprised she ever laid in his bed after that."

"Granna made it clear we were to keep that carving of yours in our family until our bloodline no longer exists in this world." He sounded distracted while he spoke and picked up a knight, shook his head, and set it back down.

A look of ire was planted on his face when he turned to his friend. "You are a conniving, devious man." He yanked the leather cord from his neck and laid it on the board. "The game is yours, Lady Darya. Take your prize."

She examined the ring. "What have I won, exactly?"

Edwind strode to her side, reaching for her hand. "I have been waiting a long time to get that back."

Before he could grab the weighty silver, she closed her fingers around it. "I won the game. It seems the ring is now mine. We should try to get some sleep before dawn. I'm sure your father has a long day planned for us."

Darya bid the men goodnight and walked out, leaving Edwind to stare helplessly after her. She knew she only had a short time to get to the room before Edwind caught up to her.

By the time he burst through the door, she had gotten her dress untied and slipped it to the floor, so she was wearing only the necklace from their wedding day. She held the heavy ring out in one hand.

"That was not what I had in—" The sentence was sliced away by the sight that confronted him when he stepped over the threshold.

"That ring." His brain seemed to struggle to make the right words come out of his mouth. "Family. Years."

She glanced at her palm. "I could be persuaded to return it to its rightful owner. For a price."

With each step he took toward the bed, he discarded a piece of clothing until he, too, was as naked as his beautiful wife. He began his plea to win back the ring from the woman who held it hostage. With each touch of his hand and the beckoning of his mouth and urging of his body, he was, at last, able to convince her to accept his offer.

The cool breath of morning wafted into the open balcony doors, sweeping over the exhausted lovers that lay intertwined atop a mass of blankets on the floor. She worked the ring on Edwind's finger. "What would have happened if I didn't win it back from Varic?"

"It would have returned to me, eventually."

"If it was so important, why did you wager it at all?"

He frowned. "I wasn't the one who lost it, to begin with."

She stared at him, expecting him to explain.

"It's a story for another time," he said, sweeping her hair from her face.

After a long minute of studying his face, she said, "How old are you?"

"Do you really want to know?"

"I asked, didn't I? You carved that piece of wood for Varic's grandfather." She looked over the stones of their room. "A place this size would have taken decades to complete."

"You know your architecture."

"I know my history. Did you forget where I came from?"

He gave her one of his patented cocked half-smiles. "I'm seventy-two."

"Wow. You look good for an old guy."

His body shook with silent laughter. "This old guy can still keep up with you."

She dropped her head to the side. Dawn was peeking through the veil of darkness. "So much for getting some rest before we leave."

"I suppose we should gather our things." He went around the room, retrieving his clothes. When he was dressed, he headed for the door. "I'll make sure the other old men are up and ready to go."

They shared a lingering kiss before he left her to dress. She finished brushing her hair and putting it in a braid when someone knocked on her door. Thinking it was Edwind, she pulled on the metal knob, barely looking up.

Had she been paying better attention, she might have stopped Lerin from covering her nose and mouth with that sickly sweet spelling rag. A heavy blanket of shadows crowded around her vision and sucked away what little fight she had left. No matter how much she tried to claw her way back into consciousness, she kept slipping down the dark, dank hole of oblivion.

Chapter 18

EDWIND BALANCED TWO CUPS of tea in one hand and a loaf of sweet bread in the other when he backed into the bedroom. If he and his wife couldn't get any sleep after their full night of lovemaking, he would make sure they had something warm and satisfying on their bellies for the journey ahead.

"This should help keep you awake, my love," he said to the empty room. He set the food and tea on the table so he could bend down to pick up Darya's comb. A flash of light drew his gaze to the floor where his mother's pendant lay half-hidden behind a bedpost. His nostrils flared at the distinct odor in the air that made the already fading grin fall away, and the happy swell of his heart sank into the pit of his stomach.

He ran from the room, yelling for his father and grandfather.

"What's wrong?" Horsa asked.

"It's Darya. I think someone has taken her."

"Taken?"

Edwind practically leaped down to the ground floor. "Varic!" He swung his head around, searching for his friend.

Horsa stepped into his line of sight, and Edwind said, "Our room smells of aconite, and I found Mother's pendant at the foot of the bed."

"What is all this yelling?" The men looked at the top of the stairs where Lerin came sauntering into view, covering her mouth to hide a petite yawn. "It's too early for all this ruckus."

Hengist eyed Edwind. "I thought you were supposed to be gone from here."

"This is my home, too. I shouldn't have to leave if I do not wish it." She crossed her arms. "Now, what is all the yelling about?"

"Darya is missing," Edwind said. "Did you see or hear anything?"

Her mouth dropped open. "I've been in my room, sleeping. Oh, dear. I hope she's alright."

"Where's Varic?"

She waved off the question, bouncing down the stairs. "He's probably on one of his morning walks. He will return soon." She stepped to his side and tried to put her arm in his. "Maybe she went back home. She said she was leaving. I guess this was all too much for the poor girl."

The speed with which Edwind turned on her and the intensity of the anger in his gaze made her flinch and step away from him. "She didn't leave. She certainly would not have gone home." He snatched her hands, bringing them to his face. He pushed her up against the wall so hard that her head snapped against the stone, making her cry in pain.

"Edwind." Horsa reached for him.

"What did you do to her?" Edwind struggled to control his fury.

"I—" she squeaked out.

"What do you think you're doing touching my sister like that?" Varic tried to rip Edwind away from Lerin, but Edwind was too lost in his anger to be moved.

"Still yourself," Hengist told Varic. "That spoiled sister of yours is about to learn what it means to betray my family."

Varic frowned at Hengist. "What is going on here?"

Edwind didn't take his focus off Lerin. "Darya is missing, and your sister reeks of the aconite I smelled in our room." He shook the woman again. "What have you done to her?"

Lerin averted her eyes from his steely glare. "He said he was here to take her back to her cousin. She was meant to marry another man but ran away."

He released her arms and took a step back. "What are you talking about?"

"Who told you this?" Hengist asked.

"The man tasked with finding her."

"Who is this man?" Hengist demanded.

"He said his name was Eron Tyr."

"Where did he take her?" Hengist's voice matched Edwind's dangerous quiver.

She shook her head. "I don't know."

He stepped toward her.

"I swear. I was only supposed to make sure she was unconscious." She looked at Edwind. "Why do you still care for her when she lied to you?"

Edwind's anger bubbled over. "Darya didn't lie, you foolish woman." The fear on his face was reflected in his words. "If he wanted her unconscious, surely he doesn't mean to kill her."

"Eron has done a lot of questionable things," Hengist said, "but I've never known him to kill for sport or money."

"Not even he would be reckless enough to take to the sky among so many people," Horsa told them.

Edwind started for the door. "When I find her, we will meet at The Three Maidens." He fought to control the dragon that wanted to lash out at Lerin. To Varic, he said, "If I ever lay eyes on your sister again, it will be the last time she ever draws breath in her body."

"Edwind, wait." Varic rushed to catch up to him. "Let me give you my men to help search for your wife. Your secrets are safe with them. You have my word."

He held the man's gaze for a moment longer before rushing through the streets toward the city gates. Varic called to his guards, giving the order to follow Edwind.

Darya clawed her way out of the depths of the drug-induced unconsciousness to a searing pain shooting up her neck with each steady bounce of her head bobbing up and down. A heavy arm was anchored around her chest, holding her upright, and a rope was tied around her wrists, binding them to what she guessed was part of a saddle. Judging from the misty, muted fog of sheer cloth over her eyes, she had been blindfolded as well.

She tried to hold her neck still to keep her head from being jostled any more than it already was, but she barely had the strength to lift it off her chest. When she tested her grip against the ropes around her wrists, the man at her back shifted.

"Easy, girl," came a silken voice in her ear, but it wasn't Mark who spoke to her. She felt something sharp press into her side. "It's not my intent to harm you, but I won't have you using that witchery of yours on me."

She moved her head to the side, struggling to raise her chin from her chest again. Whatever Lerin used to knock her out lingered in her blood, sapping her energy. From the feel of the fading sun on her face and the songs of the twilight insects, she'd slept through the whole day in her captor's arms. There was no telling how far they'd traveled in that amount of time.

Beneath her, the winded steed relayed what he could of their journey through the unfamiliar territory. It couldn't tell her where she was. All she knew was the poor horse had been pushed to the brink of exhaustion for most of the day.

Darya offered the tired equine what little comfort she could, but the horse was made for this kind of work. It was duty-bound to serve whoever rode in its saddle. Even a hired mercenary.

She struggled against the ropes that were already chafing her skin, it only made them bite into her even more. "Who are you?"

Her head throbbed at the sound of her own voice. The slow and steady trot jostled her queasy gut, and before she could stop the coming tide of nausea that rose from her cramping stomach, she flung herself forward, thinking she was going to fly off the horse when she vomited up bile and acid.

The man tightened his arm around her and made a disgusted sound. "That ignorant woman. I told her not to use so much aconite. It's a potent herb. A little goes a long way to subdue a woman of your stature."

"Get—" She gagged, and her stomach lurched again. "Get your fucking hands off me."

His laughter shook her body with his, threatening to let loose another round of heaving. Instead of responding, he put a water skin in her mouth. The water was warm and stale, but it helped get the awful taste off her tongue. She spits the nasty liquid to the side, prompting him to let out a sharp curse. There was a petty sense of satisfaction that her aim had been true.

"That wasn't very ladylike," he said.

She let her head fall forward, trying to concentrate on the world around her. Somewhere in the distance, she picked up on a pack of wolves calling to each other. The muffled whispers of the smaller animals didn't speak of a dragon coming through their home to rescue her.

She was uncomfortable being so close to the man at her back, so she tried scooting away, but he tightened his grip on her. "You can ride up here in my arms, or I can drag you on the ground behind me." Any levity that was in his voice earlier was gone.

"Where are you taking me?"

More whispers filled the silence between them. The faint voices of the forest animals brought a secret comfort to her. She wondered if she could use them to get a message to Edwind somehow. But what good would that do since he couldn't understand them?

The blackness of her vision opened to a sweeping landscape of trees, rocks, and grass that bobbed in time with the footsteps of the horse on which they rode. Her heart pounded in her chest at this new and unfamiliar sensation. The horse bobbed his head in time with his trot, sweeping his gaze along the dim landscape.

"What's made you so excited, Lady Darya?"

Her body stiffened at her captor's words. She knew of only a handful of people who could hear another heartbeat like that and fought to calm herself. "I've been abducted by a stranger. I'm bound, blindfolded, and you won't tell me why you've taken me hostage. Am I not supposed to be scared?"

"Are you scared?"

"Yes," she said, truthfully.

"Good. That will keep you alive." He readjusted himself in the saddle, pulling the blade from her side. "We are approaching a river. I am going to lead the horse upstream. Don't try anything stupid."

Her captor eased off his steed, coming around to the front of the stallion, patting his companion reassuringly. Darya got a clear image of the face from the horse's perspective. She noted his dark demeanor matched his black soul. Her vision was drawn to the rounded scar that puckered along his left temple, and she hoped he felt every ounce of the pain when he got that wound.

The dagger he used to subdue her glinted off the remaining rays of the day. She'd never seen a black blade like that before. It was a little longer than the length of his forearm and curved into a vicious tip, but the most unusual aspect of it was how much it resembled a raven's feather. She imagined that when the serrated blade was lodged into the meaty parts of a human body, those breaks in the steel would eviscerate whatever it came in contact with.

He moved toward her, and she noticed a matching dragon's wing hilt on the other side of his belt. He pulled the reins over the horse's head and took a moment to study her. He paused at the thick cloth that cut off her vision. She was relieved that he didn't linger on other parts of her body.

When he was beside her, she noted he was tall like Edwind but leaner.

She braced herself for his touch, and he rested his hand on the small of her back and urged the horse forward. They followed the flow of the stream for what she guessed to be half a mile. Once they were on dry land again, her captor took a moment to ring out the water from his pants. Instead of rejoining her in the saddle, he walked beside her for the remainder of their trek until he announced they would rest for a while.

He pulled her to the ground. "If you try to run, you know I'll catch you before you can get very far. You won't like what will happen when I do."

"Will it be worse than what you are planning to do with me, anyway?"

Through the horse's vision, she saw him frown at the ground. "Would you care for something to eat?"

That was the second time he ignored her question about her fate. "Do you think I'm really in the mood to eat? I want you to tell me the truth about why you've abducted me."

"Does it matter?"

"Did Mark hire you?"

His sudden silence gave her the answer. When he spoke again, his voice didn't give away his emotions. "You are but a job."

She had the horse scan the trees. The power of the earth thrummed beneath her feet, yet she wasn't confident enough to use it when she was blind and bound. If she could reach out to the wolves moving through the forest, maybe they could distract her kidnapper so she could get loose of the ropes.

An idea came to her, albeit a reckless one, but she was desperate. "I have to pee."

He kept his sights on the reins he was wrapping around a thin tree. "So, pee."

"Can't a girl have some privacy?"

"You must think I'm a fool." He took hold of her arm, leading her to a clump of brambles.

She jumped and kicked at him when a hand went to the base of her dress. "What are you doing?"

"Helping you."

"Like hell you are."

"I'll look away. I promise."

"Touch me like that again, and I'll give you a matching scar on the other side of your face."

His hands left her body, and she felt him tug at the blindfold. "How do you know about my scar? Can you see through this thing?"

She clamped her mouth shut.

A hand was at the back of her neck, dragging her toward the horse. Panic made her scramble to grab onto the strength of the earth that waited for her command. A thick, gnarled clump of brushwood sprang from the ground and snaked up his legs. He confirmed her suspicions when he transformed into a dragon and broke free of her weak attempt to bind him.

Her head swam from the amount of magic she took in, and she stumbled toward the horse in a feeble attempt to flee. Something big and heavy shoved her forward, tripping her and sending her to the ground.

Damn you, woman. She heard him say.

She let out a scared cry that coincided with the stallion's high-pitched whinny. He reared up and pawed at the dragon standing over her.

"Calm down." The man came back to himself, sidling away from those dangerous hooves.

The horse continued to tear at the dirt over Darya while she curled herself into a tight ball, waiting for her captor to follow through on his earlier promise.

Instead, he jerked her to her feet and ripped away the blindfold. She squinted at the moonlight that danced across her blurry vision. It took a few seconds for the scenery to come into focus. A familiar face swam into view before he re-wrapped her wrists in more rope, tighter this time.

He poised one of the onyx blades under her chin, the deadly point digging into her frail flesh. "What are you, Lady Darya? What is this power you possess?"

"Fuck you." Her voice quivered with the fear of what he was going to do to her, and fearful tears trailed down her cheeks.

"I just might." His eyes lingered over her breasts. "If you don't tell me what you are."

She averted her head, no longer able to hold his gaze. She hated the way her body trembled against him. Out in the far reaches of the forests, she heard the distant call of a pack of wolves. Their voices yipped into the night, reaching out to her. She let her head fall back and shook out a laughing sob.

He snatched the horse's broken reins with one hand, keeping her wrists secure in his other hand. "Stop your crying. I may do a lot of vile things, but I would never force myself on a woman."

She knew better than to confess her tears didn't come from fear.

"I've proven I will overpower you if you try to use your magic on me, witch."

Keeping her head turned away from him, she said, "I'm not a witch."

"I don't care. I am stronger than you. We've wasted enough time." He tried to pull her to the horse, but she fought to hold her ground. "I grow weary of your obstinance. I don't know how Edwind puts up with you."

The weight of her glare made him flinch. "You know my husband?"

His face betrayed the surprise her words elicited. "We have a past."

"Who are you?" she asked again.

He kept silent.

"Do you even know the monster you're working for?"

He grabbed her by the arm. "I was hired to do a job. I am going to do it."

"You dragons think you are so powerful because of the beasts you carry within, but brute strength isn't all there is in this world."

Her words made him pause.

The baying of more than a dozen wolves echoed from all around them. Eron's gaze darted from tree to tree, trying to pinpoint the lupine voices that spoke to one another. When his gaze landed on Darya again, her toothy sneer made his own smile disappear.

Understanding swept over him. "That lucky dragon got himself a druidae."

She leaned into him. "A druidae goddess."

His lips parted, but before he could speak, a half-dozen wolves leaped out of the trees in unison. One second, the man was standing in front of her; the next, he was on the ground, being rolled away in a blur of teeth and fur. Another wolf was at Darya's side, chewing the ropes that bound her.

As soon as her arms were loose, she wriggled herself free and followed the wolf that helped her escape. A black dragon landed with a heavy thump, blocking her path. His leathery lips were pulled back into a snarl, showing off curved, vicious teeth.

She was ready for him that time and yanked at a line of power connected to a boulder sitting at the top of a steep hill. It punched him in the side, pushing him out of her way, leaving an opening for her to escape.

She ran for the trees and the promise of safety with the other wolves that waited for her there. She hadn't gone but a few feet when another dragon came crashing through the forest into her path. The wolves swung around toward the new interloper.

"No," she cried, running to her husband.

Edwind scooped her up in his arms. "My love. Thank the gods you're safe." His gentle touch became a possessive hug, and he pushed her behind him.

The black dragon stood atop a rocky cliff where the wolves couldn't reach him. He watched them with a stony expression.

"Eron Tyr," Edwind bellowed. "I am going to tear your limbs from your body and feed your organs to the beasts of the underworld."

The dragon chuckled, then Eron stood before them. "You always were so dramatic, old friend."

"I am not your friend."

Darya peeked around Edwind's back. "That is Eron Tyr?"

Edwind pulled her closer to him. "Yes. I don't know how he became entangled in our lives, but I'm going to make sure he never lays a hand on you again."

The wolves circled the cliff, waiting for their chance to attack. If he wouldn't have flown away, she could break apart the rock and watched him fall to his doom.

"That is one hell of a woman you have there." Eron pointed at them with a dagger. "I don't know if my employer realizes the challenge that awaits him."

Edwind turned his head to the side. "I want you to run from this place. Go back across the river. Have your wolves take you to the men who wait there. They will escort you to Atleny. I will return when I've taken care of this black-hearted bastard."

She latched onto his arm, refusing to let him go. "I'm not leaving your side. If you stay, I stay."

His enraged expression landed on the cliffs. "For once, will you please do as I say?"

One of her hands found its way to the side of his face and turned it, so he had to look at her again. "If you think I'm abandoning you to fight any battle alone, you must not believe in how much I truly love you."

Eron made a gagging sound. "I'm going to be sick, watching you two fondle each other."

Darya looked past him to the sky. Her lips curled into a sneer. "Gouge out his eyes!" she yelled.

Eron's flippant demeanor hardened into surprise before spinning on one foot and was knocked off the cliff by a handful of eagles that dived in silent unison. He morphed into his dragon, heading straight for Darya and Edwind.

Edwind had his wife in his arms and in the air, flying her away from the other dragon in the span of a few heartbeats. The birds did their best to slow Eron's pursuit with heavy blows of their own sharp claws to his dark scales.

They tore at his wings, making him screech in rage or pain, or both, but Eron wouldn't be distracted from his prize. He spotted Edwind rounding a distant mountain and shot into the night after them.

Edwind dove into a thick patch of brambles that emanated a powerful cinnamon scent, making Darya's eyes water. He wrapped her in a tight embrace, trying to calm her thundering heartbeat. Eron's heavy wings beat at the air above them, searching for where they hid.

He landed with a heavy thump, sending a flock of blackbirds into the sky. Eron wanted them to know he was there. He hoped Darya's panic would give away their hiding spot.

Edwind felt her heart race against his arm, so he pressed his lips to the side of her neck and whispered in her ear. "Keep calm, my love. He won't find us here."

She relaxed, but only a little.

They could hear Eron searching the thickets surrounding them. Edwind kept himself loose, prepared to launch them into the air at the first hint that the other man might have found them.

Darya closed her eyes, listening to some of the smaller animals skittering through the trees. They told her exactly where the other dragon was going. Some of them bound through the debris of the forest floor to draw his attention away from them. When their distraction worked, and Eron followed the false trail, she to let go of most of her fear.

Another few minutes went by, and she whimpered in his chest. Edwind pulled her closer, but she fought against him. "He's gone," she said.

"How do you know?"

"The animals. They say he is across the valley."

He helped her out of the underbrush, sweeping away dirt and debris from her hair and dress. "We need to find a safe place to stay for the night. I'll figure out exactly where we are in the morning." He tried to keep the frustration out of his voice, but it still bled through in his words. "It could take us weeks to get back to where we are supposed to meet my father." He ran a hand through his hair and let out a soft curse.

More voices from the forest made her turn away from him.

"Stay here while I find some water," he said. When she didn't respond to him, he turned. "Darya, are you listening to me?"

She shook herself from communing with the animals. "There's a cave near here and a stream through those trees." Her voice was cold and emotionless.

He took her by the hand. "I'm not angry with you."

Rounding on him, she said, "Well, I'm mad at you, acting as though you're the only one who can protect us. Just because I can't wield a sword or change into a giant beast doesn't mean I can't offer something useful."

He stared at her for a long time before his expression softened. "My god, Darya. Do you really think I can't see how special and amazing you are? Why do you think I want to protect you so fiercely? Your life is more precious to me than anything else on this earth."

"Like I said, I don't always need your protection."

"I will never stop trying to keep you safe. You cannot ask me to change who I am." He laid a forceful kiss on her.

She pulled back from him. "Quit trying to distract me with those damn lips of yours."

"Then stop arguing with me, stubborn woman." He kissed her again, softer that time.

"I think I've proven I am quite capable of taking care of myself. I held my own against Eron, didn't I?"

He chuckled, running a hand down the side of her frazzled hair. "Yes, my love. I was impressed with your use of that boulder. Come. Let's find this cave so that I may pay homage to my warrior goddess."

The midday sun was beating down on Eron by the time he made it back to the port city where Mark waited for him. It didn't take long to find the little worm in a run-down tavern taking advantage of the local brew and women. A pretty brunette sat on his lap, helping him pour another cup of ale. When Eron approached the table, he snatched the cup from the woman's hand, taking a long drink.

"Did you find her?" Mark asked, pushing the woman away, ignoring her protests.

"I did." Eron pulled the chair back from the table to keep plenty of distance between himself and the other man.

"Good. Where is she? Did you bring her here?"

"You failed to mention she was a druidae." He finished the ale. "And a goddess."

There was a genuine surprise on Mark's face, but his expression quickly turned to irritation. "What does that matter? I paid you to do a job. Where is she?"

Leaning forward, Eron said, "I don't have her."

"What?" Mark's voice rose an octave, drawing the attention of a few of the surrounding patrons.

"I will tell you where to find her. You can fight her dragon and powers to get what you want. As for me, I've fulfilled my end of the bargain."

Mark's eyes lost focus, and their usual chestnut color morphed into dangerous storm clouds. "You will take us to the girl, skamelar."

The words of his mother froze the blood in his veins. Eron sat there, staring at the creature before him, unable to take in a breath. No one else knew the nasty little pet name she used to call her son when she was in a particularly foul mood. "Who are you?"

"I am the one who will destroy you and everything you hold dear if you do not obey my commands. Until you have delivered the seedling, you are beholden to me and my vassal."

Eron sat back in the chair, debating whether to run his blade through the man's heart.

Whatever entity held Mark captive smiled and motioned for Eron's belt. "Do you think you are fast enough, dragon?"

He wasn't accustomed to being on the receiving end of threats, nor did he like the idea of this creature knowing him so intimately. There was no doubt in his mind that even if he killed Mark, the thing that lived inside his head would send someone else in his place.

Eron may not be in good standing with his old friend, but he still cared enough for the man to regret his decision to deliver Edwind's wife to this monster and the sadistic god he served.

Mark's eyes were back to normal when the barmaid returned with another tankard and refilled their cups. He slid his gaze and his hands over her lush, round bottom. "I'm afraid I won't be able to partake in your delicious bounty tonight after all, sweetheart. My friend and I must leave after we finish our drinks."

Chapter 19

HORSA PULLED A PIECE of roasted rabbit off the fire. He stared at the charred meat, not as hungry as he had been when he put it on to cook. He was too worried about Edwind and Darya. It had been over three weeks since they parted ways.

He refused to believe that a foul dragon for hire could best his son or the goddess he married. Hengist was inclined to think the same thing.

The sounds of a bickering couple brought him out of his stupor. Edwind crested the hill to the west, with Darya following a few feet behind. Their faces told of the long road they'd traveled to get there.

"See," Edwind said, motioning to his father. "Didn't I tell you we were close?"

The look she gave him was one Horsa recognized from his time with Diana. There was no mistaking the remains of their lover's quarrel etched in her furious stare. She stormed past her husband, turning her icy gaze on Horsa.

He noted the usual pink tint to her complexion was missing. In its place was a pale pallor with dark circles rimming tired, drooping eyes. He got to his feet, ready to embrace the two younglings.

She stared longingly at the food in his hand, and he held it out to her. "Are you hungry?"

She reached for it, but drew back, covering her mouth, and rushed into the forest.

Edwind looked after her, opened his mouth as if to speak, then shook his head, snatching a piece of meat from the open flames instead before plopping down beside the fire.

"Are you two alright?" Horsa asked, staring after Darya.

Edwind paused the violent gnawing long enough for him to say, "That woman is going to drive me mad."

"What happened? Did Eron hurt her?"

"What? No, of course not." He finished off the meat and threw the bones in the fire. "After we got away from him, it put us weeks behind you. Until a few days ago, I thought everything was fine. We were both road weary, sure, but good."

He grabbed another piece of food off the spit and a drink from the kettle that was steeping over the flames. "One morning, it was as if I woke up next to a stranger. We argue over the smallest things. She's stopped eating, and when she does take in food, she can't keep it in her stomach. Every time I try to bring up my concerns about how ill she is getting, she runs off crying. It's like she doesn't want to be around me anymore. I don't know what I've done."

Horsa studied the young man, suspecting the truth of their situation. "I wouldn't worry too much about her well-being. She is a strong woman."

"How can I not worry? She gets weaker by the day, and she won't let me help her. I can't lose her. Not like this."

Horsa tried to keep the laughter out of his voice. "I promise she is in no danger of dying, my boy."

His father's words struck a fresh wave of fear that showed in his pallid complexion. "What if the power inside her is doing this? What if it's too much for her, and it kills her as it did before? I won't let that happen. By the gods, I will make her listen to reason this time."

Edwind threw down the meat and the cup and ran through the trees after his wife.

Darya inhaled deep, soothing breaths, forcing the nausea to recede back into the pit of her stomach. She was so tired of being sick. Every day it was the same. From the moment she woke to the time she went to bed, she couldn't even think of food without her gut clenching into a tight ball. At first, she wondered if she'd picked up a virus from somewhere, but this had been going on for nearly a week now with no signs of letting up. She didn't know how much more her body could take.

Then there was the annoying way Edwind kept hovering over her when all she wanted was to have a few minutes to herself. Was that too much to ask? Every time she lost her temper, she would regret it immediately. She loved her husband with all her heart, but it was like she had no control over herself anymore.

She reached out to a nearby tree, taking comfort in the strength it provided. A single thought kept working its way into the forefront of her mind, and when it did, she shoved it away. The doctors made it clear. There was no chance that her body would recover from that kind of damage.

Her gaze slid down to her belly, to that symbol of a barren woman who was never supposed to conceive a child of her own. She closed her eyes, trying to calculate her last cycle.

With all that had happened, she hadn't realized she had missed her period by two weeks.

Impossible.

Edwind came stomping through the trees, pushing past branches at a half-run. The expression of fear on his face almost made her double over and vomit right then and there.

"Is something wrong? Did Mark find us?"

He ignored her question. "I cannot continue to watch you wither away in this sickness of yours while you ignore my attempts to help you. Father says you are in no danger, but I see how ill you've become. I won't stand for you pushing me away any longer. I—"

"I think I'm pregnant," she blurted out before he could go on.

He opened his mouth to say something else, but he closed it just as quickly. His gaze wandered down to her belly, and he took a half step back.

It wasn't the reaction she expected. She thought he'd be more excited. Maybe he was serious when he said he didn't want children.

"I don't know for sure," her voice was small. "I was told it would never happen for me, but I'm showing every symptom. The nausea, the mood swings."

Still, he stared wide-eyed and silent.

"Edwind, please say something."

He dropped to his knees and pulled her against him so fast that if he hadn't been there to hold her up, she would have lost her balance and fallen over. He laid an ear against her belly and closed his eyes.

"What are you doing?"

"Quiet, woman," he whispered. His hands tightened around her hips as his body trembled against hers. When he looked up at her again, his jade eyes shimmered in the sunlight with unshed tears. "My love, that is the most beautiful sound I've ever heard."

"What do you hear?"

"Our child's heartbeat," he said.

She lost herself in his kiss, letting go of the anger and frustration of the last few days. None of that mattered anymore, for she carried inside her the manifestation of their love. A miracle of life that connected them more deeply than anything else they had yet to experience.

Edwind pushed to his feet, kissing her one last time. "I was so scared you were dying."

"I thought I was for a while." She wrapped herself around him. "I still can't believe it's real. Are you sure you heard a heartbeat?"

His body shook with soft laughter. "Oh yes. It's faint, but it has a strong little dragon heartbeat."

She pulled back and caught his gaze. "What is this going to mean for our baby? It's going to have god-blood and dragon-blood. Has there ever been such a being?"

"I don't know. We will ask Grandfather when he returns. First, I want to tell my father the good news."

"What's all this?" Hengist flipped the satchel he'd been carrying over his shoulder onto the ground by the fire.

Horsa was spinning Darya in an excited hug.

"Careful, Father," Edwind said. "Her stomach is still quite delicate."

Horsa set her down and turned to Hengist. "I'm going to be a grandfather. Finally."

"It was bound to happen, the way those two go at each other," Hengist mumbled.

"Grandfather, don't be so crude."

He shrugged. "I can't say I'm surprised, regardless."

Darya said, "I don't understand how it's even possible."

Hengist snorted. "With the god-blood that flows inside you and staved off Arawn himself, do you think it couldn't heal that broken womb of yours?"

She blinked at him, feeling foolish that the thought hadn't occurred to her before.

He motioned to the sun hanging in the west. "We will stay one more night and start for the temple tomorrow. We should be able to reach it within the week. Edwind, why don't you take your wife to the falls? Let the girl rinse off her journey."

Edwind led Darya through the trees toward the sound of water breaking against the rock. "This is why we call it the Three Maidens."

He pushed past thick foliage, opening a path leading to the enclosed valley. It was walled off by full leafy vegetation flanking a triple waterfall flowing into a single, clear pool below. The rush of water echoed off the surrounding rocks, vibrating the ground with its thundering roar.

"It's beautiful." She turned in a slow, mesmerized circle, taking in the entire scene.

When she came back around to face him, he tucked a finger under her chin and turned up her face. "Not as beautiful as you are, my love. Knowing you carry our child changes everything."

"I still have a destiny to fulfill."

"This I know, but you must promise you won't fight me when I try to protect you."

"I can't do that."

He stared at her, a frown pulling at his features.

She sighed. "Fine. I promise not to be so stubborn."

When his smile returned, so did hers. "Wait here. I'll grab us clean clothes." He kissed the side of her neck before disappearing the way they came.

When he was gone, she took off her dress and waded into the cool, clear water, giving into the heavy flow of falls cascading down on her tired muscles, washing away the last few weeks of travel.

A pair of hands slipped over her shoulders, down her arms, and around the front of her waist. It had been a long time since Edwind touched her like that. She tried to turn around, but he held her against his chest.

"Let me enjoy the feel of you a while longer."

She smiled her acquiescence. His fingers floated across her skin in a light dance of delicate touches, taking his time at her breasts.

"Easy with those," she murmured. "They're a little sore."

"I will be extra gentle." He led her to the water's edge, laying her on one of the flat rocks there. True to his word, his touch was tender, and he traced his lips down her neck, pausing to circle her stiff peaks with light kisses.

She shivered in anticipation as he made his way down her belly until he reached the heat of her desire. With each flick of his tongue, she squirmed and writhed, and by the time he summoned the full force of her excitement, she'd worked her fingers deep into his hair, anchoring herself against the orgasm that threatened to shatter her from the inside out. He clung to her hips, holding her in place while she bucked against each wave of ecstasy he demanded.

Only when she was calm again did he traverse her body until he hovered over her parted lips. "I've missed the sounds you make when you give yourself to me."

"I'm sorry I've been so moody. I guess I haven't been myself."

He pushed inside her with a satisfied groan. "Oh, my love. I forgive you." He devoured her mouth and kept pace with the urging of her hands and hips.

She threw her head back and welcomed the shards of lightning that swept through her quivering body. They moved as one being again, losing themselves in the sounds of rushing water and the caress of the afternoon sun kissing their naked bodies until they were no longer thirsting for each other's touch.

They lay in the calm afterglow of their lovemaking, Edwind leaning on one elbow so he could trace his fingers along her belly.

She wrinkled her nose at him. "Why are you looking at me like that?"

"Can I not admire the beauty of my wife?"

With a roll of her eyes, she kissed him on the cheek and got back into the water to finish the bath she was promised.

Eron heard the frantic cries of the woman when he approached Mark's room. The sounds she made were not that of someone receiving the kinds of pleasure this establishment was meant for. Anger spurned him forward, and he shoved the door open to find the worm on top of a fragile little pale-haired beauty with one hand wrapped around her slender neck. She bucked at him, but Mark was too strong for her petite frame.

There was no hesitation between the doorway and the bed when Eron made those two long strides to grab the helot and throw him off the girl. "How dare you touch her with such beastly intention?" he raged.

A sliver of storm clouds passed over Mark's gaze, denoting the ire of the god that was ever-present in his mind. "I was just having a little fun with the whore here."

Eron looked at the trembling woman, pulling at the furs on the bed. "Get out."

As if waiting for that very command, she bolted from the room, ignoring the dress that lay in tatters on the floor.

"I haven't gotten my money's worth out of her yet." Mark was on his feet, grabbing for his shirt.

A new wave of anger drove Eron forward. One of the raven daggers was already in his hand, but before he reached the other man, he was across the room in a heap against the far wall. His vision warbled from the force with which he banged his head.

Mark strode to Eron's side, kneeling beside him. "Never raise a weapon against me or my vassal, or I will pluck the teeth from your head and use them to scrape the flesh from your living body." Cernunnos' blazing blue eyes bore into him, making it hard for Eron to hold his stare.

"Your helot is here to do a job," Eron said, fighting to keep his voice steady. "Maybe you should keep him on task and not fucking every woman that will spread her legs for him."

The god that puppeted Mark sat back on his haunches. A humorless smile parted his lips, making Eron's stomach roll uncomfortably. "He does get distracted easily. Perhaps you will make a better servant for my needs."

Eron pushed himself farther into the wall, easing his hand to the other dagger that still rested in its sheath.

Cernunnos scrutinized Eron's movements and made a disappointed sound. "Maybe not. You are much too willful for my taste." He backed off, giving Eron room to stand.

A thin line of blood oozed from one of Mark's nostrils, and he swayed when the god left his conscious mind. "Where is she?" He asked, wiping at the blood that fell over his top lip.

On his feet again, Eron snatched his weapon from the ground before heading to the door. He thought briefly about lying. The idea of giving over Darya to this fiend and the creature he served made his skin crawl. If he got caught in a lie, he didn't know if he could stop the god from killing him.

He should not have gone back to Atleny, but he knew Lady Lerin would give him whatever information she had. "They are meeting at The Three Maidens."

"Is that a tavern near here?"

He looked down and to the side, unable to meet the man's stare. "No. Get dressed and be ready to leave before dusk."

Darya woke to Edwind resting his head on her stomach. There was a contented grin on his face as he lay there with his eyes closed. She ran her fingers through his hair, bringing him out of his meditative thoughts. "Are you listening to our baby's heartbeat again?"

He kissed her belly a few times before crawling to her side. "It grows stronger every day."

"In my time, we have the technology to see the baby in my womb."

"That is an amazing feat. How is it possible?"

"I don't have the technical ability to explain how sonograms work, but doctors can put a moving picture on a television screen, and you can see the outline of the baby inside me."

He took one of her hands, running a thumb over the back of it. "Are you sure you don't want to go back to nineteen eighty-two?"

"Even if I knew how, I wouldn't leave this place. Sure, I'm going to miss some things like indoor plumbing. You haven't lived until you've experienced the magic of a hot shower, but all that is a small sacrifice for you and our baby." She pulled him on top of her. "I have everything I want and need right here."

Footsteps halted their impassioned exploration, and Edwind sat up, searching the surrounding trees.

"Good. You two are awake," Hengist said from somewhere out of view. "We should eat and be on our way."

"Food actually sounds good right now," she said.

With her belly full of the first proper meal in days, Darya enjoyed the lazy morning, relaxing by the fire as she watched the other men gather their belongings for the journey ahead. Every time she tried to make a move to help, Edwind pushed her back to the ground, insisting she not lift a finger.

It was only a matter of time before they had it out over this ridiculous notion that she shouldn't do any kind of manual labor simply because she was with child. For now, though, she appreciated the rest her body needed and let her husband pamper her as the doting father-to-be.

All the calm left her when she saw Horsa's head snap to attention and jumped into a defensive stance over her.

"Get Darya away from here," he told Edwind. "Now, boy."

Edwind took her by the hand and had her on her feet before Hengist's thick dragon body lumbered into the trees toward an unseen enemy.

"What's going on?" Darya was frantic to find the danger they faced, but Edwind had her encased in a protective cocoon of arms.

"I think Eron found us," Horsa said. "I'd recognize his stench anywhere."

Edwind pushed Darya into his father's arms. "Take her and get to safety. I'm going to make sure he doesn't bother us again."

"No," she said, "you aren't leaving me alone."

"You promised not to fight me."

She pressed her lips together so tight they nearly disappeared. Her eyes glistened with fearful tears. "If you get yourself killed, I'll hunt you down in the underworld and make you regret leaving me."

He kissed her, and she imprinted the feel of him in her memory. "I'd expect nothing less." He turned to his father. "Make sure we know how to find you."

Darya watched, helpless, as her heart disappeared into the trees.

Horsa took her hand, urging her away from that spot. "We need to go."

Before they could take more than a few steps, a brown-speckled hawk shot through the air. Mark landed a few feet in front of them. Horsa was between him and Darya, his outstretched wings making a barrier between them.

Darya peered around the massive body, protecting her from the man she used to know. His disheveled appearance was nothing as she remembered. He wore a leather band across his face where the falcon tore out his eye. Unkempt scruff lined his haggard features. His one remaining eye no longer held the life it once had. Now it looked like that of a dead man.

"Give me the woman," he demanded.

Horsa's response was to let out a loud warning growl.

"The master I serve does not fear you, dragon."

Reaching for the veins of power in the earth, she sent tendrils of foliage up his legs and around his torso. Mark's dull gaze flared to life in surprise. To her horror, he grinned, and his visage changed from that of Mark to the horned god Cernunnos for just a moment; and the vines were gone.

When Mark spoke again, it wasn't his voice that came out of his mouth. "That is my power you seek to usurp, seedling."

Horsa leaped at the man, but his inhuman speed easily sidestepped the attack and shoved both hands into the side of the dragon, sending it sliding across the ground and into the woods.

Darya dove for Horsa's side, but Cernunnos was already moving Mark forward, ready to cut her off. She tried to turn away from his outstretched arms and was almost free of his reach when he jumped at her, tackling her to the ground.

"Finish it." The ancient god growled. His sapphire eye glowed with fury. "Now." Mark reached for the dagger on his hip.

A symphony of growls echoed around them, and the god who held Mark hostage froze.

His hands went slack as he studied the surrounding trees.

Cernunnos looked down at her again. Genuine fear lay in his gaze. "Druidae," he whispered. "You carry her power as well."

She saw him try to retreat away from her, back to wherever he went to hide, but just like how he held her in the vision, she latched on to him, keeping him trapped inside Mark. "You're not going anywhere." Her hands squeezed the sides of the man's face, and she could feel Cernunnos fighting to escape her grasp.

"You do not possess the power to hold me here."

She knew he was probably right. Already, her arms shook with the exertion it took to keep him trapped. "I'll kill you for what you've done."

His laughter spat blood on her face. "You will kill this body, but I will still live on to hunt you down."

Even after all Mark had done, she couldn't bring herself to take his life. She didn't want his blood on her hands, so she released the hold on Cernunnos and pulled away. As soon as she did, the monster was gone.

Mark got to his feet, staggering back a few steps. His eye was once again his own. He stared down at her, blinking the remnants of his master out of his consciousness. He wiped at his mouth, pulling back a blood-smeared fist. "You should have killed me."

Horsa burst through the trees. His crimson scales were like raging flames in the afternoon sunlight as he loped toward Darya.

Mark took another step away from her, then he was in the air, disappearing over the waterfalls.

Horsa skidded to a stop at her side, helping her to her feet. "Are you alright? Did he hurt you?"

She shook her head. Whatever calm facade she'd been holding onto cracked wide open, and the fissure of tears flowed down her cheeks.

Horsa took hold of her arms. "We need to get you to safety."

"No." She tried to pull back. "I'm going to find Edwind. I need to know he is okay."

"I promise there is no man, beast, or god in creation safer than your husband is right now."

She gave him a questioning look.

"If he sees fit, one day, my father will tell you of his days as a death dragon and what it means for him still. Eron is a fool to cross him." He held out his hand. "Now, will you allow me to keep my promise to my son?"

With a deep reluctance in her heart, she put her hand in his.

Chapter 20

SHADOWS DANCED ACROSS THE narrow chamber as Darya paced the length of the jagged rock wall, eyeing the darkness beyond the opening. Horsa had been gone for a long time.

Too long.

He promised to be back by now. What if they got past Edwind and Hengist and found their hiding place? There was nowhere for her to run. She was trapped.

Footsteps echoed from somewhere in the tunnels, making her scramble for the power of the earth. If anyone but Horsa came through that opening, she was prepared to send the weight of the mountain on top of them.

When Horsa's face appeared from the darkness, she let out her breath along with the magic she was holding. "Did you find them?" she asked.

He stepped around the fire, refusing to meet her stare. His clothes were damp and carried the scent of the summer storm that still clung to him.

She started for the dark tunnel. "I'm going after them."

"No. You need to wait here, where you are safe. They will return."

"It's been two days." She clenched her hands into fists, struggling to keep her temper under control. The flames of the fire roiled in time with her emotions. "They should have been back already."

"They will return," he said again.

She rushed into the darkness, ignoring Horsa's pleas. A harsh wind blew heavy rains into the mouth of the cave. The dreary, overcast sky reflected the weight in her chest.

Horsa joined her on the other side of the opening, and they watched the horizon in an uneasy silence for a few minutes. Darya crossed her arms, refusing to look away from the hillside. "Are you sure they can find us?"

"I left markers."

"What if they got separated?"

"My father would sacrifice his own life before abandoning his grandson, and there has yet to be a creature that's found a way to kill that old dragon."

The figure of a man crested over the hill in the distance. It was impossible to make out who it was through the veil of rain. She leaned closer to the opening. "There's someone out there."

"I'd recognize that weathered face anywhere," Horsa said.

"Hengist?"

He nodded.

"Where's Edwind? I don't see him." She ran out into the deluge, slipping out of Horsa's reach.

When Hengist saw her running toward him, he glanced over his shoulder. Her husband rushed over the hill past the elder dragon.

"Edwind!" she yelled.

The moment Edwind spotted her, he let his dragon loose so he could race across the field. When he was within his wife's grasp, he swept her up in his arms, showering her with a flurry of kisses. She locked her arms around his neck and refused to release her hold on him.

The storm had washed away a lot of the blood from the numerous cut and gashes on his upper body. What remained of his shirt lay in tatters at his waist. "What happened? Did Eron and Mark do all this?"

"Bah." Hengist snorted. "Those two weaklings led us into a group of dragon hunters."

She scrunched up her face. "Dragon hunters?"

Hengist spat on the ground. "Let's hope you never have the displeasure of dealing with them. It's fortunate we got away with as little bloodshed as we did. Unfortunately, Eron and Mark escaped as well."

Edwind grabbed hold of Darya's hand, leading her back to the open mouth of the cave.

"Come, let's get under shelter before we all drown."

They followed Horsa through the tunnels to the fire. Edwind sat down with his wife in his lap and began wringing the excess water from her hair and clothes. "I was worried we wouldn't make it back before they found you again."

"We may have been able to lose them in all the chaos," Hengist said, "but you know Eron can track us. We need to get Darya to the temple sooner than later."

"You two need rest," she objected.

Edwind cupped her face in his hands. "I want to take you back to Didean and forget about Cernunnos and Mark and all of this nonsense, and we can raise our child, never to think about this stupid quest again." Darya started to argue, but he went on. "I know Cernunnos will never stop until you kill him. To do that, we need to get you to the temple and reach the destiny that waits for you there."

She squeezed his hand. "How far away are we?"

Horsa nodded to the east. "I'd say another half day's journey. As soon as the rain lets up, we will be on our way."

When the group set out for the temple, Edwind kept them going at a grueling pace, pushing through branches and brush while making sure none of them snagged Darya's clothes and skin. She was having a hard time keeping up with him. Horsa and Hengist were at her back, and the few times she dared look over her shoulder, she saw them struggling almost as much as she was.

At one point, Edwind stopped so suddenly that Darya bounced into him, having to grab onto his waist to keep from falling back to the ground.

"What is it?" Hengist asked. His eyes shone with the afternoon sun peeking through the thick canopy of leaves above their head.

Edwind turned a slow circle, one arm holding her to his back. "I think we are being followed."

Horsa lifted his nose in the air, taking in a deep breath. "Damn them," he said. "Take Darya to the temple. Your grandfather and I will stay back and search the forest."

Edwind didn't hesitate. He held tight to his wife's hand and took off running. They fled through the trees, not caring that the outreaching branches scraped at their faces and arms.

The temple wasn't much farther now. Its call sang to her from the depths of the ground she walked on. Though she didn't pull at the power, she opened herself to it and let it push her faster until she was running ahead of Edwind.

By the time the sacred place loomed into view, they were both panting and covered in sweat. He squeezed her hand, making her slow down and releasing the power back into the earth. They were near a clearing, where Darya could see remnants of ancient stone reflecting the light like a beacon that guided them forward.

Something big and black knocked Edwind out of her grasp. In the following heartbeat, someone snatched her from behind, securing their arm around her chest as the cold kiss of a blade was lodged under her jawline.

She forced her head to the side and saw Edwind being dragged to the ground. Eron snapped an iron shackle around his throat and secured it with a heavy lock. Thick, sharp spikes threatened to pierce the delicate flesh at his neck, making dimples where they rested.

"Edwind," she tried to scream his name, but fear made her voice come out frail and broken.

Mark's grip on her tightened. "There's no escape this time."

She wasn't sure who was speaking to her. His voice was too raspy to tell if it was God or man behind those hoarse words.

Edwind bucked and punched at the man on top of him, but Eron slipped an arm between Edwind's arms and back, yanking him to his feet.

"Get this shackle off me," Edwind growled.

Eron held a blade, ready to pierce his lung. "Don't fight me, old friend. You know what will happen if you bring out your dragon with that thing around your neck."

"Damn you, Eron. Let me save her." He pulled against the other man, but Eron shared Edwind's dragon's strength and kept him in place.

Darya grabbed at Mark's arm. "Don't do this, please," she begged.

"I'm sorry. It's not about Annie anymore." Mark let the knife fall away from her neck and used the hilt to hit himself on the forehead. "He's in my head. All the time. He won't let me go."

Fear, anger, and helplessness threatened to rip her apart. There was a moment of clarity, and she scrambled to take in the power beneath her feet. Vines sprouted from the earth and snaked up Mark's legs, to his torso and out across his arms, tearing him away from her body. She leaned forward as if to run, but the tendrils disintegrated, and he tightened his hold once again.

"Your stolen magic will not save you, seedling." There was no doubt who controlled Mark now when the knife was at her throat again.

The blade bit into her skin, making her cry out. She held her stare steady on her husband, who writhed and cursed the man at his back. She wanted his face to be the last one she saw before leaving this world. "I love you."

"DARYA!" Edwind roared.

The ground trembled from the weight and ferocity of Edwind's hulking dragon body loping over the terrain to reach them. His mouth was wide open, ready to chomp down on Mark's vulnerable head.

Mark froze, then threw Darya to the side, preparing for Edwind's incoming blow. Edwind was within a few feet of the man when Mark's body jerked to the side, a feathered onyx blade lodged to the hilt in his neck. His eyes swirled from sapphire to brown as his life's blood spurted in long arterial bursts in time with his slowing heartbeat. He dropped to his knees when his strength left him.

Darya scrambled away from the dying man, watching the life fade from his dark eyes. Edwind had her in his arms within seconds, dragging her to safety.

He wiped away the blood from the shallow cut on her neck. "My love," he whispered, enveloping her in a tight embrace.

Eron sauntered up to Mark's corpse with the steel shackle in one hand. He knelt to retrieve his dagger, tearing away flesh when he yanked it from the dead man. After wiping the blood and bits on Mark's shirt, he put it back on the hilt of his belt. "I was never going to let him kill her. I needed him distracted. I needed that thing inside his head distracted."

Edwind released Darya before unleashing his dragon on Eron. He shrieked, and Eron barely had time to match the incoming blow with a claw of his own. The two dragons flailed at each other, knocking down trees and gouging the earth with their claws.

Horsa and Hengist came running through the forest, pulling her out of the path of destruction.

"Should we help?" Horsa asked.

Eron jumped out of Edwind's reach, holding out his hands in a placating manner. "Would you control yourself?"

"You've gone too far," Edwind said, his voice breaking from the cacophony of emotions that twisted his features. "I will kill you for abducting my wife and giving her over to that monster."

"I made sure she stayed alive, you idiot. I made sure you both lived."

Darya seized her husband's arm, pulling his face to hers. She cut off his anger with a kiss.

When she leaned back, she said, "I don't care about Eron or what he did to me. None of that matters right now." She nodded over her shoulder. "Our destiny is through those trees."

He tried to look at Eron, but she held his gaze on her. "He doesn't matter anymore."

He lowered his eyes to the place where his child grew inside her. "You're right. You and our baby are safe. Let's finish this so we can go home."

Edwind and Darya approached the entrance to the forest temple, being careful in the thick foliage. Tight-knit limbs threatened to choke out the midday sun above their heads. Her gaze wandered up the pale bark of the roots that wrapped around the open doorway where her fate waited. Thin beams of muted light trickled through the intertwined foliage, and when she moved her body in and out of the glow, she could feel the power of the sacred sanctuary flow through her.

"Do you want me to go in with you?"

She entwined her fingers with his. "I think I have to do this alone. No harm will come to me. Not here."

Horsa and Hengist pushed their way through the under-brush.

"Good. You haven't gone inside yet," Hengist said. "I want-ed to warn you about what you may be facing."

"There's nothing malicious about this place."

"Your people put too much faith in your gods and goddesses. These beings you worship are not as infallible as they would have you to believe."

"You've told me that on more than one occasion."

There was a hint of a smile that curled his lips. "Whatever Gaia says to you, do not take her words as the only truth."

She clung to Edwind's hand as she stepped up to the darkened entryway. "I know that what waits for me beyond the threshold is our destiny, but I'm still scared of what I'll find."

He gave her his strength by way of his embrace. "Go, my love, so that we may return home and face what comes next together."

It took her a long time to let go of him. At last, she made herself turn toward the darkness of the archway. She took one step, then another, and another until she passed from this realm to the next.

The transition from the forest to the temple was like falling off a cliff. Her body jerked forward into a vast, black oblivion. She flailed her arms, trying to find something, anything to grab onto to stop the descent into the maddening nothingness.

The impenetrable darkness gave way to wavering shards of light that lanced across her sight, cutting through the veil of the oily pitch. Familiar patterns shimmered throughout her vision, but she was helpless to stop what was coming.

She hit the water with so much force that what little breath was in her lungs pushed out in a quick huff. Her arms thrashed wildly in panicked sweeping motions to get her head above the waves.

Trembling fingers found the comforting pressure of sand that she used to pull herself forward toward where she hoped was the shore. As soon as her face felt the sweet cool breeze of fresh air, she coughed out a mouthful of saltwater, retching and trying to catch her breath.

She got far enough out of the water that she could lie down without the fear of the waves sweeping her back into the sea.

It took her a few minutes to gather the strength to get up on her hands and knees. Surely, there was a less horrifying way for Gaia to have brought her there.

The sting of salt made her vision hazy, but she had a distinct impression that she recognized some of the landscape. There was a small shape running toward her from inland. Her vision was clear enough for her to recognize the two-story building she never thought she'd see again.

Not in this year.

Not without Edwind.

"Miss Darya." The little boy's voice cut through her confusion.

She looked over her shoulder at the vast, open ocean. This wasn't right. She didn't belong here. Not anymore.

Marcos was at her side. His small hands were trying to help her off the ground. "Come on. They're waiting for you."

The concerned look on the little boy's touch quelled her need to lash out. "Who is waiting for me?"

"Horsa and Ronwen." He helped her get to her feet. Taking her by the hand, he pulled her toward the Dragon's Rest.

But not Edwind. Not her husband. Her heart threatened to shatter right then in there. If not for the anger that boiled her blood, she didn't know if she could have made the short trek to the inn.

Chapter 21

Familiar faces greeted Darya when she entered the dining room of the Dragon's Rest. With every breath she took, the tightness in her chest squeezed her lungs until she thought she would suffocate in her grief. Her eyes filled to the point of overflowing, tears streaming down her sand-encrusted cheeks. It didn't matter if they were from sadness or anger; they still came from a place of loss.

"Why am I here?" She pushed away the towel someone handed her, instead focusing her gaze on Ronwen. "Send me back to Edwind."

Her usual sour expression softened, and she turned an uncertain glance at Horsa.

"She can't," Horsa said. "Your destiny led you here."

Fury flared inside her, and glowing embers in the fireplace erupted into roaring flames, making everyone in the room jump. "My destiny is with my husband."

He took a step toward her. "There's so much we wanted to tell you before you went to the past, so much you should have been prepared for. You were never meant to stay—"

"How can you say that? I'm carrying his child. I can't do this without him. I won't do it without him. Now, return me to Edwind." Her anger bled away, leaving only desperation. "Please."

"My love."

The sound of the voice that she had left a thousand years in the past brough her around to the open patio doors.

A man with her husband's face stood there. He had Edwind's jade eyes and snarky half-smile. His hair was clipped short to his head, and his once full beard was now trimmed neat and tight against his sharp jaw.

"I can't believe it. My wife has been rendered speechless." He closed the distance between them. His kiss drew an involuntary cry of relief from her, which opened a floodgate of tears. "I've missed you so much." His arms trembled as he held tight to her.

The words he spoke brought her back from the edge of emotional insanity. "How did you get here?"

"You two are going to have a powerful little goddess," Horsa said.

She stared into her husband's eyes. "What is he talking about?"

Edwind smiled. "Not long after you stepped into the temple, our daughter came to us. She told me you were never coming back. Not to nine eighty-two."

Her gaze fell to her belly. "I don't understand. Our baby—our daughter—came to you? From when?"

"She couldn't say," Horsa told Darya. "She was only there to give Edwind a choice to stay in nine eighty-two or travel to the future with you."

"There was no choice." Edwind ran the back of his fingers down her cheek. "You are my home, Darya. Both of you."

"What about Gita? Saebbi? This should have been my decision. I should have been able to stay." She turned her renewed anger toward Ronwen. "What is so important that I had to come back? There's nothing for me here. I have no family. No friends."

The look Horsa gave her stilled her anger. "We are your family, child. We have always been and will always be your tribe. You are meant to carry on our bloodline in this time and place as Gita did back then."

Edwind distracted her with his damnable lips. Whatever thought had been ready to leave her mouth got lost on the tip of his tongue, and it reminded her she had the most important part of her life in her arms.

"I don't know if Marcos needs to be seeing this," Mrs. Beal said in a hushed voice.

Edwind broke their kiss, keeping his gaze locked on his wife. "I've waited a long time for that kiss."

Darya took a step back, studying his appearance more closely. "How long have you been here?"

"Despite your daughter's power," Ronwen said, "she miscalculated the portal to send Edwind to us. Instead of bringing him to this moment to join you, she sent him a year before your arrival to Broughied."

"A year?"

"One long, lonely year," Edwind said.

"So, you've been here the whole time I was here?"

He nodded.

An epiphany dawned on her. "It was you in the trees that first day."

"You don't know how hard it was to watch you walking these streets and not be able to go to you. But you weren't the woman I fell in love with."

She shook her head, trying to get her discombobulated thoughts in order. "On the beach with Dino?"

"I wasn't going to let another man touch you, even if you were not yet mine."

Horsa put his arms around the couple. "Take your wife home. She needs her rest."

"Home?" she asked.

Edwind smiled. "I have so much to show you, my love."

He settled Darya into the passenger seat of a Mercedes painted in the same shade of burnt copper as the bricks that made up the Dragon's Rest, then slid behind the wheel.

"You can drive?"

"It was an odd experience at first." He took her hand and kissed the back of her fingers. "There were a lot of things I struggled with when I first arrived."

The motion of the car going around one corner after another had her stomach twisting in on itself. She closed her eyes against the strange sensation, but that made her nausea worse.

Squeezing his hand, she leaned for the door. "Stop the car."

He pulled to the side of the road and was at her door in a matter of seconds. It took all her willpower to keep the roiling in her gut from working up and out of her mouth. Edwind had a hand at her back, rubbing in small circles, his palm warming her skin.

"I've never been car sick before." She rested her head on his shoulder. "Then again, I've never been pregnant before."

"We aren't that far from home. I'll carry you if need be."

She ran her fingers through his short hair. "A year in the modern world hasn't changed you at all."

He was careful to keep his kiss light, barely brushing his lips against hers. "I've missed this."

When she was sure she wouldn't be sick again, he returned to the driver's seat. She leaned on his arm as he shifted gears through the winding, lush countryside. He pulled the car up a winding dirt path. Tall, reedy grass swayed in a soft breeze preceding their arrival.

Her mouth dropped open in stunned awe when the house came into view. "That's your house?"

"Our house, my love."

The car came to a stop in front of a two-story red brick cottage that had the look of something built in the late forties or early fifties. Even in the dusk of twilight, Darya could tell that the shutters that flanked the shaded windows had been newly repainted a pale yellow, her favorite color. The deep, rich red and brown-colored bricks, though weather-worn, were free of the telltale aged dirt and grime she'd seen on some of the other buildings in the village.

She paused at the front door, peering into the flowerbeds on either side of the entryway. The scent of the fresh blooms reminded her of the gardens on Didean.

"Mrs. Beal helped me plant them, but I don't have the talent you do," he said.

She patted his arm. "They aren't beyond saving."

He pushed open the heavy wooden door that reminded her of one she'd seen in the castle on the island. "Welcome home." He led her over the threshold.

She squinted her eyes at the harsh light that assaulted her vision.

"I know." He dimmed the bulbs as they walked past the entryway to the living room. "It took me a while to get used to this strange lighting."

As she looked over the decorations, they struck a familiar chord with her. "Is some of this stuff mine?"

"Don't be angry. Father had Janine send over your things after you left for Broughied."

She turned in a slow circle. Horsa knew there would be no going back to Dallas. "My clothes?"

"They are in our room." He pulled her toward the stairs. "Come. I want you to see the nursery."

He led her to a door that was decorated with pale pink and yellow roses. When she stepped inside, she sucked in a sharp breath. "It's all so beautiful." She traced the intricate carvings of the baby furniture that lined each wall.

"I made each piece just for her."

He took her by the hand again. "I've been waiting for so long to share this room with you."

The master suite waited like a throne room. There was a king-size bed on the far wall draped in sheer white curtains. A set of double doors led to a small balcony overlooking the ocean. When she bypassed the bed for the bathroom, the disappointed look he gave her was fleeting.

She opened the glass door and turned on the water. Patting his face, she said, "I haven't had a shower in a very long time. You're going to have to indulge me." She unbraided her hair before untying her dress.

Edwind watched her with hungry eyes.

She was about to drop her clothes on the floor when she said, "Have you never thought about the fun we could have in here together?"

His hands were already unbuttoning his shirt and pants before she stepped under the water. The moan that left her lips when the hot water struck her body was nearly euphoric. "I didn't think I'd ever feel anything like this again."

"You weren't lying when you said modern plumbing was a thing of pure magic."

His self-control lasted for as long as it took her to wash her hair before his hands began tracing the contours of her curves. He moved over her skin like a blind man trying to capture the image of her body with his fingers rather than with his eyes.

Soon, touch wasn't enough to slake the desire to relearn every delicious inch of her. Lonely lips that yearned for the velvet smoothness of her breasts traced around his favorite buds.

His chest rumbled when he ran his palms over her hips and tucked a hand between her legs. "Forgive me if I am not the fierce lover you desire." He turned her around, bracing her against the tiled seat. "But I will make sure you are satisfied before the night is over."

He grabbed her hips and plunged inside her, eliciting a ravenous groan. His professions of love came in quick whispers in the old tongue, culminating in a frantic release that nearly took him to his knees, leaving him heaving at her back.

She turned around and tenderly traced the sharp line of his jaw with her fingers. "Maybe this slippery shower isn't the best place to get out all of your pent-up sexual frustration."

His smile tugged at her heart like it had the first time she saw it. He turned off the water and helped her dry off before leading her to the bed. He tried to push her back on the duvet, but she smacked his hands away from her.

"What are you doing?" he asked.

She urged him onto his back and straddled his waist. "You've been waiting a long time for me. Shouldn't I be the one satisfying your every need?"

The amber in his eyes flared to life as his mouth worked in wordless sounds when she slid her lips down his chest in delicate kisses. He pulled at her arm, but she pushed his hand aside. His whole body jerked when she took his hardness into her mouth.

"Woman, you play a dangerous game."

She didn't respond with words, instead running her tongue around his tip, letting him slide back into her mouth. He sat up, swung her around, and pulled her legs over his shoulders. "You will not deny me your pleasure while you take mine."

They lost themselves to each other until time held no meaning. Neither of them could recall leaving that place of togetherness until, at last, they were forced apart when their bodies couldn't sustain any more of the longing they felt for one another.

They lay in each other's arms, Edwind running a hand up and down one of her arms. "I want you still, but I just don't have the strength."

She pulled him into her for a kiss. "I'm not going any-where."

"No, sweet druidae. I won't let anything tear us apart again."

Sunrise had come and gone when Darya woke to the feel of her husband's gentle caressing as she swept a hand lightly along her arm Even though she kept her eyes closed, she felt his gaze on her, as light as the touch of his fingers on her skin. The grin that curled her lips came as her pulse quickened.

"I could lie here staring at your smile for the rest of eternity," Edwind said.

"How long have you been watching me?"

"Since before the sun was up. I keep thinking this is all a dream, and when I wake, you will be gone."

She got up on one elbow and leaned into him. "It's not a dream."

He was on top of her, his mouth at her neck and moving down her shoulders. "You're lucky I value your needs over my own pleasure. I distracted you from dinner last night. You must be starving." He slid off her and made his way across the room to a dark cherry wood chest of drawers.

"My appetite was very much satisfied. It's hard to believe I've been gone from your life for a year, yet for me, it's been less than a day," she said.

He returned to the bed with a pair of blue jeans and a black t-shirt that looked wholly out of place on him. He sat down on the edge of the bed, the smile on his face not quite reaching his eyes. "There were times I wanted to go to America and make you remember me. Of course, Father would remind me how dangerous it was for you to meet me before you traveled to nine eighty-two. I wouldn't do anything to risk this; us."

She sat up, running the tips of her fingers against the softness of his beard, and he slid a hand up to one of her breasts. "I better head downstairs and start breakfast before I can no longer control myself. You're going to love my blueberry pancakes."

"Those happen to be my favorite. How did you know?"

"I've learned a lot about you over the last year, Darya Laine."

She fell back onto the bed. "There is a reason I never divulged that information."

"It's a lovely name, befitting a ravishing goddess." He leaned over, stealing one last kiss before standing.

"Did our daughter tell you her name?"

He shook his head. "She said we will figure it out."

"What will she look like?"

"Beautiful, just like her mother."

When he was gone, Darya looked through the clothes hanging in the wardrobe. All her dresses were there. Her t-shirts and shorts were in the chest of drawers, plus some new pieces she didn't recognize. She chose a strapless plumb and teal gingham sundress and a pair of white sandals. Instead of putting her hair in its usual braid, she grabbed a hairband from the bathroom and put it in a loose ponytail.

On her way to the nursery, she stepped inside to get a better view of the furniture. She ran a finger over the filigree, and it struck a chord of familiarity. The same talented hands that made the baby furniture had chiseled the game pieces from the island.

She headed downstairs and paused by the game table, grabbing a pale white knight. The board was an exact replica of the one they shared their first kiss over, but the pieces were the same ones from all those years ago. She set the knight back where he belonged and strode through the living room to the kitchen, where her dutiful husband moved between the cabinets and stovetop with the nimble finesse of a man forced to live the life of a bachelor.

She felt guilty for not being there for him, even if the circumstances were out of her control. What if she could warn their daughter about the mistake she was going to make? Would it change anything for them now?

While she stood there contemplating the delicate nuances of time travel and what the ramifications would be if they changed the outcome of the past, Edwind turned from his pancake-making and swept her up in a hug.

"That dress looks amazing on you." He kissed her cheek and whispered in her ear, "It would look much better on the floor."

She pulled back. "Did you carve the pieces on the chess table?"

"How did you know?"

"I recognized your work from the nursery. Is there anything you can't do?"

"I can't call upon the power of the earth. I'm simply a man with idle hands." He intertwined his fingers in hers. "Now I have something much better to do with them."

Leading him to the couch, she pushed him down and straddled his lap. Eager hands worked at the belt of his jeans to free him from their restrictive confines.

"What about breakfast?" he asked, pulling the dress above her head.

"I'm suddenly not very hungry for food." She captured his lips, quieting any more protests.

Later, when her hunger for her husband was fulfilled, she lay nestled into the back of the plush leather cushions of the couch, with Edwind resting his head on her belly. "I've missed the sound of her heartbeat."

She ran her fingertips along the contours of his shoulders. After kissing her stomach one last time, he held himself over her, eyes roaming the beauty of her naked curves. "I love you."

She didn't have time to respond when the front door opened, and a gruff voice boomed, "Edwind, my boy."

Edwind looked up from his position over his wife. "Grandfather? What are you doing here?"

Hengist ignored the naked couple on the couch, following the smell of food coming from the kitchen. "I'm here to see the woman carrying my great-grandchild. Now hurry and get dressed. Your father isn't far behind me."

Edwind took the blanket off the back of the couch, holding it up so she could dress out of view of the kitchen. His face burned with embarrassment. "I thought he was coming over later in the day."

When they were fully clothed, they joined the old dragon in the dining room. Hengist threw his arms around Darya. "Child, it is good to hold you again."

"It must have been hard not to give me that hug on the plane."

He laughed. "You remember that?"

"When Gaia sent me back, all of my memories returned."

"How did you get in here, anyway?" Edwind asked. "I keep the doors locked."

"Your grandfather is a dragon of many talents."

"Uh, huh." There was a knock at the door. "That must be Father."

When they were alone, Hengist leaned into her. "I'm glad to see him smiling again."

"I can't help but feel a guilty about what happened. I should have been here."

"This is the way things are meant to be."

"Shouldn't we warn our daughter in the future? Can we tell her to be more careful when she sends him back?"

Hengist's smile vanished. "Horsa and I and others of our kind are bound by fate's laws, and so shall you be when it comes to what you know of the past and the future. If you try to change anything that is meant to happen, the consequences will be far worse than whatever benefit you seek. Promise me you will never attempt to alter it."

She expected him to start smiling again, as he often did when he tried to get the point across. The desperate look in his eyes chilled her blood. "Okay. I promise."

His smile returned, and he cupped her cheeks in his palms. "There's so much I wish I could tell you two. Many wonderful things are in store for you and your children."

"Children?"

There was a mischievous twinkle in those jade jewels. "Oops. I wasn't supposed to say that."

Edwind returned to the kitchen with his father and Ronwen in tow. Horsa gave Darya a quick peck on the cheek before his gaze wandered to where the smell of pancakes hung in the air. "Is that food for everyone?"

Edwind rolled his eyes. "Sure. I can make more."

Chapter 22

When everyone finished eating, Hengist, Horsa, and Ronwen walked to the back porch while Darya stayed in the kitchen to help Edwind clean up the mess from breakfast. Moving side by side with him was awkward at first. He had been so used to having the small space to himself for so long that her presence seemed to hinder his progress rather than help. At one point, she had to step away when she noticed him getting frustrated.

He put down the dish he was drying and turned to her. "Are you alright?"

"I don't know. It's like I don't belong here. Like I don't fit into your life anymore."

The sad expression that fell over his face made her guilt even worse. "How can you say that? I've been counting the days until you came back to me."

As she stood there, staring into the eyes of the man she loved more than anything else in the world, she considered shoving aside her insecurities just so she didn't have to confront him with her own feelings.

She tucked herself into his arms. "I know it will take time to get back to where we were before...." She let the sentence fall off with a long sigh. "I feel like I'm in the way of this life you've had to build for yourself. It's silly, I know, but I can't help it."

He tried to look her in the eyes, but she hung on to him, unable to meet his stare. "What if I had listened to you, and we returned to the island instead of going to the temple? You wouldn't have had to leave your family and your home."

"You are my home, Darya." He hugged her tight to him. "I promised I would travel a thousand years to be with you, and that is what I have done."

She untangled herself from his waist and kissed his cheek. "Go on out to the porch with the others. I'll finish here. It will give me time to learn where everything goes." He hesitated, but she pushed him out of the kitchen. "Go," she insisted. "Let me get acquainted with my new home."

When he was gone, she took her time going through each cabinet and memorizing how Edwind had arranged every-thing. He had been meticulous about the layout of the dish-es, keeping the most used utensils, pots, and pans within arm's reach of the stove top. Everything was organized in a way that made it easy to go from oven to plate to drink to the table. It was the most coordinated kitchen she'd ever seen. Much more so than the chaos she kept in her old apartment.

Once the dishes were clean and put away, Darya went to join the others on the porch only to find Horsa and Ronwen lost in their own conversation while Hengist was leaned back in one of the wicker chairs with his feet propped up on the rail. His eyes were fixed on the ocean. She followed his gaze and saw Edwind strolling along the beach. By the time she reached the water's edge, he was searching the horizon as if trying to find his old home among the waves.

"There you are," she said, tucking her arm into his.

He smiled, but it fell too quickly.

"What's wrong?"

"I was just thinking about the island and what it looks like after all this time."

"You haven't been there yet?"

He shook his head, returning to his vigil over the ocean. "I've been trying to convince myself to go, but I couldn't bear the thought of what I'll find." Pulling her closer, he said, "Will you come with me?"

"Of course. I'll go anywhere with you."

When they arrived on the island, he flew them to where his home once stood. Now there were only a few stones left of the grand castle. So much of the landscape had changed over the last thousand years. The cliff where she sank the ships had long since crumbled into the sea below. The valley where the village once sprawled across the open fields was overgrown with tall, reedy grass.

Time had erased nearly everything of Edwind's past.

She stood back and let him walk among the memories of his childhood. She couldn't imagine how much he must miss Gita and Saebbi. Her heart ached for their loss as well.

Watching him stroll through the ruin of his home manifested the name of their child. "I know what we are going to call her."

He reached up, wiping at the wetness forming at the corners of his eyes. "Who?"

"Our daughter."

He made the short hike up the hill to where she stood. "Tell me, my love."

"Brigita Diane."

He took her face in his hands and let his lips say what he could not, then turned her back to his chest so they could both watch the lazy waves of the ocean. He kept drawing in a deep breath, holding it for a few seconds, then letting it out with a long sigh.

"What's on your mind?" she asked, finally.

After another deep breath, he said, "I've been thinking about this for a while now. When Mark showed up at the inn, Father found a priestess to place wards around The Dragon's rest and our house to protect us from dangers such as Cernunnos and his ilk."

She rolled in his arms to face him. "Protect us how?"

"As long as we stay within the bounds of those walls, no harm will come to us."

"That's great. At least Cernunnos can't get to us in our sleep."

"Exactly." He shifted his stance.

"Are you sure you're alright? You're acting strange."

"Like I said, I've been contemplating this for almost as long as you've been gone. What if you didn't have to kill Cernunnos? You and Brigita wouldn't have to face such dangers."

She stepped away from him, moving herself in front of his field of vision. "What are you saying? That I should let that monster go on torturing and raping more women for the sake of my own safety?"

"And our daughter's safety as well."

"I can't believe you're really suggesting this. You didn't see what he did to those women. What he did to my mother, and how it affected her afterward."

He took her by the shoulders, his expression set in a hard determination. "I don't care about other people. I only care for you and my family."

"Even if I agreed to this ridiculous notion, you can't expect us to stay in that house for the rest of our lives. I won't be held prisoner in my own home, nor will I allow my children to live that way, either."

"You won't be a prisoner. I can have Father make more wards."

"No, Edwind. I won't agree to it. I have a destiny to fulfill, and it's freeing those people. My people. Just like you had a duty to protect those on this island, I have to think about my mother's friends and family that are cursed to that sadistic god." She jerked away from him.

"You barely survived the last attempt on your life."

"But I did survive, and I will do so again."

He crossed his arms, refusing to give in. "I'm sorry, but I won't allow you to go through with it. I will do whatever I have to do to keep you and Brigita safe."

"You won't allow me?" Her volatile emotions pulled at the tendrils of power at her feet. "And how do you think you will stop me?"

"I've made up my mind, Darya. This is one battle I cannot not concede."

It took a great deal of self-control not to lash out at him, and she knew if she didn't get away from this conversation, she would lose her temper. "Take me home." Her voice was dangerously quiet.

"Not until you agree to my terms."

"Take me home!" she yelled. The ground shook, and a shallow crevice split the grass between them.

Jumping backward from the violent outburst, he shouted back, "Fine!"

Darya threw open the sliding glass door expecting the house to be empty, but Horsa, Ronwen, and Hengist were still sitting around the table drinking tea when she entered. They took one look at her red face, then at Edwind storming up the walk behind her, and knew the real storm had yet to come.

"We're not done," he said, slamming the sliding door closed. "We are far from done, woman."

"There's nothing more to discuss." Her eyes raked over faces staring at them from the dining room table. "Why don't we ask them what they think about your ridiculous idea?"

Edwind said, "Oh, no. You're not involving anyone else. This is between us."

She whirled on him. "It's not our decision, Edwind. It's mine. This is my destiny. I'm the one who was born with his blood running through my veins. You don't get a say."

He pointed his finger at her stomach. "That is my child you carry inside you, so that gives me just as much bloody say as you."

Horsa stepped up beside them. "Stop it. Both of you."

They turned their anger on him.

"What happened between you two?" Hengist asked them.

Darya shoved her hands in her arms and turned away while Edwind told his father about his plan to keep her from having to fulfill her fate. "It's the only way to guarantee their safety," he finished.

Ronwen stepped forward. "And Cernunnos will be left to brutalize more women,"

"Exactly," Darya said. "Shouldn't our daughter's presence in the past prove we survive this fight?"

"Or it means you did as I asked and gave up on this stupid quest." Edwind shot back.

Hengist let out a sigh. "I agree with Darya. This is her destiny."

Edwind let out a frustrated growl and started for the door again. "Destiny be damned."

"Where are you going?" Horsa asked.

"I can't stay here any longer while my family is led down a path to certain death." Tears dripped down his cheeks, and he turned his grief on Darya. "I gave up everything for you. For both of you. I lost my sister, my best friend, and my home. Now you want me to stand by and lose my wife and child as well? Why can't you give this to me after everything I've sacrificed for you? Maybe it was a mistake coming here. I would have been better off staying in nine eighty-two, so I wouldn't have to watch my family be destroyed like this." He clamped his mouth shut, realizing the full force of what he had just said.

Darya reeled backward at the bitterness of his tirade.

Hengist moved in between them, squeezing Edwind's shoulder. "Hold your tongue, you stupid man."

"Don't you dare put your hands on him," Horsa warned.

The sting of Edwind's words plucked tears from Darya's eyes, forcing them down heated cheeks. She glanced around the room, looking for an escape, but there was no place for her to go. There was no sanctuary to be had there.

Horsa continued to argue with his father. "He makes a valid point. He's given up a lot for her."

"What about what she's had to sacrifice?" Hengist said. "Her whole life has been leading to this one moment. She didn't have a choice in any of it. Edwind chose to be here with her."

Horsa leaned into his father. "And now she is willing to put her life and that of her own child in unnecessary danger when there is another option to be considered?"

Darya's gaze swept over Edwind, yet his eyes stayed fixed on the ground. All she wanted him to do was tell her he didn't mean what he said. That he didn't regret coming here to be with her. Instead, he turned from the room and disappeared outside.

So that was his answer.

She looked at Hengist and Horsa, who were still locked in their own quarrel. Ronwen went to her side, her expression betraying the first hint of empathy Darya had seen since meeting the stoic woman.

"Give him time to calm down."

"Send him back," Darya said, surprised at the calmness of her own voice. "When he returns, send him back to where he really wants to be." She started for the door.

"Where are you going?" Ronwen asked.

"I need to be alone."

"He didn't mean it."

"He's made his choice." Without looking back, Darya ran for the forest, where she hoped to find some comfort among their branches.

She made it a few yards into the shaded woods before her legs gave out, and she fell to her knees, giving into the despair that threatened to consume her. If not for the child that grew in her womb, she would have opened up the earth and let it swallow her whole.

She lay on the soft dirt, taking in its sweet, wet scent as she fed it with her misery and tears. She was so lost in her pain she didn't feel the ground rise beneath her upper body and cradle her head on a pair of dirt-encrusted legs.

A gentle hand pushed away the hair from her face. "Poor little seedling."

The sound of that familiar voice comforted Darya, and she reached over the creature's legs. "I should have listened to you," she said. "I should have made Edwind take me back to the island."

"It is true. I wanted to keep you away from this place. I knew what it would mean for you to return."

"I should have listened," Darya said again.

"You followed the path you were meant to take, druidae." Delicate fingers traced through dark hair. "Not even a mother's love could save her son from the death he so rightly deserves."

Darya tried to sit up, but those small hands kept her still.

"He wasn't always so lost, my Cernunnos. He was once a gentle protector of my lands. When his mate and child were murdered, it killed the goodness in him. I wish I had been strong enough to take away his grief, but I thirsted for retribution as well. Only when I tasted the suffering and the blood he spilled for that vengeance did I know the Weaver was right to pass her judgment on him."

"I don't want this burden anymore. I want my family back. I want my husband back." Darya's body quaked with a new torrent of agony. "It isn't fair that I have to sacrifice so much for such a despicable creature."

Flidais stopped stroking the young woman's hair. "Love is sacrifice, druidae. I must sacrifice my child for the sake of those who endure such horrors at his hands. I do not have the strength to do what you must, but I will make sure the way is open for you to reach your destiny."

Darya closed her eyes, squeezing out fresh tears at the feel of a light kiss on her cheek.

"Your heart will heal. As will mine."

When Darya opened her eyes again, she was no longer in the cradle of her grandmother's lap but lying on solid ground again, staring at an empty clearing.

She lay there, watching the light fade from the sky. There was no escaping what had to be done, so she got to her feet and started back for the house. When the back door came into view, it was nearly too much, and she had to force her feet to continue the last few yards.

Everything was quiet when she walked into the empty house. She bypassed the dining room and went to the set of keys hanging by the front door. By the time Edwind returned—if he returned—she would be on her way to finishing what fate intended for her.

She only hoped he knew how much she loved him and would carry that love with him, no matter where he ended up.

Edwind sat on the beach of the home he no longer recognized, letting the tide wash over his feet. He wished for those the waves to take him back a thousand years so he could talk to his sister again and receive her counsel. He missed the sound of her voice so much.

He hung his head, surrendering to the swirl of dark thoughts in his mind. What if he made a mistake coming to nineteen eighty-two? Maybe he wasn't supposed to come back to Darya.

He quickly dismissed that notion. There was no destiny or fate that would lead him away from his wife and their child.

"Edwind."

He lifted his gaze at the sound of his grandfather's voice. "I want to be alone."

"We all want a lot of things in this life, boy." He sat down beside his grandson.

"I'm not ready to go back. I don't know if I ever will be."

"I'm not here to take you home."

They sat in silence for a while, listening to the crashing of the waves on a nearby cluster of rocks until Hengist took the rock he had been holding, flung it into the sea and said, "I am going to tell you this, then you and I will never speak of it again."

Edwind's silent stare prompted his grandfather to go on.

"I've told you some stories of my time as Arawn's death dragon, but I never explained why I was allowed to lay that mantle down until it is passed on to my successor." He stared across the horizon, his eyes losing focus. "Your father had a sister."

Edwind's mouth dropped open, unsure of how to respond or even if he should say anything at all.

"They loved each other dearly. Much like you and Gita." His smile held both joy and sadness. "One of my assignments from Arawn took me to a time in the future, and I saw what was in store for my precious Niara. I didn't want to see her fated to that life, so when I returned, I spoke with Horsa about what was to come. He agreed with me, and we set out to change her destiny."

He turned his gaze back on Edwind, tears glistening in his sea foam eyes. "Your father and I learned you cannot circumvent the will of fate for our own selfish desires."

"What happened?"

"We meant to stop her from being bonded to a horrible dragon. He was a selfish tyrant that ruled his lands through fear and death. I thought that Niara would have been miserable had she given herself over to him. In my self-righteous pride, I failed to consider that he might actually make her happy, nor did I consider she would be a conduit for which he might be redeemed."

Hengist paused again, more tears gathering in his eyes. "By the time Horsa and I found the dragon, Niara was already his. We didn't know it, so when we killed him, she felt his death as if it was her own."

He inhaled a deep breath before pushing on. "It is a horrible thing to suffer the loss of one's mate under any circumstances, but to do so by the hands of your own father and brother is something she could not abide. When she took her own life, her mother never forgave us. Soon after that, Onae lost her will to live and simply faded away."

Edwind looked down at the surf crashing between his legs for a while before saying, "Why are you telling me this?"

"Because, boy, no matter how much you want to alter Darya's destiny, it remains the same. If you fight to change it, are you prepared to accept the consequences?"

"What if I'm supposed to stop her from killing Cernunnos?"

"Do you really think so much care was used to ensure she made it to this point in time to have her fate derailed by someone as insignificant as you?"

Edwind glared at his grandfather. "I am not insignificant."

"In the grand scheme of things, you are. To your wife, though, you are the most important person in her life, and look at how you've treated her." Hengist stood and dusted the sand from his jeans. "We all have our part to play in this, but yours is vital to Darya's survival." He put a hand on Edwind's shoulder. "You were always meant to be the one to walk this path by her side."

Edwind's brows furrowed into confusion.

"Of all the places in all of time, did you ever wonder why she showed up on your island?"

"I—" He dropped his head, considering the question.

"Your mother knew she would come for you. That's why she left that silly trunk locked away in her room for Darya to find."

"I've never regretted coming here. If I could have bonded myself to her, I would have."

"But you did. Even if it isn't the same connection we dragons share, your love is just as strong and unbreakable."

Edwind turned his head toward his true home. His stomach rolled at the impact of how vile his words had been. "What have I done?"

"Nothing that cannot be undone."

Edwind launched into the air, racing across the waves. He had to get to Darya and tell her how wrong he was to say those things to her. He landed on two feet and sprinted for the house. Inside, a clammy wave of nausea swept over him in the absence of his wife's presence.

He rushed upstairs to find their bedroom empty. Downstairs, he ran to the front door and nearly fell to his knees when he saw the car was no longer parked in the driveway.

Rushing back inside, he called his father. "Darya is gone. Is she with you?"

There was a pause before Horsa replied. "No. Ronwen said she was quite upset when you left, but we knew you two needed some time to calm down before reconciling. Perhaps she is still in the forest."

"The car is gone." Edwind felt the plastic of the phone crack under the pressure of his panic. "I'm coming there. If Darya shows up, tell her I'm on my way."

He set off on foot, knowing The Dragon's Rest was only a few minutes away at a full sprint across the beach.

Horsa waited for him outside the balcony. His expression confirmed Darya wasn't there.

"Where could she have gone?" Horsa asked.

"She doesn't know anyone else here. Do you think she went to the airport? Could she be trying to return to America?"

Ronwen stepped outside with a couple of drinks in her hands. "Did you find her?"

"No. I was hoping she came here," Edwind said.

Setting the cups on a table, she looked out over the ocean. A muffled whimper parted her lips. "Oh, no." Wide, fearful eyes turned on Edwind. "I can feel her thread unraveling."

"Unraveling? What does that mean? Is she in danger?"

She reached for Horsa. "She isn't supposed to face Cernunnos alone. How could she have been so reckless to run off on her own?"

The implication of her words made Edwind's body sway to the side. "This is my fault. I said those horrible things to her. I didn't mean them. I was just so scared."

"She doesn't know where to find the grove," Horsa said. "How can she possibly get to his sanctuary without us?"

"She carries his blood inside her. His power will lead her to where he hides."

Edwind took off around the building.

Horsa rushed after him. "Where are you going?"

"After my wife and child. I promised I would always be there for them."

"As will I." Horsa grabbed his son's arm, nodding to the car under the awning. "She doesn't know where she is going, but we do. Maybe we can get there before she does."

Chapter 23

THE TAINT OF THE Stag was strong on the wind and in the ground. It reeked of his grotesque power and spoke to that place inside Darya that shared his blood. The glimmer of power that she had felt when gathering the breath of the earth was but a candle flame among the torrent of wildfire that waited to drown her with its dangerous seduction.

What if she couldn't defeat him? She barely had control of the little magic she could touch. How did she expect to kill a being that had been born of the very magic that petrified her? The fear of what she was about to face made her want to turn around and drive back to Broughied.

But another kind of death waited for her if she returned to that house.

At least here, in her father's sanctuary, she had a chance to make right the horrors he inflicted on those poor people. Remembering the reason she was there, Darya left the dirt path and ventured into the shade of the forest.

She'd gone only a few steps into the cover of the trees when she heard the faint whispers of the smaller creatures. They told her of a safe route to the camp that lay ahead. She moved in and out of the last of the sun's rays.

Despite the assurance of the woodland animals, she kept her pace slow and purposeful until she spotted the first hint of the wall of timber that denoted her destination. She crouched lower to the ground to evaluate her next move. A dirt road rounded out of view, and she assumed it led to the main entrance to the camp, but she couldn't just walk up and demand entry. Surely, there had to be another way for her to get inside unnoticed.

She had taken a few steps from her hiding spot when a hand shot out from the shadows, covering her mouth so she couldn't yell out. The unseen foe yanked her off her feet and out of sight of the encampment, and the shock of being dragged through the woods left her helpless to the man who had her wrapped in a relentless bear hug.

It took her a few seconds to gather enough calm to pull at the power of the earth, but the man squeezed an arm around her chest. "Do not use your magic here if you wish us to stay alive."

The desperation in his voice made what little of the earth she'd gathered slip through her grasp. He released his grip on her, sending her sprinting forward a few feet before turning on her would-be captor. The face she saw peering at her through the dim light of the canopied forest turned her legs to rubber.

Tiernen stood before her, holding up empty hands to convey he was unarmed, though the knife he'd used on her rested in its sheath at his side. "I am not here to harm you, druidae."

"You're dead. They said you were dead."

His jaw flexed and said, "Your people are much more forgiving than mine."

In the dying light of day, she could make out the remnants of the vicious scars that marred the left side of his neck where Dash had ripped out his throat. "I'm not so benevolent." The power of the earth lay at her fingertips, ready to lash out at him if he tried to come after her.

"I am no longer a slave to that monster. You are safe with me."

"Like hell I am. You're tethered to him, the same as Mark was."

He donned a patient smile and turned his head to the side, pointing to where Cernunnos' sigil had been burned into his scalp. "When I died, so did his power over me." He nodded past her. "We need to leave this place before we are discovered."

"I can't leave. Not until I kill Cernunnos and put an end to his curse."

"You can't defeat him alone. Where are your people? Where is your husband?"

At the mention of Edwind, the wound in her heart threatened to break open again. "This is my destiny."

"You have the spirit of a fierce warrior, but no matter how righteous your cause, you are not meant to fight this battle alone." He held out his hand. "That child that grows inside you is meant for great things. Do not deny her the chance to make her mark in this world."

Darya's eyes fell to her belly. She'd nearly let grief devour her will to live. It wasn't her life that mattered. It was the daughter that would one day grow up and travel a thousand years into the past to reunite with her parents.

Only for them to be torn apart again.

She clamped down on the wave of despair that welled inside her. "I can't ask anyone else to fight this battle for me. Especially Edwind. He's lost so much already. He deserves to be happy in the life he's chosen."

"This is the life I choose."

Darya spun around at the sound of her husband's voice. The mere sight of him quelled the raging storm of emotions that threatened to crack her wide open. "But you said—"

He pulled her into his arms and held her with the strength and tenderness she so desperately needed from him. "Bloody hell. I didn't mean it. I was scared and angry." He tucked a strand of hair behind her ear, fighting back his own pain. "I've never regretted coming here to be with you."

She shook her head. "I can't give you what you want. I can't walk away from this."

"I know," he said, moving into her again, but she pushed herself away while still staying in his embrace.

"I can't live with myself knowing I have the chance to put an end to their torture."

"Darya, I know." He kissed her forehead. "It was selfish of me to ask it of you."

She buried her face in his chest to muffle her cries of relief.

Horsa went to Tiernen's side. "Have you been here all this time?"

Tiernen shrugged. "I am in your debt for giving me my freedom."

Edwind tightened his embrace around Darya, his hold firm yet gentle. "Thank you for protecting my wife and child."

"She is far from safe, dragon. Do not abandon her again."

Darya felt his chest rumble, and she squeezed him, bringing his focus back to her.

Tiernen moved with an unnatural speed, his arm shooting out and snatching an arrow from the air before it reached Darya's back. In a fluid roll of his torso, he flung it at the woman standing atop the wall. She quickly dropped out of view, and the arrow whistled past the space where her head used to be.

He turned to Darya. "Your destiny has come for you, druidae."

Edwind snatched Darya off the ground, turning his back so he was between her and the camp, and thrust her behind a group of saplings. She glanced to her left, where Tiernen hid beside them.

His face twisted into a feral grimace. "The men of this tribe are bound to The Stag's will. They will defend his grove with their lives." His expression turned into a concerned frown. To Edwind he said, "I would like to see them unharmed, but do what you must to keep yourselves alive."

The gate swung inward, and a line of men with swords and bows rushed out. Edwind pressed Darya to one of the oak trees. "Stay here until I come back for you." He didn't give her a chance to argue before joining Tiernen.

Horsa bound through the trees, twilight making his scales take on a deep crimson hue as if they were molten lava. He stomped toward the group of men who, at seeing the hulking beast, lost some of their resolve. That hesitation gave Tiernen and Edwind the opportunity to rush through their ranks and pick them apart, one by one.

Ronwen joined Darya behind the cedar.

"Aren't you going to help them?" Darya asked.

"I'm not allowed to interfere."

Darya stared at her like she'd grown a second head. A mixture of indignant anger and disbelief made her want to lash out at the goddess with her powers but reigned in her temper. "What have you been doing all this time?"

"I made sure things happened the way they were supposed to, and they did. Now it's up to you to finish your journey."

"Don't you know how it's going to end?"

Ronwen's concern vanished, replaced by indifference. "I know how it could end. Those threads have yet to be woven."

A half-dozen men hurried from around the other side of the wooden barrier, attempting to ambush Edwind and the others. Darya shot Ronwen one last look, but the woman was gone.

Turning back to the new threat, she lashed out, raising a shallow wall of earth to trip them up. She managed to take the first few men in line off their feet, but the others were nimble enough to avoid their fallen brethren and kept running for their target.

A pack of wolves burst through the trees. Streaks of white and coppery silver overtook the men as their teeth sank into arms and legs and whatever else they could latch on to.

"Don't kill them." Darya left the safety of her wooded shield.

The biggest of the pack dropped a leg from his mouth, and when the man tried to run, another wolf barred his way with bared fangs.

Fearful eyes darted from the wolves to where Darya was approaching them. Behind her, the ground shook from the half-dozen brown bears lumbering into view. Even though she couldn't see them, she knew there were more predators waiting in the shadows of the thick brush. Yet it wasn't her command they heeded. They spoke of their true mistress, Flidais.

"If you try to run," Darya warned, "I can't promise I'll be able to control them."

A few of the wolves stayed behind with the men when she hurried to the gates, where Edwind and Tiernen did their best to neutralize who they could without killing anyone. Edwind's fierce expression softened into surprise when he saw the bears and wolves at her back.

He rushed to her side. "I told you to wait where it was safe."

A silver wolf came around to her side. Its chest rumbled a warning. Darya laid a hand on its head, but it was her husband she spoke to. "I am going into there to finish this." She held out her other hand. "Right now, I need your strength, not your protection."

She saw the reluctant acceptance melt his features into a tender smile. "Very well."

When he took hold of her arm, a cluster of bears rushed past them into the fray with Tiernen and Horsa. The wolves padded through the open gates ahead of Darya and Edwind, clearing the way before them. They made it through the heart of the camp to the communal fire.

A frail voice spoke from somewhere among the simple log houses. "Polly, is that you?" The old woman that came into view looked anything but threatening. However, Edwind stepped in front of his wife, ready to defend her.

Darya peeked around him to find a tall, studying the woman. Her hair was white with age, but her dark eyes were sharp and clear. Behind her, two young women grabbed her arms.

"Have you come back to us?" the old woman asked.

Darya stepped around Edwind. "I'm not Polly," she said. "I'm her daughter, Darya."

"Daughter?" The old woman jerked free of the two younger girls.

Seeing the map of wrinkles that told the story of her age, Darya assumed she was Polly's mother, or maybe her grand-mother.

"Nan, who is Polly?" The girl who spoke shared Darya's dark hair and sharp chin.

"She was my sister."

"How is that possible?" Edwind asked. "How can she be your mother's sister?"

Darya shook her head. The same questions were running through her mind as well. "When was Polly chosen as a bride?"

"She was taken from us when I was only ten. I remember we celebrated the new century that year."

Darya looked over her shoulder at Edwind. "They did the same thing to my mother as they did to me; hid her in the annals of time."

The last of Darya's hatred dissipated like a thick fog in the harsh light of the sun, replaced by a deep regret that she wasn't able to comfort her mother for what she had lost. "What's your name?"

"Dara."

"She named me after you," Darya mused.

"Where is Polly? Where is my sister?"

Darya couldn't bring herself to admit the horrible truth about her mother's death, but the old woman saw the truth in her niece's eyes.

"You are the one my grandson spoke of. When the woman he loved was killed by the horned god, he told me of her visions."

"Darya," Edwind said softly. "We need to go before we are found."

Dara pointed over his shoulder. "His grove is just through those trees."

"Be mindful of the succubus," one of the girls told Darya. "She is dangerous to you, but more so to your man." To Edwind, she added, "Don't let her touch you."

Dara turned her gaze to the man running up behind them. Her eyes widened, and he held his arms out to shield her granddaughters. "We were told you were dead."

Tiernen ignored her. "Come with me. I will take you to the grove."

"I'll come back for you," Darya promised her family.

Edwind took her by the hand, sprinting after Tiernen into the darkness of the forest.

Chapter 24

"Stay behind me, Druidae." Tiernen studied the surrounding forest with those sharp gray eyes of his. "Edwind, keep at your wife's back. Boudica is an opportunist. She will strike at the first sign of weakness."

Darya felt safe in her husband's presence. She reached for him, squeezing his hand when he took hold of hers. The wolves stayed by her side, keeping their sights locked on the surrounding woods. Every so often, one of them would pause long enough to raise a nose in the air before returning to the others.

"They sense someone out there, watching us," she said.

Tiernen nodded. "As do I."

Edwind let go of her hand, and the ground shook with the weight of his dragon stalking behind them. *There are only a handful of men out there. Nothing we can't handle.*

The wolves moved as one and darted into the trees after the unseen threat, followed by the sound of men's fearful screams.

Tiernen came to a stop when they reached a set of bone markers. "This is the entrance to his sanctuary. However, I can no longer open the way." He met Darya's stare. "You are of his blood. You should be able to get us through."

The sound of wings fluttering through the air drew her attention to the limbs high in a tree beside her. The white falcon stared at her with its pale, round orbs. It was then Darya understood the connection she had with it. "There's no need for me to do anything. My grandmother will open the way."

Tiernen levied a questioning look on her.

She pointed to the fowl. "Flidais has been with me this whole time."

Edwind stepped up beside her, following her finger. "That was her on the island?" The anger in his voice wasn't lost on Darya.

"She doesn't mean us harm. She was only trying to protect her son."

"Perhaps that is what she wishes to do now."

"I don't think so. She is ready to end this curse as much as we are." Darya approached the markers. A whisper of cool wind swept over her. "It's open."

Tiernen stepped in between the bones and vanished.

Edwind grabbed Darya's hand. "We will go together."

The transition from one realm to the next sent a wave of nausea through her. It wasn't as painful as the portal, but she had to take a few seconds to regain her footing when she was on the other side.

"That was unpleasant," Edwind muttered.

"We must keep moving." Tiernen was ahead of them, looking over the dusky landscape.

Darya's blood sang with the power that tried to seep into her bones. She had to be careful if she tried to pull at it if she didn't want to be overwhelmed like she had been on the island.

"I should have known you would find a way back to us."

Tiernen turned in a slow circle, searching for the melodious voice that came from everywhere at once. "I am not here to join you, succubus. I've come to put an end to the misery you bring to these people."

Sultry laughter echoed around them. "I make their pain so pleasurable. As I did for you, Na Fianna. Let me show you again how much fun we can have together."

A hand snaked up from behind him, running along his shoulder, making his vision lose focus for a few seconds. Shaking himself, Tiernen broke free of her grasp, bringing up his dagger. "I will not succumb to your temptation, helot."

Boudica's mouth split in a hungry grin. "I think you will." She pushed aside the weapon, taking hold of his other wrist.

Edwind stepped forward, but Darya held on to his arm. "Don't go near her," she said.

Boudica turned her stare on the other woman. "Your dragon will not yield to my power. His love for you is sickeningly pure." Looking back at Tiernen, she added, "But I know how to turn this one's desire into something fierce and deadly. Now, be a good lover and kill him for me."

Edwind took hold of his dragon before Tiernen had his dagger raised to strike. Keep behind me. He ordered, throwing a desperate glance over a wing at Darya.

She stayed at his left flank, testing the power that begged to be let loose inside her.

Instead of the thin vines she'd been able to summon before, thick stalk-like sprouts sprang up from beneath their feet, nearly impaling Tiernen. He easily sidestepped them, cutting down each trunk that jutted from the earth.

Edwind swept his tail through the open air, knocking Tiernen back, but he was on his feet in a matter of seconds, rushing forward once again. On his way across the expanse between them, Darya saw the lack of awareness in his gray eyes. Whatever Boudica had done to him took away his free will.

She tracked his footsteps, preparing to push up the earth to throw him away from her husband, but she didn't get the chance before a hand wrapped around her braid and yanked her to the ground. The succubus straddled her chest, an expression of murderous glee glowing in her eyes. Their honey color flashed to a deep shade of blue, and Darya knew Cernunnos watched from inside his slave's mind. Boudica's connection to the god gave her an inhuman strength that made it impossible for Darya to buck her off.

Darya! Edwind bound across the field toward the two women. He was a few yards away when Tiernen rushed him from the side, rolling him out of the way.

Tiernen sidestepped the dark claw that raked the air in front of him. He used his momentum to swing around and jump onto Edwind's back, sending the dragon into a roll to dislodge the unwelcome interloper.

Darya gripped Boudica's wrist, using what power she dared gather from the earth, and twisted the leaves and debris into a tight cyclone to blind the woman on top of her.

"Bitch!" Cernunnos' voice boomed from Boudica's mouth, and waved a hand, dispelling the wind. "You will not best me in my own sanctuary."

Boudica withdrew a curved hunting knife from her waistband. She used her free hand to press Darya into the soft grass. The knife, along with the hand that had been holding it, disappeared into a spray of misting blood. Boudica's mouth was agape in a silent scream as she stared at the bloody stump.

Flidais crouched in a deadly stance a few feet away, her feral eyes fixed on the succubus. "You are a vile creature, Boudica of Icine."

Darya took advantage of the distraction and bucked the woman off her.

"You dare trespass in this sacred grove?" It was hard to tell who spoke those words, but Boudica's eyes were her own.

"Go." Flidais ordered to Darya. "End your people's suffering."

Boudica reached for Darya, but Flidais was already in between them. A giant black bear took the place of the God Mother and lunged at her. Boudica tried to duck away, but razor-sharp claws dug into her back, sending her sprawling to the ground.

Darya scanned the landscape. Edwind stumbled out of the trees, bloodied but alive. Tiernen followed behind him, and she called out to her husband. Edwind didn't pay any attention to the limping man behind him.

Tiernen ambled in the opposite direction toward the bear that rested a heavy paw on Boudica's bloodied back. "I've waited a long time for this," he said and lifted a short sword above the frightened woman.

"You will die for this," Boudica said through gritted teeth. "Cernunnos will make sure you suffer—"

He cut her words short when he dislodged her head from her neck.

Flidais peered through wild, matted hair at Tiernen. "I can end your suffering, Na Fianna."

"Not yet," he said. "I still have much to atone for."

Flidais shrugged. "Penance is a waste of your talent." She turned those wild eyes on Darya. "I will not aid you any further." She shot into the sky, disappearing over the trees.

Tiernen studied at bone markers, then looked at Edwind. "I need to make sure the others are safe."

Edwind nodded and turned to his wife. "Let's finish this, my love."

She glanced over her shoulder to where she felt the pull of the deity that shared her blood. Shoving down the fear that begged her to retreat, grabbed Edwind's hand and began the final journey to her destiny.

Darya followed the path that called her forth to meet her fate. Edwind was by her side, studying the surrounding trees. She spotted a crudely carved ancient stone. The archaic text that had been chiseled into the rock wasn't meant for mortal men to comprehend their meaning, but she understood what they said.

It was the grave of the woman Cernunnos had loved.

"Etaine," Darya whispered.

"What?"

"That was her name. Cernunnos' mate. This is her grave." As soon as Darya took a step toward the marker, she felt a new presence nearby.

Laughter echoed from all around them.

Edwind squeezed her hand. "Careful."

A set of antlers appeared from behind a cluster of trees. Cernunnos strode into the open. His hidden face focused on Darya. "So, my seedling has come to fulfill the will of the Weaver."

Darya fought to hold her ground. His presence pushed at her with each step he took. The same letters carved in the stone decorated the aged, yellowed bone that hid his features, and a wave of disgust swept over her. "That's her skull you wear."

His demeanor changed from arrogant to something darker.

"You use her face to hide your own, you fucking coward."

"I wear her bones to remind those mortals of what they stole from me."

"They've suffered enough at your hands."

He made a move toward her. Edwind was already in motion to intercept. Cernunnos matched the dragon's speed and threw his arms out to meet the beast's blow, knocking Edwind across the grass, where he landed against a cluster of rocks.

Darya sprinted for her husband, but Cernunnos used her panic to get his arms around her waist, dragging her to the grave. The ground rumbled beneath her feet as the earth gave way to a set of brittle bones.

She cried out in pain when he forced her head down.

"Look at them. Look at what they did to my family. There is no punishment vile enough to atone for their deaths."

She twisted her face away from the gruesome sight of what remained of Etaine and the child that had been growing inside her.

"It's not your place to punish them," she snarled.

"I made it my place!" His roar shook her to the core.

Refusing to give in to her fear, she forced herself to meet his stare. "What you've done is far more despicable. Even your mother wants this torture to end."

He growled and drew back his hand to strike her but let go of her hair and spun around just as a sword came slicing through the air where he once stood. Edwind's forward momentum carried him past the taller man, and Cernunnos kicked him in the side, sending Edwind across the field again.

Despite the fear of losing control, Darya drew on the dangerous power beneath her feet and sent a thick barbed vine shooting up from the dirt where it wrapped around one of the horned god's legs. Cernunnos forgot about the other man, focusing his fury on Darya.

Blood bloomed on his pants where the thorns dug into his flesh. His eyes flashed a bright blue, and he was free. "This is my realm. That is my magic you fumble over."

Darya watched in horror as the same thorny shoots wrapped around her arms and legs. She screamed from the agony of her skin being sliced open by the thick, unforgiving barbs. Cernunnos knelt in front of her, taking her chin in one hand.

She snatched her face out of his grasp, gritting her teeth to keep her pain inside. "I'm going to kill you." Her voice lacked the conviction she hoped to convey. The vines twisted ever so slightly, and she let out another pathetic cry.

The old god chuckled. "You may do just that, seedling, but you will know my grief before you take my life."

Edwind was back on his feet, running for his wife. Cernunnos snatched the man up by his neck, lifting him off the ground so that his toes barely brushed over the grass. Edwind's expression betrayed his disbelief.

"No, no, youngling." Cernunnos cooed. "There will be no calling on your dragon."

Darya fought to free herself from her deadly confines, but the fiery agony that bit at her skin prevented her from gathering enough strength to break the magic that held her down.

"Edwind." Her voice shook with more fear than pain.

Cernunnos snatched the sword from Edwind's hand, inspecting the blade.

"Get away from him," she whimpered. She searched the forest for help, but there were no creatures among those trees. They'd been banished long ago to keep Flidais out of his shrine.

Cernunnos drew back, holding Darya's gaze, and shoved the blade through Edwind's chest.

"NO!" Darya ignored the searing pain that set her skin on fire and yanked against the deadly restraints. She opened herself to the energy that bubbled up from the dirt beneath her, letting it fill every crevice of her being, no longer fearing the consequences of what it would do to her. The thorns that bound her body withered to husks and crumbled to the ground. She scrambled on hands and knees to the place where Edwind lay.

Cernunnos let her get as far as Edwind's legs before snatching her off the ground. "Now you will know the agony of watching your heart die," he said. "But I will show you the mercy I was denied and send you to the afterlife with him."

An agonized wail clawed its way out of her open mouth. She tried to keep her eyes locked on her husband, but her gaze was ripped away when Cernunnos brought her face around to his. The smirk on his lips wavered before falling away completely from the unbridled fury blazing in her eyes.

She pushed all the despair and anger and fear that coursed through her veins into the hands that were now latched onto the ancient god's wrists. She welcomed the maniacal rage that emanated from somewhere deep inside her, radiating outward in a gush of savage madness.

So lost was she in the frenzy of her wrath that she didn't notice Cernunnos' veins casting an orange glow from beneath his pale skin until smoke plumed from his flesh. As the magic rushed forth, she knew it didn't come from the earth. The power she called on manifested from inside her; from that part of her she created with the man that now lay dead at her feet.

The expression on Cernunnos' face betrayed the pain and fear he felt. He tried to shake himself loose from her grip, but she refused to relinquish her hold.

She squeezed even harder, letting out another mournful bellow. With her cry came more agony, and with that agony came more fire that she forced inside him. His skin glowed with her pain and misery until the flames engulfed his entire body. His wails were lost in the fire's roar that spiraled into the air, burning them both from the inside out.

The world came alive with the brightness of the very sun itself, and the memories of all the women that had come before filled Darya's senses until her own screams drowned them out.

Then the light was gone. Silence swallowed the world around her.

Darya opened her eyes. She was on her back, staring into the face of her husband. His pallid features sent a pang of grief through her heart.

She rolled over to the smoking remains of the dead god, whose mouth was set into a horrified expression of the terrible way in which he perished. She looked at her own skin that was untouched by the fire. Her body shook with another weak sob.

Why was she still alive? Why was she not in the underworld with her family? She didn't want to live, not without Edwind.

Drawing on the strength of the earth, she dug her fingers into the ground, pulling herself toward her love. She was careful not to touch the sword protruding from his chest and nestled herself into his arm.

"Don't leave me." Her whole body shook with sorrow. "I can't face this world without you."

"Darya." Horsa's voice came to her out of the fog of her grief. "Edwind."

She was only slightly aware of a pair of hands pulling her from the ground, and she clung to Edwind's arm. "Don't take him away," she cried.

Horsa knelt beside her. "Oh, my sweet child, I'm not trying to take him from you."

Ronwen ran into view, and Darya scrambled away from Horsa. "Call on Arawn. Tell him to bring Edwind back to me."

She looked from Darya to the charred body of Cernunnos.

"I did what you wanted," Darya shrieked. "Now give him back to me."

When Ronwen didn't say anything, Darya shoved away the tears that had gathered in her eyes. "Bring him back to me."

Horsa took Darya by the hand. "That's not within her power. Not even Arawn can give you what you ask."

"Why not? He brought me back from the dead. Why can't he do the same for Edwind?"

"Because he's not dead."

Darya swayed to the side, refusing to believe the words she was hearing. "He's alive?"

Horsa set Darya's hand on Edwind's chest. "He is gravely injured, but he still lives."

Her whole body trembled when she felt the slow but steady beating of his heart. She bent forward, kissing his forehead and running her hands down his face. "You're alive," she whispered.

Hengist and Tiernen ran into the clearing. The elder dragon rushed to Edwind's side, resting a hand on the sword. His movements were slow and purposeful when he drew the blade from his grandson's chest, then he covered the wound to stymie the bleeding.

"We need to get him to the island." Horsa insisted.

Darya latched onto Edwind's arm. "What? No. He needs proper medical care."

"Your modern medicine can't do anything for him," Hengist said. "I will take him to the caves on the island where his dragon will heal his body."

"For how long?"

"I can't say for sure. Time is all we can give him."

"But he will be alright?" Darya asked.

"Yes."

"Can I visit him?"

"Of course." Horsa helped her to stand. "Any time you wish."

Darya kissed Edwind one last time before letting his hand slip away. For the second time, she was helpless to watch her love disappear into the sky.

Horsa urged her forward. "Let's get you home."

Chapter 25

Darya sat in the wicker chair on the back porch, staring across the horizon, willing Edwind to return to her. Every breeze carried with it the tangy nip of the salty ocean, reminding her of what her life was missing. Even after nearly a month of healing, she still couldn't close her eyes without reliving the horrors of that day in the grove, and there was no one there to comfort her when the nightmares came.

She studied the pink remnants of the cuts on her arms, but there was one wound that refused to heal. Not until her husband returned. Every time she woke in the middle of the night, she thought she could hear him running up the stairs, and when he wasn't there, her heart would break all over again.

She spent most of her days on the back porch, watching the ocean, hoping to see his silhouette among the clouds. When she visited the island, she begged him to wake up and come home with her, but his dragon continued to slumber, refusing to do as she commanded.

The door to the kitchen opened, and Horsa stepped outside, following her gaze across the sea. "Your dinner is ready."

"I'm not hungry."

"You can't waste away out here waiting for Edwind to return. We will go to the island tomorrow."

She readjusted herself in the chair, so she was facing away from him while keeping her sights on the rolling waves.

"You need to keep up your strength. Not only for yourself, but for Brigita."

Tears overflowed onto her cheeks. "Don't you dare use our child to manipulate me."

Horsa let out a frustrated sigh. "You aren't the only one who's suffering."

Heat snaked up her body and burned her face. Her lips trembled from the shame he brought to the surface. "I never said I was."

"You're acting like it. My father and I have lived through more losses and heartache than you can possibly fathom, girl, and we've had to endure; we can endure because of the lives that continue to build each new generation."

She finally met his stare and her face twisted with the sorrow that swallowed her heart. Horsa pulled her out of the chair and wrapped her in a tender embrace, stroking her back and murmuring comforting words to console her grief.

When she quieted, he said, "No matter what the future holds, one day you are going to raise a daughter who is brilliant, compassionate, and powerful, just like her mother. That is what you must focus on now."

Giving the ocean one last longing glance, she followed Horsa inside. The smell of the food made her stomach rumble. Ronwen was in the kitchen, pouring water from a kettle into three cups.

She set one of them in front of Darya and took her seat beside Horsa. "I spoke with Tiernen today." She kept her tone casual. "He says Dara has taken a leadership role among their people. They are healing from their imprisonment, but there's a lot of uncertainty and fear of what the future holds for them."

"Is he staying in the camp?" Horsa asked.

"For a while. I don't know if they can ever truly trust him, given his role as their warden."

"I'm sure your aunt would like to see you." Horsa rested his hand on Darya's arm. "So would the rest of your kin."

Darya pushed the medley of vegetables around her plate. She looked forward to getting to know her new family, but the thought of leaving the house and possibly missing Edwind when he returned made her hesitant to go anywhere. "Who will be here when he comes back?"

"Ronwen or I will be here. Or my father."

She eyed Horsa, frowning.

"I'll take you to the camp tomorrow after we return from the island," he said. "It's time you join the world again."

Horsa was right. She needed to get away from this place, if only for a little while. She felt like a prisoner trapped in her own longing and grief. There was nothing else she could do for Edwind. As frustrating as it was, time and patience were the only things that were going to bring him home.

Edwind woke in darkness.

His body ached as if he had been buried beneath the weight of mountains. His breath came in shallow gulps, and for a moment, he wasn't sure if he was still dreaming. The last thing he remembered was Darya's scream. The sword piercing his chest. The world fading to black.

He pressed a trembling hand to his heart. The scar was there. But he was alive.

"Darya." The name cracked in his throat, echoing in the emptiness surrounding him.

He ran through the tunnels until he came to the nearly blinding light of the late afternoon sun shining down on the white sands of the island.

The image of his wife's frightened face drove him to the frothy sea foam covered beach outside the cave. His whole body shook with the fear of what had happened to her. Was she still alive? If she lived, had she given birth to their daughter yet? Ignoring the uneasy thoughts in his mind, he took to the sky.

When he reached the mainland, he made the trek to his home on foot. He ran up to the back of the house and nearly fell over himself when he saw his wife kneeling in a small garden sweeping at the dirt around the flowers. When she stood, her belly was big and round with child.

Joyful tears clouded his vision.

He started for her, but his steps were halted by the sound of the sliding glass door opening. A little girl ran outside. Her dark hair bounced over her shoulders, wide eyes shining bright and clear, reflecting the spring meadows of his Didean.

"Mummy." Her voice carried the music of the wind.

"You are supposed to be napping," Darya said.

Dino followed the little girl outside. "Someone decided she wanted to help her mother in the garden."

"Brigita Diane, what am I going to do with you?" She gave the little girl a warm smile, then kissed Dino tenderly on the cheek. "I'm almost finished out here, anyway. She can help me with the last of the lilies." She patted her extended belly. "I think our little one is ready for a nap, too."

Dino placed a hand on hers before pressing his mouth to her lips. "I'll make you a cup of tea."

Edwind staggered backward. He'd been gone too long. How could he have slept for so many years? Didn't Darya know he would have come back to her? His heart cried out for the family that was no longer his, and in a fit of despair, he ran his hands through his hair, releasing his grief in a heavy, miserable wail.

Edwind's body spasmed, jerking himself out of the night-mare. He scanned the blackness. There was a surreal sense of relief that he was again inside the caves under the island. He didn't hesitate and sprinted through the dark tunnels, following the scent of the ocean and the crashing of the surf against the rock.

Instead of sunlight, a moonless sky blanketed by count-less brilliant stars greeted him. He didn't dare ponder how long he'd been asleep or if Darya was still alive.

She lived. He could feel her, even now.

As soon as he reached land, he sprinted for the house, flinging open the sliding glass door. "Darya." His gaze swept over the empty living room. "My love. I'm home."

He darted for the stairs, ready to take his wife in his arms, but movement from the kitchen made him pause. He glanced over his shoulder.

Darya stood at the end of the bar, her face set in an expression of disbelief. In one hand, she held a bowl of ice cream and, in the other, a spoon. The light blue gown she wore showed off her growing belly.

She let both the bowl and spoon clatter to the counter. "Is this a dream? Please don't let this be another dream."

He strode up to her and took her face in his hands, melting into their kiss. "I'm really here, my love. I've come back to you." He laid a hand on her stomach. "Is this our Brigita?"

Shock gave way to concern. "Yes, of course."

He pulled her into him. "Thank the gods."

She tightened her arms around him. "What happened? Why would you think this isn't our child?"

"Nothing. It was just a stupid dream." He kissed her again and asked, "How long have I been asleep?"

"Almost five months. I visited and watched you heal, but you never woke."

"I'm here now." He swept her from the ground and headed for the stairs.

"Where are you going? You can't be tired after sleeping for so long."

"It's not sleep I need."

In their bedroom, he laid her on the bed, careful not to put his full weight on her. She hesitated when he tried to remove her gown.

"I look so different from what you remember."

He stilled her protests with more kisses. "You are even more beautiful than the last time I saw you." He slid the gown over her head, his eyes alight with love.

"Don't you ever leave me again, you big, dumb dragon," she whispered.

"Never again, my beautiful, stubborn goddess."

Epilogue

DARYA LEANED AGAINST THE open door of the nursery, watching Edwind rock their daughter to sleep. Brigita clung to his finger, her tiny mouth forming a tight pucker as she gave into her full belly. Whatever the infant dreamed of when she slept, Darya hoped their daughter knew how much she was cherished.

"We made this perfect little girl," he said, bringing her tiny hand to his lips.

Darya went to his side. "It took a thousand years, but she's finally here."

A hint of sadness edged into his smile. "I wish Gita and Saebbi could have met her."

"Who knows, maybe one day they will." Horsa slipped past Darya, holding a pale pink dragon in one hand and a bottle of dark liquid in the other.

"What do you know, old man?" Darya asked.

"I know a lot of things." He held up the stuffed dragon. "For my granddaughter." Then the ale. "For my son."

He put the dragon in the crib and the ale on the dresser before pulling a jewelry box out of a shirt pocket and handing it to Darya. "Gita wanted me to give this to you. It belonged to my mother and is the matching pendant to that ring you wear."

Darya ran a finger over the familiar knot-work, ignoring his sidestep of her question. There were so many times she wanted to ask Ronwen to take them back, if only for a short while, but every time she brought it up to Edwind, he refused to entertain the idea. He said it was too dangerous. Perhaps, one day, he would change his mind, and they would get to return to that place and time where their love began.

"Thank you." She hugged Horsa and let him put the pendant around her neck.

He stepped up beside Edwind. "May I hold my granddaughter now?"

Edwind hesitated before prying his finger out of his daughter's firm grip. "Be gentle. You have to support her neck. Make sure—"

"I know how to hold a baby. I managed to keep you and your sister alive."

Darya took her husband by the hand before he could argue. "Let your father spend some time with Brigita while we finish our game."

Edwind conceded with a kiss. Before they left the room, he turned back to his father. "Thank you for looking after my family."

Horsa didn't look away from the sleeping infant and shushed Edwind. "You're going to wake this precious child. Go."

Darya pulled her husband from the nursery and down the stairs, where they sat at the newly refinished chess board. She made her play and waited for Edwind to decide his next move.

He glanced up. "What?"

She struggled to find the right words to express the love she felt for her new family. Every day, she found new ways to adore them even more.

His lips curved into a mischievous smirk. "Stop trying to distract me."

She reached across the table, brushing the back of her hand against his arm. "If I wanted to distract you, we would be upstairs in our bed."

He lifted a tawny eyebrow. "Don't tempt me, druidae."

They settled into a comfortable silence as she reflected on the many roads she'd taken to reach this place. She would go through every struggle, suffer every ounce of pain all over again, as long as she found her way to this moment.

To Edwind.

To Brigita.

To their love.

A Word From The Author

Thank you for reading *Destiny Awakened*. I hope you enjoyed the journey as much as I cherished creating it. If you
have a moment, I'd be grateful if you could share your honest review on your favorite platform. Your feedback means
the world to me!
  With gratitude,
  C. A. Hollister
  www.cahollister.net

Also by C. A. Hollister

Destiny Unbound: Laws of Fate Book 1
  Imperfect Illusions

About the Author

C.A. Hollister's roots are deeply planted in the rich soil of a small North East Texas town, where family gatherings buzzed with the warmth of shared stories and the joy of cooking together. This nurturing environment sparked her imagination, leading her to create her own unique universes from a very young age. In her storytelling, she blends the familiar with the fantastical, weaving tales that resonate with raw emotion and explore the universal longing for connection and love. Her approach to writing marries the everyday with the extraordinary, inviting readers into worlds where magic touches the mundane, and where characters' desires and heartaches echo our own.